"DO YOU MIND THE LIGHT IN YOUR EYES?"

—*Katherine Lauderdale.*

THE COMPLETE WORKS OF
F. MARION CRAWFORD
In Thirty-two Volumes ✒ *Authorized Edition*

Katharine Lauderdale

BY

F. MARION CRAWFORD

WITH FRONTISPIECE

P. F. COLLIER & SON
NEW YORK

THE COMPLETE WORKS OF F. MARION CRAWFORD

—22—

KATHARINE LAUDERDALE

CONTENTS

CONTENTS

KATHARINE LAUDERDALE.

CHAPTER I.

"I PREFER the dark style, myself — like my cousin," said John Ralston, thoughtfully.

"And you will therefore naturally marry a fair woman," answered his companion, Hamilton Bright, stopping to look at the display in a florist's window. Ralston stood still beside him.

"Queer things — orchids," he observed.

"Why?" Nothing in the world seemed queer or unnatural to Bright, who was normally constituted in all respects, and had accepted the universe without comment.

"I am not sure why. I think the soul must look like an orchid."

"You are as bad as a Boston girl," laughed Bright. "Always thinking of your soul! Why should the soul be like an orchid, any more than like a banana or a turnip?"

"It must be like something," said Ralston, in explanation.

"If it's anything, it's faith in a gaseous state, my dear man, and therefore even less visible and less like anything than the common or market faith, so to say — the kind you get at from ten cents to a dollar the seat's worth, on Sundays, according to the charge at the particular place of worship your craving for salvation leads you to frequent."

1

"I prefer to take mine in a more portable shape,'
answered Ralston, grimly. " By the bottle — not by the
seat — and very dry."

" Yes — if you go on, you'll get one sort of faith — the
lively evidence of things unseen — snakes, for instance."

Bright laughed again as he spoke, but he glanced at
his friend with a look of interest which had some anxiety
in it. John Ralston was said to drink, and Bright was
his good angel, ever striving to be entertained unawares,
and laughing when he was found out in his good intentions. But if Bright was a very normal being, Ralston
was a very abnormal one, and was, to some extent, a weak
man, though not easily influenced by strong men. A
glance at his face would have convinced any one of that
— a keen, nervous, dark face, with those deep lines from
the nostrils to the corners of the mouth which denote
uncertain, and even dangerous tempers — a square, bony
jaw, aggressive rather than firm, but not coarse — the
nose, aquiline but delicate — the eyes, brown, restless,
and bright, the prominence of the temples concealing the
eyelids entirely when raised — the forehead, broad, high,
and visibly lean like all the features — the hair, black
and straight — the cheek bones, moderately prominent.
Possibly John Ralston had a dash of the Indian in his
physical inheritance, which showed itself, as it almost
always does, in a melancholic disposition, great endurance
and an unnatural love of excitement in almost any shape,
together with an inborn idleness which it was hard to
overcome.

Nothing is more difficult than to convey by words what
should be understood by actual seeing. There are about
fifteen hundred million human beings alive to-day, no two
of whom are exactly alike, and we have really but a few
hundreds of words with which to describe any human

being at all. The argument that a few octaves of notes furnish all the music there is, cannot be brought against us as a reproach. We cannot speak a dozen words at once and produce a single impression, any more than we can put the noun before the article as we may strike any one note before or after another. So I have made acknowledgment of inability to do the impossible, and apology for not being superhuman.

John Ralston was dark, good-looking, nervous, excitable, enduring, and decidedly dissipated, at the age of five and twenty years, which he had lately attained at the time of the present tale. Of his other gifts, peculiarities and failings, his speech, conversation and actions will give an account. As for his position in life, he was the only son of Katharine Ralston, widow of Admiral Ralston of the United States Navy, who had been dead several years.

Mrs. Ralston's maiden name had been Lauderdale, and she was of Scotch descent. Her cousin, Alexander Lauderdale, married a Miss Camperdown, a Roman Catholic girl of a Kentucky family, and had two children, both daughters, the elder of whom was Mrs. Benjamin Slayback, wife of the well-known member of Congress. The younger was Katharine Lauderdale, named after her father's cousin, Mrs. Ralston, and she was the dark cousin whom John admired.

Hamilton Bright was a distant relative to both of these persons. But by his father's side he had not originally belonged to New York, as the others did, but had settled there after spending some years of his early youth in California and Nevada, and had gone into business. At four and thirty he was the junior partner in the important firm of Beman Brothers and Company, Bankers, who had a magnificent building of their own in Broad Street, and

were very solidly prosperous, having shown themselves
to be among the fittest to survive the financial storms of
the last half century. Ralston's friend was a strong,
squarely built, very fair man, of what is generally called
the Saxon type. At first sight, he inspired confidence,
and his clear blue eyes were steady and true. He had
that faculty of looking almost superhumanly neat and
spotless under all circumstances, which is the prerogative
of men with straight, flaxen hair, pink and white complex-
ions, and perfect teeth. It was easy to predict that he
would become too stout with advancing years, and he was
already a heavy man, though not more than half an inch
taller than his friend and distant cousin, John Ralston.
But no one would have believed at first sight that he was
nine years older than the latter.

The nature of friendship between men has been almost
as much discussed as that of love between man and
woman, but with very different results. He laughs at
the idea of friendship who turns a little pale at the memory of love. At all events, most of us feel that friendship is generally a less certain and undeniable thing,
inasmuch as it is harder to exclude from it the element
of personal interest and advantage. The fact probably
is, that no one person can possibly combine all the elements supposed to make up what every one means by
friendship. It would be far more reasonable to construct
one friendship out of many persons, securing in each of
them one at least of the qualities necessary. For instance,
the discreet man, to whom it is safe to tell secrets when
they must be told at all, is not as a matter of course the
man most capable of giving the best advice; nor, if a
certain individual is extremely generous and ready to
lend all he has to his friend, does it follow that he pos-
sesses the tough, manly nature that will face public scorn

rather than abandon that friend in his hour of need. Some men, too, want sympathy in their troubles, and will have it, even at the cost of common sense. Others need encouragement; others, again, need most of all to be told the unpleasant truth about themselves in the most pleasant form practicable. Altogether it seems probable that the ideal friend must either be an altogether superhuman personage, or a failure in so far as his own life is concerned.

Hamilton Bright approached as nearly to that ideal as his humanity would allow. He did not in the least trouble himself to find out why he liked Ralston, and wished to be of service to him, and he wisely asked for nothing whatever in return for what he gave. But he was very far from looking up to him, and perhaps even from respecting him as he wished that he might. He simply liked him better than other men, and stood by him when he needed help, which often happened.

They left the florist's window and walked slowly up Fifth Avenue. John Ralston was a born New Yorker and preferred his own city to any other place in the world with that solid, satisfactory, unreasoning prejudice which belongs especially to New Yorkers and Parisians, and of which it is useless to attempt any explanation. Hamilton Bright, on the contrary, often wished himself away, and in spite of his excessively correct appearance even the easy formality of American metropolitan life was irksome to him. He had loved the West, and in the midst of great interests and advantages, he regretted his former existence and daily longed for the clearer air and bolder breath of Nevada. The only objects about which he ever displayed much enthusiasm were silver and cattle, about which Ralston knew nothing and cared less.

"When is it to be?" asked Bright after a long silence.

Ralston looked at him quickly.

"What?" he asked in a short tone.

Bright did not answer at once, and when he spoke his voice was rather dull and low.

"When are you going to be married? Everybody knows that you are engaged."

"Then everybody is wrong. I am not engaged."

"Oh — I thought you were. All right."

Another pause followed and they walked on.

"Alexander Junior said I was a failure," observed Ralston at last. "That was some time ago."

"Oh — was that the trouble?"

Bright did not seem to expect any reply to the question, but his tone was thoughtful.

"Yes," answered Ralston, with a short, discontented laugh. "He said that I was of no use whatever, that I never did anything and never should."

"That settled it, I suppose."

"Yes. That settled it. There was nothing more to be said — on his side, at least."

"And how about your side?"

"We shall see."

Ralston shut his lips viciously and his clean-cut, prominent chin looked determined enough.

"The fact is," said his friend, "that Alexander Junior was not so awfully far wrong — about the past, at all events. You never did anything in your life except make yourself agreeable. And you don't seem to have succeeded in that with him."

"Oh, he used to think me agreeable enough," laughed the younger man. "He used to play billiards with me by the month for his liver, and then call me idle for playing with him. I suppose that if I had given up billiards he would have been impressed with the idea that I was about to reform. It wouldn't have cost me much. I hated the stupid game and only played to amuse him."

"All the same — I wish I had your chances — I mean, I wish I may have as good a chance as you, when I think of getting married."

"My chances!" Ralston did not smile now, and his tone was harsh as he repeated the words. He glanced at his companion. "When will that be?" he asked after a moment's pause. "Why don't you get married, Ham? I've often wondered. But then — you're so cursedly reasonable about everything! I suppose you'll stick to the single ticket as long as you have strength to resist, and then you'll marry a nurse. Wise man!"

"Thank you. You're as encouraging as usual."

"You don't need encouragement a bit, old man. You're so full of it anyhow, that you can spare a lot for other people. You have a deuced good effect on my liver, Ham. Do you know it? You ought to look pleased."

"Oh, yes. I am. I only wish the encouragement might last a little longer."

"I can't help being gloomy sometimes — rather often, I ought to say. I fancy I'm a born undertaker, or something to do with funerals. I've tried a lot of other things for a few days and failed — I think I'll try that. By the by, I'm very thirsty and here's the Hoffman House."

"It's not far to the club, if you want to drink," observed Bright, stopping on the pavement.

"You needn't come in, if you think it's damaging to your reputation," answered Ralston.

"My reputation would stand a good deal of knocking about," laughed Bright. "I think my character would bear three nights a week in a Bowery saloon and spare time put in now and then in a University Place bar, without any particular harm."

"By Jove! I wish mine would!"

"It won't," said Bright. "But I wasn't thinking of your reputation, nor of anything especial except that things are generally better at a club than at a hotel."

"The Brut is good here. I've tried it — often. Come along."

"I'll wait for you outside. I'm not thirsty."

"I told you so," retorted Ralston. "You're afraid somebody will see you."

"You're an idiot, Jack!"

Thereupon Bright led the way into the gorgeous bar, a place probably unique in the world. A number of pictures by great French masters hang on the walls — pictures unrivalled, perhaps, in beauty of execution and insolence of conception. The rest is a blaze of polished marble and woodwork and gleaming metal.

Ralston nodded to the bar-tender.

"What will you have? " he asked, turning to Bright.

"Nothing, thanks. I'm not thirsty."

"Oh — all right," answered Ralston, discontentedly. "I'll have a pint of Irroy Brut with a bit of lemon peel in it. Champagne isn't wine — it's only a beverage," he added, turning to Bright as though to explain his reasons for wanting so much.

"I quite agree with you," said Bright, lighting a cigar. "Champagne isn't wine, and it's not fit to drink at the best. Either give me wine that is wine, or give me whiskey."

"Whichever you like."

"Did you say whiskey, sir ?" enquired the bar-tender, who was in the act of rubbing the rim of a pint glass with a lemon peel.

"Nothing, thank you. I'm not thirsty," answered Bright a third time.

"Hallo, Bright, my little man! What are you doing here ? Oh — Jack Ralston — I see."

The speaker was a very minute and cheerful specimen of human New York club life, — pink-cheeked, black-eyed, neat and brisk, not more than five feet six inches in height, round as a little barrel, with tiny hands and feet. He watched Ralston, as soon as he noticed him. The bartender had emptied the pint bottle of champagne into the glass and Ralston had set it to his lips with the evident intention of finishing it at draught.

"Hold on, Jack!" cried Frank Miner, the small man. "I say — easy there! You'll have apoplexy or something — I say — "

"Don't speak to a man on his drink, Frank," said Bright, calmly. "When I drove cattle in the Nacimiento Valley we used to shoot for that."

"I shall avoid that place," answered Miner.

Ralston drew a long breath as he set down the empty glass.

"I wanted that," he said, half to himself. "Hallo, Frank — is that you? What will you have?"

"Nothing — now — thank you," answered Miner. "I've satisfied my thirst and cured my tendency to vice by seeing you take that down. You're a beautiful sight and an awful example for a thirsty man. Get photographed, Jack — they could sell lots of copies at temperance meetings. Heard the story about the temperance tracts? Stop me if you have. Man went out to sell teetotal tracts in Missouri. Came back and his friends were surprised to see him alive. 'Never had such a good time in my life,' said he. 'Every man to whom I offered a tract pulled out a pistol and said, "Drink or I'll shoot." And here I am.' There's a chance for you, Jack, when you get stuck."

Bright and Ralston laughed at the little man's story and all three turned and left the bar-room together.

"Seen the old gentleman lately?" enquired Frank Miner, as they came out upon the pavement.

"Do you mean uncle Robert?" asked Bright.

"Yes — cousin Robert, as we call him."

"It always amuses me to hear a little chap like you calling that old giant 'cousin,'" said Bright.

"He likes it. It makes him feel frisky. Besides, he is a sort of cousin. My uncle Thompson married Margaret Lauderdale — "

"Oh, yes — I know all about the genealogy," laughed Bright.

"Who was Robert Lauderdale's own cousin," continued Miner. "And as Robert Lauderdale is your great-uncle and Jack Ralston's great-uncle, that makes you second cousins to each other and makes me your — let me see — both — "

"Shut up, Frank!" exclaimed Ralston. "You've got it all wrong again. Uncle Robert isn't Bright's great-uncle. He's first cousin to your deceased aunt Margaret, who was Bright's grandmother, and you're first cousin to his mother and first cousin, once removed, to him; and he's my third cousin and you're no relation to me at all, except by your uncle's marriage, and if you want to know anything more about it you have your choice between the family Bible and the Bloomingdale insane asylum — which is a quiet, healthy place, well situated."

"Well then, what relation am I to my cousin Robert?" asked Miner, with a grin.

"An imaginary relation, my dear boy."

"Oh, I say! And his being my very own aunt by marriage's own cousin is not to count for anything, because you two are such big devils and I am only a light weight, and you could polish your boots with me if I made a fuss! It's too bad! Upon my word, brute force rules society as much as it ever did in the middle ages. So there goes my long-cherished claim upon a rich relation. However, you've destroyed the illusion so often before that I know how to resurrect it."

"For that matter," said Bright, "the fact is about as illusory as the illusion itself. If you insist upon being considered as one of the Lauderdale tribe, we're glad to have you on your own merits — but you'll get nothing out of it but the glory — "

"I know. It gives me a fictitious air of respectability to be one of you. Besides, you should be proud to have a man of letters — "

"Say an author at once," suggested Ralston.

"No. I'm honest, if I'm anything, — which is doubtful. A man of letters, I say, can be useful in a family. Suppose, for instance, that Jack invented an electric street-dog, or — "

"What ? " enquired Ralston, with a show of interest. "An electric what ? "

"I was only thinking of something new," said Miner, thoughtfully.

"I thought you said, an electric street-dog — "

"I did — yes. Something of that sort, just for illustration. I believe they had one at Chicago, with an india-rubber puppy, — at least, if they didn't, they ought to have had it, — but anything of the kind would do — self-drying champagne — anything ! Suppose that Jack invented something useful like that, I could write it up in the papers, and get up advertisements for it, and help the family to get rich."

"Is that the sort of literature you cultivate ? " asked Bright.

"Oh, no ! Much more flowery — quite like the flowers of the field in some ways, for it cometh up — to the edi-

tor's office — in the morning, and in the evening, if not
sooner, it is cut down — by the editor — dried up, and
withered, or otherwise disposed of, so that it cannot be
said to reach the general public."

"Not very paying, I should think."

"Well — not to me. But of course, if there were not
so much of it offered to the magazines and papers, there
wouldn't be so many people employed by them to read
and reject articles. So somebody gets a living out of it.
I console myself with the certainty that my efforts help
to keep at least one man in every office from starvation.
I spoke to cousin Robert about it and he seemed rather
pleased by the idea, and said that he would mention it
to his brother, old Mr. Alexander, who's a philanthropist — "

"Call him cousin Alexander," suggested Ralston.
"Why do you make any distinction?"

"Because he's not the rich one," answered Miner, im-
perturbably. "He'll be promoted to be my cousin, if the
fortune is left to him."

"Then I'm afraid he'll continue to languish among
your non-cousin acquaintances."

"Why shouldn't he inherit the bulk of the property?"
enquired Miner, speaking more seriously.

"Because he's a philanthropist, and would spend it all
on idiots and 'fresh air funds,' and things of that sort."

"There is Alexander Junior," suggested Miner. "He's
careful enough, I'm sure. I suppose it will go to him."

"I doubt that, too," said Bright. "Alexander Junior
goes to the opposite extreme. However, Jack knows
more about that than I do — and is a nearer relation,
besides."

"Ham is right," answered John Ralston, thoughtfully.
"Cousin Sandy is the most villainous, infernal, steel-trap-

fingered, patent-locked old miser that ever sat down in a
cellar chinking money bags."

"There's a certain force about your language," observed
Miner.

"I believe he's not rich," said Bright.   "So he has an
excuse."

"Poor!" exclaimed Ralston, contemptuously.   "I'm
poor."

"I wish I were, then — in your way," returned Miner.
"That was Irroy Brut, I noticed.   It looked awfully good.
It's true that you haven't two daughters, as your cousin
Sandy has."

"Nor a millionaire son-in-law — like Ben Slayback, —
Slayback of Nevada he is, in the Congressional Record,
because there's another from somewhere else."

"He wears a green tie," said Miner, softly.   "I saw him
two years ago, before he and Charlotte were married."

"I know," answered Ralston.   "Cousin Katharine
hates him, I believe.   Uncle Robert will probably leave
the whole fortune in trust for Slayback's children.   There's
a little boy.   They say he has red hair, like his father,
and they have christened him Alexander — merely as an
expression of hope.   It would be just like uncle Robert."

"I don't believe it," said Bright.   "But as for Slayback, don't abuse him till you know him better.   I knew
him out West, years ago.   He's a brick."

"He is precisely the colour of one," retorted Ralston.

"Don't be spiteful, Jack."

"I'm not spiteful.   I daresay he's full of virtue, as all
horrid people are — inside.   The outside of him is one of
nature's finest failures, and his manners are awful always
— and worse when he tries to polish them for the evening.
He's a corker, a thing to scare sharks with — it doesn't
follow that he's been a train-wrecker or a defaulting cash-

ier, and I didn't say it did. Oh, yes — I know — handsome is that puts its hand into its pocket, and that sort of thing. Give me some soda water with a proverb in it — that confounded Irroy wasn't dry enough."

Frank Miner looked up into Bright's eyes and smiled surreptitiously. He was walking between his two taller companions. Bright glanced at Ralston's lean, nervous face, and saw that the lines of ill-temper had deepened during the last quarter of an hour. It was not probable that a pint of wine could alone have any perceptible effect on the man's head, but it was impossible to know what potations had preceded the draught.

"No," said Bright. "Such speeches as that are not spiteful. They're foolish. Besides, Slayback's a friend of mine."

Miner looked up again, but in surprise. Ralston turned sharply on Bright.

"I say, Ham—" he began.

"All right, Jack," Bright interrupted, striding steadily along. "We're not going to quarrel. Stand up for your friends, and I'll stand up for mine. That's all."

"I haven't any," answered Ralston, growing suddenly gloomy again.

"Oh! Well — so much the better for you, then."

For a few moments no one spoke again. Miner broke the silence. He was a cheerful little soul, and hated anything like an unpleasant situation.

"Heard about the cow and the collar-stud, Jack?" he enquired, by way of coming to the rescue.

"Chestnut!" growled Ralston.

"Of course," answered Miner, who was nevertheless convinced that Ralston had not heard the joke. "I wasn't going to tell it. It only struck me just then."

"Why?" asked Bright, who failed to see any con-

"I want to leave a card on some people at the Imperial," he said. "I'll be back in a moment." And he disappeared within.

Bright and Miner stood waiting outside.

"Do you believe that — about leaving a card?" asked Miner, after a pause.

"I don't know," answered Bright.

"Because I think he's got the beginning of a 'jag' on him now. He's gone in for something short to settle that long drink. Pity, isn't it?"

Bright did not answer at once.

"I say, Frank," he said at last, "don't talk about Jack's drinking — there's a good fellow. He'll get over it all right, some day."

"People do talk about it a good deal," answered Miner. "I don't think I'm worse than other people, and I'll try to talk less. But it's been pretty bad, lately. The trouble is, you can't tell just how far gone he is. He has a strong head — up to a certain point, and then he's a fiend, all at once. And he's always quarrelsome, even when he's sober, so that's no sign."

"Poor chap! He inherits it to some extent. His father could drink more than most men, and generally did."

"Yes. I met a man the other day — a fellow in the Navy — who told me they had no end of stories of the old Admiral. But no one ever saw him the worse for it."

"That's true enough. But no nerves will last through two generations of whiskey."

"I suppose not." Miner paused. "You see," he continued presently, "he could have left his card in half the time he's been in there. Come in. We shall find him at the bar."

"No," said Bright. "I won't spy on him. I shouldn't like it myself."

"And he says he has no friends!" exclaimed Miner, not without admiration.

"Oh, that's only his way when he's cross. Not that his friends are of any use to him. He'll have to work out his own salvation alone — or his own damnation, poor devil!"

Before Miner made any answer, Ralston came out again. His face looked drawn and weary and there were dark shadows under his eyes. He stood still a moment on the threshold of the door, looked deliberately to the left, towards Broadway, then to the right, along the street, and at last at his friends. Then he slowly lighted a cigarette, brushed a tiny particle of ash from the sleeve of his rough black coat and came out upon the pavement, with a quick, decided step.

"Now then, I'm ready for the undertaker," he said, with a sour smile. "Sorry to have kept you waiting so long," he added, as though by an afterthought.

"Not a bit," answered Miner, cheerfully.

Bright said nothing, and his quiet, healthy face expressed nothing. But as they went towards the crossing of Broadway, he was walking beside Ralston, instead of letting little Frank Miner keep his place in the middle.

CHAPTER II.

IT was between three and four o'clock, and Broadway was crowded, as it generally is at that time in the afternoon. In the normal life of a great city, the crowd flows and ebbs in the thoroughfares as regularly as the blood in a living body. From that mysterious, grey hour, when the first distant rumble is heard in the deserted streets, jast before the outlines of the chimneys become distinct against the clouds or the murky sky, when the night-worker and the man of pleasure, the day-labourer and the dawn, all meet for a brief moment at one of the crossings in daily life's labyrinth, through all the four and twenty hours in which each pulsation is completed, until that dull, far-off roll of the earliest cart echoes again, followed within a few minutes by many others,— round and round the clock again, wth unfailing exactness, you may note the same rise and fall of the life-stream.

The point at which Ralston and his companions crossed Broadway is a particularly busy one. It is near many of the principal theatres; there are a number of big hotels in the neighbourhood; there are some fashionable shops; it is only one short block from the junction of Broadway and Sixth Avenue, where there is an important station of the elevated road, and there are the usual carts, vans and horse-cars chasing each other up and down, and not leaving even enough road for two carriages to pass one another on either side of the tracks. The streams of traffic meet noisily, and thump and bump and jostle through the difficulty, and a man standing there may watch the expression change in all the faces as they approach the point. The natural look disappears for a moment; the eyes glance nervously to the right and left; the lips are set as though for an effort; the very carriage of the body is different, as though the muscles were tightened for an exertion which the frame may or may not be called upon to make instantly without warning. It is an odd sight, though one which few people see, every one being concerned to some extent for his own safety, and oblivious of his neighbour's dangers.

Ralston and the others stood at the corner waiting for an opportunity to pass. There was a momentary inter-

ruption of the line of vehicles on the up-town side, which
was nearest to them. Ralston stepped forward first
toward the track. Glancing to the left, he saw a big
express cart coming up at full speed, and on the other
track, from his right as he stood, a horse-car was coming
down, followed at some distance by a large, empty van.
The horse-car was nearest to him, and passed the corner
briskly. A small boy, wheeling an empty perambulator
and leading a good-looking rough terrier by a red string,
crossed towards Ralston between the horse-car and the
van, dragging the dog after him, and was about to cross
the other track when he saw that the express cart rattling
up town was close upon him. He paused, and drew back
a little to let it pass, pulling back his perambulator,
which, however, caught sideways between the rails. At
the same instant the clanging bell and the clatter of a
fire engine, followed by a hook and ladder cart, and
driven at full speed, produced a sudden commotion, and
the man who was driving the empty van looked backward
and hastened his horses, in order to get out of the way.
In the confusion the little boy and his perambulator were
in danger of annihilation.

Ralston jumped the track, snatched the boy in one arm
and lifted the perambulator bodily with his other hand,
throwing them across the second pair of rails as he
sprang. He fell at full length in the carriage way. He
lay quite still for a moment, and the horses of the empty
van stuck out their fore-feet and stopped with a plunge
close beside him. The people paused on the pavement,
and one or two came forward to help him. There is no
policeman at this crossing as a rule, as there is one a
block higher, at the main corner. Ralston was not hurt,
however, though he had narrowly escaped losing his foot,
for the wheel of one of the vehicles had torn the heel

from his shoe. He was on his legs in a few moments, holding the terrified boy by the collar, and lecturing him roughly upon the folly of doing risky things with a perambulator. Meanwhile the horse-cars and wagons which had blocked the crossing having moved off in opposite directions, Bright and Frank Miner ran across. Bright was very pale as he passed his arm through Ralston's and drew him away. Miner looked at him with silent admiration, having all his life longed to be the hero of some such accident.

"I wish you wouldn't do such things, Jack," said Bright, in his calm voice. "Are you hurt?"

"Not a bit," answered Ralston, who seemed to have enjoyed the excitement. "The thing almost took off my foot, though. I can't walk. Come over to the Imperial again. I'll get brushed down, and take a cab. Come along — I can't stand this crowd. There'll be a reporter in a minute."

Without further words the three recrossed the street to the hotel.

"I don't suppose the most rigid doctor would object to my having something to drink after that tumble," observed Ralston, as they passed through the crowded hall.

"Every man is the best judge of what he wants," answered Bright.

Few people noticed, or appeared to notice, Ralston's dilapidated condition, his smashed hat, his dusty clothes and his heelless shoe. He found a hall-boy who brushed him, and little Frank Miner did his best to restore the hat to an appearance of respectability.

"All right, Frank," said Ralston. "Don't bother — I'm going home in a cab, you know."

He led the way to the bar, swallowed half a tumbler of whiskey neat, and then got into a carriage.

"See you this evening," he said briefly, as he nodded to Bright and Miner, and shut the cab door after him.

The other two watched the carriage a moment, as it drove away, and then looked at one another. Miner had a trick of moving his right ear when he was puzzled. It is rather an unusual peculiarity, and his friends knew what it meant. As Bright looked at him the ear began to move slowly, backwards and forwards, with a slight upward motion. Bright smiled.

"You needn't wag it so far, Frank," he said. "He's going home. It will be all right now."

"I suppose so — or I hope so, at least. I wonder if Mrs. Ralston is in."

"Why?"

"The trouble with you intelligent men is that you have no sense," answered the little man. "He's had another drink — four fingers it was, too — and he's been badly shaken up, and he had the beginning of a 'jag' on before, and he's going home in a rolling cab, which makes it worse. If he meets his mother, there'll be a row. That's all. Even when I was a boy it wasn't good form to be drunk before dinner, and nobody drinks now — at least, not as they used to. Well — it's none of my business."

"It's everybody's business," said Bright. "But a harder man to handle I don't know. He'll either come to grief or glory, or both together, one of these days. It's not the quantity he takes — it's the confounded irregularity of him. I'm going to the club — are you coming?"

"I may as well correct my proofs there as anywhere else. Pocket's full of them." Miner tapped his round little chest with an air of some importance.

"Proofs, eh? Something new?"

"I've worn them out, my boy. They're incapable of

returning me with thanks any more — until next time. I've worn them out, heel and toe, — right out."

"Is it a book, Frank?"

"Not yet. But it's going to be. This is the first — a series of essays, you know — this is the wedge, and I've got it in, and I am going to drive it for all I'm worth, and when there are six or seven they'll make a book, together with some other things — something in the same style, — which have appeared before."

"I'm very glad, old man. I congratulate you. Go in and win."

"It's an awful life, though," said Frank Miner, growing suddenly grave.

Bright glanced at the neat, rotund little figure, at the pink cheeks and bright eyes, and he smiled quietly.

"It's not wearing you to the bone yet," he observed.

"Oh — that's no sign! Look at Napoleon. He had rather my figure, I believe. What's the good of getting thin about things, anyhow? It's only unhappy people who get thin. You work hard enough, Ham, in your humdrum way — oh, I don't envy your lot! — and you're laying it on, Ham, you're laying it on steadily, year after year. You'll be a fat man, Ham — ever so much fatter than I am, because there's twice as much of you, to begin with. Besides, you've got a big chest and that makes a man look stout. But then, you don't care, do you? You're perfectly happy, so you get fat. So would Apollo, if he were a successful banker, and gave up bothering about goddesses and things. As for me, I about keep my weight. Given up bread, though — last summer. Bad thing, bread."

So Miner chattered on as he walked by his friend's side, towards the club. There was no great talent in him, though he had drifted into literature, and of in-

dustry he had not so much as he made people believe.
But he possessed the treasure of cheerfulness, and dis-
pensed it freely in his conversation, whereas in his
writings he strove at the production of gruesome and
melancholy tales, stories of suffering and horror, the
analysis of pain and the portraiture of death in many
forms. The contradiction between the disposition of
literary men and their works is often a curious study.

Mrs. Ralston was at home that afternoon, or rather, to
be accurate in the social sense, she was in, and had given
orders to the general effect that only her particular
friends were to be admitted. This, again, is a statement
susceptible of misapprehension, as she had not really any
particular friends in the world, but only acquaintances
in divers degrees of intimacy, who called themselves her
friends and sometimes called one another her enemies.
But of such matters she took little heed, and was at no
pains to set people right with regard to her private opinion of them. She did many kind things within society's
limits and without, but she was wise enough to expect
nothing in return, being well aware that real gratitude is
a mysterious cryptogam like the truffle, and indeed
closely resembling the latter in its rarity, its spontaneous
growth, its unprepossessing appearance, and in the fact
that it is more often found and enjoyed by the lower
animals than by man.

It may be as well to elucidate here the somewhat
intricate points of the Lauderdales' genealogy and connections, seeing that both have a direct bearing upon the
life of Katharine Lauderdale, of John Ralston, and of
many others who will appear in the course of this epi-
sodic history.

In old times the primeval Alexander Lauderdale, a
younger son of an honourable Scotch family, brought his

wife, with a few goods and no particular chattels, to. New York, and they had two sons, Alexander and Robert, and died and were buried. Of these two sons the elder, Alexander, did very well in the world, married a girl of Dutch family, Anna Van Blaricorn, and had three sons, and he and his wife died and were buried beside the primeval Alexander.

Of these three sons the eldest was Alexander Lauderdale, the philanthropist, of whom mention has been made, who was alive at the time this story begins, who married a young girl of Puritan lineage and some fortune. She died when their only son, Alexander Lauderdale Junior, was twenty-two years of age. The latter married Emma Camperdown, of the Kentucky Catholic family, and had two daughters, the elder, Charlotte, married at the present time to Benjamin Slayback of Nevada, member of Congress, the younger, Katharine Lauderdale, being John Ralston's dark cousin.

So much for the first of the three sons. The second was Robert Lauderdale, the famous millionaire, the uncle Robert spoken of by Ralston and the others, who never married, and was at the time of this tale about seventy-five years of age. He originally made a great sum by a fortunate investment in a piece of land which lies in the heart of the present city of Chicago, and having begun with real estate he stuck to it like the wise man he was, and its value doubled and decupled and centupled, and no one knew how rich he was. He was the second son of the elder son of the primeval Alexander.

The third son of that elder son was Ralph Lauderdale, who was killed at the battle of Chancellorsville in the Civil War. He married a Miss Charlotte Mainwaring, whose father had been an Englishman settled somewhere in the South. Katharine, the widow of the late Admiral

Ralston, was the only child of their marriage, and her
only child was John Ralston, second cousin to Katharine
Lauderdale and Mrs. Slayback.

But the primeval Alexander had a second son Robert,
who had only one daughter, Margaret, married to Rufus
Thompson. And Rufus Thompson's sister married Livingston Miner of New York, and was the mother of
Frank Miner and of three unmarried daughters. That is
the Miner connection.

And on the Lauderdale side Rufus Thompson had one
daughter by his wife, Margaret Lauderdale; and that
daughter married Richard Bright of Cincinnati, who
died, leaving two children, Hamilton Bright and his
sister Hester, the wife of Walter Crowdie, the eminent
painter of New York. This is the relationship of the
Brights to the Lauderdales. Bright, John Ralston and
Katharine Lauderdale were all descended from the same
great-great-grandfather—the primeval Alexander. And
as there is nothing duller to the ordinary mind than
genealogy, except the laborious process of tracing it,
little more shall be said about it hereafter, and the
ingenious reader may refer to these pages when he is
in doubt.

It has been shown, however, that all these modern
individuals with whom we have to do come from a common stock, except little Frank Miner, who could only
boast of a connection by marriage. For it was a good
stock, and the families of all the women who had
married into it were proud of it, and some of them
were glad to speak of it when they had a chance.
None of the Lauderdales had ever come to any great
distinction, it is true, except Robert, by his fabulous
wealth. But none of them had ever done anything dishonourable either, nor even approaching it. There had

not even been a divorce in the family. Some of the men had fought in the war, and one had been killed, and, through Robert, the name was a power in the country. It was said that there had never been any wild blood in the family either, until Ralph married Miss Mainwaring, and that John Ralston got all his faults from his grandmother. But that may or may not be true, seeing that no one knows much of the early youth of the primeval Alexander before he came to this country.

It is probably easier for a man to describe a man than a woman. The converse may possibly be true also. Men see men, on the whole, very much as they are, each man being to each other an assemblage of facts which can be catalogued and referred to. But most men receive from woman an indefinite and perhaps undefinable impression, besides, and sometimes altogether at variance with what is merely visible. It is very hard to convey any idea of that impression to a third person, even in the actual presence of the woman described; it is harder still when the only means are the limited black and white of printed English.

Katharine Lauderdale, at least, had a fair share of beauty of a certain typical kind, a general conception of which belongs to everybody, but her aunt Katharine had not even that. No one ever called Katharine Ralston beautiful, and yet no one had ever classed her among pretty girls when she had been young. Between the two, between prettiness and beauty, there is a debatable country of brown-skinned, bright-eyed, swift-like women of aquiline feature, and sometimes of almost man-like energy, who succeed in the world, and are often worshipped for three things — their endurance, their smile and their voice. They are women who by laying no claim to the immunities of womanhood acquire a direct right to consideration for their own sakes. They also may often possess that mysterious gift known as charm, which is incomparably more valuable than all the classic beauty and perfection of colouring which nature can accumulate in one individual. Beauty fades; wit wears out; but charm is not evanescent.

Katharine Ralston had it, and sometimes wondered what it was, and even tried to understand herself by determining clearly what it was not. But for the most part she thought nothing about it, which is probably the best rule for preserving it, if it needs any sort of preservation.

Outwardly, her son strongly resembled her. He had from her his dark complexion, his lean face and his brown eyes, as well as a certain grace of figure and a free carriage of the head which belong to the pride of station — a little exaggerated — which both mother and son possessed in a high degree. Katharine Ralston did not talk of her family, but she believed in it, as something in which it was good to believe from the bottom of her heart, and she had brought up John to feel that he came from a stock of gentlemen and gentlewomen who might be bad, but could not be mean, nor anything but gentle in the vague, heraldic sense of that good word.

She was a sensible woman and saw her son's faults. They were not small, by any means, nor insignificant by their nature, nor convenient faults for a young gentleman about town, who had the reputation of having tried several occupations and of having failed with quite equal brilliancy in all. But they were not faults that estranged him from her, though she suffered much for his sake in a certain way. She would rather ha re had him a drunkard, a gambler, almost a murderer, than have seen him turn out a hypocrite. She would far

rather have seen him killed before her than have known
that he had ever lied to save himself, or done any of
the mean little sins, for which there may be repentance
here and forgiveness hereafter, but from the pollution
of which honour knows no purification.

Religion she had none whatever, and frankly owned
the fact if questioned directly. But she made no profession of atheism and gave no grounds for her unbelief.
She merely said that she could not believe in the existence of the soul, an admission which at once settled all
other kindred points, so far as she was concerned. But
she regretted her own position. In her childhood, her
ideas had been unsettled by the constant discussions
which took place between her parents. Her father, like
all the Lauderdales, had been a Presbyterian. Her
mother had been an Episcopalian, and, moreover, a
woman alternately devout and doubting. Katharine
shared neither the prejudices nor the convictions of
either. Then she had married Admiral Ralston, a man,
like many officers of the Navy, of considerable scientific
acquirements, and full to overflowing of the scientific
arguments against religion, which were even more popular in his day than they are now. What little hold the
elder Katharine had still possessed upon an undefined
future state was finally destroyed by her sailor husband's
rough, sledge-hammer arguments. In the place of religion she set up a sort of code of honour to which she
rigidly adhered, and in the observance of which she
brought up her only son.

It is worth remarking that until he finally left college
she encouraged him to be religious, if he would, and
regularly took him to church so long as he was a boy.
She even persuaded his father not to talk atheism before
him; and the admiral, who was as conservative as only

republicans can be, was quite willing to let the young
fellow choose for himself what he should believe or reject
when he should come to years of discretion. Up to the
age of twenty-one, Jack had been a remarkably sober
and thoughtful young fellow. He began to change soon
after his father died.

Ralston let himself in with his key when he got home
and went upstairs, supposing that his mother was out,
as she usually was at that hour. She heard his footstep,
however, as he passed the door of her own sitting-room,
on the first landing, and having no idea that anything
was wrong, she called to him.

"Is that you, Jack?"

Ralston stopped and in the dusk of the staircase realized for the first time that he was not sober. He made an
effort when he spoke, answering through the closed door.

"It's all right, mother; I'll be down in a few minutes."

Something unusual in the tone of his voice must have
struck Mrs. Ralston. He had made but two steps forward when she opened the door, throwing the light full
upon him.

"What's the matter, Jack?" she asked, quietly.

Then she saw his face, the deep lines, the drawn
expression, the shadows under the eyes and the unnatural dull light in the eyes themselves. And in the
same glance she saw that his hat was battered and that
his clothes were dusty and stained. She knew well
enough that he drank more than was good for him, but
she had never before seen him in such a state. The
broad daylight, too, and the disorder of his clothes made
him look much more intoxicated than he really was.
Katharine Ralston stood still in silence for a moment,
and looked at her son. Her face grew a little pale just
before she spoke again.

"Are you sober enough to take care of yourself?" she asked rather harshly, for there was a dryness in her throat.

John Ralston was no weakling, and was, moreover, thoroughly accustomed to controlling his nerves, as many men are who drink habitually — until the nerves themselves give way. He drew himself up and felt that he was perfectly steady before he answered in measured tones.

"I'm sorry you should see me just now, mother. I had a little accident, and I took some whiskey afterwards to steady me. It has gone to my head. I'm very sorry."

That was more than enough for his mother. She came swiftly forward, and gently took him by the arm to lead him into her room. But Ralston's sense of honour was not quite satisfied.

"It's partly my fault, mother. I had been taking others things before, but I was all right until the accident happened."

Mrs. Ralston smiled almost imperceptibly. She was glad that he should be so honest, even when he was so far gone. She led him through the door into her own room, and made him sit down in a comfortable chair near the window.

"Never mind, Jack," she said, "I'm just like a man about understanding things. I know you won't do it again."

But Ralston knew his own weakness, and made no rash promises then, though a great impulse arose in his misty understanding, bidding him then and there make a desperately solemn vow, and keep it, or do away with himself if he failed. He only bowed his head, and sat down, as his mother bid him. He was ashamed, and he was a man to whom shame was particularly bitter.

Mrs. Ralston got some cold water in a little bowl, and bathed his forehead, touching him as tenderly as she would have touched a sick child. He submitted readily enough, and turned up his brows gratefully to her hand.

"Your head is a little bruised," she said. "Were you hurt anywhere else? What happened? Can you tell me now, or would you rather wait?"

"Oh, it was nothing much," answered Ralston, speaking more easily now. "There was a boy, with a perambulator, getting between the cars and carts. I got him out of the way, and tumbled down, because there wasn't even time to jump. I threw myself after the boy — somehow. The wheel took off the heel of my boot, but I wasn't hurt. I'm all right now. Thank you, mother dear. There never was anybody like you to understand."

Mrs. Ralston was very pale again, but John could not see her face.

"Don't risk such things, Jack," she said, in a low voice. "They hurt one badly."

Ralston said nothing, but took her hand and kissed it gently. She pressed his silently, and touched his matted hair with her tightly shut lips. Then he got up.

"I'll go to my room, now," he said. "I'm much better. It will be all gone in half an hour. I suppose it was the shaking, — but I did swallow a big dose after my tumble."

"Say nothing more about it, my dear," answered Mrs. Ralston, quietly.

She turned from him, ostensibly to set the bowl of water upon a table. But she knew that he could not be perfectly himself again in so short a time, and if he was still unsteady, she did not wish to see it — for her own sake.

"Thank you, mother," he said, as he left the room.

She might have watched him, if she had chosen to do so, and she would have seen nothing unusual now — nothing but his dusty clothes and the slight limp in his gait, caused by the loss of one low heel. He was young, and his nerves were good, and he had a very strong incentive in the shame he still felt. Moreover, under ordinary circumstances, even the quantity he had drunk would not have produced any visible bodily effect on him, however it might have affected his naturally uncertain temper. It was quite true that the fall and the excitement of the accident had shaken him.

He reached his own room, shut the door, and then sat down to look at himself in the glass, as men under the influence of drink very often do, for some mysterious reason. Possibly the drunken man has a vague idea that he can get control over himself by staring at his own image, and into the reflection of his own eyes. John Ralston never stayed before the mirror longer than was absolutely necessary, except when he had taken too much.

But to-day he was conscious that, in spite of appearances, he was rapidly becoming bodily sober. If it had all happened at night, he would have wound up at a club, and would probably have come home in the small hours, in order to be sure of not finding his mother downstairs, and he would have been in a very dubious condition. But the broad light, the cold water, his profound shame and his natural nerve had now combined to restore him, outwardly at least, and so far as he was conscious, to his normal state.

He bathed, looked at the clock, and saw that it was not yet five, and then dressed himself as though to go out. But, before doing so, he sat down and smoked a cigarette. He felt nervously active now, refreshed and able to face anything. Before he had half finished smoking he had made up his mind to show himself to his mother and then to go for a walk before dinner.

He glanced once more at the mirror to assure himself that he was not mistaken, and was surprised at the quick change in his appearance. His colour had come back, his eyes were quiet, the deeper lines were gone from his face — lines which should never have been there at five and twenty. He turned away, well pleased, and went briskly down the stairs, though it was already growing dark, and the steps were high. After all, he thought it was probably the loss of the heel from his shoe that had made him walk unsteadily. Such an absurd accident had never happened to him before. He knocked at the door of his mother's sitting-room, and she bade him come in.

"You see, mother, it was nothing, after all," he said, going up to her as she sat before the fire.

She looked up, saw his face, and then smiled happily.

"I'm so glad, Jack," she answered, springing to her feet and kissing him. "You have no idea how you looked when I saw you there on the landing. I thought you were really — quite — but quite, quite, you know, my dear boy."

She shook her head, still smiling, and holding botl his hands.

"I'm going for a bit of a walk before dinner," he said. "Then we'll have a quiet evening together, and I shall go to bed early."

"That's right. The walk will do you good. You're quite wonderful, Jack!" She laughed outright — he looked so perfectly sober. "Don't drink any more whiskey to-day!" she added, not half in earnest.

"Never fear!" And he laughed too, without any suspicion of himself.

He walked rapidly down the street in the warm glow of the evening, heedless of the direction he took. By fate or by habit, he found himself a quarter of an hour later opposite to Alexander Lauderdale's house. He paused, reflected a moment, then ascended the steps and rang the bell.

"Is Miss Katharine at home?" he enquired of the girl who opened the door.

"Yes, sir. She came in a moment ago."

John Ralston entered the house without further question.

CHAPTER III.

RALSTON entered the library, as the room was called, although it did not contain many books. The house was an old-fashioned one in Clinton Place, which nowadays is West Eighth Street, between Fifth Avenue and Sixth Avenue, a region respectable and full of boarding houses. In accordance with the customs of the times in which it had been built, the ground floor contained three good-sized rooms, known in all such houses as the library, the drawing-room or 'parlour,' and the dining-room, which was at the back and had windows upon the yard. The drawing-room, being under the middle of the house, had no windows at all, and was therefore really available only in the evening. The library, where Ralston waited, was on the front.

There was an air of gravity about the place which he had never liked. It was not exactly gloomy, for it was on too small a scale, nor vulgarly respectable, for such objects as were for ornament were in good taste, as a few engravings from serious pictures by great masters, a good portrait of the primeval Alexander Lauderdale, a small bronze reproduction of the Faun in the Naples museum, two or three fairly good water-colours, which were apparently views of Scotch scenery, and a big blue china vase with nothing in it. With a little better arrangement, these things might have gone far. But the engravings and pictures were hung with respect to symmetry rather than with regard to the light. The stiff furniture was stiffly placed against the wall. The books in the low shelves opposite to the fireplace were chiefly bound in black, in various stages of shabbiness, and Ralston knew that they were largely works on religion, and reports of institutions more or less educational or philanthropic. There was a writing table near the window, upon which a few papers and writing materials were arranged with a neatness not business-like, but systematically neat for its own sake — the note paper was piled with precision upon the middle of the blotter, upon which lay also the penwiper, and a perfectly new stick of bright red sealing-wax, so that everything would have to be moved before any one could possibly write a letter. The carpet was old, and had evidently been taken to pieces and the breadths refitted with a view to concealing the threadbare parts, but with effect disastrous to the continuity of the large green and black pattern. The house was heated by a furnace and there was no fire in the grim fireplace. That was for economy, as Ralston knew.

For the Lauderdales were evidently poor, though the old philanthropist who lived upstairs was the only living brother of the arch-millionaire. But Alexander Senior spent his life in getting as much as he could from Robert in order to put it into the education of idiots, and would cheerfully have fed his son and daughter-in-law and Katharine on bread and water for the sake of educating one idiot more. The same is a part of philanthropy when it becomes professional. Alexander Junior had a magnificent reputation for probity, and was concerned in business, being connected with the administration of a great Trust Company, which brought him a fixed salary. Beyond that he assured his family that he had never made a dollar in his life, and that only his health, which indeed was of iron, stood between them and starvation, an argument which he used with force to crush any frivolous tendency developed in his wife and daughter. He had dark hair just turning to a steely grey, steel-grey eyes, and a long, clean-shaven, steel-grey upper lip, but his eyebrows were still black. His teeth were magnificent, but he had so little vanity that he hardly ever smiled, except as a matter of politeness. He had looked pleased, however, when Benjamin Slayback of Nevada had led his daughter Charlotte from the altar. Slayback had loved the girl for her beauty and had taken her penniless; and uncle Robert had given her a few thousands for her bridal outfit. Alexander Junior had therefore been at no expense for her marriage, except for the cake and decorations, but it was long before he ceased to speak of his expenditure for those items. As for Alexander Senior, he really had no money except for idiots; he wore his clothes threadbare, had his overcoats turned, and secretly bought his shoes of a little Italian shoemaker in South Fifth Avenue. He was said to be over eighty years of age, but was in reality not much older than his rich brother Robert.

It would be hard to imagine surroundings more uncongenial to Mrs. Alexander Junior, as Katharine Lauderdale's mother was generally called. An ardent Roman Catholic, she was bound to a family of rigid Presbyterians; a woman of keen artistic sense, she was wedded

to a man whose only measure of things was their money-
value; a nature originally susceptible to the charm of all
outward surroundings, and inclining to a taste for modest
luxury rather than to excessive economy, she had married
one whom she in her heart believed to be miserly. She
admitted, indeed, that she would probably have married
her husband again, under like circumstances. The child
of a ruined Southern family, loyal during the Civil War,
she had been brought early to New York, and almost as
soon as she was seen in society, Alexander Lauderdale
had fallen in love with her. He had seemed to her, as
indeed he was still, a splendid specimen of manhood; he
was not rich, but was industrious and was the nephew of
the great Robert Lauderdale. Even her fastidious people
could not say that he was not, from a social point of view,
of the best in New York. She had loved him in a girlish
fashion, and they had been married at once. It was all
very natural, and the union might assuredly have turned
out worse than it did.

Seeing that according to her husband's continual assur-
ances they were growing poorer and poorer, Mrs. Alexander had long ago begun to turn her natural gifts to
account, with a view to making a little money wherewith
to provide herself and her daughters with a few harmless
luxuries. She had tried writing and had failed, but she
had been more successful with painting, and had produced
some excellent miniatures. Alexander Junior had at first
protested, fearing the artistic tribe as a whole, and dread-
ing lest his wife should develop a taste for things Bohemian, such as palms in the drawing-room, and going to the
opera in the gallery rather than not going at all. He did
not think of anything else Bohemian within the range of
possibilities, except, perhaps, dirty fingers, which disgusted him, and unpunctuality, which drove him mad.

But when he saw that his wife earned money, and ceased to ask him for small sums to be spent on gloves and perishable hats, he rejoiced greatly, and began to suggest that she should invest her savings, placing them in his hands at five per cent interest. But poor Mrs. Alexander never was so successful as to have any savings to invest. Her husband accepted gratefully a miniature of the two girls which she once painted as a surprise and gave him at Christmas, and he secretly priced it during the following week at a dealer's, and was pleased when the man offered him fifty dollars for it, — which illustrates Alexander's thoughtful disposition.

This was the household in which Katharine Lauderdale had grown up, and these were the people whose characters, temperaments, and looks had mingled in her own. So far as the latter point was concerned, she had nothing to complain of. It was not to be expected that the children of two such handsome people should be anything but beautiful, and Charlotte and Katharine had plenty of beauty of different types, fair and dark respectively. Charlotte was most like her mother in appearance, but more closely resembled her father in nature. Katharine had inherited her father's face and strength of constitution with many of her mother's gifts, more or less modified and, perhaps, diminished in value. At the time when this history begins, she was nineteen years old, and had been what is called 'out' in society for more than a year. She therefore, according to the customs of the country and age, enjoyed the privilege of receiving alone the young gentlemen of her set who either admired her or found pleasure in her conversation. Of the former there were many; of the latter, a few.

Ralston stood with his back to the empty fireplace, staring at the dark mahogany door which led to the regions of the staircase. He had only waited five minutes, but he was in an impulsive frame of mind, and it had seemed a very long time. At last the door opened. Katharine entered the room, smiled and nodded to him, and then turned and shut the door carefully before she came forward.

She was a very beautiful girl. No one could have denied that, in the main. Yet there was something puzzling in the face, primarily due, perhaps, to the mixture of races. The features were harmonious, strong and, on the whole, noble and classic in outline, the mouth especially being of a very pure type, and the curved lips of that creamy, salmon rose-colour occasionally seen in dark persons — neither red, nor pink, nor pale. The very broadly marked dark eyebrows gave the face strength, and the deep grey eyes, almost black at times, had an oddly fixed and earnest look. In them there was no softness on ordinary occasions. They expressed rather a determination to penetrate what they saw, not altogether unmixed with wonder at the discoveries they made. The whole face was boldly outlined, but by no means thin, and the skin was perceptibly freckled, which is unusual with dark people, and is the consequence of a red-haired strain in the inheritance. The primeval Alexander had been a red-haired man, and Robert the Rich had resembled him before he had grown grey. Charlotte Slayback had christened the latter by that name. She had a sharp tongue, and called the primeval one Alexander the Great, her grandfather Alexander the Idiot, and her father Alexander the Safe. Katharine had her own opinions about most of the family, but she did not express them so plainly.

She was still smiling as she met Ralston in the middle of the room.

"You look happy, dear," he said, kissing her forehead softly.

"I'm not," she answered. "I'm glad to see you. There's a difference. Sit down."

"Has there been any trouble?" he asked, seating himself in a little low chair beside the corner of the sofa she had chosen.

"Not exactly trouble — no. It's the old story — only it's getting so old that I'm beginning to hate it. You understand."

"Of course I do. I wish there were anything to be done — which you would consent to do." He added the last words as though by an afterthought.

"I'll consent to almost anything, Jack."

The smile had vanished from her face and she spoke in a despairing tone, fixing her big eyes on his, and bending her heavy eyebrows as though in bodily pain. He took her hand — firm, well-grown and white — in his and laid it against his lean cheek.

"Dear!" he said.

His voice trembled a little, which was unusual. He felt unaccountably emotional and was more in love than usual. The tone in which he spoke the single word touched Katharine, and she leaned forward, laying her other hand upon his other one.

"You do love me, Jack," she said.

"God knows I do," he answered, very earnestly, and again his voice quavered.

It was very still in the room, and the dusk was creeping toward the high, narrow windows, filling the corners, and blackening the shadowy places, and then rising from the floor, almost like a tide, till only the faces of the two young people seemed to be above it, still palely visible in the twilight.

Suddenly Katharine rose to her feet, with a quick-drawn breath which was not quite a sigh.

"Pull down the shades, Jack," she said, as she struck a match and lit the gas at one of the stiff brackets which flanked the mantelpiece.

Ralston obeyed in silence. When he came back she had resumed her seat in the corner of the sofa, and he sat down beside her instead of taking the chair again.

He did not speak at once, though it seemed to him that his heart had never been so full before. As he looked at the lovely girl he felt a thrill of passionate delight that ran through him and almost hurt him, and left him at last with an odd sensation in the throat and a painful sinking at the heart. He did not reflect upon its meaning, and he certainly did not connect it with the reaction following what he had made his nerves bear during the day. He was sincerely conscious that he had never been so deeply, truly in love with Katharine before. She watched him, understanding what he felt, smiling into his eyes, but silent, too. They had known each other since they had been children, and had loved one another since Katharine had been sixteen years old, — more than three whole years, which is a long time for first love to endure, unless it means to be last as well as the first.

"You said you would consent to almost anything," said Ralston, after a long pause. "It would be very simple for us to be married, in spite of everybody. Shall we? Shall we, dear?" he asked, repeating the question.

"I would almost do that —" She turned her face away and stared at the empty fireplace.

"Say, quite! After all, what can they all do? What is there so dreadful to face, if we do get married? We must, one of these days. Life's not life without you —

and death wouldn't be death with you, darling," he added.

"Are you in earnest, Jack, — or are you making love to me ? "

She asked the question suddenly, catching his hands and holding them firmly together, and looking at him with eyes that were almost fierce. The passion rose in his own, with a dark light, and his face grew pale. Then he laughed nervously.

"I'm only laughing, of course — you see I am. Why must you take a fellow in earnest ? "

But there was nothing in his words that jarred upon her. He could not laugh away the truth from his look, for truth it was at that moment, whatever its source.

"I know — I understand," she said, in a low voice. "We can't live apart, you and I."

"It's like tearing out fingers by the joints every time I leave you," Ralston answered. "It's the resurrection of the dead to see you — it's the glory of heaven to kiss you."

The words came to his lips ready, rough and strong, and when he had spoken them, hers sealed every one of them upon his own, believing every one of them, and trusting in the strength of him. Then she pushed him away and leaned back in her corner, with half-closed eyes.

"I don't know why I ever ask if you're in earnest, dear," she said. "I know you are. It would kill me to think that you're playing. Women are always said to be foolish — perhaps it's in that way — and I'm no better than the rest of them. But you don't spoil me in that way. You don't often say it as you did just now."

"I never loved you as I do now," said Ralston, simply.

"I feel it."

"But I wish — well, impossibilities."

"What ? Tell me, Jack. I shall understand."

"Oh — nothing. Only I wish I could find some way of proving it to you. But people always say that sort of thing. We don't live in the middle ages."

"I believe we do," answered Katharine, thoughtfully. "I believe people will say that we did, hundreds of years hence, when they write about us. Besides — Jack — not that I want any proof, because I believe you — but there is something you could do, if you would. I know you . wouldn't like to do it."

It flashed across Ralston's mind that she was about to ask him to make a great sacrifice for her, to give up wine for her sake, having heard, perhaps — even probably — of some of his excesses. He was nervous, overwrought and full of wild impulses that day, but he knew what such a promise would mean in his simple code. He was not in any true sense degraded, beyond the weakening of his will. In an instant so brief that Katharine did not notice his hesitation he reviewed his whole life, so familiar to him in its worse light that it rose instantaneously before him as a complete picture. He felt positively sure of what she was about to ask him, and as he looked into her great grey eyes he believed that he could keep the pledge he was about to give her, that it would save him from destruction, and that he should thus owe his happiness to her more wholly than ever.

"I'll do it," he answered, and the fingers of his right hand slowly closed till his fist was clenched.

"Thank you, dear one," answered Katharine, softly. "But you mustn't promise until you know what it is."

"I know what I've said."

"But I won't let you promise. You wouldn't forgive me — you'd think that I had caught you — that it was a trap — all sorts of things."

Ralston smiled and shook his head. He felt quite sure

of her and of himself. And it would have been better for her and for him, if she had asked what he expected.

"Jack," she said, lowering her voice almost to a whisper, "I want you to marry me privately — quite in secret — that's what I mean. Not a human being must know, but you and I and the clergyman."

John Ralston looked into her face in thunderstruck astonishment. It is doubtful whether anything natural or supernatural could have brought such a look into his eyes. Katharine smiled, for the idea had long been familiar to her.

"Confess that you were not prepared for that!" she said. "But you've confessed it already."

"Well — hardly for that — no."

The look of surprise in his face gradually changed into one of wondering curiosity, and his brows knit themselves into a sort of puzzled frown, as though he were trying to solve a difficult problem.

"You see why I didn't want you to promise anything rashly," said Katharine. "You couldn't possibly foresee what I was going to ask any more than you can understand why I ask it. Could you?"

"No. Of course not. Who could?"

"I'm not going to ask any one else to, you may be sure. In the first place, do you think it wrong?"

"Wrong? That depends — there are so many things —" he hesitated.

"Say what you think, Jack. I want to know just what you think."

"That's the trouble. I hardly know myself. Of course there's nothing absolutely wrong in a secret marriage. No marriage is wrong, exactly, if the people are free."

"That's the main thing I wanted to know," said Katharine, quietly.

"Yes — but there are other things. Men don't think it exactly honourable to persuade a girl to be married secretly, against the wishes of her people. A great many men would, but don't. It's somehow not quite fair to the girl. Running away is all fair and square, if people are ready to face the consequences. Perhaps it is that there are consequences to face — that makes it a sort of pitched battle, and the parents generally give in at the end, because there's no other way out of it. But a secret marriage — well, it doesn't exactly have consequences, in the ordinary way. The girl goes on living at home as though she were not married, deceiving everybody all round — and so must the man. In fact it's a kind of lie, and I don't like it."

Ralston paused after this long speech, and was evidently deep in thought.

"All you say is true enough — in a sense," Katharine answered. "But when it's the only way to get married at all, the case is different. Don't you think so yourself? Wouldn't you rather be secretly married than go on like this — as this may go on, for ten, fifteen, twenty years — all our lives?"

"Of course I would. But I don't see why —"

"I do, and I want to make you see. Listen to my little speech, please. First, we are both of age — I am so far as being married is concerned, and we have an absolute right to do as we please about it — to be married in the teeth of the lions, if that's not a false metaphor — or something — you know."

"In the jaws of hell, for that matter," said Ralston, fervently.

"Thank you for saying it. I'm only a girl and mustn't use strong languáge. Very well, we have a perfect right to do as we please. That's a great point. Then we have only to choose, and it becomes a matter of judgment."

"You talk like print," laughed Ralston.

"So much the better. We have made up our minds that we can't live without each other, so we must be married somehow. You don't think it's not — what shall I say? — not quite like a girl for me to talk in this way, do you? We have talked of it so often, and we decided so long ago!"

"What nonsense! Be as plain as possible."

"Because if you do — then I shall have to write it all to you, and I can't write well."

Ralston smiled.

"Go on," he said. "I'm waiting for the reasons."

"They could simply starve us, Jack. We've neither of us a dollar in the world."

"Not a cent," said Ralston, very emphatically. "If we had, we shouldn't be where we are."

"And your mother can't give you any money, and my father won't give me any."

"And I'm a failure," Ralston observed, with sudden grimness and hatred of himself.

"Hush! You'll be a success some day. That's not the question. The point is, if we tried to get married openly, there would be horrible scenes first, and then war, and starvation afterwards. It's not a pretty prospect, but it's true."

"I suppose it is."

"It's so deadly true that it puts an open marriage out of the question altogether. If there were nothing else to be done, it would be different. I'd rather starve than give you up. But there is a way out of it. We can be married secretly. In that way we shall avoid the scenes and the war."

"And then wait for something to happen ?   We should be just where we are now.   To all intents and purposes you would be Spinster Lauderdale and I should be Bachelor Ralston.   I don't see that it would be the slightest improvement on the present situation — honestly, I don't. I'm not romantic, as people are in books.   I don't think it would be sweeter than life to call you wife, and when we're married I shall call you Katharine just the same. I don't distrust you.   You know I don't.   I'm not really afraid that you'll go and marry Ham Bright, or Frank Miner, nor even the most desirable young man in New York, who has probably proposed to you already.   I'm not vain, but I know you love me.   I should be a brute if I doubted it — "

" Yes — I think you would, dear," said Katharine, with great directness.

" So that since I'm to wait for you till ' something happens ' — never mind to whom, and long life to all of them ! — I'd rather wait as we are than go through it with' a pack of lies to carry."

"I like you, Jack — besides loving you.   It's quite another feeling, you know.   You're such a man !"

" I wish I were half what you think I am."

" I'll think what I please.   It's none of your dear business.   But you haven't heard half I have to say yet.   I'll suppose that we're married — secretly.   Very well.   That same day, or the next day, and as soon as possible, I shall go to uncle Robert and tell him the whole truth."

"To uncle Robert !" exclaimed Ralston, who had not yet come to the end of the surprises in store for him. "And ask him for some money, I suppose ?   That won't do, Katharine.   Indeed it won't.   I should be letting you go begging for me.   That's the plain English of it.   No, no !   That can't be done."

"You'll find it hard to prevent me from begging for you, or working for you either, if you ever need it," said Katharine. There was a certain grand simplicity about the plain statement.

"You're too good for me," said Ralston, in a low voice, and for the third time there was a quiver in his tone. Moreover, he felt an unaccustomed moisture in his eyes which gave him pleasure, though he was ashamed of it.

"No, I'm not — not a bit too good for you. But I like to hear — I don't know why it is, but your voice touches me to-day. It seems changed."

Ralston was truthful and honourable. If he had himself understood the causes of his increased emotion, he would have hanged himself rather than have let Katharine say what she did, without telling her what had happened. He drank, and he knew it, and of late he had been drinking hard, but it was the first time that he had ever spoken to Katharine Lauderdale when he had been drinking, and he was deceived by his own apparent soberness beyond the possibility of believing that he was on the verge of being slightly hysterical. Let them who doubt the possibility of such a case question those who have watched a thousand cases.

There was a little pause after Katharine's last words. Then she went on, — explaining her project.

"Uncle Robert always says that nobody understands him as I do. I shall try and make him understand me, for a change. I shall tell him just what has happened, and I shall tell him that he must find work for you to do, since you're perfectly capable of working if you only have a fair chance. You never had one. I don't call it a chance to put an active man like you into a gloomy law office to copy fusty documents. And I don't call it giving you a chance to glue you to a desk in **Beman Brothers'**

bank. You're not made for that sort of work. Of course
you were disgusted and refused to go on. I should have
done just the same."

"Oh, you would — I'm quite sure!" answered Ralston,
with conviction.

"Naturally. Not but that I'm just as capable of working as you are, though. To go back to uncle Robert. It's
just impossible, with all his different interests, all over
the country, and with his influence — and you know what
that is — that he should not have something for you to
do. Besides, he'll understand us. He's a great big man,
on a big scale, a head and shoulders mentally bigger than
all the rest of the family."

"That's true," assented Ralston.

"And he knows that you don't want to take money
without giving an equivalent for it."

"He's known that all along. I don't see why he should
put himself out any more now — "

"Because I'll make him," said Katharine, firmly. "I
can do that for you, and if you torture your code of
honour into fits you can't make it tell you that a wife
should not do that sort of thing for her husband. Can
you?"

"I don't know," answered Ralston, smiling. "I've
tried it myself often enough with the old gentleman.
He says I've had two chances and have thrown them up,
and that, after all, my mother and I have quite enough
to live on comfortably, so he supposes that I don't care
for work. I told him that enough was not nearly so
good as a feast. He laughed and said he knew that,
but that people couldn't stand feasting unless they worked
hard. The last time I saw him, he offered to make
Beman try me again. But I couldn't stand that."

"Of course not."

"I can't stand anything where I produce no effect, and am not to earn my living for ever so long. I wasn't to have any salary at Beman's for a year, you know, because I knew nothing about the work. And it was the same at the lawyer's office — only much longer to wait. I could work at anything I understood, of course. But I suppose I do know precious little that's of any use. It can't be helped, now."

"Yes, it can. But you see my plan. Uncle Robert will be so taken off his feet that he'll find you something. Then the whole thing will be settled. It will probably be something in the West. Then we'll declare ourselves. There'll be one stupendous crash, and we shall disappear from the scene, leaving the family to like it or not, as they please. In the end they will like it. There would be no lies to act — at least, not after two or three days. It wouldn't take longer than that to arrange things."

"It all depends on uncle Robert, it seems to me," said Ralston, doubtfully. "A runaway match would come to about the same thing in the end. I'll do that, if you like."

"I won't. It must be done in my way, or not at all. If we ran away we should have to come back to see uncle Robert, and we should find him furious. He'd tell us to go back to our homes, separately, till we had enough to live on — or to go and live with your mother. I won't do that either. She's not able to support us both."

"No — frankly, she's not."

"And uncle Robert would be angry, wouldn't he? He has a fearful temper, you know."

"Yes — he probably would be raging."

"Well, then?"

"I don't like it, Katharine dear — I don't like it."

"Then you can never marry me at all, Jack. At least, I'm afraid not."

"Never?" Ralston's expression changed suddenly.

"There's another reason, Jack dear. I didn't want to speak of it — now."

CHAPTER IV.

RALSTON said nothing at first. Then he looked at Katharine as though expecting that she should speak again and explain her meaning, in spite of her having said that she had not meant to do so.

"What is this other reason?" he asked, after a long pause.

"It would take so long to tell you all about it," she answered thoughtfully. "And even if I did, I am not sure that you would understand. It belongs — well — to quite another set of ideas."

"It must be something rather serious if it means marriage now, or marriage never."

"It is serious. And the worst of it is that you will laugh at it — and I am sure you will say that I am not honest to myself. And yet I am. You see it is connected with things about which you and I don't think alike."

"Religion?" suggested Ralston, in a tone of enquiry.

Katharine bowed her head slowly, sighed just audibly and looked away from him as she leaned back. Nothing could have expressed more clearly her conviction that the subject was one upon which they could never agree.

"I don't see why you should sigh about it," said Ralston, in a tone which expressed relief rather than perplexity. "I often wonder why people generally look so sad when they talk about religion. Almost everybody does."

"How ridiculous!" exclaimed Katharine, with a little laugh. "Besides, I wasn't sighing, exactly — I was only wishing it were all arranged."

"Your religion?"

"Don't talk like that. I'm in earnest. Don't laugh at me, Jack dear — please!"

"I'm not laughing. Can't you tell me how religion bears on the matter in hand? That's all I need to know. I don't laugh at religion — at yours or any one else's. I believe I have a little inclination to it myself."

"Yes, I know. But — well — I don't think you have enough to save a fly — not the smallest little fly, Jack. Never mind — you're just as nice, dear. I don't like men who preach."

"I'm glad of it. But what has all this to do with our getting married?"

"Listen. It's perfectly clear to me, and you can understand if you will. I have almost made up my mind to become a Catholic —"

"You?" Ralston stared at her in surprise. "You — a Roman Catholic?"

"Yes — Holy Roman Catholic and Apostolic. Is that clear, Jack?"

"Perfectly. I'm sorry."

"Now don't be a Puritan, Jack —"

"I'm not a Puritan. I haven't a drop of Puritan blood. You have, Katharine, for your grandmother was one of the real old sort. I've heard my father say so."

"You're just as much a Lauderdale as I am," retorted Katharine. "And if Scotch Presbyterians are not Puritans, what is? But that isn't what I mean. It's the tendency to wish that people were nothing at all rather than Catholics."

"It's not that. I'm not so prejudiced. I was thinking of the row — that's all. You don't mean to keep that a secret, too? It wouldn't be like you."

"No, indeed," answered Katharine, proudly.

"Well — you've not told me what the connection is between this and our marriage. You don't suppose that it will really make any difference to me, do you? You can't. And you're quite mistaken about my Puritanism. I would much rather that my wife should be a Roman Catholic than nothing at all. I'm broad enough for that, anyhow. Of course it's a serious matter, because people sometimes do that kind of thing and then find out that they have made a mistake — when it's too late. And there's something ridiculous and undignified about giving it up again when it's once done. Religion seems to be a good deal like politics. You may change once — people won't admire you — I mean people on your old side — but they will tolerate you. But if you change twice — "

"I'm not going to change twice. I've not quite, quite made up my mind to change once, yet. But if I do, it will make things — I mean, our marriage — almost impossible."

"Why?"

"The Catholics do everything they can to prevent mixed marriages, Jack, — especially in our country. You would have to make all sorts of promises which you wouldn't like, and which I shouldn't want you to make — "

Ralston laughed, suddenly comprehending her point of view.

"I see!" he exclaimed.

"Of course you see. It's as plain as day. I want to make sure of you — dear," — she laid her hand softly on his, — "and I also want to be sure of being perfectly free to change my mind about my religion, if I wish to. It's a stroke of diplomacy."

"I don't know much about diplomatic proceedings," laughed Ralston, "but this strikes me as — well — very intelligent, to say the least of it."

Katharine's face became very grave, and she withdrew her hand.

"You mean that it does not seem to you perfectly honest," she said.

"I didn't say that," he answered, his expression changing with hers. "Of course the idea is that if you are married to me before you become a Catholic, your church can have nothing to say to me when you do."

"Of course — yes. You couldn't be called upon to make any promises. But if I should decide, after all, not to take the step, there would be no harm done. On the contrary, I shall have the advantage of being able to put pressure on uncle Robert, as I explained to you before."

"I didn't say I thought it wasn't honest," said Ralston. "It's rather deep, and I'm always afraid that deep things may not be quite straight. I should like to think about it, if you don't mind."

"I want you to decide. I've thought about it."

"Yes — but —"

"Well? Suppose that, after thinking it over for ever so long, you should come to the conclusion that I should not be acting perfectly honestly to my conscience — that's the worst you could discover, isn't it? Even then — and I believe it's an impossible case — it's my conscience and not yours. If you were trying to persuade me to a secret marriage because you were afraid of the consequences, it would be different —"

"Rather!" exclaimed Ralston, vehemently.

"But you're not. You see, the main point is on my account, and it's I who am doing all the persuading, for that reason. It may be un — un — what shall I call it — not like a girl at all. But I don't care. Why shouldn't I tell you that I love you? We've both said it often enough, and we both mean it, and I mean to be married to you. The religious question is a matter of conviction. You have no convictions, so you can't understand — "

"I have one or two — little ones."

"Not enough to understand what I feel — that if religion is anything, then it's everything except our love. No — that wasn't an afterthought. It's not coming between you and me. Nothing can. But it's everything else in life, or else it's nothing at all and not worth speaking of. And if it is — if it really is — why then, for me, as I look at it, it means the Catholic Church. If I talk as though I were not quite sure, it's because I want to be quite on the safe side. And if I want you to do this thing — it's because I want to be absolutely sure that hereafter no human being shall come between us. I know all about the difficulties in these mixed marriages. I've made lots of enquiries. There's no question of faith, or belief, or anything of the sort in their objections. It's simply a matter of church politics, and I daresay that they are quite right about it, from their point of view, and that if one is once with them one must be with them altogether, in policy as well as in religion. But I'm not as far as that yet. Perhaps I never shall be, after all. I want to make sure of you — oh, Jack, don't you understand? I can't talk well, but I know just what I mean. Tell me you understand, and that you'll do what I ask!"

"It's very hard!" said Ralston, bending his head and looking at the carpet. "I wish I knew what to do."

Woman-like, she saw that she was beginning to get the advantage.

"Go over it all, dear. In the first place, it's entirely for my sake, and not in the least for yours. So you can't say there's anything selfish in it, if you do it for me, can you? You don't want to do it, you don't like it, and if you do it you'll be making a sacrifice to please me."

"In marrying you!" Ralston laughed a little and then became very grave again.

"Yes, in marrying me. It's a mere formality, and nothing else. We're not going to run away afterwards, nor meet in the dark in Gramercy Park, nor do anything in the least different from what we've always done, until I've got what I want from uncle Robert. Then we'll acknowledge the whole thing, and I'll take all the blame on myself, if there is any —"

"You'll do nothing of the kind," interrupted Ralston.

"Unless you tell a story that's not true, you won't be able to find anything to blame yourself with," answered Katharine. "So it will be all over, and it will save no end of bother — and expense. Which is something, as neither of us, nor our people, have any money to speak of, and a wedding costs ever so much. I needn't even have a trousseau — just a few things, of course — and poor papa will be glad of that. You needn't laugh. You'll be doing him a service, as well as me. And you see how I can put it to uncle Robert, don't you? 'Uncle Robert, we're married — that's all. What are you going to do about it?' Nothing could be plainer than that, could it?"

"Nothing!"

"Now he will simply have to do something. Perhaps he'll be angry at first, but that won't last long. He'll get over it and laugh at my audacity. But that isn't the main point. It's perfectly conceivable that you might work and slave at something you hate for years and years, until we could get married in the regular way. The principal question is the other — my freedom afterwards to do exactly as I please about my religion without any possibility of any one interfering with our marriage."

"Katharine! Do you really mean to say that if you were a Catholic, and if the priests said that we shouldn't be married, you would submit?"

"If I couldn't, I couldn't," Katharine answered. "If I were a Catholic, and a good Catholic, — I wouldn't be a bad one, — no marriage but a Catholic one would be a marriage at all for me. And if they refused it, what could I do? Go back? That would be lying to myself. To marry you in some half regular way — "

"Hush, child! You don't know what you're talking about!"

"Yes, I do — perfectly. And you wouldn't like that. So you see what my position is. It's absolutely necessary to my future happiness that we should be quietly married some morning — to-morrow, if you like, but certainly in a day or two — and that nobody should know anything about it, until I've told uncle Robert."

"After all," said Ralston, hesitating, "it will be very much the same thing as though we were to run away, provided we face everybody at once."

"Very much better, because there'll be no scandal — and no immediate starvation, which is something worth considering."

"It won't really be a secret marriage, except for the mere ceremony, then. That looks different, somehow."

"Of course. You don't suppose that I thought of taking so much trouble and doing such a queer thing just for the sake of knowing all to myself that I was married, do you? Besides, secrets are always idiotic things. Somebody always lets them out before one is ready. And it's not as though there were any good reason in the world why we should not be married, except the money question. We're of age — and suited to each other — and all that."

"Naturally!" And Ralston laughed again.

"Well, then — it seems to me that it's all perfectly clear. It amounts to telling everybody the day after, instead of the day before the wedding. Do you see?"

"I suppose I ought to go on protesting, but you do make it very clear that there's nothing underhand about it, except the mere ceremony. And as you say, we have a perfect right to be married if we please."

"And we do please — don't we?"

"With all our hearts," Ralston answered, in a dreamy tone.

"Then when shall it be, Jack?" Katharine leaned towards him and touched his hand with her fingers as though to rouse him from the reverie into which he seemed to be falling.

The touch thrilled him, and he looked up suddenly and met her glance. He looked at her steadily for a moment, and once more he felt that odd, pleasurable, unmanly moisture in his eyes, with a sweeping wave of emotion that rose from his heart with a rush as though it would burst his throat. He yielded to it altogether this time, and catching her in his arms drew her passionately to him, kissing her again and again, as though he had never kissed her before. He did not understand it himself, and Katharine was not used to it. But she loved him, too, with all her heart, as it seemed to her. She had proved it to him and to herself more completely within the last half hour, and she let her own arms go round him. Then a deep, dark blush which she could feel, rose slowly from her throat to her cheeks, and she instinctively disentangled herself from him and drew gently back.

"Remember that it's for my sake — not for yours, dear," she said.

Her grey eyes were as deep as the dusk itself. Vaguely she guessed her power as she gave him one more long look, and then rose suddenly and pretended to busy herself with the single light, turning it up a little and then down. Ralston watched the springing curves that outlined her figure as she reached upward. He was in many ways a strangely refined man, in spite of all his sins, and of his besetting sin in particular, and refinement in others appealed to him strongly when it was healthy and natural. He detested the diaphanous type of semi-consumptive with the angel face, man or woman, and declared that a skeleton deserved no credit for looking refined, since it could not possibly look anything else. But he delighted in delicacy of touch and grace of movement when it went with such health and strength as Katharine had.

"You are the most divinely beautiful thing on earth," he said quietly.

Katharine laughed, but still turned her face away from him.

"Then marry me," she said, laughing. "What a speech!" she cried an instant later. "Just fancy if any one could hear me, not knowing what we've been talking about!"

"You were just in time, then," said Ralston. "There's some one coming."

Katharine turned quickly, listened a moment, and distinguished a footfall on the stairs outside the door. She nodded, and came to his side at once.

"You will, Jack," she said under her breath. "Say that you will — quick!"

Ralston hesitated one moment. He tried to think, but her eyes were upon him and he seemed to be under a spell. They were close together, and there was not much light in the room. He felt that the shadow of something unknown was around them both — that somewhere in the room a sweet flower was growing, not like other flowers, not common nor scented with spring — a plant full of softly twisted tendrils and pale petals and in-turned stamens — a flower of moon-leaf and fire-bloom and dusk-thorn — drooping above their two heads like a blossom-laden bough bending heavily over two exquisite statues — two statues that did not speak, whose faces did not change as the night stole silently upon them — but they were side by side, very near, and the darkness was sweet.

It was only an instant. Then their lips met.

"Yes," he whispered, and drew back as the door opened. Mrs. Lauderdale entered the room.

"Oh, are you there, Jack?" she asked, but without any surprise, as though she were accustomed to find him with Katharine.

"Yes," answered Ralston, quietly. "I've been here ever so long. How do you do, cousin Emma?"

"Oh, I'm so tired!" exclaimed Mrs. Lauderdale. "I've been working all day long. I positively can't see."

"You ought not to work so hard," said Ralston. "You'll wear your eyes out."

"No, I'm strong, and so are my eyes. I only wanted to say that I was tired. It's such a relief!"

Mrs. Lauderdale had been a very beautiful woman, and

was, indeed, only just beginning to lose her beauty. She
was much taller than either of her daughters, but of a
different type of figure from Katharine, and less evenly
grown, if such an expression may be permitted. The
hand was typical of the difference. Mrs. Lauderdale's
was extremely long and thin, but well made in the
details, though out of proportion in the way of length
and narrowness as a whole. Katharine's hand was firm
and full, without being what is called a thick hand.
There was a more perfect balance between flesh and
bone in the straight, strong fingers. Mrs. Lauderdale
had been one of those magnificent fair beauties occasionally seen in Kentucky, — a perfect head with perfect but
small features, superb golden hair, straight, clear eyes,
a small red mouth, — great dignity of carriage, too, with
the something which has been christened 'dash' when
she moved quickly, or did anything with those long
hands of hers, — a marvellous constitution, and the dazzling complexion of snow and carnations that goes with
it, very different from the softer 'milk and roses' of the
Latin poet's mistress. Mrs. Lauderdale had always
been described as dazzling, and people who saw her for
the first time used the word even now to convey the
impression she made. Her age, which was known only
to some members of the family, and which is not of the
slightest importance to this history, showed itself chiefly
in a diminution of this dazzling quality. The white was
less white, the carnation was becoming a common pink,
the gold of her hair was no longer gold all through, but
distinctly brown in many places, though it would certainly never turn grey until extreme old age. Her
movements, too, were less free, though stately still, —
the brutal word 'rheumatism' had been whispered by the
family doctor, — and to go back to her face, there were

undeniably certain tiny lines, and many of them, which were not the lines of beauty.

It was a brave, good face, on the whole, gifted, sometimes sympathetic, and oddly cold when the woman's temper was most impulsive. For there is an expression of coldness which weakness puts on in self-defence. A certain narrowness of view, diametrically opposed to a corresponding narrowness in her husband's mind, did not show itself in her features. There is a defiant, supremely satisfied look which shows that sort of limitation. Possibly such narrowness was not natural with Mrs. Lauderdale, but the result of having been systematically opposed on certain particular grounds throughout more than a quarter of a century of married life. However that may be, it was by this time a part of her nature, though not outwardly expressed in any apparent way.

She had not been very happy with Alexander Junior, and she admitted the fact. She knew also that she had been a good wife to him in every fair sense of the word. For although she had enjoyed compensations, she had taken advantage of them in a strictly conscientious way. Undeniable beauty, of the kind which every one recognizes instantly without the slightest hesitation, is so rare a gift that it does indeed compensate its possessor for many misfortunes, especially when she enjoys amusement for its own sake, innocently and without losing her head or becoming spoiled and affected by constant admiration. Katharine Lauderdale had not that degree of beauty, and there were numerous persons who did not even care for what they called 'her style.' Her sister Charlotte had something of her mother's brilliancy, indeed, but there was a hardness about her face and nature which was apparent at first sight. Mrs. Alexander had always remained the beauty of the family, and indeed the beauty of the society to which she belonged, even after her daughters had been grown up. She had outshone them, even in a world like that of New York, which does not readily compare mothers and daughters in any way, and asks them out separately as though they did not belong to each other.

She had not been very happy, and apart from any purely imaginary bliss, procurable only by some miraculous changes in Alexander Junior's heart and head, she believed that the only real thing lacking was money. She had always been poor. She had never known what seemed to her the supreme delight of sitting in her own carriage. She had never tasted the pleasure of having five hundred dollars to spend on her fancies, exactly as she pleased. The question of dress had always been more or less of a struggle. She had not exactly extravagant tastes, but she should have liked to feel once in her life that she was at liberty to throw aside a pair of perfectly new gloves, merely because when she put them on the first time one of the seams was a little crooked, or the lower part was too loose for her narrow hand. She had always felt that when she had bought a thing she must wear it out, as a matter of conscience, even if it did not suit her. And there was a real little pain in the thought, of which she was ashamed. Small things, but womanly and human. Then, too, there was the constant chafing of her pardonable pride when ninety-nine of her acquaintances all did the same thing, and she was the hundredth who could not afford it — and the subscriptions and the charity concerts and the theatre parties. It was mainly in order to supply herself with a little money for such objects as these that she had worked so hard at her painting for years — that she might not be obliged to

apply to her husband for such sums on every occasion.
She had succeeded to some extent, too, and her initials
had a certain reputation, even with the dealers. Many
people knew that those same initials were hers, and a
few friends were altogether in her confidence. Possibly
if she had been less beautiful, she would have been
spoken of at afternoon teas as 'poor Mrs. Lauderdale,'
and people would have been found — for society has its
kindly side — who would have half-surreptitiously paid
large sums for bits of her work, even much more than
her miniatures could ever be worth. But she did not
excite pity. She looked rich, as some people do to their
cost. People sympathized with her in the matter of
Alexander Junior's character, for he was not popular.
But no one thought of pitying her because she was poor.
On the contrary, many persons envied her. It must be
'such fun,' they said, to be able to paint and really
sell one's paintings. A dashing woman with a lot of
talent, who can make a few hundreds in half an hour
when she chooses, said others. What did she spend the
money on? On whatever she pleased — probably in
charity, she was so good-hearted. But those people did
not see her as Jack Ralston saw her, worn out with a
long day's work, her eyes aching, her naturally good
temper almost on edge; and they did not know that
Katharine Lauderdale's simple ball gowns were paid for
by the work of her mother's hands. It was just as well
that they did not know it. Society has such queer fits
sometimes — somebody might have given Katharine a
dress. But Ralston was in the secret and knew.

"One may be as strong as cast-steel," he said. "Even
that wears out. Ask the people who make engines.
You'll accomplish a great deal more if you go easy and
give yourself rest from time to time."

"Like you, Jack," observed Mrs. Lauderdale, not
unkindly.

"Oh, I'm a failure. I admitted the fact long ago.
I'm only fit for a bad example, — a sort of moral scare-
crow."

"Yes. I wonder why?" Mrs. Lauderdale was tired
and was thinking aloud. "I didn't mean to say that,
Jack," she added, frankly, realizing what she had said,
from the recollection of the sound of her own voice, as
people sometimes do who are exhausted or naturally
absent-minded.

"It wasn't exactly complimentary, mother," said
Katharine, coldly. "Besides, is it fair to say that a
man is a failure at Jack's age? Patrick Henry was a
failure at twenty-three. He was bankrupt."

"Patrick Henry!" exclaimed Ralston. "What do you
know about Patrick Henry?"

"Oh, I've been reading history. It was he who said,
'Give me liberty, or give me death.'"

"Was it? I didn't know. But I'm glad to hear of
somebody who got smashed first and celebrated afterwards. It's generally the other way, like Napoleon and
Julius Cæsar."

"Cardinal Wolsey, Alexander the Great, and John
Gilpin. It's easy to multiply examples, as the books
say."

"You're much too clever for me this evening. I must
be going home. My mother and I are going to dine all
alone and abuse our neighbours all the evening."

"How delightful!" exclaimed Katharine, thinking of
the grim family table at which she was to sit as usual
— there had been some fine fighting in Charlotte's unmarried days, but Katharine's opposition was generally of
the silent kind.

"Yes," answered Ralston. "There's nobody like my mother. She's the best company in the world. Good night, cousin Emma. Good night, Katharine."

But Katharine followed him into the entry, letting the library door almost close behind her.

"It will be quite time enough, if you come and tell me on the evening before it is to be," she whispered hurriedly. "There's no party to-morrow night, but on Wednesday I'm going to the Thirlwalls' dance."

"Will any morning do?" asked Ralston, also in a whisper.

"Yes, any morning. Now go—quick. That's enough, dear—there, if you must. Go—good night—dear!"

The process of leave-taking was rather spasmodic, so far as Katharine was concerned. Ralston felt that same strange emotion once more as he found himself out upon the pavement of Clinton Place. His head swam a little, and he stopped to light a cigarette before he turned towards Fifth Avenue.

Katharine went back into the library, and found her mother sitting as the two had left her, and apparently unconscious that her daughter had gone out of the room.

"He's quite right, mother dear. You are trying to do too much," said Katharine, coming behind the low chair and smoothing her mother's beautiful hair, kissing it softly and speaking into the heavy waves of it.

Mrs. Lauderdale put up one thin hand, and patted the girl's cheek without turning to look at her, but said nothing for a moment.

"It's quite true," Katharine said. "You mustn't do it any more."

"How smooth your cheek is, child!" said Mrs. Lauderdale, thoughtfully.

"So is yours, mother dear."

"No — it's not. It's full of little lines. Touch it — you
can feel them — just there. Besides — you can see them."   .

"I don't feel anything — and I don't see anything,"
answered Katharine.

But she knew what her mother meant, and it made her
a little sad — even her. She had been accustomed all
her life to believe that her mother was the most beautiful woman in the world, and she knew that the time had
just come when she must grow used to not believing it
any longer.   Mrs. Lauderdale had never said anything
of the sort before. She had been supreme in her way,
and had taken it for granted that she was, never refer-
ring to her own looks under any circumstances.

In the long silence that followed, Katharine quietly
went and closed the shutters of the windows, for Ralston
had only pulled down the shades. She drew the dark
curtains across for the evening, lit another gaslight, and
remained standing by the fireplace.

"Thank you, darling," said Mrs. Lauderdale.

"I do wish papa would let us have lamps, or shades,
or something," said Katharine, looking disconsolately
at the ground-glass globes of the gaslights.

"He doesn't like them — he says he can't see."

There was a short pause.

"Oh, mother dear! what in the world does papa like,
I wonder?"   Katharine turned with an impatient movement as she spoke, and her broad eyebrows almost met
between her eyes.

"Hush, child!"   But the words were uttered wearily
and mechanically — Mrs. Lauderdale had pronounced
them so often under precisely the same circumstances
during the last quarter of a century.

Katharine sighed, a little out of impatience and to
some extent in pity for her mother. But she stood look-

ing across the room at the closed door through which
Ralston and she had gone out together five minutes
earlier, and she could still feel his last kiss on her
cheek. He had never seemed so loving as on that day,
and she had succeeded in persuading him, against his
instinctive judgment, to promise her what she asked,
— the maddest, most foolish thing a girl's imagination
could long for, no matter with what half-reasonable
excuse. But she had his promise, which, as she well
knew, he would keep — and she loved him with all her
heart. The expression of mingled sadness and impatience vanished like a breath from a polished mirror.
She was unconscious that she looked radiantly happy, as
her mother gazed up into her face.

"What a beautiful creature you are!" said Mrs. Lauderdale, in a tone unlike her natural voice.

CHAPTER V.

KATHARINE had no anxiety about the future, and it
seemed to her that she had managed matters in the wisest
and most satisfactory manner possible. She had provided, as she thought, against the possibility of any subsequent interference with her marriage in case she should
see fit to take the step of which she had spoken. The
combination seemed perfect, and even a sensible person,
taking into consideration all the circumstances, might
have found something to say in favour of a marriage
which should not be generally discussed. Ralston and
Katharine, though not rich, were decidedly prominent
young people in their own society, and their goings and

comings interested the gossips and furnished food for conversation. There were many reasons for this. Neither of them was exactly like the average young person in the world. But the great name of Lauderdale, which was such a real power in the financial world, contributed most largely to the result. Every one who bore it, or who was as closely connected with it as the Ralstons, was more or less before the public. Most of the society paragraph writers in the newspapers spoke of the family, collectively and individually, as often as they could find anything to say about it, and as a general rule the tone of their remarks was subdued and laudatory, and betrayed something very like awe. The presence of the Lauderdales and the Ralstons was taken for granted in all accounts of big parties, first nights at the opera and Daly's, and of other similar occasions. From time to time a newspaper man in a fit of statistics calculated how many dollars of income accrued to Robert Lauderdale at every minute, and proceeded to show how much each member of the family would have if it were all equally divided. As Robert the Rich had made his money in real estate, and his name never appeared in connection with operations in Wall Street, he was therefore not periodically assailed by the wrathful chorus of the sold and ruined, abusing him and his people to the youngest of the living generation, an ordeal with which the great speculators are familiar. But from time to time the daily papers published wood-cuts supposed to be portraits of him and his connections, and the obituary notice of him — which was, of course, kept ready in every newspaper office — would have given even the old gentleman himself some satisfaction. The only member of the family who suffered at all for being connected with him was Benjamin Slayback, the member of Congress.

If he ever dared to hint at any measure implying expenditure on the part of the country, he was promptly informed by some Honourable Member on the other side, that it was all very well for him to be reckless, with the whole Lauderdale fortune at his back, but that ordinary mortals had to content themselves with ordinary possibilities. The member from California called him the Eastern Crœsus, and the member from Massachusetts called him the Western Millionaire, and the member from Missouri quoted Scripture at him, while the Social-Democrat member from Somewhere — there was one at that time, and he was a little curiosity in his way — called him a Capitalist, than which epithet the social-democratic dictionary contains none more biting and more offensive in the opinion of its compilers. Altogether, at such times the Honourable Slayback of Nevada had a very bad quarter of an hour because he had married Charlotte Lauderdale, — penniless but a Lauderdale, very inadequately fitted out for a bride, though she was the grand-niece of Robert the Rich. Slayback of Nevada, however, had a certain rough dignity of his own, and never mentioned those facts. He had plenty of money himself and did not covet any that belonged to his wife's relations.

"I'm not as rich as your uncle Robert," he said to her on the day after their marriage, "and I don't count on being. But you can have all you want. There's enough to go round, now. Maybe you wouldn't like to be bothering me all the while for little things? Yes, that's natural; so I'll just put something up to your credit at Riggs's and you can have a cheque-book. When you've got through it, tell Riggs to let me know. You might be shy of telling me."

And Benjamin Slayback smiled in a kindly fashion

not at all familiar to his men friends, and on the following day Charlotte received a notice from the bank to the
effect that ten thousand dollars stood to her credit.
Never having had any money of her own, the sum seemed
a fortune to her, and she showed herself properly grateful, and forgave Benjamin a multitude of small sins, even
such as having once worn a white satin tie in the evening, and at the opera, of all places.

Katharine was perfectly well aware that the smallest
actions of her family were subjects for public discussion,
and she knew how people would talk if it were ever discovered that she had been secretly married to John Ralston. On the other hand, the rest of the Lauderdales
were in the same position, and would be quite willing,
when they were acquainted with the facts, to say that
the marriage had been a private one, leaving it to be supposed that they had known all about it from the first.
She had no anxiety for the future, therefore, and believed
that she was acting with her eyes open to all conceivable
contingencies and possibilities. Matters were not,
indeed, finally settled, for even after she was married
she would still have the interview with her uncle to
face; but she felt sure of the result. It was so easy for
him to do exactly what he pleased, as it seemed to her, to
make or unmake men's fortunes at his will, as she could
tie and untie a bit of string.

And her confidence in Ralston was boundless. Considering his capacities, as they appeared to her, his failure to do anything for himself in the two positions which
had been offered to him was not to be considered a failure at all. He was a man of action, and he was an exceptionally well-educated man. How could he ever be
expected to do an ordinary clerk's work? It was absurd to suppose that he could change his whole char-

acter at a moment's notice, and it was an insult to expect
that he should change it at all. It was a splendid
nature, she thought, generous, energetic, brave, averse
to mean details, of course, as such natures must be,
impatient of control, independent and dominating.
There was much to admire in Ralston, she believed,
even if she had not loved him. And perhaps she was
right, from her point of view. Of his chief fault she
really knew nothing. The little she had heard of his
being wild, as it is called, rather attracted than repelled
her. She despised men whom she looked upon as 'duf-
fers' and 'muffs.' Even her father, whose peculiarities
were hard to bear, was manly in his way. He had been
good at sports in his youth, he was a good rider, and
could be trusted with horses that did not belong to him,
which was fortunate, as he had never possessed any of
his own; he was a good shot, as she had often heard, and
he periodically disappeared upon solitary salmon-fishing
expeditions on the borders of Canada. For he was a
strong man and a tough man, and needed much bodily
exercise. The only real 'muff' there had ever been in
the family Katharine considered to be her grandfather,
the philanthropist, and he was so old that it did not
matter much. But the tales he told of his studious
youth disgusted her, for some occult reason. All the
other male relations were manly fellows, even to little
Frank Miner, who was as full of fight as a cock-sparrow,
in spite of his diminutive stature. Benjamin Slayback,
too, was eminently manly, in an awkward, constrained
fashion. Hamilton Bright was an athlete. And John
Ralston could do all the things which the others could
do, and did most things a trifle better, with a certain
finished 'style' which other men envied. He was eminently the kind of man whose acquaintances at the club

will back for money in every contest requiring skill and strength.

It was no wonder that Katharine admired him. But she told herself that her admiration had nothing to do with her love. There was much more in him than the world knew of, and she was quite sure of it. Her ideals were high, and Ralston fulfilled most of them. She always fancied that there was something knightly about him, and it appealed to her more than any other characteristic.

She felt that he could be intimate without even becoming familiar. There is more in that idea than appears at first sight, and the distinction is not one of words. Up to a certain point she was quite right in making it, for he was naturally courtly, as well as ordinarily courteous, and yet without exaggeration. He did certain things which few other men did, and which she liked. He walked on her left side, for instance, whenever it was possible, if they chanced to be together in the street. She had never spoken of it to him, but she had read, in some old book on court manners, that it was right a hundred years ago, and she was pleased. They had been children together, and yet almost since she could remember he had always opened the door for her when she left a room. And not for her only, but for every woman. If she and her mother were together when they met him, he always spoke to her mother first. If they got into a carriage he expected to sit on the left side, even if he had to leave the pavement and go to the other door to get in. He never spoke of her simply as ' Katharine' if he had to mention her name in her presence to any one not a member of the family. He said 'my cousin Katharine,' or 'Miss Lauderdale,' according to circumstances.

They were little things, all of them, but by no means absurd in her estimation, and he would continue to do them all his life. She supposed that his mother had taught him the usages of courtesy when he had been a boy, but they were a part of himself now. How many men, thought Katharine, who believed themselves 'perfect gentlemen,' and who were undeniably gentlemen in every essential, were wholly lacking in these small matters! How many would have called such things old-fashioned nonsense, who had never so much as noticed that Ralston did them all, because he did them unobtrusively, and because, in reality, most of them are founded on perfectly logical principles, and originally had nothing but the convenience of society for their object. Katharine had thought it out. For instance, most men, being right-handed, have the more skilful hand and the stronger arm on the lady's side, with which to render her any assistance she may need, if they find themselves on her left. There was never any affectation of fashion about really good manners, Katharine believed, and everything appertaining thereto had a solid foundation in usefulness. During Slayback's courtship of her sister she had found numberless opportunities of contrasting what she called the social efficiency of the man who knew exactly what to do with the inefficiency of him who did not; and, on a more limited scale, she found such opportunities daily when she saw Ralston together with other men.

He had a very high standard of honour, too. Many men had that, and all whom she knew were supposed to have it, but there were few whom she felt that she could never possibly suspect of some little meanness. That was another step to the pedestal on which she had set up her ideal.

But perhaps one of the chief points which appealed to

her sympathy was Ralston's breadth of view, or absence
of narrowness. He had spoken the strict truth that
evening when he had said that he never laughed at any
one's religion, and, next to love, religion was at that
time uppermost in Katharine Lauderdale's mind. At
her present stage of development everything she did,
saw, read and heard bore upon one or the other, or both,
which was not surprising considering the atmosphere in
which she had grown up.

Alexander Junior had never made but one sacrifice
for his wife, and that had been of a negative description.
He had forgiven her for being a Roman Catholic, and
had agreed never to mention the subject; and he had
kept his word, as indeed he always did on the very rare
occasions when he could be induced to give it. It is
needless to say that he had made a virtue of his conduct
in this respect, for he systematically made the most of
everything in himself which could be construed into a
virtue at all. But at all events he had never broken his
promise. In the days when he had married Emma Camperdown there had been little or no difficulty about marriages between Catholics and members of other churches,
and it had been understood that his children were to
be brought up Presbyterians, though nothing had been
openly said about it. His bride had been young, beautiful and enthusiastic, and she had believed in her heart
that before very long she could effect her husband's con-
version, little dreaming of the rigid nature with which
she should have to deal. It would have been as easy to
make a Roman Catholic of Oliver Cromwell, as Mrs.
Lauderdale soon discovered to her sorrow. He did not
even consider that she had any right to talk of religion
to her children.

Charlotte Lauderdale grew up in perfect indifference.

Her mind developed young, but not far. In her childhood she was a favourite of old Mrs. Lauderdale,— formerly a Miss Mainwaring, of English extraction, and the
mother of Mrs. Ralston,— and the old lady had taught
her that Presbyterians were no better than atheists, and
that Roman Catholics were idolaters, so that the only
salvation lay in the Episcopal Church. The lesson had
entered deep into the girl's heart, and she had grown up
laughing at all three; but on coming to years of discretion she went to an Episcopal church because most of
her friends did. She enjoyed the weekly fray with her
father, whom she hated for his own sake in the first
place, and secondly because he was poor, and she once
went so far as to make him declare, in his iron voice,
that he vastly preferred Catholics to Episcopalians, — a
declaration which she ever afterwards cast violently in
his teeth when she had succeeded in drawing him into a
discussion upon articles of faith. Her mother never had
the slightest influence over her. The girl was quick-
witted and believed herself clever, was amusing and
thought she was witty, was headstrong, capricious and
violent in her dislikes and was consequently convinced
that she had a very strong will. She married Slayback
for three reasons, — to escape from her family, because
he was rich, and because she believed that she could do
anything she chose with him. She was not mistaken
in his wealth, and she removed herself altogether from
the sphere of the Lauderdales, but Benjamin Slayback
was not at all the kind of person she had taken him for.

Katharine was altogether different from her sister.
She was more habitually silent, and her taste was never
for family war. She thought more and read less than
Charlotte, who devoured literature promiscuously and
trusted to luck to remember something of what she read.

Indeed, Katharine thought a great deal, and often reasoned correctly from inaccurate knowledge. In a healthy way she was inclined to be melancholic, and was given to following out serious ideas, and even to something like religious contemplation. Everything connected with belief in transcendental matters interested her exceedingly. She delighted in having discussions which turned upon the supernatural, and upon such things as seem to promise a link between the hither and the further side of death's boundary, — between the cis-mortal and the trans-mortal, if the coining of such words be allowable. In this she resembled nine-tenths of the American women of her age and surroundings. The mind of the idle portion of American society to-day reminds one of a polypus whose countless feelers are perpetually waving and writhing in the fruitless attempt to catch the very smallest fragment of something from the other side, wherewith to satisfy the mortal hunger that torments it.

There is something more than painful, something like an act of the world's soul-tragedy, in this all-pervading desire to know the worst, or the best, — to know anything which shall prove that there is something to know. There is a breathless interest in every detail of an 'experience' as it is related, a raising of hopes, a thrilling of the long-ready receptivity as the point is approached; and then, when the climax is reached and past, there is the sudden, almost agonizing relapse into blank hopelessness. The story has been told, but nothing is proved. We know where the door is, but before it is a screen round which we must pass to reach it. The screen is death, as we see it. To pass it and be within sight of the threshold is to die, as we understand death, and there lies the boundary of possible experience, for, so far as we know, there is no other door.

The question is undoubtedly the greatest which humanity can ask, for the answer must be immortality or annihilation.   It seems that a certain proportion of mankind,
driven to distraction by the battle of beliefs, has actually
lost the faculty of believing anything at all, and the
place where the faculty was aches, to speak familiarly.

That, at least, was how it struck Katharine Lauderdale, and it was from this point of view that she seriously contemplated becoming a Catholic.   If she did so,
she intended to accept the Church as a whole and refuse,
forever afterwards, to reopen the discussion.   She never
could accept it as her mother did, for she had not been
brought up in it, but there were days when she felt that
by a single act of will she could bind herself to believe
in all the essentials, and close her eyes to the existence
of the non-essentials, never to open them again.   Then,
she thought, she should never have any more doubts.

But on other days she wished that there might be
another way.   She got odd numbers of the proceedings
of a society devoted to psychological researches, and
read with extreme avidity the accurately reported evidence of persons who had seen or heard unusual sights
or sounds, and studied the figures illustrating the experiments in thought transference.   Then the conviction
came upon her that there must be another door besides
the door of death, and that, if she were only patient, she
might be led to it or come upon it unawares.   She knew
far too little of even what little there is to be known, to
get any further than this vague and not unpleasant
dream, and she was conscious of her ignorance, asking
questions of every one she met who took the slightest
interest in psychical enquiries.   Of course, her attempts
to gain knowledge were fruitless.   If any one who is
willing to be a member of civilized society knew any-

thing definite about what we call the future state, the
whole of civilized society would know it also in less than
a month.   Every one can be quite sure of that, and no
one need therefore waste time in questioning his neighbour in the hope of learning anything certain.

There were even times when her father's rigid and
merciless view of the soul pleased her, and was in sympathy with her slightly melancholic temperament.   The
unbending, manly quality of the Presbyterian belief
attracted her by its strength — the courage a man must
have to go through life facing an almost inevitable hell
for himself and the positive certainty of irrecoverable
damnation for most of those dearest to him.   If her
father was in earnest, as he appeared to be, he could not
have the slightest hope that her mother could be saved.
At that idea Katharine laughed, being supposed to be a
Presbyterian herself.   Nevertheless, she sometimes liked
his hard sayings and doings, simply because they were
hard.   Hamilton Bright had often told her that she had
a lawyer's mind, because she could not help seeing things
from opposite sides at the same time, whereupon she
always answered that though she despised prejudices,
she liked people who had them, because such persons were
generally stronger than the average.   Ralston, who had
not many, and had none at all about religious matters,
was the man with whom she felt herself in the closest
sympathy, a fact which went far to prove to Bright that
he was not mistaken in his judgment of her.

On the whole, in spite of the declaration she had made
to Ralston, Katharine Lauderdale's state was sceptical,
in the sense that her mind was in a condition of suspended judgment between no less than five points of
view, the Presbyterian, the Catholic, the deistic, the
psychologic, and the materialistic.   It was her misfor-

tune that her nature had led her to think of such matters
at all, rather than to accept some existing form of belief
and to be as happy as she could be with it from the first,
as her mother had done: and though her intelligence was
good, it was as totally inadequate to grapple with such
subjects as it was well adapted to the ordinary requirements of worldly life. But she was not to be blamed for
being in a state of mind to which her rather unusual
surroundings had contributed much, and her thoughtful
temperament not a little. If anything, she was to be
pitied, though the mighty compensation of a genuine
love had grown up year by year to neutralize the elements of unhappiness which were undoubtedly present.

It is worth noticing that at this time, which opened
the crucial period of her life, she doubted her own religious convictions and her own stability of purpose, but
she did not for a moment doubt the sincerity of her love
for John Ralston, nor of his for her, as she conclusively
proved when she determined to risk her whole life in such
a piece of folly as a secret marriage.

When she came down to dinner on that memorable
evening, she found her father and mother sitting on
opposite sides of the fireplace. Alexander Junior was
correctly arrayed in evening dress, and his clothes fitted
perfectly upon his magnificent figure. The keen eye of
a suspicious dandy could have detected that they were
very old clothes, and Mr. Lauderdale would not have felt
at all dismayed at the discovery of the fact. He prided
himself upon wearing a coat ten years, and could tell the
precise age of every garment in his possession. He tied
his ties to perfection also, and this, too, was an economy, for such was his skill that he could wear a white
tie twice, bringing the knot into exactly the same place
a second time. Mont Blanc presented not a more spot-

less, impenetrable, and unchanging front than **Alexander Junior's** shirt. He had processes of rejuvenating his shoes known to him alone, and in the old days of evening gloves, his were systematically aned and rematched, and the odd ones laid aside to replace possible torn ones in the future, constituting a veritable survival of the fittest. Five and twenty years of married life had not taught him that a woman could not possibly do the same with her possessions, and he occasionally enquired why his wife did not wear certain gowns which had been young with her daughters. He never put on the previously mentioned white tie, however, unless some one was coming to dinner. When the family was alone, he wore a black one. As he was not hospitable, and did not encourage hospitality in his wife, though he praised it extravagantly in other people, and never refused a dinner party, the black tie was the rule at home. Black ties last a long time.

Katharine noticed the white one this evening, and was surprised, as her mother had not spoken to her of any guest.

"Who is coming to dinner?" she asked, looking at her father, almost as soon as she had shut the door.

Mr. Lauderdale's steel-grey upper lip was immediately raised in a sort of smile which showed his large white teeth — he had defied the dentist from his youth up, and his smile was hard and cold as an electric light.

"Ah, my dear child," he answered in a clear, metallic voice, "I am glad you notice things. Little things are always worth noticing. Walter Crowdie is coming to dinner to-day. In fact, he is rather late — "

"With Hester?" asked Katharine, quickly. Hester Crowdie was Hamilton Bright's sister, and Katharine liked her.

"No, my dear, without Hester. We could hardly ask two people to our every-day dinner."

"Oh — it's only Mr. Crowdie, then," said Katharine in a tone of disappointment, sitting down beside her mother.

"I hope you'll be nice to him, Katharine," said Mr. Lauderdale. "There are many reasons — "

"Oh, yes! I'll be nice to him," answered the young girl, with a short, quick frown that disappeared again instantly.

"I don't like your expression, my child," said Alexander Junior, severely, "and I don't like to be interrupted. Mr. Crowdie is very kind. He wishes to paint your portrait, and he proposes to give us the study he must make first, which will be just as good as the picture itself, I have no doubt. Crowdie is getting a great reputation, and a picture by him is valuable. One can't afford to be rude to a man who makes such a proposal."

"No," observed Mrs. Lauderdale as though speaking to herself. "I should really like to have it. He is a great artist."

"I haven't the least intention of being rude to him," answered Katharine. "What does he mean to do with my portrait — with the picture itself when he has painted it — sell it?"

"He would have a perfect right to sell it, of course — with no name. He means to exhibit it in Paris, I believe, and then I think he intends to give it to his wife. You always say she is a great friend of yours."

"Oh — that's all right, if it's for Hester," said Katharine. "Of course she's a friend of mine. Hush! I hear the bell."

"When did Mr. Crowdie talk to you about this?" asked Mrs. Lauderdale, addressing her husband.

"This morning — hush! Here he is."

Alexander Junior had an almost abnormal respect for
the proprieties, and always preferred to stop talking
about a person five minutes before he or she appeared.
It was a part of his excessively reticent nature.

The door opened and Walter Crowdie appeared, a pale
young man with heavy, red lips and a bad figure. His
eyes alone redeemed his face from being positively repulsive, for they were of a very beautiful blue colour and
shaded by extremely long brown lashes. A quantity of
pale hair, too long to be neat, but not so long as worn
by many modern musicians, concealed the shape of his
head and grew low on his forehead. The shape of the
face, as the hair allowed it to be seen, resembled that of
a pear, wide and flaccid about the jaws and narrowing
upwards towards the temples. Crowdie's hands were
small, cushioned with fat, and of a dead white — the
fingers being very pointed and the nails long and polished. His shoulders sloped like a woman's, and were
narrow, and he was heavy about the waist and slightly
in-kneed. He was too fashionable to use perfumes, but
one instinctively expected him to smell of musk.

Both women experienced an unpleasant sensation when
he entered the room. What Mr. Lauderdale felt it is
impossible to guess, but as Katharine saw the two shake
hands she was proud of her father and of the whole
manly race from which she was descended.

Last of all the party came Alexander Senior, taking
the utmost advantage of age's privilege to be late. Even
he, within sight of his life's end, contrasted favourably
with Walter Crowdie. He stooped, he was badly dressed,
his white tie was crooked, and there were most evident
spots on his coat; his eyes were watery, and there were
wrinkles running in all directions through the eyebrows,

the wrinkles that come last of all; he shambled a little as he walked, and he certainly smelt of tobacco smoke. He had not been the strongest of the three old brothers, though he was the eldest, and his faculties, if not impaired, were not what they had been. But the skull was large and bony, the knotted and wrinkled old hands were manly hands, and always had been, and the benevolent old grey eyes had never had the womanish look in them which belonged to Crowdie's.

But the young man was quite unconscious of the unfavourable impression he always produced upon Mrs. Lauderdale and her daughter, and his languishing eyelids moved softly and swept his pale cheeks with their long lashes as he looked from one to the other and shook hands.

Alexander Junior, whose sense of punctuality had almost taken offence, rang the bell as his father entered, and a serving girl, who lived in terror of her life, drew back the folding doors a moment later.

CHAPTER VI.

THE conversation at dinner did not begin brilliantly. Mrs. Lauderdale was tired, and Katharine was preoccupied; as was natural, old Mr. Lauderdale was not easily moved to talk except upon his favourite hobby, and Alexander Junior was solemnly and ferociously hungry, as many strong men are at regular hours. As for Crowdie, he always felt a little out of his element amongst his wife's relations, of whom he stood somewhat in awe, and he was more observant than communicative at first.

Katharine avoided looking at him, which she could easily
do, as she sat between him and her father. As usual, it
was her mother who made the first effort to talk.

"How is Hester?" she asked, looking across at
Crowdie.

"Oh, very well, thanks," he answered, absently.
"Oh, yes, — she's very well, thank you," he added,
repeating the answer with a little change and more animation. "She had a cold last week, but she's got over
it."

"It was dreadful weather," said Katharine, helping
her mother to stir the silence. "All grandpapa's idiots
had the grippe."

"All Mr. Lauderdale's what?" asked Crowdie. "I
didn't quite catch — ".

"The idiots — the asylum, you know."

"Oh, yes — I remember," said the young man, and his
broad red lips smiled.

Alexander Senior, whose hand shook a little, had eaten
his soup with considerable success. He glanced from
Katharine to the young artist, and there was a twinkle
of amusement in the kindly old eyes.

"Katharine always laughs at the idiots, and talks as
though they were my personal property." His voice was
deep and almost musical still — it had been a very gentle
voice in his youth.

"Not a very valuable property," observed Alexander
Junior, fixing his eye severely on the serving girl, who
forthwith sprang at Mrs. Lauderdale's empty plate as
though her life depended on taking it away in time.

The Lauderdales had never kept a man-servant. The
girl was a handsome Canadian, very smart in black and
white.

"Wouldn't it be rather an idea to insure all their lives,

and make the insurance pay the expenses of the asylum?" enquired Crowdie, gravely looking at Alexander Junior.

"Not very practical," answered the latter, with something like a smile.

"Why not?" asked his father, with sudden interest. "That strikes me as a very brilliant idea for making charities self-supporting. I suppose," he continued, turning to his son, "that the companies could make no objections to insuring the lives of idiots. The rate ought to be very reasonable when one considers the care they get, and the medical attendance, and the immunity from risk of accident."

"I don't know about that. When an asylum takes fire, the idiots haven't the sense to get out," observed Alexander Junior, grimly.

"Nonsense! Nonsense, Alexander!" The old man shook his head. "Idiots are just as — well, not quite as sensible as other people, — that would be an exaggeration — but they're not all so stupid, by any means."

"No — so I've heard," said Crowdie, gravely.

"So stupid as what, Mr. Crowdie?" asked Katharine, turning on him rather abruptly.

"As others, Miss Lauderdale — as me, for instance," he answered, without hesitation. "Probably we both meant — Mr. Lauderdale and I — that all idiots are not so stupid as the worst cases, which are the ones most people think of when idiots are mentioned."

"Exactly. You put it very well." The old philanthropist looked pleased at the interruption. "And I repeat that I think Mr. Crowdie's idea of insuring them is very good. Every time one dies, — they do die, poor things, — you get a sum of money. Excellent, very excellent!"

His ideas of business transactions had always been

hazy in the extreme, and his son proceeded to set him right.

"It couldn't possibly be of any advantage unless you had capital to invest and insured your own idiots," said Alexander Junior. "And that would just amount to making a savings bank on your own account, and saving so much a year out of your expenses for each idiot. You could invest the savings, and the interest would be all you could possibly make. It's not as though the idiots' families paid the dues and made over the policies to you. There would be money in that, I admit. You might try it. There might be a streak of idiocy in the other members of the patient's family which would make them agree to it."

The old man's gentle eyes suddenly lighted up with ill temper.

"You're laughing at me, Alexander," he said, in a louder voice. "You're laughing at me!"

"No, sir; I'm in earnest," answered the son, in his cool, metallic tones.

"Don't the big companies insure their own ships?" asked the philanthropist. "Of course they do, and they make money by it."

"I beg your pardon. They make nothing but the interest of what they set aside for each ship. They simply cover their losses."

"Well, and if an idiot dies, then the asylum gets the money."

"Yes, sir. But an idiot has no intrinsic value."

"Why, then the asylum gets a sum of money for what was worth nothing, and it must be very profitable — much more so than insuring ships."

"But it's the asylum's own money to begin with —"

"And as for your saying that an idiot has no intrinsic

value, Alexander," pursued the old man, going off on another track, "I won't have you say |such things. I won't listen to them. An idiot is a human being, sir, and has an immortal soul, I'd have you to know, as well as you or I. And you have the assurance to say that he has no intrinsic value! An immortal soul, made for eternal happiness or eternal suffering, and no intrinsic value! Upon my word, Alexander, you forget yourself! I should not have expected such an inhuman speech from you."

"Is the ' vital spark of heavenly flame ' a marketable commodity?" asked Crowdie, speaking to Katharine in a low voice.

"Idiots have souls, Mr. Crowdie," said the philanthropist, looking straight across at him, and taking it for granted that he had said something in opposition.

"I've no doubt they have, Mr. Lauderdale," answered the painter. "I never thought of questioning the fact."

"Oh! I thought you did. I understood that you were laughing at the idea."

"Not at all. It was the use of the word 'intrinsic' as applied to the value of the soul which struck me as odd."

"Ah — that is quite another matter, my dear sir," replied the old gentleman, who was quickly appeased. "My son first used the word in this discussion. I'm not responsible for it. The younger generation is not so careful in its language as we were taught to be. But the important point, after all, is that idiots have souls."

"The soul is the only thing anybody really can be said to have as his own," said Crowdie, thoughtfully.

Katharine glanced at him. He did not look like the kind of man to make such a speech with sincerity. She wondered vaguely what his soul would be like, if she could see it, and it seemed to her that it would be something strange — white, with red lips, singing an evil song, which she could not understand, in a velvet voice, and that it would smell of musk. The side of her that was towards him instinctively shrank a little from him.

"I am glad to hear you say that, Mr. Crowdie," said the philanthropist, with approbation. "It closes the discussion very fittingly. I hope we shall hear no more of idiots not having souls. Poor things! It is almost the only thing they have that makes them like the rest of us."

"People are all so different," replied the artist. "I find that more and more true every day. And it takes a soul to understand a soul. Otherwise photography would take the place of portrait painting."

"I don't quite see that," said Alexander Junior, who had employed the last few minutes in satisfying his first pangs of hunger, having been interrupted by the passage of arms with his father. "What becomes of colour in photography?"

"What becomes of colour in a charcoal or pen and ink drawing?" asked Crowdie. "Yet either, if at all good, is preferable to the best photograph."

"I'm not sure of that. I like a good photograph. It is much more accurate than any drawing can be."

"Yes — but it has no soul," objected Crowdie.

"How can an inanimate object have a soul, sir?" asked the philanthropist, suddenly. "That is as bad as saying that idiots — "

"I mean that a photograph has nothing which suggests the soul of the original," said Crowdie, interrupting and speaking in a high, clear tone. He had a beautiful tenor voice, and sang well; and he possessed the power of making himself heard easily against many other voices.

"It is the exact representation of the person," argued Alexander Junior, whose ideas upon art were limited.

"Excuse me. Even that is not scientifically true. There can only be one point in the whole photograph which is precisely in focus. But that is not what I mean. Every face has something besides the lines and the colour. For want of a better word, we call it the expression — it is the individuality — the soul — the real person — the something which the hand can suggest, but which nothing mechanical can ever reproduce. The artist who can give it has talent, even if he does not know how to draw. The best draughtsman and painter in the world is only a mechanic if he cannot give it. Mrs. Lauderdale paints — and paints well — she knows what I mean."

"Of course," said Mrs. Lauderdale. "The fact that there is something which we can only suggest but never show would alone prove the existence of the soul to any one who paints."

"I don't understand those things," said Alexander Junior.

"Grandpapa," said Katharine, suddenly, "if any one asserted that there was no such a thing as the soul, what should you answer?"

"I should tell him that he was a blasphemer," answered the old gentleman, promptly and with energy.

"But that wouldn't be an argument," retorted the young girl.

"He would discover the force of it hereafter," said her father. The electric smile followed the words.

Crowdie looked at Katharine and smiled also, but she did not see.

"But isn't a man entitled to an argument?" she asked. "I mean — if any one really couldn't believe that he had a soul — there are such people —"

"Lots of them," observed Crowdie.

"It's their own fault, then, and they deserve no mercy — and they will find none," said Alexander Junior.

"Then believing is a matter of will, like doing right," argued the young girl. "And a man has only to say, 'I believe,' and he will believe, because he wills it."

But neither of the Lauderdales had any intention of being drawn out on that point. They were good Presbyterians, and were Scotch by direct descent; and they knew well enough what direction the discussion must take if it were prolonged. The old gentleman put a stop to it.

"The questions of the nature of belief and free will are pretty deep ones, my dear," he said, kindly, "and they are not of the sort to be discussed idly at dinner."

Strange to say, that was the species of answer which pleased Katharine best. She liked the uncompromising force of genuinely prejudiced people who only allowed argument to proceed when they were sure of a logical result in their own favour. Alexander Junior nodded approvingly, and took some more beef. He abhorred bread, vegetables, and sweet things, and cared only for what produced the greatest amount of energy in the shortest time. It was astonishing that such iron strength should have accomplished nothing in nearly fifty years of life.

"Yes," said Crowdie, "they are rather important things. But I don't think that there are so many people who deny the existence of the soul as people who want to satisfy their curiosity about it, by getting a glimpse at it. Hester and I dine out a good deal — people are very kind, and always ask us to dinners because they know I can't go out to late parties on account of my work — so we are always dining out; and we were saying only to-day that at nine-tenths of the dinners we go to the conversation sooner or later turns on the soul, or psychical research, or Buddhism, or ghosts, or something of the sort. It's odd, isn't it, that there should be so much talk about those things just now? I think it shows a kind of general curiosity. Everybody wants to get hold of a soul and study its habits, as though it were an ornithorynchus or some queer animal — it is strange, isn't it?"

"I don't know," said Mrs. Lauderdale, suddenly joining in the conversation. "If you once cut loose from your own form of belief there's no particular reason why you should be satisfied with that of any one else. If a man leaves his house without an object there's nothing to make him go in one direction rather than in another."

"So far as that is concerned, I agree with you," said Alexander Junior.

"There is truth to direct him," observed the philanthropist.

"And there is beauty," said Crowdie, turning his head towards Mrs. Lauderdale and his eyes towards Katharine.

"Oh, of course!" exclaimed the latter. "If you are going to jumble the soul, and art, and everything, all together, there are lots of things to lead one. Where does beauty lead you, Mr. Crowdie?"

"To imagine a vain thing," answered the painter with a soft laugh. "It also leads me to try and copy it, with what I imagine it means, and I don't always succeed."

"I hope you'll succeed if you paint my daughter's portrait," remarked Alexander Junior.

"No," Crowdie replied thoughtfully, and looking at Katharine quite directly now. "I shan't succeed, but if Miss Lauderdale will let me try, I'll promise to do my very best. Will you, Miss Lauderdale? Your father said he thought you would have no objection."

"I said you would, Katharine, and I said nothing about objections," said her father, who loved accurate statements.

Katharine did not like to be ordered to do anything and the short, quick frown bent her brows for a second.

"I am much flattered," she said coldly.

"You will not be, when I have finished, I fear," said Crowdie, with quick tact. "Please, Miss Lauderdale, I don't want you to sit to me as a matter of duty, because your father is good enough to ask you. That isn't it, at all. Please understand. It's for Hester, you know. She's such a friend of yours, and you're such a friend of hers, and I want to surprise her with a Christmas present, and there's nothing she'd like so much as a picture of you. I don't say anything about the pleasure it will be to me to paint you — it's just for her. Will you?"

"Of course I will," answered Katharine, her brow clearing and her tone changing.

She had not looked at him while he was speaking, and she was struck, as she had often been, by the exquisite beauty of his voice when he spoke familiarly and softly. It was like his eyes, smooth, rich and almost woman-like.

"And when will you come?" he asked. "To-morrow? Next day? Would eleven o'clock suit you?"

"To-morrow, if you like," answered the young girl. "Eleven will do perfectly."

"Will you come too, Mrs. Lauderdale?" Crowdie asked, without changing his manner.

"Yes — that is — not to-morrow. I'll come one of these days and see how you are getting on. It's a long time since I've seen you at work, and I should enjoy it ever so much. But I should rather come when it's well begun. I shall learn more."

"I'm afraid you won't learn much from me, Mrs. Lauderdale. It's very different work from miniature — and I have no rule. It seems to me that the longer I paint the more hopeless all rules are. Ten years ago, when I was working in Paris, I used to believe in canons of art, and fixed principles, and methods, and all that sort of thing. But I can't any more. I do it anyhow, just as it seems to come — with anything — with a stump, a brush, a rag, hands, fingers, anything. I should not be surprised to find myself drawing with my elbow and painting with the back of my head! No, really — I sometimes think the back of my head would be a very good brush to do fur with. Any way — only to get at the real thing."

"I once saw a painter who had no arms," said the old gentleman. "It was in Paris, and he held the brushes with his toes. There is an idiot in the asylum now, who likes nothing better than to pull his shoes off and tie knots in a rope with his feet all day long."

"He is probably one of us," suggested Crowdie. "We artists are all half-witted. Give him a brush and see whether he has any talent for painting with his toes."

"That's an idea," answered the philanthropist, thoughtfully. "Transference of manual skill from hands to feet," he continued in a low, dreamy voice, thinking aloud. "Abnormal connections of nerves with next adjoining brain centres — yes — there might be some-thing in it — yes — yes —"

The old gentleman had theories of his own about nerves and brain centres. He had never even studied anatomy, but he speculated in the wildest manner upon the probability of impossible cases of nerve derangement and imperfect development, and had long believed him-self an authority on the subject.

The dinner was quite as short as most modern meals. Old Mr. Lauderdale and Crowdie smoked, and Alexander Junior, who despised such weaknesses, stayed in the dining-room with them. Neither Mrs. Lauderdale nor Katharine would have objected to smoking in the library, but Alexander's inflexible conservatism abhorred such a practice.

"I can't tell why it is," said Katharine, when she was alone with her mother, "but that man is positively repulsive to me. It must be something besides his ugliness, and even that ought to be redeemed by his eyes and that beautiful voice of his. But it's not. There's something about him — " She stopped, in the sheer impossibility of expressing her meaning.

Her mother said nothing in answer, but looked at her with calm and quiet eyes, rather thoughtfully.

"Is it very foolish of me, mother? Don't you notice something, too, when he's near you?"

"Yes. He's like a poisonous flower."

"That's exactly what I wanted to say. That and — the title of Tennyson's poem, what is it? Oh — 'A Vision of Sin' — don't you know?"

"Poor Crowdie!" exclaimed Mrs. Lauderdale, laughing a little, but still looking at Katharine.

"I wonder what induced Hester to marry him."

"He fascinated her. Besides, she's very fond of music, and so is he, and he sang to her and she played for him. It seems to have succeeded very well. I believe they are perfectly happy."

"Oh, perfectly. At least, Hester always says so. But did you ever notice — sometimes, without any special reason, she looks at him so anxiously? Just as though she expected something to happen to him, or that he should do something queer. It may be my imagination."

"I never noticed it. She's tremendously in love with him. That may account for it."

"Well — if she's happy — " Katharine did not finish the sentence. "He does stare dreadfully, though," she resumed a moment later. "But I suppose all artists do that. They are always looking at one's features. You don't, though."

"I? I'm always looking at people's faces and trying to see how I could paint them best. But I don't stare. People don't like it, and it isn't necessary. Crowdie is vain. He has beautiful eyes and he wants every one to notice them."

"If that's it, at all events he has the sense to be vain of his best point," said Katharine. "He's not an artist for nothing. And he's certainly very clever in all sorts of ways."

"He didn't say anything particularly clever at dinner, I thought. By the bye, was the dinner good? Your father didn't tell me Crowdie was coming."

"Oh, yes; it did very well," answered Katharine, in a reassuring tone. "At least, I didn't notice what we had. He always takes away my appetite. I shall go and steal something when he's gone. Let's sit up late, mother — just you and I — after papa has gone to bed, and we'll light a little wee fire, and have a tiny bit of supper, and make ourselves comfortable, and abuse Mr. Crowdie just as much as we like. Won't that be nice? Do!"

"Well — we'll see how late he stays. It's only a quarter past nine yet. Have you got a book, child? I am going to read that article about wet paintings on pottery — I've had it there ever so long, and the men won't come back for half an hour at least."

Katharine found something to read, after handing her mother the review from the table.

"Perhaps reading a little will take away the bad taste of Crowdie," said Mrs. Lauderdale, with a laugh, as she settled herself in the corner of the sofa.

"I wish something would," answered Katharine, seating herself in a deep chair, and opening her book.

But she found it hard to fix her attention, and the book was a dull one, or seemed so, as the best books do when the mind is drawn and stretched in one direction. Her thoughts went back to the twilight hour, when Ralston had been there, and to the decided step she was about to take. The only wonder was that she had been able to talk with a tolerable continuity of ideas during dinner, considering what her position was. Assuredly it was a daring thing which she meant to do, and she experienced the sensation familiar even to brave men — the small, utterly unreasoning temptation to draw back just before the real danger begins. Most people who have been called upon to do something very dangerous, with fair warning and in perfectly cold blood, know that little feeling and are willing to acknowledge it. It is not fear. It is the inevitable last word spoken by the instinct of self-preservation.

There are men who have never felt it at all, rare instances of perfectly phlegmatic physical recklessness. They are not the ones who deserve the most credit for doing perilous deeds. And there are other men, even fewer, perhaps, who have felt it, but have ceased to feel it, in whom all love of life is so totally and hopelessly dead that even the bodily, human impulse to avoid death can never be felt again. Such men are very dangerous in fight. 'Beware of him who seeks death,' says an ancient Eastern proverb. So many things which seem impossible are easy if the value of life itself be taken out of the balance. But with the great majority of the human race that value is tolerably well defined. The poor Chinaman who sells himself, for the benefit of his family, to be sliced to death in the stead of the rich criminal, knows within an ounce or two of silver what his existence is worth. The bargain has been made so often by others that there is almost a tariff. It is not a pleasant subject, but, since the case really happens, it would be a curious thing to hear theologians discuss the morality of such suicide on the part of the unfortunate wretch. Would they say that he was forfeiting the hope of a future reward by giving himself to be destroyed for money, of his own free will? Or would they account it to him for righteousness that he should lay down his life to save his wife and children from starving to death? For a real case, as it is, it certainly presents difficulties which approach the fantastic.

It was very quiet in the room, as it had been once or twice when there had been a silence between Katharine and Ralston a few hours earlier. The furniture was all just as it had been — hardly a chair had been turned. The scene came back vividly to the young girl's imagination, and the sound of Ralston's voice, just trembling with emotion, rang again in her ears. That had been the sweetest of all the many sweet hours she had spent with him since they had been children. Her book fell upon her knees and her head sank back against the cushion. With lids half drooping, she gazed at a point she did not see. The softest possible light, the exquisite, trembling radiance of spotless maidenhood's divinest dream, hovered about the lovely face and the girlish lips just parted to meet in the memory of a kiss.

Suddenly, from the next room, as the three men came towards the closed door of the library, Crowdie's laugh broke the stillness, high, melodious, rich. Some men have a habit of laughing at anything which is said just as they leave the dining-room.

Katharine started as though she had been stung. She was unconscious that her mother had ceased reading, and had been looking at her for several minutes, wondering why she had never fully appreciated the girl's beauty before.

"What's the matter, dear?" she asked, as she saw the start and the quick expression of resentment and repulsion.

"It's that man's voice—it's so beautiful and yet—ugh!" She shivered as the door opened and the three men came in.

"You've not been long," said Mrs. Lauderdale, looking up at Crowdie. "I hope they gave you a cigar in there."

"Oh, yes, thanks—and a very good one, too," added the artist, who had not succeeded in smoking half of the execrable Connecticut six-for-a-quarter cigar which the philanthropist had offered him.

It seemed natural enough to him that a man who devoted himself to idiots should have no taste, and he would have opened his eyes if he had been told that the Connecticut tobacco was one of the economies imposed by Alexander Junior upon his long-suffering father. The old gentleman, however, was really not very particular, and his sufferings were not to be compared with those of Balzac's saintly charity-maniac, when he gave up his Havanas for the sake of his poor people.

Crowdie looked at Katharine, as he answered her mother, and continued to do so, though he sat down beside the latter. Katharine had risen from her seat, and was standing by the mantelpiece, and Mrs. Lauderdale was sitting at the end of the sofa on the other side of the fireplace, under the strong, unshaded light of the gas.

She made an effort to talk to her guest, for the sake of sparing the girl, though she felt uncomfortably tired, and was looking almost ill.

" Did you talk any more about the soul, after we left ? " she asked, looking at Crowdie.

" No," he answered, still gazing at Katharine, and speaking rather absently. " We talked — let me see — I think — " He hesitated.

" It couldn't have been very interesting, if you don't remember what it was about," said Mrs. Lauderdale, pleasantly. " We must try and amuse you better than they did, or you won't come near us again."

" Oh, as far as that goes, I'll come just as often as you ask me," answered Crowdie, suddenly looking at his shoes.

But he made no attempt to continue the conversation. Mrs. Lauderdale felt a little womanly annoyance. The constant and life-long habit of being considered by men to be the most important person in the room, whenever she chose to be considered at all, had become a part of her nature. She made up her mind that Crowdie should not only listen and talk, but should look at her.

" What are you doing now ? Another portrait ? " she asked. " I know you are always busy."

" Oh, yes — the wife of a man who has a silver mine somewhere. She's fairly good-looking, for a wonder."

His eyes wandered about the room, and, from time to time, went back to Katharine. Old Mr. Lauderdale was going to sleep in an arm-chair, and Alexander Junior was reading the evening paper.

" Does your work always interest you as it did at first ? " asked Mrs. Lauderdale, growing more and more determined to fix his attention, and speaking softly. " I mean — are you happy in it and with it ? "

His languid glance met hers for an instant, with an odd look of lazy enquiry. He was keen and quick of intuition, and more than sufficiently vain. There is a certain tone of voice in which a woman may ask a man if he is happy which indicates a willingness to play at flirtation. Now, it had never entered the head of Walter Crowdie that Mrs. Lauderdale could possibly care to flirt with him. Yet the tone was official, so to say, and he had some right to be surprised, the more so as he had never heard any man — not even the famous club-liar, Stopford Thirlwall — even suggest that she had ever really flirted with any one, or do anything worse ·than dance to the very end of every dancing party, and generally amuse herself in an innocent way to an extent that would have ruined the constitutions of most women not born in Kentucky. Even as he turned to look at her, however, he realized the absurdity of the impression he had received, and his eyes went mechanically back to Katharine's profile. The smile that moved his heavy, red mouth was for himself, as he answered Mrs. Lauderdale's question.

"Oh, yes," he said, quite naturally. "I love it. I'm perfectly happy." And again he relapsed into silence.

Mrs. Lauderdale was annoyed. She turned her head, under the glaring light, towards the carved pillar at the right of the fireplace. An absurd little looking-glass hung by a silken cord from the mantelpiece to the level of her eyes — one of those small Persian mirrors set in a case of embroidery, such as are used for favours at cotillons.

She saw very suddenly the reflection of her own face. The glass was perhaps a trifle green, which made it worse, but she stared in a sort of dumb horror, realizing in a single moment that she had grown old, that the lines had deepened until every one could see them, that the eyes looked faded, the hair dull, the lips almost shrivelled, the once dazzling skin flaccid and sallow — that the queenly beauty was gone, a perishable thing already perished, a memory now and worse than a memory, a cruelly bitter regret left in the place of a possession half divine that was lost for ever and ever, dead beyond resurrection, gone beyond recall.

That was the most terrible moment in Mrs. Lauderdale's life. Fate need not have made it so appallingly sudden — she had prepared for it so long, so conscientiously, trying always to wean herself from a vanity the sternest would forgive. And it had seemed to be coming so slowly, by degrees of each degree, and she had thought it would be so long in coming quite. And now it was come, in the flash of a second. But the bitterness was not passed.

Instinctively in the silence she looked up before her and saw her daughter's lovely face. Her head reeled, her sight swam. A great, fierce envy caught at her heart with iron fingers and wrung it, till she could have screamed, — envy of her who was dearest to her of all living things — of Katharine.

CHAPTER VII.

JOHN RALSTON had given his word to Katharine and he intended to keep it. Whenever he was assailed by doubts he recalled by an act of will the state of mind to which the young girl had brought him on Monday evening, and how he had then been convinced that there was

no harm in the secret marriage. He analyzed his position, too, in a rough and ready way, with the intention
of proving that the clandestine ceremony could not be of
any advantage to himself, that it was therefore not from
any selfish motive that he had undertaken to have it performed, and that, consequently, since the action itself
was to be an unselfish one, there could be nothing even
faintly dishonourable in it. For he did not really believe
that old Robert Lauderdale would do anything for him.
On the contrary, he thought it most likely that the old
man would be very angry and would bid the young
people abide by the consequences of their doings. He
would blame Ralston bitterly. He would not believe
that he had been disinterested. He would say that he
had married Katharine, and had persuaded her to the
marriage in the hope of forcing his uncle to help him,
out of consideration for the girl. And he would refuse
to do anything whatsoever. He might even go so far as
to strike the names of both from his will, if he had left
them a legacy, which was probable. But, to do Ralston
justice, so long as he was sure of his own motives he had
never cared a straw for the opinions others might form
of them, and he was the last man in the world to assume
a character for the sake of playing on the feelings of a
rich relation. If Robert Lauderdale should send for
him, and be angry, and reproach him with what he had
done, John was quite capable of answering that he had
acted from motives which concerned himself only, that
he was answerable to no one but Katharine herself and
that uncle Robert might make the best of it at his leisure.
The young man possessed that sort of courage in abundance, as every one knew, and being aware of it himself,
he suspected, not without grounds of probability, that
the millionaire was aware of it also, and would simply

leave him alone to his own devices, refusing Katharine's request, and never mentioning the question again. That the old man would be discreet, was certain. With a few rare exceptions, men who have made great fortunes unaided have more discretion than other people, and can keep secrets remarkably well.

The difficulty which presented itself to Ralston at once was a material one. He did not in the least know how such an affair as a secret marriage should be managed. None of his close acquaintances had ever done anything so unusual, and although he knew of two cases which had occurred in New York society, the one in recent years and the other long ago, he had no means of finding out at short notice how the actual formalities necessary had been fulfilled in either case. He knew, however, that a marriage performed by a respectable clergyman of any denomination was legal, and that a certificate signed by him was perfectly valid. He had heard of marriages before a Justice of the Peace, and even of declarations made before respectable witnesses and vouched for, which had been legal marriages beyond dispute, but he did not like the look of anything in which there was no religious ceremony, respectfully indifferent though he was to all religion. The code of honour, which was his only faith, is connected, and not even very distantly, with Christianity. There are honourable men of all religions under the sun, including that of Confucius, but we do not associate the expression 'the code of honour' with non-Christians — which is singular enough, considering the view the said code takes of some moral questions.

There must be a marriage service, therefore, thought Ralston, and it must be performed in New York. There was no possibility of taking Katharine into a neighbouring State, and he had no wish to do so for many reasons.

He was not without foresight, and he intended to be able to prove at any future time that the formality, the whole formality, and nothing but the formality of the ceremony had been fulfilled. It was not easy. He racked his recollections in vain, and he read all the newspapers published that morning with an interest he had certainly never felt in them before, in the hope of finding some account of a case similar to his own. He thought of going to a number of clergymen, of the social type, with whom he had a speaking acquaintance, and of laying the facts before each in turn, until one of them consented to marry him. But though many of them were excellent men, he had not enough confidence in their discretion. He laughed to himself when he thought that the only men he knew who seemed to possess the necessary quali- ties for such a delicate affair were Robert the Rich himself and Hamilton Bright, whom Ralston secretly suspected of being somewhat in love with Katharine on his own account. It was odd, he thought, that of all the family Bright alone should resemble old Robert, physi- cally and mentally, but the resemblance was undeniable, though the relationship only consisted in the fact that Bright was descended from old Robert Lauderdale's grandfather, the primeval Alexander often mentioned in these pages.

Ralston turned the case over and over in his mind. He thought of going to some dissenting minister quite unknown to him, and trying what eloquence could do. He had heard that some of them were men of heart to whom one could appeal in trouble. But he knew very well that every one of them would tell him to do the thing openly, or not at all, and the mere idea revived his own scruples. He wondered whether there were not churches where the marrying was done by batches of

four and five couples on a certain Sunday in the month,
as babies are baptized in some parts of the world, and
whether he and Katharine could not slip in, as it were by
mistake, and be married by a man who did not even know
their names. But he laughed at the idea a moment later,
and went on studying the problem.

Another of his ideas was to consult a detective, from a
private office. Such men would, in all likelihood, know
a good deal about runaway couples. And this seemed
one of the wisest plans which had suggested itself, though
it broke down for two reasons. He hated the thought of
getting at his result by the help of a man belonging to
what he considered a mean and underhand profession;
and he reflected that such men were always on the look-
out for private scandals, and that he should be putting
himself in their power. At last he decided to consult a
lawyer. Lawyers and doctors, as a rule, were discreet, he
thought, because their success depended on their discretion. He could easily find a man whom he had never seen,
honest and able to keep a secret, who would give him the
information he wanted in a professional way and take a
fee for the trouble. This seemed to him honourable and
wise. He wished everything to be legal, and the best
way to make it so was to follow a lawyer's directions.
There was not even a doubt but that the said lawyer, if
requested, would make a memorandum of the case, and
take charge of the document which was to prove that
Katharine Lauderdale had become the lawful wife of
John Ralston. There were lists and directories in which
he could find the names of hundreds of such men. He
was in his native city, and between the names and the
places of business he thought he could form a tolerably
accurate opinion of the reputation and standing of some,
if not of all, of the individuals.

In the course of a couple of hours he had found what
he wanted — a lawyer whose name was known to him as
that of a man of good reputation and a gentleman, one
whom he had never seen and who had probably never
seen him, old enough, as he knew, to have a wide experience, yet not so old as to be justified in assuming airs of
vast moral superiority in order to declare primly that he
would never help a young man to commit an act of folly.
For folly it was, as Ralston knew very well in his heart.

He lost no time, and within half an hour was inter-
viewing the authority he had selected, for, by a bit of
good luck, he was fortunate enough to meet the lawyer
at the door of his office, just returning from luncheon.
Otherwise he might have had some difficulty in gaining
immediate admittance. He found him to be a grave,
keen personage of uncertain age, who laid his glasses
beside him on his desk whenever he spoke, and put
them on again as soon as he had done. He wiped them
carefully when Ralston had explained what he wanted,
and then paused a moment before replying. Ralston
was by no means prepared for what he said.

"I presume you are a novelist."

The lawyer looked at him, smiled pleasantly, looked
away and turned his glasses over again.

The young man was inclined to laugh. No one had
ever before taken him for a man of letters. He hesitated,
however, before he answered, wondering whether he had
not better accept the statement in the hope of getting
accurate information, rather than risk a refusal if he said
he was in earnest. The lawyer took his hesitation for
assent.

"Because, in that case, it would not be at all difficult
to manage," he continued, without waiting any longer
for a reply. "Lots of things can happen in books, you

see, and you can wind up the story and publish it before
the people in the book who are to be kept in the dark
have found out the secret. In real life, it is a little
different, because, though it's very easy to be married,
it's the duty of the person who marries you to send a
certificate or statement of the marriage to the office
where the record of statistics is kept."

"Oh!" ejaculated Ralston, and his face fell. "I didn't
know that."

"Yes. That's necessary, on pain of a fine. And yet
the marriage may remain a secret a long while—for a
lifetime under favourable circumstances.. So that if you
are writing a story you can let the young couple take
the chances, and you can give them in their favour."

"Well—how, exactly?" asked John. "That sort of
thing isn't usual, I fancy."

"Not usual—no." The lawyer smiled. "But there
are more secret marriages than most people dream of.
If your hero and heroine must be married in New York,
it is easy enough to do it. Nobody will marry them
without afterwards making out the certificate, which
is recorded. If anybody suspects that they are married,
it is the easiest thing in the world to find out that the
marriage has been registered. But if nobody looks for
it, the thing will never be heard of. It's a thousand to
one against anybody's finding it out by accident."

"But if it were done in that way it would be absolutely
legal and could never be contested?"

"Of course—perfectly legal. But it's not so in all
States, mind you."

"I wanted to know about New York," said Ralston.
"It couldn't possibly take place anywhere else."

"Oh—well—in that case, you know all there is to be
known."

'I'm very grateful," said John, rising. "I've taken up a great deal of your valuable time, sir. May I—"

In considerable doubt as to what he should do, he thrust his hand into his breast-pocket and looked at the lawyer.

"My dear sir!" exclaimed the latter, rising also. "How can you think of such a thing? I'm very glad indeed to have been of service to—a young novelist."

"You're exceedingly kind, and I thank you very much," said Ralston, shaking the outstretched hand, and making for the door as soon as possible.

He had not even given his name, which had been rather rude on his part, as he was well aware. At all events, the lawyer would not be able to trace him, which was a point to his advantage.

Oddly enough he felt a sense of satisfaction when he thought over what he had learned. He could tell Katharine that a really secret marriage was wholly impossible, and perhaps when she knew that she was running a risk of discovery she would draw back. He should be glad of that. Realizing the fact, he was conscious for the first time that he was seeking a way out of the marriage and not a way into it, and a conflict arose in his mind. On the one hand he had given Katharine his word that he would do what she asked, and his word was sacred, unless she would release him from the promise. On the other side stood that intimate conviction of his own that, in spite of all her arguments, it was not a perfectly honourable thing to do, on its own merits. He could not help feeling glad that a material difficulty stood in the way of his doing what she required of him.

In any case he must see her as soon as possible. He ascertained without difficulty that they need not show evidence that they had resided in New York during any particular period, nor were there any other formalities to be fulfilled. He went home to luncheon with his mother — it was on the day after he had given his promise to Katharine, for he had lost no time—and he went out again before three o'clock, hoping to find the young girl alone.

To his annoyance he found her with her mother in the library. Mrs. Lauderdale was generally at work at that hour, if she was at home, but to-day she, who was always well, had a headache and was nervous and altogether different from herself. Katharine saw that she was almost ill, and insisted upon staying at home with her, to read to her, or to talk, as she preferred, though Mrs. Lauderdale begged her repeatedly to go away and make visits, or otherwise amuse herself as she could. But the young girl was obstinate; she saw that her mother was suffering and she had no intention of leaving her that afternoon. Alexander Junior was of course at his office, and the philanthropist was in his own quarters upstairs, probably dozing before the fire or writing reports about idiots.

It was clear to Ralston in five minutes that Mrs. Lauderdale was not only indisposed, but that she was altogether out of temper, a state of mind very unusual with her. She found fault with little things that Katharine did in a way John had never noticed before, and as for himself, she evidently wished he had not come. There was a petulance about her which was quite new. She was not even sitting in her usual place, but had taken the deep arm-chair on the other side of the fireplace, and turned her back to the light.

"You seem to be as busy as usual, Jack," she observed, after exchanging a few words.

"I'm wishing I were, at all events," he answered. "You must take the wish for the deed."

"They say that there's always plenty of work for any one who wants it," answered Mrs. Lauderdale, coldly.

"If you'll tell me where to find it—"

"Why don't you go to the West, as young Bright did, and try to do something without help? Other men do."

"Bright took money with him," answered Ralston.

"Did he? Not much, then, I fancy. I know he lived a hard life and drove cattle—"

"And bought land in wild places which he found in the course of his cattle driving. The driving was a means of getting about—not unpleasant, either—and he had some money to invest. I could do the same, if I had any."

"You know it's quite useless, mother," said Katharine, interposing before Mrs. Lauderdale could make another retort. "You all abuse him for doing nothing, and yet I hear you all say that every profession is overcrowded, and that nobody can do anything without capital. If uncle Robert chose, he could make Jack's fortune by a turn of his hand."

"Of course—he could give him a fortune outright and not feel it—unless he cared what became of it."

There was something so harsh about the way in which she spoke the last words that Ralston and Katharine looked at each other. Ralston did not lose his temper, however, but tried to turn the subject with a laugh.

"My dear cousin Emma," he said, "I'm the most hopeless case living. Please talk about somebody who is successful. There are lots of them. You've mentioned Bright already. Let us praise him. That will make you feel better."

To this Mrs. Lauderdale said nothing. After waiting a moment Ralston turned to Katharine.

"Are you going out this afternoon?" he asked, by way of hinting that he wanted to see her alone.

"No," said Mrs. Lauderdale, answering for her. "She says she means to stay at home and take care of me. It's ever so good of her, isn't it?"

"Yes," answered Ralston, absently.

It struck Katharine that, considering that her mother had been trying for half an hour to persuade her to go out, it would have been natural to propose that she should go for a short walk with John, and that the answer had come rather suddenly.

"But you can't stay at home all day," said Ralston, all at once. "You'll be having a headache yourself. Won't you let Katharine come with me for half an hour, cousin Emma? We'll walk twice round Washington Square and come right back. She looks pale."

"Does she?" Mrs. Lauderdale glanced at the girl's face. "I don't think so," she continued. "Besides—"

"What is it?" asked Ralston, as she hesitated and stopped. "Isn't it proper? We've often done it."

Mrs. Lauderdale rose from her chair and stood up, tall and slim, with her back to the mantelpiece. The light fell upon her face now, and Ralston saw how tired and worn she looked. Immediately she turned her back to the window again, and looked at him sideways, resting her elbow on the shelf.

"What is the use of you two going on in this way?" she asked suddenly.

There was an awkward silence, and again Katharine and Ralston looked at one another. They were momentarily surprised out of speech, for Mrs. Lauderdale had always taken their side, if not very actively, at least in a kindly way. She had said that Katharine should marry the man she loved, rich or poor, and that if she chose to wait for a poor man, like Ralston, to be able to support her, that was her own affair. The violent opposition had come from Katharine's father when, a year previously, the two had boldly told him that they loved each other and wished to be married. Alexander Junior did not often lose his temper, but he had lost it completely on that occasion, and had gone so far as to say that Ralston should never enter the house again, a verdict which he had been soon forced to modify. But he had said that he considered John an idle good-for-nothing, who would never be able to support himself, let alone a wife and children; that his, Alexander's, daughter should never marry a professional dandy, who was content to let his widowed mother pay his extravagant tailor's bills, and who played poker at the clubs as a source of income; that it was not enough of a recommendation to be half a Lauderdale and to skim the cream from New York society in the form of daily invitations — and to have the reputation of being a good polo player with other people's horses, a good yachtsman with other people's yachts, and of having a strong head for other people's wines. Those were not the noble qualities Alexander Junior looked for in a son-in-law. Not at all, sir. He preferred Benjamin Slayback of Nevada. The Lauderdales were quite able to make society accept Benjamin Slayback of Nevada, because Benjamin Slayback of Nevada was quite able to stand upon his own feet anywhere, having worked for all he had, like a man, and having pushed himself into the forefront of political life by sheer energy and ability, and having as good a right and as good a chance in every way as any man in the country. No, he was certainly not a Lauderdale. If Lauderdales were to go on marrying Lauderdales and no one else, there would soon be an end of society. He advised John Ralston to go to

Nevada and marry Benjamin Slayback's sister, if she would look at him, which was more than doubtful, considering that he was the most atrociously idle young ne'er-do-weel — here Alexander's Scotch upper lip snapped like a steel trap — that ever wasted the most precious years of life between the society of infatuated women by day, sir, and the temptations of the card-table and the bottle by night — the favourite of fine ladies, the boon companion of roisterers and the sport of a London tailor.

Which was a tremendous speech when delivered at close quarters in Alexander Junior's metallic voice, and in his most irately emphatic manner, while the grey veins swelled at his grey temples, and one iron hand was clenched ready to strike the palm of the other when the end of the peroration was reached. He allowed himself, as a relation, even more latitude in his language than he would have arrogated to himself as Katharine's father. He met John Ralston not only as the angry stage father meets the ineligible and determined young suitor, but as one Lauderdale meeting another — the one knowing himself to be irreproachable, upbraiding the other as the disgrace of the family, the hardened young sinner, and the sport of his tailor. That last expression had almost brought a smile to Ralston's angry face.

He had behaved admirably, however, under such very trying circumstances, and afterwards secretly took great credit to himself for not having attacked him whom he wished for a father-in-law with the furniture of the latter's own library, the chairs being the only convenient weapons in the room. Alexander the Safe, as his own daughter called him, could probably have killed John Ralston with one back-hander, but John would have liked to try him in fight, nevertheless. Instead of doing anything of the kind, however, John drew back two

steps, and said as much as he could trust himself to say
without foaming at the mouth and seeing things in
scarlet.   He said that he did not agree with his cousin
Alexander upon all the points the latter had mentioned,
that he did not care to prolong a violent scene, and he
wished him good morning.   Thereupon he had left the
house, which was quite the wisest thing he could do, for
when Alexander was alone he found to his extreme
annoyance that he had a distinct sensation of having
been made almost ridiculous.   But he soon recovered
from that, for whatever the secret main-spring of his
singular character might be, it was certainly not idle
vanity.

Mrs. Lauderdale had consoled Katharine, and Ralston
too, for that matter, as well as she could, and with sincere
sympathy.   Ralston continued to come to the house very
much as he pleased, and Mr. Lauderdale silently tolerated
his presence on the rare occasions of their meeting.   He
had certainly said more than enough to explain his point
of view, and he considered the matter as settled.   It was
really not possible to keep a man who was his cousin altogether away, and he suffered also from a delusion common to many fathers, which led him to think that no one
would ever dare to act against his once clearly expressed
wishes.

Between Katharine and her mother and Ralston there
remained a sort of tacit understanding.   There was no
formal engagement, of course, which would have had to
be concealed from Mr. Lauderdale, but Mrs. Lauderdale
meant that the two young people should be married if
they continued to love one another, and she generally
left them as much together as they pleased when Ralston
came.

It was, therefore, not strange that they should both be

surprised by the nature of her sudden question as she stood by the fireplace looking sideways at Ralston, with her back to the light.

"What is the use?" asked Katharine, repeating the words in astonishment and emphasizing the last one.

"Yes. What is the use? It is leading to nothing. You never can be married, and you know it by this time. You had much better separate at once. It will be easier for you now, perhaps, than by and by. You are both so young!"

"Excuse me, cousin Emma," said Ralston, "but I think you must be dreaming."

He spoke very quietly, but the light was beginning to gleam in his eyes. His mother was said to have a very bad temper, and John was like her in many respects. But Mrs. Lauderdale continued to speak quite calmly.

"I have been thinking about you two a great deal lately," she said. "I have made a mistake, and I may as well say so at once, now that I have discovered it. You wouldn't like me to go on letting you think that I approved of your engagement, when I don't — would you? That wouldn't be fair or honest."

"Certainly not," answered Ralston, in a low voice, and he could feel all his muscles tightening as though for a physical effort. "Have you said this sort of thing to Katharine before, or is this the first time?"

"No, she hasn't said a word," replied Katharine herself.

The girl was standing by the easy chair, her hand resting on the back of it, her face pale, her great grey eyes staring wide open at her mother's profile.

"No, I have not," said Mrs. Lauderdale. "I thought it best to wait until I could speak to you together. It's useless to give pain twice over."

"It is indeed," said Ralston, gravely. "Please go on."

"Why — there's nothing more to be said, Jack," answered Mrs. Lauderdale. "That's all. The trouble is that you'll never do anything, and you have no fortune, nor any prospect of any — until your mother —"

"Please don't speak of my mother in that connection," interrupted Ralston, his lips growing white.

"Well — and as for us, we're as poor as can be. You see how we live. Besides, you know. Old Mr. Lauderdale gets uncle Robert to subscribe thousands and thousands for the idiots, but he never suggests that they are far better off than we are. However, those are our miseries and not yours. Yours is that you are perfectly useless —"

"Mother!" cried Katharine, losing control of herself and moving a step forward.

"It's all right, dear," said Ralston. "Go on, cousin Emma. I'm perfectly useless —"

"I don't mean to offend you, Jack, and we're not strangers," continued Mrs. Lauderdale, "and I won't dwell on the facts. You know them as well as I do, and are probably quite as sorry that they really are facts. I will only ask one question. What chance is there that in the next four or five years you can have a house of your own, and an income of your own — just enough for two people to live on and no more — and — well — a home for Katharine? What chance is there?"

"I'll do something before that time," answered Ralston, with a determined look.

But Mrs. Lauderdale shook her head.

"So you said last year, Jack. I repeat — I don't want to be unkind. How long is Katharine to wait?"

"I'll wait all my life, mother," said the young girl, suddenly speaking out in ringing tones. "I'll wait till

I die, if I must, and Jack knows it. And I believe in
him, if you don't — against you all, you and papa and
uncle Robert and every one. Jack has never had a chance
that deserves to be called a chance at all. He must succeed — he shall succeed — I know he'll succeed. And I'll
wait till he does. I will — I will — if it's forever, and I
shan't be tired of waiting — it will always be easy, for
him. Oh, mother, mother — to think that you should have
turned against us! That's the hard thing!"

"Thank you, dear," said Ralston, touching her hand
lovingly.

Mrs. Lauderdale had turned her face quite away from
him now and was looking at the clock, softly drumming
with her fingers upon the mantelpiece.

"I'm sorry, Katharine," she said. "But I think it,
and I've said it — and I can't unsay it. It's far too
true."

There was a dead silence for several seconds. Then
Katharine suddenly pushed Ralston gently toward the
door.

"Go, Jack dear," she said in a low voice. "She has a
dreadful headache — she's not herself. Your being here
irritates her — please go away — it will be all right in a
day or two —"

They had reached the door, for Ralston saw that she
was right.

"No," said Mrs. Lauderdale, from the fireplace, I
shan't change my mind."

It was all so sudden and strange that Ralston found
himself outside the library without having taken leave
of her in any way. Katharine came out with him.

"There's a difficulty," he whispered quickly as he
found his coat and stick. "After it's done there has
to be a certificate saying that —"

"Katharine! Come here!" cried Mrs. Lauderdale from within, and they heard her footstep as she left the fireplace.

"Come to-morrow morning at eleven," whispered Katharine.

She barely touched his hand with hers and fled back into the library. He let himself out and walked slowly along Clinton Place in the direction of Fifth Avenue.

CHAPTER VIII.

KATHARINE went back to the library mechanically, because Mrs. Lauderdale called her and because she heard the latter's step upon the floor, but not exactly in mere blind submission and obedience. She was, indeed, so much surprised by what had taken place that she was not altogether her usual self, and she was conscious that events moved more quickly just then than her own power of decision. She was observant and perceptive, but her reason had always worked slowly. Ralston, at least, was out of the way, and she was glad that she had made him go. It had been unbearable to hear her mother attacking him as she had done.

She believed that Mrs. Lauderdale was about to be seriously ill. No other theory could account for her extraordinary behaviour. It was therefore wisest to take away what irritated her and to be as patient as possible. There was no excuse for her sudden change of opinion, and as soon as she was quite well she would be sorry for what she had said. Katharine was not more patient than most people, but she did her best.

"Is anything the matter, mother? You called so loud." She spoke almost before she had shut the door behind her.

"No. Did I? I wanted him to go away, that was all. Why should he stand there talking to you in whispers?"

Katharine did not answer at once, but her broad eyebrows drew slowly together and her eyelids contracted. She sat down and clasped her hands together upon her knee.

"Because he had something to say to me which he did not wish you to hear, mother," she answered at last.

"Ah — I thought so." Mrs. Lauderdale relapsed into silence, and from time to time her mouth twitched nervously.

She glanced at her daughter once or twice. The young girl's straight features could look almost stolid at times. Her patience had given way once, but she got hold of it again and tried to set it on her face like a mask. She was thinking now and wondering whether this strange mood were a mere caprice of her mother's, though Mrs. Lauderdale had never been capricious before, or whether something had happened to change her opinion of Ralston suddenly but permanently. In the one case it would be best to bear it as quietly as possible, in the other to declare war at once. But that seemed impossible, when she tried to realize it. She was deeply, sincerely devoted to her mother. Hitherto they had each understood the other's thoughts and feelings almost without words, and in all the many little domestic difficulties they had been firm allies. It was not possible that they were to quarrel now. The gap in life would be too deep and broad. Katharine suddenly rose and came and sat beside her mother and drew the fair, tired face to her own, very tenderly.

"Mother dear," she said, "look at me! What is the matter? Have I done anything to hurt you — to displease you? We've always loved each other, you and I — and we can't really quarrel, can we? What is it, dearest? Tell me everything — I can't understand it at all — I know — you're tired and ill, and Jack irritated you. Men will, sometimes, even the very nicest men, you know. It was only that, wasn't it? Yes — I knew it was — poor, dear, darling, sweet, tired little mother, just let your dear head rest — so, against me — yes, dear, I know — it was nothing — "

It was as though they had changed places, the mother and the daughter. The older woman's lip quivered, as her cheek rested on Katharine's breast. Slowly, almost imperceptibly, two tears gathered just within the shadowed lids, and grew and overflowed and trembled and fell — two crystal drops. She saw them fall upon the rough grey stuff of her daughter's frock, and as she lay there upon the girl's bosom with downcast eyes, she watched her own tears, in momentary apathy, and noticed how they ran, then crawled along, then stopped, caught as it seemed in the stiff little hairs of the coarse material — and she noticed that there were a few black hairs mixed with the grey, which she had not known before.

Then quite suddenly, just as they were shrinking and darkening the wool with two small spots, a great irresistible sob seemed to come from outside and run through her from head to foot, and shook her and hurt her and gripped her throat. A moment more and the flood of tears broke. Those storms of life's Autumn are chill and sharp. They are not like the showers of spring, quick, light and soft, that make blossoms fragrant and woods sweet-scented.

Katharine did not understand, and her face was gentle and full of pain as she pressed her mother to her bosom.

"Don't cry, mother — don't cry!" she repeated again and again.

"Ah, Katharine — child — if you knew!" The few words came with difficulty, as each sob rose and would not be forced back.

"No, darling — don't! There, there!" And the young girl tried to soothe her.

Suddenly it all ceased. With an impatient movement, as though she despised herself, Mrs. Lauderdale drew back, steadied herself with one hand upon the end of the sofa, turned her head away and rose to her feet.

"Go out, child — leave me to myself!" she said indistinctly, and going quickly towards the door. "Don't come after me — don't — no, don't," she repeated, not looking back, as she went out.

Left to herself, and understanding that it was better not to follow, Katharine · stood still a moment in the middle of the room, then went to the window and looked out, seeing nothing. She did not know what it all meant, but she felt that some great change which she could not comprehend had come over her mother, and that they could never be again as they had been. A mere headache, the mere fatigue from overwork, could not have produced such results. Nor was Mrs. Lauderdale really ill, as the girl's womanly instinct had told her within the last five minutes. The trouble, whatever it might be, was mental, and the tears had given it a momentary relief. But it was not over.

Katharine went out, at last, and was glad to breathe the keen air of the wintry afternoon; glad, too, to be alone with herself. She even wished that she were not

obliged to go into Fifth Avenue, where she might meet
an acquaintance, or at all events to cross it, as she
decided to do when she reached the first corner. Going
straight on, the next street was University Place, and
the lower part of that was quiet, and Waverley Place and
the neighbourhood of the old University building itself.
She could wander about there for half an hour without
going so far as Broadway, nor southwards to the pre-
cincts of the French and Italian business colonies. So
she walked slowly on, and then turned, and turned
again, round and round, backwards and forwards, meeting no one she knew, thinking all the time and idly
noticing things that had never struck her before, as,
for instance, that there is a row of stables leading westward out of University Place which is called Washington Mews, and that at almost every corner where
there is a liquor-shop there seems to be an Italian fruit-
stand — the function of the 'dago' being to give warning of the approach of the police, in certain cases, a
fact which Katharine could not be expected to know.

Just beyond the aforesaid Mews, at the corner of
Washington Square, she came suddenly upon little Frank
Miner, his overcoat buttoned up to his chin and a roll of
papers sticking out of his pocket. His fresh face was
pink with the cold, his small dark mustache glistened,
and his restless eyes were bright. The two almost ran
against one another and both stopped. He raised his
hat with a quick smile and put out his hand.

"How d'ye do, Miss Lauderdale?" he asked.

In spite of the family connection he had never got so
far as to call her Katharine, or even cousin Katharine.
The young girl shook hands with him and smiled.

"Are you out for a walk?" he asked, before she had
been able to speak. "And if so, may I come too?"

"Oh, yes — do."

She had been alone long enough to find it impossible to reach any conclusion, and of all people except Ralston, Miner was the one she felt most able to tolerate just then. His perfectly simple belief in himself and his healthy good humour made him good company for a depressed person.

"You seemed to be in such a hurry," said Katharine, as he began to walk slowly by her side.

"Of course, as I was coming to meet you," he answered promptly.

"But you didn't know — "

"Providence knew," he said, interrupting her. "It was foreordained when the world was chaos and New York was inhabited by protoplasm — and all that — that you and I should meet just here, at this very minute. Aren't you a fatalist? I am. It's far the best belief."

"Is it? Why? I should think it rather depressing."

"Why — no. You believe that you're the sport of destiny. Now a sport implies amusement of some kind. See?"

"Is the football amused when it's kicked?" asked Katharine, with a short laugh.

"Now please don't introduce football, Miss Lauderdale," said Miner, without hesitation. "I don't understand anything about it, and I know that I should, because it's a mania just now. All the men get it when the winter comes on, and they sit up half the night at the club, drawing diagrams and talking Hebrew, and getting excited — I've seen them positively sitting up on their hind-legs in rows, and waving their paws and tearing their hair — just arguing about the points of a game half of them never played at all."

"What a picture!" laughed Katharine.

"Isn't it? But it's just true. I'm going to write a book about it and call it 'The Kicker Kicked'—you know, like Sartor Resartus—all full of philosophy and things. Can you say 'Kicker Kicked' twenty times very fast, Miss Lauderdale? I believe it's impossible. I just left my three sisters—they're slowly but firmly turning into aunts, you know—I left them all trying to say it as hard as they could, and the whole place clicked as though a thousand policemen's rattles were all going at once—hard! And they were all showing their teeth and going mad over it."

"I should think so—and that's another picture."

"By the bye, speaking of pictures, have you seen the Loan Collection? It's full of portraits of children with such extraordinary expressions—they all look as though they had given up trying to educate their parents in despair. I wonder why everybody paints children? Nobody can. I believe it would take a child—who knew how to paint, of course,—to paint a child, and give just that something which real children have—just what makes them children."

She was silent for a moment, following the unexpected train of thoughts. There were delicate sides to his nature that pleased Katharine as well as his nonsense.

"That's a pretty idea," she said, after thinking of it a few seconds.

"Everybody tries and fails," answered Miner. "Why doesn't somebody paint you?" he asked suddenly, looking at her.

"Somebody means to," she replied. "I was to have gone to sit to Mr. Crowdie this morning, but he sent me word to come to-morrow instead. I suppose he had forgotten another engagement."

"Crowdie is ill," said Miner. "Bright told me so this

morning — some queer attack that nobody could understand."

"Something serious?" asked Katharine, quickly.

"Oh, no — I suppose not. Let's go and see. He lives
close by — at least, not far, you know, over in Lafayette
Place. It won't take five minutes to go across. Would
you like to go?"   .

"Yes," answered the young girl. "I could ask if he
will be able to begin the picture to-morrow."

They turned to the right at the next crossing and
reached Broadway a few moments later. There was the
usual crowd of traffic in the great thoroughfare, and they
had to wait a moment at the crossing before attempting
it. Miner thought of what he had seen on the previous
afternoon.

"Did you hear of Jack Ralston's accident yesterday?"
he asked.

Katharine started violently and turned pale. She had
not realized how the long hours and the final scene with her
mother had unstrung her nerves. But Miner was watching
the cars and carts for an opening, and did not see her.

"Yesterday?" she repeated, a moment later. "No —
he came to see us and stayed almost till dinner time.
What was it? When did it happen? Was he hurt?"

"Oh — you saw him afterwards, then?" Minor looked
up into her face — she was taller than he — with a curious expression — recollecting Ralston's condition when
he had last seen him.

"It wasn't serious, then? It had happened before he
came to our house?"

"Why — yes," answered the little man, with a puzzled
expression. "Was he all right when you saw him?"

"Perfectly. He never said anything about any accident. He looked just as he always does."

"That fellow has copper springs and patent joints inside him!" Minor laughed. "He was a good deal shaken, that's all, and went home in a cab. I should have gone to bed, myself."

"But what was it?"

"Oh — what he'd call nothing, I suppose! The cars at the corner of Thirty-second and Broadway — we were waiting, just as we are now — two cars were coming in opposite ways, and a boy with a bundle and a dog and a perambulator, and a few other things, got between the tracks — of course the cars would have taken off his head or his heels or his bundle, or something, and the dog would have been ready for his halo in three seconds. Jack jumped and picked up everything together and threw them before him and fell on his head. Wonder he wasn't killed or crippled — or both — no, I mean — here's a chance, Miss Lauderdale — come along before that van stops the way!"

There was not time to say anything as Katharine hastened across the broad street by his side, and by the time they had reached the pavement the blood had come back to her face. Her fears for Ralston's safety had been short-lived, thanks to Miner's quick way of telling the story, and in their place came the glow of pride a woman feels when the man she loves is praised by men for a brave action. Miner glanced at her as he landed her safely from the crossing and wondered whether Crowdie's portrait would do her justice. He doubted it, just then.

"It was just like him," she said quietly.

"And I suppose it was like him to say nothing about it, but just to go home and restore his shattered exterior and put on another pair of boots and go and see you. You said he looked as though nothing had happened to him?"

"Quite. We had a long talk together. I should certainly not have guessed that anything had gone wrong."

"Ralston's an unusual sort of fellow, anyhow," said Miner, enigmatically. "But then — so am I, so is Crowdie — do you like Crowdie? Rude question, isn't it? Well, I won't ask it, then. Besides, if he's to paint your picture you must have a pleasant expression — a smile that goes all round your head and is tied with a black ribbon behind — you know?"

"Oh, yes!" Katharine laughed again, as she generally did at the little man's absurd sayings.

"But Crowdie knows," he continued. "He's clever — oh, to any extent — big things and little things. All his lions roar and all his mosquitoes buzz, just like real things. The only thing he can't do is to paint children, and nobody can do that. By the bye, I'm repeating myself. It doesn't take long to get all round a little man like me. There are lots of things about Crowdie, though. He sings like an angel. I never heard such a voice. It's more like a contralto — like Scalchi's as it was, though she's good still, — than like a tenor. Oh, he's full of talent. I wish he weren't so queer!"

"Queer? How do you mean?"

"I don't know, I'm sure. There's something different from other people. Is he a friend of yours? I mean, a great friend?"

"Oh, no — not at all. I'm very fond of Mrs. Crowdie. She's a cousin, you know."

"Yes. Well — I don't know that I can make you understand what I mean, though. Besides, he's a very good sort of fellow. Never heard of anything that wasn't all right about him — at least — nothing particular. I don't know. He's like some kind of strange, pale, tropical fruit that's gone bad at the core and might

be poisonous.   Horrid thing to say of a man, isn't
it?"

"Oh, I know just what you mean!" answered Katharine, with a little movement of disgust.

Miner suddenly became thoughtful again, and they
reached the Crowdies' house, — a pretty little one, with
white stone steps, unlike the ordinary houses of New
York.   Lafayette Place is an unfashionable nook, rather
quiet and apparently remote from civilization.   It has,
however, three dignities, as the astrologers used to say.
The Bishop of New York has his official residence on
one side of it, and on the other is the famous Astor
Library.   A little further down there was at that time a
small club frequented by the great publishers and by
some of their most expensive authors.   No amateur ever
twice crossed the threshold alive.

Miner rang the bell, and the door was opened by an
extremely smart old man-servant in livery.   The Crowdies were very prosperous people.   Katharine asked if
Hester were at home.   The man answered that Mrs.
Crowdie was not receiving, but that he believed she
would wish to see Miss Katharine.   He had been with
the Ralstons in the Admiral's lifetime and had known
Katharine since she had been a baby.   Crowdie was
very proud of him on account of his thick white hair.

"I'll go in," said the young girl.   "Good-bye, Mr.
Miner — thank you so much for coming with me."

Miner trotted down the white stone steps and Katharine went into the house, and waited some minutes in the
pretty little sitting-room with the bow-window, on the
right of the entrance.   She was just thinking that possibly Hester did not wish to see her, after all, when the
door opened and Mrs. Crowdie entered.   She was a pale,
rather delicate-looking woman, in whose transparent

features it was hard to trace any resemblance to her athletic brother, Hamilton Bright. But she was not an insignificant person by any means. She had the Lauderdale grey eyes like so many of the family, but with more softness in them, and the eyebrows were finely pencilled. An extraordinary quantity of silky brown hair was coiled and knotted as closely as possible to her head, and parted low on the forehead in heavy waves, without any of the ringlets which had been fashionable for years. There were almost unnaturally deep shadows under the eyes, and the mouth was too small for the face and strongly curved, the angles of the lips being very cleanly cut all along their length, and very sharply distinct in colour from the ivory complexion. Altogether, it was a passionate face—or perhaps one should say impassioned. Imaginative people might have said that there was some· thing fatal about it. Mrs. Crowdie was even paler than usual to-day, and it was evident that she had undergone some severe strain upon her strength.

"Oh, I'm so glad to see you, dear!" she said, kissing the young girl on both cheeks and leading her to a small sofa just big enough to accommodate two persons, side by side.

"You look tired and troubled, Hester darling," said Katharine. "I met little Frank Miner and he told me that Mr. Crowdie had been taken ill. I hope it's nothing serious?"

"No—yes—how can I tell you? He's in his studio now, as though nothing had happened—not that he's working, for of course he's tired—oh, it has been so dreadful—I wish I could cry, but I can't, you know. I never could. That's why it hurts so. But I'm so glad you've come. I had just written a note to you and was going to send it, when Fletcher came up and said you were here. It was one of my intuitions—I'm always doing those things.''

It was so evidently a relief to her to talk that Katharine let her run on till she paused, before asking a question.

''What was the matter with him? Tell me, dear.''

Mrs. Crowdie did not answer at once, but sat holding the young girl's hand and staring at the fire.

''Katharine,'' she said at last, ''I'm in great trouble. I want a friend—not to help me, for no one can—I must bear it alone—but I must speak, or it will drive me mad.''

''You can tell me everything if you will, Hester,'' said Katharine, gravely. ''It will be quite safe with me. But don't tell me, if you are ever going to regret it.''

''No—I was thinking—''

Mrs. Crowdie hesitated and there was a short silence. She covered her eyes for an instant with one small hand —her hands were small and pointed, but not so thin as might have been expected from her face—and then she looked at her companion. The strong, well balanced features apparently inspired her with confidence. She nodded slowly, as though reaching a conclusion within herself, and then spoke.

''I will tell you, Katharine. I'd much rather tell you than any one else, and I know myself—I should be sure to tell somebody in the end. You're like a man in some things, though you are only a girl. If I had a man friend, I think I should go to him—but I haven't. Walter has always been everything to me. Somehow I never get intimate with men, as some women do.''

''Surely—there's your brother, Hester. Why don't you go to him? I should, in your place.''

''No, dear. You don't know—Hamilton never approved of my marriage. Didn't you know? He's such a good fellow that he wouldn't tell any one else so. But he—well—he never liked Walter, from the first, though I must say Walter was very nice to him. And about the arrangements—you know I had a settlement—Ham insisted upon it—so that my little fortune is in the hands of trustees—your father is one of them. As though Walter would ever have touched it! He makes me spend it all on myself. No, dear—I couldn't tell my brother —so I shall tell you.''

She stopped speaking and leaned forward, burying her face in her hands for a moment, as though to collect her thoughts. Then she sat up again, and looked at the fire while she spoke.

''It was last night,'' she said. ''He dined with you, and I stayed at home all by myself, not being asked, you see, because it was at a moment's notice—it was quite natural, of course. Walter came home early, and we sat in the studio a long time, as we often do in the evening. There's such a beautiful light, and the big fireplace, and cushions—and all. I thought he smoked a great deal, and you know he doesn't usually smoke much, on account of his voice, and he really doesn't care for it as much as some men do. I wish he did—I like the smell of it, and then a man ought to have some little harmless vice. Walter never drinks wine, nor coffee—nothing but Apollinaris. He's not at all like most men. He never uses any scent, but he likes to burn all sorts of queer perfumes in the studio in a little Japanese censer. I like cigars much better, and I always tell him so,—and he laughs. How foolish I am!'' she interrupted herself. ''But it's such a relief to talk —you don't know!''

''Go on, dear—I'm listening,'' said Katharine, humouring her, and speaking very gently.

''Yes—but I must tell you now.''

Katharine saw how she straightened herself to make
the effort, and sitting close beside her, so that they
touched one another, she felt that Hester was pressing
back against the sofa, while she braced her feet against
a footstool.

"It was very sudden," she said in a low voice. "We
were talking — I was saying something — all at once his
face changed so — oh, it makes me shudder to think of it.
It seemed — I don't know — like — almost like a devil's
face! And his eyes seemed to turn in — he was all purple — and his lips were all wet — it was like foam — oh,
it was dreadful — too awful!"

Katharine was startled and shocked. She could say
nothing, but pressed the small hand in anxious sympathy.
Hester smiled faintly, and then almost laughed, but instantly recovered herself again. She was not at all a
hysterical woman, and, as she said, she could never cry.

"That's only the beginning," she continued. "I won't
tell you how he looked. He fell over on the divan and
rolled about and caught at the cushions and at me — at
everything. He didn't know me at all, and he never
spoke an articulate word — not one. But he groaned,
and seemed to gnash his teeth — I believe it went on for
hours, while I tried to help him, to hold him, to keep
him from hurting himself. And then — after a long, long
time — all at once, his face changed again, little by little,
and — will you believe it, dear? He was asleep!"

"How strange!" exclaimed Katharine.

"Yes — wasn't it? But it seemed so merciful, and I
was so glad. And I sat by him all night and watched
him. Then early, early this morning — it was just grey
through the big skylight of the studio — he waked and
looked at me, and seemed so surprised to find himself
there. I told him he had fallen asleep — which was true,

you know — and he seemed a little dazed, and went to bed very quietly. But to-day, when he got up — it was I who sent you word not to come, because he had told me about the sitting — I told him everything, and insisted upon sending for Doctor Routh. He seemed terribly distressed, but wouldn't let me send, and he walked up and down the room, looking at me as though his heart would break. But he said nothing, except that he begged and begged me not to send for the doctor."

"And he's quite himself now, you say?"

"Wait — the worst is coming. At last he sat down beside me, and said — oh, so tenderly — that he had something to say to which I must listen, though he was afraid that it would pain me very much — that he had thought it would never be necessary to tell me, because he had imagined that he was quite cured when he had married me. Of course, I told him that — well, never mind what I said. You know how I love him."

Katharine knew, and it was incomprehensible to her, but she pressed the little hand once more.

"He told me that nearly ten years ago he had been ill with inflammatory rheumatism — that's the name of it, and it seems that it's excruciatingly painful. It was in Paris, and the doctors gave him morphia. He could not give it up afterwards."

"And he takes morphia still?" asked Katharine, anxiously enough, for she knew what it meant.

"No — that's it. He gave it up after five years — five whole years — to marry me. It was hard, he said, but he felt that it was possible, and he loved me, and he determined not to marry me while he was a slave to the poison. He gave it up for my sake. Wasn't that heroic?"

"Yes," said Katharine, gravely, and wondering whether

she had misjudged Crowdie. "It was really heroic. They say it is the hardest thing any one can do."

"He did it. I love him ten times more for it — but — this is the result of giving it up, dear. He will always be subject to these awful attacks. He says that a dose of morphia would stop one of them instantly, and perhaps prevent their coming back for a long time. But he won't take it. He says he would rather cut off his hand than take it, and he made me promise not to give it to him when he is unconscious, if I ever see him in that state again. He's so brave about it," she said, with a little choking sigh. "I've told you my story, dear."

Her face relaxed a little, and she opened and shut her hands slowly as though they had been stiffened.

Katharine sat with her half an hour longer that afternoon, sympathizing at first and then trying to divert her attention from the subject which filled all her heart and mind. Then she rose to go.

As they went out together from the little sitting-room, the sound of Crowdie's voice came down to them from the studio in the upper story. The door must have been open. Katharine and Hester stood still and listened, for he was singing, alone and to himself, high up above them, a little song of Tosti's with French words.

"Si vous saviez que je vous aime."

It was indeed a marvellous voice, and as Katharine listened to the soft, silver notes, and felt the infinite pathos of each phrase, she wondered whether, with all his success as a painter, Crowdie had not mistaken his career. She listened, spell-bound, to the end.

"It's divine!" she exclaimed. "There's no other word for it."

Hester Crowdie was paler than ever, and her soft grey eyes were all on fire. And yet she had heard him hundreds of times. Almost before Katharine had shut the glass door behind her, she heard the sound of light, quick footsteps as Hester ran upstairs to her husband.

"It's all very strange," thought Katharine. "And I never heard of morphia having those effects afterwards. But then — how should I know?"

And meditating on the many emotions she had seen in others during the last twenty-four hours, she hurried homewards.

CHAPTER IX.

MRS. LAUDERDALE had met with temptations in the course of her life, but they had not often appealed to her as they would have appealed to many women, for she was not easily tempted. A number of forms of goodness which are very hard to most people had been so easy to her that she had been good without effort, as, on the whole, she was good by nature. She had been brought up in an absolutely fixed religious belief, and had never felt any inclination to deviate from it, nor to speculate about the details of it, for her intellect was rather indolent, and in most positions in life her common-sense, which was strong, had taken the place of the complicated mental processes familiar to imaginative people like Katharine. Such imagination as Mrs. Lauderdale had was occupied with artistic matters.

Her vanity had always been satisfied quite naturally, without effort on her part, by her own great and uncontested beauty. She knew, and had always known, that

she was commonly compared with the greatest beauties
of the world, by men and women who had seen them
and were able to judge.   Social ambition never touched
her either, and she never remembered to have met with
a single one of those small society rebuffs which embitter
the lives of some women.   Nobody had ever questioned
her right, nor her husband's right, nor that of any of the
family, to be considered equal with the first.   In early
days she had suffered a little, indeed, from not being
rich enough to exercise that gift of almost boundless
hospitality which is rather the rule than the exception
among Americans, and which is said, with some justice,
to be an especial characteristic of Kentuckians.   Such
troubles as she had met with had chiefly arisen from the
smallness of her husband's income, from peculiarities of
her husband's character, and from her eldest daughter's
headstrong disposition.   And with all these her common-
sense had helped her continually.

She loved amusement and she had it in abundance, in
society, during a great part of the year.   Her talent had
helped her to procure luxuries, and she had been generous in giving a large share of them to her daughters.
She had soon learned to understand that society wanted
her for herself, and not for what she could offer it in her
own home, and she had been flattered by the discovery.
As for Alexander, he had many good qualities which she
appreciated when she compared him with the husbands
of other women.   Generosity with money was not his
strong point, but he had many others.   He loved her
tenaciously, not tenderly, nor passionately, nor in any
way that was at all romantic — if that word means anything — and certainly not blindly, but tenaciously; and
his admiration for her beauty, though rarely expressed,
found expression on such occasions in short, strong

phrases which left no manner of doubt as to his sincere conviction. She had not been happy with him, as boys and girls mean to be happy — for the rigidity of very great strength, when not combined with a corresponding intellect, is excessively wearisome in the companionship of daily married life. There is a coldness, a lack of expression and of sympathy, a Pharaoh-like, stony quality about it which do not encourage affection, nor satisfy an expansive nature. And though not imaginative, Mrs. Lauderdale was expansive. She had a few moments of despairing regret at first. She felt that she might just as well have married a magnificent, clean-built, iron-bodied, steel-jointed locomotive, as the man she had chosen, and that she could produce about as much impression on his character as she could have made upon such an engine. But she found out in time that, within certain limits, he was quite willing to do what she asked of him, and that beyond them he ran his daily course with a systematic and unvarying regularity, which was always safe, if it was never amusing. She got such amusement as she liked from other sources, and she often consoled herself for the dulness of the family dinner, when she dined at home, with the certainty that, during several hours before she went to bed, the most desirable men at a great ball would contest the honour of dancing with her. And that was all she wanted of them. She liked some of them. She took an interest in their doings, and she listened sympathetically to the story of their troubles. But it was not in her nature to flirt, nor to lose her head when she was flattered, and if she sometimes doubted whether she really loved her husband at all, she was quite certain that she could never love any one else. Perhaps she deserved no credit for her faithfulness, for it was quite natural to her.

On the whole, therefore, her temptations had been few, in reality, and she had scarcely noticed them. She had reached the most painful moment of her life with very little experience of what she could resist — the moment when she realized that the supremacy of her beauty was at an end. Of course, she had exaggerated very much the change which had taken place, for at the crucial instant when she had caught sight of her face in the mirror she had been unusually tired, considerably bored and not a little annoyed — and the mirror had a decidedly green tinge in the glass, as she assured herself by examining it and comparing it with a good one on the following morning. But the impression once received was never to be effaced; she might look her very best in the eyes of others — to her own, the lines of age being once discovered were never to be lost again, the dazzling freshness was never to come back to her skin, nor the gold to her hair, nor the bloom to her lips. And Crowdie, who was an artist, and almost a great portrait painter, could not take his eyes from Katharine, at whom no one would have looked twice when her mother had been at the height of her beauty. At least, so Mrs. Lauderdale thought.

And now, until Katharine was married and went away from home, the elder woman was to be daily, almost hourly, compared with her daughter by all who saw them together; for the first time in her life she was to be second in that one respect in which she had everywhere been first ever since she could remember, and she was to be second in her own house. When she realized it, she was horrified, and for a time her whole nature seemed changed. She clung desperately to that beauty of hers, which was, had she known it, the thing she loved best on earth, and which had reduced in her eyes

the value of everything else. She clung to it, and yet
from that fatal moment, she knew that it was hopeless
to cling to it, hopeless to try and recall it, hopeless to
hope for a miracle which, even in the annals of miracles,
had never been performed — the recall of youth. The
only possible mitigation suggested itself as a spontaneous
instinct — to avoid that cruel comparison with Katharine.
In the first hours it overcame her altogether. She could
not look at the girl. She could hardly bring herself to
speak kindly to her; though she knew that she would
willingly lay down her life for the child she loved best,
she could not lay down her beauty.

She was terrified at herself when she began to understand that something had overcome her which she felt
powerless to resist. For she was a very religious woman,
and the idea of envying her own daughter, and of almost
hating her out of envy, was monstrous. When Ralston
had come, she had not had the slightest intention of speaking as she had spoken. Suddenly the words had come to
her lips of themselves, as it were. If things went on
as they were going, Katharine would wait for Ralston
during years to come — the girl had her father's nature
in that — and Katharine would be at home, and the cruel,
hopeless comparison must go on, a perpetual and a keen
torture from which there was to be no escape. It was
simply impossible, intolerable, more than human endurance could bear. Ralston must be sent away, Katharine
must be married as quickly as possible, and peace would
come. There was no other way. It would be easy enough
to marry the girl, with her position, and the hope of some
of Robert Lauderdale's money, and with her beauty —
that terrible beauty of hers that was turning her mother's
to ugliness beside it. The first words had spoken themselves, the others had followed of necessity, and then, at

the end, had come the overwhelming consciousness of what they had meant, and the breaking down of the overstrained nerves, and the sobs and the tears, gushing out as a spring where instant remorse had rent and cleft her very soul.

It was no wonder that Katharine did not understand what was taking place. Fortunately, being much occupied with her own very complicated existence, she did not attempt any further analysis of the situation, did not accidentally guess what was really the matter, and wisely concluded that it would be best to leave her mother to herself for a time.

On the morning after the events last chronicled, Mrs. Lauderdale returned to her work, and at a quarter before eleven Katharine was ready to go out and was watching for Ralston at the library window. As soon as she saw him in the distance she let herself out of the house and went to meet him. He glanced at her rather anxiously as they exchanged greetings, and she thought that he looked tired and careworn. There were shadows under his eyes, and his dark skin looked rather bloodless.

"Why didn't you tell me that you had an accident the day before yesterday?" she asked at once.

"Who told you I had?" he enquired.

"Mr. Miner. I went out alone yesterday, after you had gone, and I met him at the corner of Washington Square. He told me all about it. How can you do such things, Jack? How can you risk your life in that way? And then, not to tell me! It wasn't kind. You seem to think I don't care. I wish you wouldn't! I'm sure I turned perfectly green when Mr. Miner told me — he must have thought it very extraordinary. You might at least have given me warning."

"I'm very sorry," said Ralston. "I didn't think it

was worth mentioning. Wasn't I all right when I came
to see you?"

He looked at her rather anxiously again — for another
reason, this time. But her answer satisfied him.

"Oh — you were 'dear' — even nicer than usual! But
don't do it again — I mean, such things. You don't
know how frightened I was when he told me. In fact,
I'm rather ashamed of it, and it's much better that you
shouldn't know."

"All right!" And Ralston smiled happily. "Now,"
he continued after a moment's thought, "I want to explain to you what I've found out about this idea of
yours."

"Don't call it an idea, Jack. You promised that you
would do it, you know."

"Yes. I know I did. But it's absolutely impossible
to have it quite a secret — theoretically, at least."

"Why?" She slackened her pace instinctively, and
then, seeing that they were just entering Fifth Avenue,
walked on more briskly, turning down in the direction of
the Square.

Ralston told her in a few words what he had learned
from the lawyer.

"You see," he concluded, "there's no way out of it.
And, of course, anybody may go to the Bureau of Vital
Statistics and look at the records."

"But is anybody likely to?" asked Katharine. "Is
the Clerk of the Records, or whatever you call him, the
sort of man who would be likely to know papa, for instance? That's rather important."

"No. I shouldn't think so. But everybody knows
all about you. You might as well be the President of
the United States as be a Lauderdale, as far as doing
anything incognito is concerned."

"There's only one President at a time, and there are twenty-three Lauderdales in the New York directory besides ourselves, and six of them are Alexanders."

"Are there? How did you happen to know that?" asked Ralston.

"Grandpapa looked them up the other day. He's always looking up things, you know — when he's not asleep, poor dear!"

"That certainly makes a difference."

"Of course it does," said Katharine. "No doubt the Clerk of the Records has seen the name constantly. Besides, I don't suppose he does the work himself. He only signs things. He probably looks at the books once a month, or something of that sort."

"Even then — he might come across the entry. He may have heard my name, too — you see my father was rather a bigwig in the Navy — and then, seeing the two together —"

"And what difference does it make? It isn't really a secret marriage, you know, Jack — at least, it's not to be a secret after I tell uncle Robert, which will be within twenty-four hours, you know. On the contrary, I shall tell him that we meant to tell everybody, and that it will be an eternal disgrace to him if he does nothing for you."

"He'll bear that with equanimity, dear. You won't succeed."

"Something will have to be done for us. When we're married and everybody knows it, we can't go on living as if we weren't — indefinitely — it would be too ridiculous. Papa couldn't stand that — he's rather afraid of ridicule, I believe, though he's not afraid of anything else. So, as I was saying, something will have to be done."

"That's a hopeful view," laughed Ralston. "But I

like the idea that it's not to be a secret for more than a day. It makes it look different."

"But I always told you that was what I meant, dear— I couldn't do anything mean or underhand. Didn't you believe me ?"

"Of course — but somehow I didn't see it exactly as I do now."

"Oh, Jack — you have no more sense than — than a small yellow dog!"

At which very remarkable simile Ralston laughed again, as he caught sight of the creature that had suggested it — a small yellowish cur sitting on the pavement, bolt upright against the railing, and looking across the street, grinning from ear to ear and making his pink tongue shake with a perfectly unnecessary panting, the very picture of canine silliness.

"Yes — that's the dog I mean," said Katharine. "Look at him — he's behaving just as you do, sometimes. But let's be serious. What am I to do? Who is going to marry us ?"

"Oh — I'll find somebody," answered Ralston, confidently. "They all say it's easy enough to be married in New York, but that it's awfully hard to be divorced."

"All the better!" laughed Katharine. "By the bye — what time is it ?"

"Five minutes to eleven," answered Ralston, looking at his watch.

"Dear me! And at eleven I'm due at Mr. Crowdie's for my portrait. I shall be late. Go and see about finding a clergyman while I'm at the studio. It can't be helped."

Ralston glanced at her in surprise. Of her sitting for her portrait he had not heard before.

"I must say," he answered, "you don't seem inclined to waste time this morning —"

"Certainly not! Why should we lose time? We've lost a whole year already. Do you think I'm the kind of girl who has to talk everything over fifty times to make up her mind? When you came, day before yesterday, I'd decided the whole matter. And now I mean — yes, you may look at me and laugh, Jack — I mean to put it through. I'm much more energetic than you seem to think. I believe you always imagined I was a lazy, pokey, moony sort of girl, with too much papa and mamma and weak tea and buttered toast in her nature. I'm not, you know. I'm just as energetic for a girl as you are for a man."

"Rather more so," said Ralston, watching her with intense admiration of her strong and beautiful self, and with considerable indifference to what she was saying, though her words amused him. "Please tell me about Crowdie and the portrait."

"Oh — the portrait? Mr. Crowdie wants to paint it for Hester. I'm going to sit the first time this morning. That's all. Here we are at the corner. We must cross here to get over to Lafayette Place."

"Well, then," said Ralston, as they walked on, "there's only one more point, and that's to find a clergyman. I suppose you can't suggest anybody, can you?"

"Hardly! You must manage that. I'm sure I've done quite enough already."

They discussed the question as they walked, without coming to any conclusion. Ralston determined to spend the day in looking for a proper person. He could easily withhold his name in every case, until he had made the arrangements. As a matter of fact, it is not hard to find a clergyman under the circumstances, since no clergyman can properly refuse to marry a respectable couple against whom he knows nothing. The matter of subsequent secrecy becomes for him more a question of taste than of conscience.

They reached the door of the Crowdie house, and Katharine turned at the foot of the white stone steps to say good-bye.

"Say you're glad, Jack dear!" she said suddenly, as she put out her hand, and their eyes met.

"Glad! Of course I'm glad — no, I really am glad now, though I wasn't at first. It looks different — it looks all right to-day."

"You don't look just as I expected you would, though," said Katharine, doubtfully. "And yet it seems to me you ought —" She stopped.

"Katharine — dear — you can't expect me to be as enthusiastically happy as though it really meant being married to you — can you?"

"But it does mean it. What else should it mean, or could it mean? Why isn't it just the same as though we had a big wedding?"

"Because things won't turn out as you think they will," answered Ralston. "At least, not soon — uncle Robert won't do anything, you know. One can't take fate and destiny and fortune and shuffle them about as though they were cards."

"One can, Jack! That's just it. Everybody has one chance of being happy. We've got ours now, and we'll take it."

"We'll take it anyhow, whether it's really a chance or not. Good-bye — dear — dear —"

He pressed her hand as he spoke, and his voice was tender and rang true, but it had not that quaver of emotion in it which had so touched Katharine on that one evening, and which she longed to hear again; and Ralston missed the wave of what had seemed like deep feeling, and wished it would come back. His nerves were perfectly steady now, though he had been late at his club on the previous evening, and had not slept much.

"I'll write you a note this afternoon," he said, "as soon as I've arranged with the clergyman. If it has to be very early, you must find some excuse for going out of the house. Of course, I'll manage it as conveniently as I can for you."

"Oh, there'll be no trouble about my going out," answered Katharine. "Nobody ever asks me where I'm going in the morning. You'll let me have the note as soon as you can, won't you?"

"Of course. Before dinner, at all events. Good-bye again, dear."

"Good-bye — until to-morrow."

She added the last two words very softly. Then she nodded affectionately and went up the steps. As she turned, after ringing the bell, she saw him walking away. Then he also turned, instinctively, and waved his hat once, and smiled, and was gone. Fletcher opened the door, and Katharine went in.

"How is Mr. Crowdie to-day — is he painting?" she asked of the servant.

"Yes, Miss Katharine, Mr. Crowdie's very well, and he left word that he expected you at eleven, Miss."

"Yes, I know — I'm late."

And she hurried up the stairs, for she had often been to the studio with Hester and with Crowdie himself, to see his pictures, and knew her way. But she knocked discreetly at the door when she had reached the upper story of the house.

"Come in, Miss Lauderdale," said Crowdie's silvery voice, and she heard his step on the polished floor as he left his work and came forward to meet her.

It seemed to her that his face was paler and his mouth redder than ever, and the touch of his soft white hand was exceedingly unpleasant to her, even through her glove.

He had placed a big chair ready for her, and she sat down as she was, with her hat and veil on, and looked about. Crowdie pushed away the easel at which he had been working. It ran almost noiselessly over the waxed oak, and he turned it with the face of the picture to the wall in a corner at some distance.

The studio was, as has been said, a very large room, occupying almost the whole upper story of the house, which was deeper than ordinary houses, though not very broad on the front. The studio was, therefore, nearly twice as long as its width, and looked even larger than it was from having no windows below, and only one door. There was, indeed, a much larger exit, by which Crowdie had his pictures taken out, by an exterior stair to the yard, but it was hidden by a heavy curtain on one side of the enormous fireplace. There were great windows, high up, on the north side, which must have opened above the roof of the neighbouring house, and which were managed by cords and weights, and could be shaded by rolling shades of various tints from white to dark grey. Over it was a huge skylight, also furnished with contrivances for modifying the light or shutting it out altogether.

So far, the description might answer for the interior of a photographer's establishment, but none of the points enumerated struck Katharine as she sat in her big chair waiting to be told what to do.

The first impression was that of a magnificent blending of perfectly harmonious colours. There was an indescribable confusion of soft and beautiful stuffs of every sort, from carpets to Indian shawls and Persian embroideries. The walls, the chairs and the divans were covered with them, and even the door which gave access to the stairs was draped and made to look unlike a door, so that when it was shut there seemed to be no way out. The divans were of the Eastern kind — great platforms, as it were, on which were laid broad mattresses, then stuffs, and then endless heaps of cushions, piled up irregularly and lying about in all directions. Only the polished floor was almost entirely bare — the rest was a mass of richness. But that was all. There were no arms, such as many artists collect in their studios, no objects of metal, save the great dull bronze fire-dogs with lions' heads, no plants, no flowers, and, excepting three easels with canvases on them, there was nothing to suggest the occupation of Walter Crowdie — nor any occupation at all. Even the little Japanese censer in which Hester said that he burned strange perfumes was hidden out of sight when not in use. There was not so much as a sketch or a drawing or a bit of modelled clay to be seen. There was not even a table with paints and brushes. Such things were concealed in a sort of small closet built out upon the yard, on the opposite side from the outer staircase, and hidden by curtains.

The total absence of anything except the soft materials with which everything was covered, produced rather a strange effect, and for some mysterious reason it was not a pleasant one. Crowdie's face was paler and his lips were redder than seemed quite natural; his womanish eyes were too beautiful and their glance was a caress — as warm velvet feels to the hand.

"Won't you let me help you to take off your veil?" he said, coming close to Katharine.

"Thank you — I can do it myself," she answered, with unnecessary coldness.

CHAPTER X.

CROWDIE stepped backward from her, as she laid her hat and veil upon her knee. He slowly twisted a bit of crayon between his fingers, as though to help his thoughts, and he looked at her critically.

" How are you going to paint me ? " she asked, regretting that she had spoken so very coldly a moment earlier.

" That's one of those delightful questions that sitters always ask," answered the artist, smiling a little. "That's precisely what I'm asking myself — how in the world am I going to paint you ? "

" Oh — that isn't what I meant! I meant — full face or side face, you know."

" Oh, yes, — of course. I was only laughing at myself. You have no idea what an extraordinary change taking off your hat makes, Miss Lauderdale. It would be awfully rude to talk to a lady about her face under ordinary circumstances. In detail, I mean. But you must forgive me, because it's my profession."

He moved about with sudden steps, stopping and gazing at her each time that he obtained a new point of view.

" How does my hat make such a difference ? " asked Katharine. " What sort of difference ? "

" It changes your whole expression. It's quite right that it should. When you have it on, one only sees the face — the head from the eyes downwards — that means the human being from the perceptions downwards. When you take your hat off, I see you from the intelligence upwards."

" That would be true of any one."

" No doubt. But the intelligence preponderates in

your case, which is what makes the contrast so strong."

"I didn't know I was as intelligent as all that!" Katharine laughed a little at what she took for a piece of rather gross flattery.

"No," answered Crowdie, thoughtfully. "That is your peculiar charm. Do you mind the light in your eyes? Just to try the effect? So? Does that tire you?"

He had changed the arrangement of some of the shades so as to throw a strong glare in her face. She looked up and the white light gleamed like fire in her grey eyes.

"I couldn't stand it long," she said. "Is it necessary?"

"Oh, no. Nothing is necessary. I'll try it another way. So." He moved the shades again.

"What a funny speech!" exclaimed Katharine. "To say that nothing is necessary —"

"It's a very true speech. Nothing is the same as Pure Being in some philosophies, and Pure Being is the only condition which is really absolutely necessary. Now, would you mind letting me see you in perfect profile? I'm sorry to bother you, but it's only at first. When we've made up our minds — if you'd just turn your head towards the fireplace, a little more — a shade more, please — that's it — one moment so —"

He stood quite still, gazing at her side face as though trying to fix it in his memory in order to compare it with other aspects.

"I want **to paint** you every way at once," he said. "May I ask — **what** do you think, yourself, is the best view of your face?"

"I'm sure I don't know," answered Katharine, with a little laugh. "What does Hester think? As it's to be for her, we might consult her."

"But she doesn't know it's for her — she thinks it's for you."

"We might ask her all the same, and take her advice. Isn't she at home?"

"No," answered Crowdie, after a moment's hesitation. "I think she's gone out shopping."

Katharine was not naturally suspicious, but there was something in the way Crowdie hesitated about the apparently insignificant answer which struck her as odd. She had made the suggestion because his mere presence was so absurdly irritating to her that she longed for Hester's company as an alleviation. But it was evident that Crowdie did not want his wife at that moment. He wanted to be alone with Katharine.

"You might send and find out," said the young girl, mercilessly.

"I'm pretty sure she's gone out," Crowdie replied, moving up an easel upon which was set a large piece of grey pasteboard. "Even if she is in, she always has things to do at this time."

He looked steadily at Katharine's face and then made a quick stroke on the pasteboard, then looked again and then made another stroke.

"What have you decided?" she enquired.

"Just as you are now, with your head a little on one side and that clear look in your eyes — no — you were looking straight at me, but not in full face. Think of what you were thinking about just when you looked."

Katharine smiled. The thought had not been flattering to him. But she did as he asked and met his eyes every time he glanced at her. He worked rapidly, with quick, sure strokes, using a bit of brown chalk. Then he took a long, new, black lead pencil, with a very fine point, from the breast-pocket of his jacket, and very care-

fully made a few marks with it. Instead of putting it
back when he used the bit of pastel again, he held the
pencil in his teeth. It was long and stuck out on each
side of his bright red lips. Oddly enough, Katharine
thought it made him look like a cat with black whisk-
ers, and the straight black line forced his mouth into a
wide grin. She even fancied that to increase the resemblance his eyes looked green when he gazed at her
intently, and that the pupils were not quite round, but
were turning into upright slits. She looked away for
a moment and almost smiled. His legs were a little
in-kneed, as those of a cat look when she stands up to
reach after anything. There was something feline even
in his little feet, which were short with a very high
instep, and he wore low shoes of dark russet leather.

"There is a smile in your eyes, but not in your face,"
said Crowdie, taking the pencil from between his teeth.
"I suppose it's rude to ask you what you are thinking
about?"

"Not at all," answered Katharine. "I was thinking
how funny you looked with that pencil in your mouth."

"Oh!" Crowdie laughed carelessly and went on with
his work.

Katharine noticed that when he next wished to dispose
of the pencil he put it into his pocket. As he had chosen
a position in which she must look directly at him, she
could not help observing all his movements, while her
thoughts went back to her own interests and to Ralston.
It was much more pleasant to think of John than of
Crowdie.

"I'm discouraged already," said Crowdie, suddenly,
after a long silence, during which he had worked rapidly.
"But it's only a first attempt at a sketch. I want a lot
of them before I begin to paint. Should you like to rest
a little?"

"Yes."

Katharine rose and came forward to see what he had been doing. She felt at once a little touch of disappointment and annoyance, which showed that she was not altogether deficient in vanity, though of a pardonable sort, considering what she saw. To her unpractised eye the sketch presented a few brown smudges, through which a thin pencil-line ran here and there.

"You don't see any resemblance to yourself, I suppose," said Crowdie, with some amusement.

"Frankly — I hope I'm better looking than that," laughed Katharine.

"You are. Sometimes you're divinely beautiful." His voice grew exquisitely caressing.

Katharine was not pleased.

"I didn't ask for impossible compliments," she said coolly.

"Now look," answered Crowdie, taking no notice of the little rebuke, and touching the smudge with his fingers. "You mustn't look too close, you know. You must try and get the effect — not what you see, but what I see."

Without glancing at her face he quickly touched the sketch at many points with his thumb, with his finger, with his bit of crayon, with his needle-pointed lead pencil. Katharine watched him intently.

"Shut your eyes a little, so as not to see the details too distinctly," he said, still working.

The face began to stand out. There was very little in the sketch, but there was the beginning of the expression.

"I begin to see something," said Katharine, with increasing interest.

"Yes — look!"

He glanced at her for a moment. Then, holding the

long pencil almost by the end and standing well back from the pasteboard, he drew a single line — the outline of the part of the face and head furthest from the eye, as it were. It was so masterly, so simple, so faultless, and yet so striking in its effect, that Katharine held her breath while the point moved, and uttered an exclamation when it stopped.

"You are a great artist!"

Crowdie smiled.

"I didn't ask for impossible compliments," he said, repeating her own words and imitating her tone, as he stepped back from the easel and looked at what he had done. "She's not so bad-looking, is she?" He fumbled in his pocket and found two or three bits of coloured pastels and rubbed a little of each upon the pasteboard with his fingers. "More life-like, now. How do you like that?"

"It's wonderful!"

"Wonderfully like?"

"How can I tell? I mean that it's a wonderful performance. It's not for me to judge of the likeness."

"Isn't it? In spite of proverbs, we're the only good judges of ourselves — outwardly or inwardly. Will you sit down again, if you are rested? Do you know, I'm almost inclined to dab a little paint on the thing — it's a lucky hit — or else you're a very easy subject, which I don't believe."

"And yet you were so discouraged a moment ago."

"That's always my way. I don't know about other artists, of course. It's only amateurs that tell each other their sensations about their daubs. We don't. But I'm always in a fit just before I'm going to succeed."

Katharine said nothing as she went back to her seat, but the expression he had just used chilled her suddenly.

She had received a vivid impression from the account Hester had given her of his recent attack, and she had unconsciously associated the idea of a fit with his ailment. Then she was amused at her own folly.

Crowdie looked at her keenly, then at his drawing, and then seemed to contemplate a particular point at the top of her head. She was not watching him, as she knew that he was not yet working again. There was an odd look in his beautiful eyes which would not have pleased her, had she seen it. He left the easel again and came towards her.

"Would you mind letting me arrange your hair a little?" he asked, stopping beside her.

Katharine instinctively raised one hand to her head, and it unexpectedly met his fingers, which were already about to touch her hair. The sensation was so inexpressively disagreeable to her that she started, lowering her head as though to avoid him, and speaking sharply.

"Don't!" she cried. "I can do it myself."

"I beg your pardon," said Crowdie, drawing back. "It's the merest trifle — but I don't see how you can do it yourself. I didn't know you were so nervous, or I would have explained. Won't you let me take the end of my pencil and just lift your hair a little? It makes such a difference in the outline."

It struck Katharine that she was behaving very foolishly, and she sat up straight in her chair.

"Of course," she said, quite naturally. "Do it in any way you like. I've a horror of being touched unexpectedly, that's all. I suppose I really am nervous."

Which was not at all true in general, though as regards Crowdie it was not half the truth.

"Thank you," he answered, proceeding to move her hair, touching it very delicately with his pointed white

fingers. "It was stupid of me, but most people don't
mind. There—if you only knew what a difference it
makes. Just a little bit more, if you'll let me—on the
other side. Now let me look at you, please—yes—
that's just it."

Katharine suffered intensely during those few moments. Something within her, of which she had never
been conscious before, but which was most certainly a
part of herself, seemed to rise up in fury, outraged and
insulted, against something in the man beside her,
which filled her with a vague terror and a positive disgust. While his soft and womanish fingers touched her
hair, she clasped her hands together till they hurt, and
repeated to herself with set lips that she was foolish and
nervous and unstrung. She could not help the sigh of
relief which escaped her lips when he had finished and
went back to his easel. Perhaps he noticed it. At all
events he became intent on his work and said nothing
for fully five minutes.

During that time she looked at him and tried to solve
the mystery of her unaccountable sensations. She
thought of what her mother had said—that Crowdie
was like a poisonous flower. He was so white and red
and soft, and the place was so still and warm, with its
masses of rich drapery that shut off every sound of life
from without. And she thought of what Miner had said
—oddly enough, in exactly the same strain, that he was
like some strange tropical fruit—gone bad at the core.
Fruit or flower, or both, she thought. Either was apt
enough.

The air was perfectly pure. It was only warm and
still. Possibly there was the slightest smell of turpen-
tine, which is a clean smell and a wholesome one. Whatever the perfumes might be which he occasionally burned,

they left no trace behind. And yet Katharine fancied they were there—unholy, sweet, heavy, disquieting, offending that something which in the young girl had never been offended before. The stillness seemed too warm—the warmth too still—his face too white—his mouth was as scarlet and as heavy as the blossom of the bright red calla lily. There was something repulsively fascinating about it, as there is in a wound.

"You're getting tired," he said at last. "I'm not surprised. It must be much harder to sit than to paint."

"How did you know I was tired?" asked Katharine, moving from her position, and looking at a piece of Persian embroidery on the opposite wall.

"Your expression had changed when I spoke," he said. "But it's not at all necessary to sit absolutely motionless as though you were being photographed. It's better to talk. The expression is like—" He stopped.

"Like what?" she asked, curious to hear a definition of what is said too often to be undefinable.

"Well—I don't know. Language isn't my strong point, if I have any strong point at all."

"That's an affectation, at all events!" laughed Katharine, becoming herself again when not obliged to look at him fixedly.

"Is it? Well—affectation is a good word. Expression is not expression when it's an affected expression. It's the tone of voice of the picture. That sounds wild, but it means something. A speech in print hasn't the expression it has when it's well spoken. A photograph is a speech in print. It's the truth done by machinery. It's often striking at first sight, but you get tired of it, because what's there is all there—and what is not there isn't even suggested, though you know it exists."

"Yes, I see," said Katharine, who was interested

in what he said, and had momentarily forgotten his personality.

"That shows how awfully clever you are," he answered with a silvery little laugh. "I know it's far from clear. There's a passage somewhere in one of Tolstoi's novels — 'Peace and War,' I think it is — about the impossibility of expressing all one thinks. It ought to follow that the more means of expression a man has, the nearer he should get to expressing everything in him. But it doesn't. There's a fallacy somewhere in the idea. Most things — ideas, anything you choose to call them — are naturally expressible in a certain material — paint, wood, fiddle-strings, bronze and all that. Come and look at yourself now. You see I've restrained my mania for oils a few minutes. I'm trying to be conscientious."

"I wish you would go on talking about expression," said Katharine, rising and coming up to the easel. "It seems very much improved," she added as she saw the drawing. "How fast you work!"

"There's no such thing as time when things go right," replied Crowdie. "Excuse me a moment. I'll get something to paint with."

He disappeared behind the curtain in the corner, to the out-built closet in which he kept his colours and brushes, and Katharine was left alone. She stood still for a few moments contemplating the growing likeness of herself. There was as yet hardly any colour in the sketch, no more, in fact, than he had rubbed on while she had watched him do it, when she had rested the first time. It was not easy to see what he had done since, and yet the whole effect was vastly improved. As she looked, the work itself, the fine pencil-line, the smudges of brown and the suggestions of colouring seemed all so slight as to be almost nothing — and yet she felt that her expression was there. She thought of her mother's laborious and minutely accurate drawing, which never reached any such effect as this, and she realized the almost impossible gulf which lies between the artist and the amateur who has tried too late to become one — in whom the evidence of talent is made unrecognizable by an excess of conscientious but wholly misapplied labour. The amateur who has never studied at all may sometimes dash off a head with a few lines, which would be taken for the careless scrawling of a clever professional. But the amateur who, too late, attempts to perfect himself by sheer study and industry is almost certainly lost as an artist — a fact which is commonly interpreted to mean that art itself comes by inspiration, and that so-called genius needs no school; whereas it only means that if we go to school at all we must go at the scholar's age and get the tools of expression, and learn to handle them, before we have anything especial to express.

"Still looking at it?" asked Crowdie, coming out of his sanctum with a large palette in his left hand, and a couple of brushes in his right. "Now I'm going to begin by spoiling it all."

There were four or five big, butter-like squeezings of different colours on the smooth surface of the board. Crowdie stuck one of his brushes through the thumb-hole of the palette, and with the other mixed what he wanted, dabbing it into the paints and then daubing them all together. Katherine sat down once more.

"I thought painters always used palette-knives," she said, watching him.

"Oh — anything answers the purpose. I sometimes paint with my fingers — but it's awfully messy."

"I should think so," she laughed, taking her position again as he looked at her.

"Yes — thank you," he said. "If you won't mind looking at me for a minute or two, just at first. I want your eyes, please. After that you can look anywhere you like."

"Do you always paint the eyes first?" asked Katharine, idly, for the sake of not relapsing into silence.

"Generally — especially if they're looking straight out of the picture. Then they're the principal thing, you know. They are like little holes — if you look steadily at them you can see the real person inside. That's the reason why a portrait that looks at you, if it's like at all, is so much more like than one that looks away."

"How naturally you explain things!" exclaimed the young girl, becoming interested at once.

"Things are so natural," answered the painter. "Everything is natural. That's one of my brother-in-law's maxims."

"It sounds like a truism."

"Everything that is true sounds like a truism — and is one. We know everything that's true, and it all sounds old because we do know it all."

"What an extraordinary way of putting it — to say that we know everything! But we don't, you know!"

"Oh, yes, we do — as far as we ever can know at all. I don't mean little peddling properties of petroleum and tricks with telephones — what they call science, you know. I mean about big things that don't change — ideas."

"Oh — about ideas. You mean right and wrong, and the future life and the soul, I suppose."

"Yes. That's exactly what I mean. In a hundred thousand ages we shall never get one inch further than we are now. A little bit more to the right, please — but go on looking at me a moment longer, if you're not tired."

"I've only just sat down again. But what you were saying — you meant to add that we know nothing, and that it's all a perfectly boundless uncertainty."

"Not at all. I think we know some things and shan't lose them, and we don't know some others and never shall."

"What kind of things, for instance?" asked Katharine.

"In the first place, there is a soul, and it is immortal."

"Lucretius says that there is a soul, but that it isn't immortal. There's something, anyhow — something I can't paint. People who deny the existence of the soul never tried to paint portraits, I believe."

"You certainly have most original ideas."

"Have I? But isn't that true? I know it is. There's something in every face that I can't paint — that the greatest painter that ever lived can't paint. And it's not on account of the material, either. One can get just as near to it in black and white as in colours, — just near enough to suggest it, — and yet one can see it. I call it the ghost. I don't know whether there are ghosts or not, but people say they've seen them. They are generally colourless, apparently, and don't stay long. But did you ever notice, in all those stories, that people always recognize the ghost instantly if it's that of a person they've known?"

"Yes. Now I think of it, that's true," said Katharine.

"Well, that's why I call the recognizable something about the living person his ghost. It's what we can't get. Now, another thing. If one is told that the best portrait of some one whom one knows is a portrait of some one else instead, one isn't much surprised. No, really — I've tried it, just to test the likeness. Most people say they are surprised, but they're not. They fall into the trap in a moment, and tell you that they see that

they were mistaken, but that it's a strong resemblance.
That couldn't happen with a real person. It happens
easily with a photograph — much more easily than with
a picture. But with a real person it's quite different, even
though he may have changed immensely since you saw
him — far beyond the difference between a good portrait
and the sitter, so far as details are concerned. But the
person — you recognize him at once. By what? By that
something which we can't catch in a picture. I call
it the ghost — it's a mere fancy, because people used to
believe that a ghost was a visible soul."

"How interesting!" exclaimed Katharine. "And it
sounds true."

"A thing must sound true to be interesting," said
Crowdie. "Excuse me a moment. I want another
colour."

He dived into the curtained recess, and Katharine
watched the disagreeable undulation of his movements
as he walked. She wondered why she was interested as
soon as he talked, and repelled as soon as he was silent.
Much of what he said was more or less paradoxical, she
thought, and not altogether unlike the stuff talked by
cynical young men who pick up startling phrases out of
books, and change the subject when they are asked to
explain what they mean. But there was something more
in what he said, and there was the way of saying it, and
there was the weight a man's sayings carry when he is a
real master of one thing, no matter how remote from the
subject of which he is speaking. Crowdie came back
almost immediately with his paint.

"Your eyes are the colour of blue fox," he remarked,
dabbing on the palette with his brush.

"Are they? They're a grey of some sort, I believe.
But you were talking about the soul."

"Yes, I know I was ; but I'm glad I've done with it. I told you that language wasn't my strong point."

"Yes — but you may be able to say lots of interesting things, besides painting well."

"Not compared with people who are good at talking. I've often been struck by that."

He stopped speaking, and made one or two very careful strokes, concentrating his whole attention for the moment.

"Struck by what ? " asked Katharine.

"By the enormous amount some men know as compared with what they can do. I believe that's what I meant to say. It wasn't particularly worth saying, after all. There — that's better ! Just one moment more, please. I know I'm tiring you to death, but I'm so interested — "

Again he executed a very fine detail.

"There !" he exclaimed. "Now we can talk. Don't you want to move about a little ?   I don't ask you to look at the thing — it's a mere beginning of a sketch — it isn't the picture, of course."

"But I want to see it," said Katharine.

"Oh, of course. But you won't like it so much now as you did at first."

Katharine saw at once that he was right, and that the painting was not in a stage to bear examination, but she looked at it, nevertheless, with a vague idea of learning something about the art by observing its processes. Crowdie stood at a little distance behind her, his palette and brushes still in his hand. Indeed, there was no place but the floor where he could have laid them down. She knew that he was there, and she was certain that he was looking at her. The strange nervousness and sense of repulsion came over her at once, but in her determination not to yield to anything which seemed so foolish, she continued to scrutinize the rough sketch on the easel.

Crowdie, on his part, said nothing, as though fearing lest the sound of his voice should disturb the graceful lines of her figure as she stood there.

At last she moved and turned away, but not towards him. Suddenly, from feeling that he was looking at her, she felt that she could not meet his eyes. She knew just what they would be like, long, languishing and womanish, with their sweeping lashes, and they attracted her, though she did not wish to see them. She walked a few steps down the length of the great room, and she was sure that those eyes were following her. An intense and quite unaccustomed consciousness overcame her, though she was never what is called shy.

She was positively certain that his eyes were fixed on the back of her head, willing her to turn and look at him; but she would not. Then she saw that she was reaching the end of the room, and that, unless she stood there staring at the tapestries and embroideries, she must face him. She felt the blood rush suddenly to her throat and just under her ears, and she knew that she who rarely blushed at all was blushing violently. She either did not know or she forgot that a blush is as beautiful in most dark women as it is unbecoming and even painful to see in fair ones. She was only conscious that she had never, in all her many recollections, felt so utterly foolish, and angry with herself, and disgusted with the light, as she did at that moment. Just as she reached the wall, she heard his footstep, and supposing that he had changed his position, she turned at once with a deep sense of relief.

Crowdie was standing before his easel again, studying what he had done, as unconcernedly as though he had not noticed her odd behaviour.

"I feel flushed," she said. "It must be very warm here."

"Is it?" asked Crowdie. "I'll open something. But if you've had enough of it for the first day, I can leave it as it is till the next sitt.ng. Can you come to-morrow?"

"Yes. That is — no — I may have an engagement." She laughed nervously as she thought of it.

"The afternoon will do quite as well, if you prefer it. Any time before three o'clock. The light is bad after that."

"I think the day after to-morrow would be better, if you don't mind. At the same hour, if you like."

"By all means. And thank you, for sitting so patiently. It's not every one who does. I suppose I mustn't offer to help you with your hat."

"Thanks, I can easily manage it," answered Katharine, careful, however, to speak in her ordinary tone of voice. "If you had a looking-glass anywhere —" She looked about for one.

"There's one in my paint room, if you don't mind."

He led the way to the curtain behind which he had disappeared in search of his colours, and held it up. There was an open door into the little room — which was larger than Katharine had expected — and a dressing-table and mirror stood in the large bow-window that was built out over the yard. Crowdie stood holding the curtain back while she tied her veil and ran the long pin through her hat. It did not take more than a minute, and she passed out again.

"That's a beautiful arrangement," she said. "A looking-glass would spoil the studio."

"Yes," he answered, as he walked towards the door by her side. "You see there isn't an object but stuffs and cushions in the place, and a chair for you — and my easels — all colour. I want nothing that has shape except what is human, and I like that as perfect as possible."

"Give my love to Hester," said Katharine, as she went out. "Oh, don't come down; I know the way."

He followed her, of course, and let her out himself. It was past twelve o'clock, and she felt the sun on her shoulders as she turned to the right up Lafayette Place, and she breathed the sparkling air with a sense of wild delight. It was so fresh and pure, and somehow she felt as though she had been in a contaminating atmosphere during the last three quarters of an hour.

CHAPTER XI.

ALEXANDER LAUDERDALE JUNIOR was a man of regular ways, as has been seen, and of sternly regular affections, so far as he could be said to have any at all. Most people were rather afraid of him. In the Trust Company which occupied his attention he was the executive member, and it was generally admitted that it owed something of its exceptional importance to his superior powers of administration, his cast-iron probity and his cold energy in enforcing regulations. The headquarters of the Company were in a magnificent granite building, on the second floor at the front, and Alexander Junior sat all day long in a spotless and speckless office, behind a highly polished table and before highly polished bookcases, upon which the light fell in the daytime through the most expensive and highly polished plate glass windows, and on winter afternoons from glittering electric brackets and chandeliers. He himself was not less perfect and highly polished in appearance than his surroundings. He was like one of those beautiful models of machinery which work silently

and accurately all day long, apparently for the mere
satisfaction of feeling their own wheels and cranks go
round, behind the show window of the shop where the
patent is owned, producing nothing, indeed, save a keen
delight in the soul of the admiring mechanician.

He was perfect in his way. It was enough to catch
one glimpse of him, as he sat in his office, to be sure that
the Trust Company could be trusted, that the widow's
portion should yield her the small but regular interest
which comforts the afflicted, and that the property of the
squealing and still cradle-ridden orphan was silently
rolling up, to be a joy to him when he should be old
enough to squander it. The Trust Company was not a
new institution. It had been founded in the dark ages
of New York history, by just such men as Alexander
Junior, and just such men had made it what it now was.
Indeed, the primeval Lauderdale, whom Charlotte Slayback called Alexander the Great, had been connected with
it before he died, his Scotch birth being counted to him
for righteousness, though his speech was imputed to him
for sin. Neither of his sons had, however, had anything
to do with it, nor his sons' sons, but his great-grandson,
Alexander the Safe, was predestined from his childhood
to be the very man wanted by the Company, and when he
was come to years of even greater discretion than he had
shown as a small boy, which was saying much, he was
formally installed behind the plate glass and the very
shiny furniture of the office he had occupied ever since.
With the appearance of his name on the Company's reports the business increased, for in the public mind all
Lauderdales were as one man, and that one man was Robert
the Rich, who had never been connected with any speculation, and who was commonly said to own half New York.
Acute persons will see that there must have been some

exaggeration about the latter statement, but as a mere
expression it did not lack force, and pleased the popular
mind. It mattered little that New York should have
enough halves to be distributed amongst a considerable
number of very rich men, of whom precisely the same
thing was said.   Robert the Rich was a very rich
man, and he must have his half like his fellow rich
men.

Alexander Junior had no more claim upon his uncle's
fortune than Mrs. Ralston.   His father was one of
Robert's brothers and hers had been the other.   Nor was
Robert the Rich in any way constrained to leave any
money to any of his relations, nor to any one in particular in the whole wide world, seeing that he had made it
himself, and was childless and answerable to no man for
his acts.   But it was probable that he would divide a
large part of it between his living brother, the philanthropist, and the daughter of his dead brother Ralph —
the soldier of the family, who had been killed at Chancellorsville.   Now as it was certain that the philanthropist, for his part, if he had control of what came to
him, would forthwith attempt to buy the Central Park as
an airing ground for pauper idiots, or do something
equally though charitably outrageous, the chances were
that his portion — if he got any — would be placed in
trust, or that it would be paid him as income by his
son, if the latter were selected to manage the fortune.
This was what most people expected, and it was certainly what Alexander Junior hoped.

It was natural, too, and in a measure just. The male
line of the Lauderdales was dying out, and Alexander
Junior would be the last of them, in the natural succes-
sion of mortality, being by far the youngest as he was
by far the strongest. It would be proper that he should

administer the estate until it was finally divided amongst the female heirs and their children.

He was really and truly a man of spotless probity, in spite of the suspicion which almost inevitably attaches to people who seem too perfect to be human. On the surface these perfections of his were so hard that they amounted to defects. It is aggressive virtue that chastises what it loves — by its mere existence. But neither his probity, nor his exterior mechanical superiority, so to say, was connected with the mainspring of his character. That lay much deeper, and he concealed it with as much skill as though to reveal its existence would have ruined him in fortune and reputation, though it would probably have affected neither the one nor the other. The only members of the family who suspected the truth were his daughter Charlotte and Robert the Rich.

Charlotte, who was afraid of nothing, not even of certain things which she might have done better to respect, if not to fear, said openly in the family, and even to the face of her father, that she did not believe he was poor. Thereupon, Alexander Junior usually administered a stern rebuke in his metallic voice, whereat Charlotte would smile and change the subject, as though she did not care to talk of it just then, but would return to it by and by. She had magnificent teeth, and, when she chose, her smile could be almost as terribly electric as Alexander's own.

As for Robert Lauderdale, he had more accurate knowledge, but not much. Like many eminently successful men he had an unusual mastery of details, and an unfailing memory for those which interested him. He knew the exact figure of his nephew's salary from the Trust Company, and he was able to calculate with tolerable exactness, also, what the Lauderdales spent, what Mrs. Lauderdale earned and how much the annual surplus must be. He knew also that Alexander Junior's mother, who had thoroughly understood her husband, the philanthropist, had left what she possessed to her only son, and only a legacy to her husband. Her property had been owned in New England; the executor had been a peculiarly taciturn New England lawyer, and Alexander had never said anything to any one else concerning the inheritance. His mother had died after he had come of age, but before he had been married, and there were no means whatever of ascertaining what he had received. The philanthropist and his son had continued to live together, as they still did; but the old gentleman had always left household matters and expenses in his wife's charge, and had never in the least understood, nor cared to understand, the details of daily life. He had his two rooms, he had enough to eat and he spent nothing on himself, except for the large quantity of tobacco he consumed and for his very modest toilet. As for the cigars, Alexander had brought him down, in the course of ten years, by very fine gradations, from the best Havanas which money could buy to 'old Virginia cheroots,' at ten cents for a package of five, — a luxury which even the frugal inhabitant of Calabrian Mulberry Street would consider a permissible extravagance on Sundays. Alexander, who did not smoke, saw that the change had not had any ill effect upon his father's health, and silently triumphed. If the old gentleman's nerves had shown signs of weakness, Alexander had previously determined to retire up the scale of prices to the extent of one cent more for each cigar. In the matter of dress the elder Alexander pleased himself, and in so doing pleased his son also, for he generally forgot to

get a new coat until the old one was dropping to pieces,
and he secretly bought his shoes of a little Italian shoemaker in the South Fifth Avenue, as has been already
noticed; the said shoemaker being the unhappy father
of one of the philanthropist's most favourite and un-
promising idiots.

But of old Mrs. Lauderdale's money, nothing more
was ever heard, nor of several thousand dollars yearly,
which, according to old Robert's calculations, Alexander
Junior saved regularly out of his salary.

Yet the youngest of the Lauderdale men was always
poor, and his wife worked as hard as she could to earn
something for her own little pleasures and luxuries.
Robert the Rich had once been present when Alexander
Junior had borrowed five dollars of his wife. It had
impressed him, and he had idly wondered whether
the money had ever been returned, and whether Alexander did not manage in this way to extract a contribu-
tion from his wife's earnings, as a sort of peace-offering
to the gold-gods, because she wasted what she got by
such hard work, in mere amusement and hats, as Alexander cruelly put it. But Robert, who had a broader
soul, thought she was quite right, since, next to true
love, those were the things by which a woman could
be made most happy. It is true that Robert the Rich
had never been married. As a matter of fact, Alexander Lauderdale never returned the small sums he
succeeded in borrowing from his wife from time to time.
But he kept a rigidly accurate account of them, which
he showed her occasionally, assuring her that she 'might
draw on him' for the money, and that he credited her
with five per cent interest so long as it was 'in his
hands' — which were of iron, as she knew — and
further, that it would be to her advantage to invest

all the money she earned in the same way, with him.
A hundred dollars, he said, would double itself in
fourteen years, and in time it would become a thousand,
which would be 'a nice little sum for her.' He had
a set of expressions which he used in speaking of money,
wherewith he irritated her exceedingly. More than
once she asked him to give her a trifle out of what she
had lent him, when she was in a hurry, or really
had nothing. But he invariably answered that he had
nothing about him, as he always paid everything by
cheque, — which was true, — and never spent but ten
cents daily for his fare in the elevated road to and from
his office. He lunched somewhere, she supposed, during
the day, and would need money for that; but in this
she was mistaken, for his strong constitution needed
but two meals daily, breakfast at eight and dinner at
half-past seven. At one o'clock he drank a glass of
water in his office, and in fine weather took a turn
in Broad Street or Broadway. He sometimes, if hard
pressed by her, said that he would include what she
wanted in the next cheque he drew for household
expenses — and he examined the accounts himself every
Saturday afternoon — but he always managed to be alone
when he did this, and invariably forgot to make any
allowance for the purpose of paying his just debts.

Robert Lauderdale knew, therefore, that there must
be a considerable sum of money, somewhere, the property
of Alexander Junior, unless the latter had privately
squandered it. This, however, was a supposition which
not even the most hopelessly moonstruck little boy
in the philanthropist's pet asylum would have entertained for a moment. The rich man had watched his
nephew narrowly from his boyhood to his middle age,
and was a knower of men and a good judge of them, and

he was quite sure that he was not mistaken. Moreover, he knew likewise Alexander's strict adherence to the letter of truth, for he had proved it many times, and Alexander had never said that he had no money. But he never failed to say that he was poor — which was a relative term. He would go so far as to say that he had no money for a particular object, clearly meaning that he would not spend anything in that direction, but he had never said that he had nothing. Now the great Robert was not the man to call a sum of several hundred thousands a nothing, because he had so much more himself. He knew the value of money as well as any man living. He used to say that to give was a matter of sentiment, but that to have was a matter of fact, — probably meaning thereby that the relation between length of head and breadth of heart was indeterminate, but that although a man might not have fifty millions, if he had half a million he was well enough off to be able to give something to somebody, if he chose. But Robert the Rich was fond of rather enigmatical sayings. He had seen the world from quite an exceptional point of view and believed that he had a right to judge it accordingly.

He had watched his nephew during more than thirty years, and one half of that period had sufficed to bring him to the conclusion that Alexander Junior was a thoroughly upright but a thoroughly miserly person, and the remaining half of the time had so far confirmed this judgment as to make him own that the younger man was not only miserly, but in the very most extended sense an old-fashioned miser in the midst of a new-fashioned civilization, and therefore an anachronism, and therefore, also, not a man to be treated like other men.

Robert had long ago determined that Alexander should

have some of the money to do with as he pleased. His sole idea would be to hoard it and pile it up to fabulous dimensions, and if anything happened to it he would probably go mad, thought the great man. But the others were also to have some of it, more or less according to their characters, and it was interesting to speculate upon their probable actions when they should be very rich. None of them, Robert believed, were really poor, and certainly Alexander Junior was not. If they had been in need, the old gentleman would have helped them with actual sums of money. But they were not. As for Mrs. Lauderdale and her daughters, they really had all that was necessary. Alexander did not starve them. He did not go so far as that — perhaps because in his social position it would have been found out. His wife was an excellent housekeeper, and old Robert liked the simplicity of the little dinners to which he occasionally came without warning, asking for 'a bite,' as though he were a poor relation. He loved what was simple and, in general, all things which could be loved for their own sake, and not for their value, and which were not beyond his rather limited æsthetic appreciation.

It was a very good thing, he thought, that Mrs. Lauderdale should do a little work and earn a little money. It was an interest and an occupation for her. It was fitting that people should be willing to do something to earn money for their charities, or even for their smaller luxuries, though it was very desirable that they should not feel obliged to work for their necessities. If everybody were in that position, he supposed that every one would be far happier. And Mrs. Lauderdale had her beauty, too. Robert the Rich was fond of her in a fatherly way, and knowing what a good woman she was, he had determined to make her a compensation when she should lose her good looks. When her beauty departed, she should be made rich, and he would manage it in such a way that her husband should not be able to get hold of any of her wealth, to bury with what Robert was sure he had, in secret and profitable investment. Alexander Junior should have none of it.

As for his elder brother, the philanthropist, Robert Lauderdale had his own theories. He did not think that the old man's charities were by any means always wise ones, and he patronized others of his own, of which he said nothing. Robert thought that too much was done for the deserving poor, and too little for the undeserving poor, and that the starving sinner might be just as hungry as the starving saint — a point of view not popular with the righteous, who covet the unjust man's sunshine for themselves and accuse him unfairly of bringing about cloudy weather, though every one knows that clouds, even the very blackest, are produced by natural evaporation.

But it was improbable, as Robert knew, that his brother should outlive him, and he contributed liberally to the support and education of the idiots, and his brother was mentioned in the will in connection with a large annuity which, however, he had little chance of surviving to enjoy.

There were plenty of others to divide the vast inheritance when the time should come. There were Mrs. Lauderdale and her two daughters, and her baby grandson, Charlotte's little boy. And there was Katharine Ralston and there was John. And then there were the two Brights and their mother, whose mother had been a Lauderdale, so that they were direct relations. And there were the Miners — the three old-maid sisters and little Frank Miner, who really seemed to be struggling hard to make a living by literature — not near connections, these Miners, but certainly included in the tribe of Lauderdales on account of their uncle's marriage with the millionaire's first cousin — whom he remembered as 'little cousin Meg' fifty years ago. Robert the Rich always smiled — a little sadly — when he reached this point in the enumeration of the family, and was glad that the Miners were in his will.

The Miners would really have been the poorest of the whole connection, for their father had been successively a spendthrift bankrupt, a drunkard and a lunatic — which caused Alexander Junior to say severely that Livingston Miner had an unnatural thirst for emotions; but a certain very small investment which Frank Miner had made out of the remnants of the estate had turned out wonderfully well. Miner had never known that old Lauderdale had mentioned the investment to old Beman, and that the two great men had found the time to make it roll over and over and grow into a little fortune at a rate which would have astonished persons ignorant of business — after which they had been occupied with other things, each in his own way, and had thought nothing more about the matter. So that the Miners were comparatively comfortable, and the three old maids stayed at home and 'took care' of their extremely healthy brother instead of going out as governesses — and when they were well stricken in old-maidhood they had a queer little love story all to themselves, which perhaps will be told some day by itself.

The rich man made few presents, for he had few wants, and did not understand them in others. He was none the less on that account a generous man, and would often have given, had he known what to give; but those who expressed their wishes were apt to offend him by expressing them too clearly. The relations all lived in good houses and had an abundance of bread and a suf ficient allowance of butter, and John Ralston was the only one in connection with whom he had heard mention of a tailor's bill — John Ralston was more in the old gentleman's mind than any one knew. What did the others all want? Jewels, perhaps, and horses and carriages and a lot of loose cash to throw out of the window. That was the way he put it. He had never kept a brougham himself until he was fifty years of age. It was true that he had no womankind and was a strong man, like all his tribe. But then, many of his acquaintances who might have kept a dozen horses, said it was more trouble than it was worth, and hired what they wanted. His relations could do the same — it was a mere curiosity on their part to experience the sensation of looking rich. Robert Lauderdale knew the sensation very well and knew that it was quite worthless. Of course, he thought, they all knew that at his death they would be provided for — even lazy Jack, as he mentally nick-named Ralston. At least, he supposed that they knew it. They should have a fair share of the money in the end.

But he was conscious, and acutely conscious, that most of them wanted it, and he had very little belief in the disinterested affection of any of them. Even the old philanthropist, if he had been offered the chance by a playful destiny, would have laid violent hands on it all for his charities, to the exclusion of the whole family. His son would have buried it in his own Trust Company, and longed to have it for that purpose, and for no other. Jack Ralston wanted to squander it; Hamilton Bright wanted to do banking with it and to out-Rothschild the Rothschilds in the exchanges of the world. Crowdie, whom Robert the Rich detested, wanted his wife to have it in order that he might build marble palaces with it on the shores of more or less mythic lakes. Katharine Ralston would have liked some of it because she liked to be above all considerations of money, and her husband's death had made a great difference in her income. Mrs. Lauderdale wanted it, of course, and her ideal of happiness would be realized in having three or four princely establishments, in moving with the seasons from one to the other and in always having her house full of guests. She was born in Kentucky — and she would be a superb hostess. Perhaps she should have a chance some day. Charlotte Slayback wanted as much as she could get because her husband was rich, and she had nothing, and she had good blood in her veins, but an abundance of evil pride in her heart. There was Katharine Lauderdale, about whom the great man was undecided. He liked her and thought she understood him. But of course she wanted the money too — in order to marry lazy Jack — and wake up love's young dream with a jump, as he expressed it familiarly. She should not have it for that purpose, at all events. It would be much better that she should marry Hamilton Bright, who was a sensible fellow. Had not Ralston been offered two chances, at both of which he had pitiably failed? He had no idea for doing anything more for the boy at present. If he ever got any of the money it should be from his mother. The two Katharines were out and out the best of the tribe. He had a great mind to tear up his old will and divide the whole fortune equally between Katharine Ralston and Katharine Lauderdale. No doubt there would be a dispute about the will in any case — he might just as well follow his inclinations, if he could not prevent fighting.

And then, when he reached that point, he was suddenly checked by a consideration which does not present itself to ordinary men. As he leaned back in his leathern writing chair, while his knotted fingers played with the cork pen-holder he used, his great head slowly bowed itself, and he sat long in deep thought.

It was all very well for him to play at being just a capricious old uncle with some money to leave, as he pleased, to this one or that one, as old uncles did in story books, making everybody happy in the end. That was all very well. He had his little likes and dislikes, his attachments and his detestations, and he had a right to have them, as smaller men had. A little here and a little there would of course give pleasure and might even make happiness. But how much would it need to make them all rich, compared with their present position? Robert Lauderdale did not laugh as he answered the question to himself. One year's income alone, divided amongst them, would give each a fortune. The income of two years would give them wealth. And the capital would remain — the vast possession which in a few years he must lay down forever, which at any moment might be masterless, for he was an old man, over seventy years of age. If he had a son, it would be different. Things would follow their natural course for good or evil, and he would not himself be to blame for what happened. But he had no one, and the thing he must leave to some one was great power in its most serviceable form — money.

He had been face to face with the problem for years and had not solved it. It is a great one in America, at the present day, and Robert Lauderdale knew it. He was well aware that he and a score of others, some richer, some less rich than himself, were execrated by a certain proportion of the community and pointed out as the

disturbers of the equal distribution of wealth. He was
made personally sure of the fact by hundreds of letters,
anonymous and signed, warning him of the approaching
destruction of himself and his property. People who
did not even know that he was a bachelor, threatened to
kidnap his children and keep them from him until he
should give up his wealth. He was threatened, entreated,
admonished, preached at and held up to ridicule by every
species of fanatic which the age produces. He was not
afraid of any of them. He did not have himself guarded
by detectives in plain clothes and athletes in fashionable
coats, when he chose to walk in the streets, and he did
not yield to the entreaties of women who wrote to him
from Texas that they should be perfectly happy if he
would send them grand pianos to the addresses they
gave. He was discriminating, he was just according to
his light and he tried to do good, while he took no notice
of those who raved and abused him. But he knew that
there was a reason for the storm, and was much more
keenly alive to the difficulties of the situation than any
of his anonymous correspondents.

He had in his own hands and at his absolute disposal
the wealth which, under a proper administration, would
perpetually supply between seven and eight thousand
families with the necessaries of life. He had made that
calculation one day, not idly, but in the endeavour to
realize what could really be done with so much money.
He was not a visionary philanthropist like his brother,
though he helped him in many of his schemes. He was
not a saint, though he was a good man, as men go. He
had not the smallest intention of devoting a gigantic
fortune exclusively to the bettering of mankind, for he
was human. But he felt that in his lonely wealth he
was in a measure under an obligation to all humanity —

that he had created for himself a responsibility greater
than one man could bear, and that he and others like
him had raised a question, and proposed a problem which
had not before been dreamt of in the history of the world.
He, an individual with no especial gifts besides his keen
judgment in a certain class of affairs, with nothing but
his wealth to distinguish him from any other individual,
possessed the equivalent of a sum of money which would
have seemed very large in the treasury of a great nation,
or which would have been considered sufficient as a re-
serve wherewith to enter upon a great war. And there
were others in an exactly similar position. He knew
several of them. He could count half a dozen men who,
together with himself, could upset the finances of the
world if they chose. It needed no tortuous reasoning
and but little vanity to show him that he and they did
not stand towards mankind as other men stood. And
the thought brought with it the certainty that there was
a right course for him to pursue in the disposal of his
money, if he could but see it in the right light.

This was the man whom all the Lauderdale tribe called
uncle Robert, and to whom Katharine intended to appeal
as soon as she had been secretly married to John Ralston, and from whom she felt sure of obtaining what she
meant to ask. He was capable of surprising her.

'You have a good house, good food, good clothes — and
so has your husband. What right have you, Katharine
Lauderdale, or Mrs. John Ralston, to claim more than
any member of each of the seven or eight thousand families whom I could support would get in the distribution?'

That was the answer she might receive — in the form
of a rather unanswerable question.

CHAPTER XII.

THE afternoon which followed the first sitting in Crowdie's studio seemed very long to Katharine. She did all sorts of things to make the time pass, but it would not. She even set in order a whole drawer full of ribbons and gloves and veils and other trifles, which is generally the very last thing a woman does to get rid of the hours.

And all the time she was thinking, and not sure whether it would not be better to fight against her thoughts. For though she was not afraid of changing her mind she had a vague consciousness that the whole question might raise its head again and face her like a thing in a dream, and insist that she should argue with it. And then, there was the plain and unmistakable fact that she was on the eve of doing something which was hardly ever done by the people amongst whom she lived.

It was not that she was timid, or dreaded the remarks which might be made. Any timidity of that sort would have checked her at the very outset. If the man she loved had been any one but Jack Ralston, whom she had known all her life, she could never have thought of proposing such a thing. Oddly enough, she felt that she should blush, as she had blushed that morning at the studio, at the mere idea of a secret marriage, if Ralston were any one else. But not from any fear of what other people might say. Not only had the two been intimate from childhood — they had discussed during the last year their marriage, and all the possibilities of it, from every point of view. It was a subject familiar to them, the difficulties to be overcome were clear to them both, they had proposed all manner of schemes for overcoming them, they had talked for hours about running away together and had been sensible enough to see the folly of such a thing. The mere matter of saying certain words and of giving and receiving a ring had gradually sunk into insignificance as an event. It was an inevitable formality in Ralston's eyes, to be gone through with scrupulous exactness indeed, and to be carefully recorded and witnessed, but there was not a particle of romance connected with it, any more than with the signing and witnessing of a title-deed or any other legal document.

Katharine had a somewhat different opinion of it, for it had a real religious value in her eyes. That was one reason why she preferred a secret wedding. Of course, the moment would come, sooner or later, for they were sure to be married in the end, publicly or privately. But in any case it would be a solemn moment. The obligations, as she viewed them, were for life. The very words of the promise had an imposing simplicity. In the church to which she strongly inclined, marriage was called a sacrament, and believed to be one, in which the presence of the Divine personally sanctified the bond of the human. Katharine was quite willing to believe that, too. And the more she believed it, the more she hated the idea of a great fashionable wedding, such as Charlotte Slayback had endured with much equanimity. She could imagine nothing more disagreeable, even painful, than to be the central figure of such an exhibition.

That holy hour, when it came at last, should be holy indeed. There should be nothing, ever thereafter, to disturb the pure memory of its sanctity. A quiet church, the man she loved, herself and the interpreter of God. That was all she wanted — not to be disturbed in the greatest event of her life by all the rustling, glittering, flower-scented, grinning, gossiping crowd of critics, whose ridiculous presence is considered to lend marriage a dignity beyond what God or nature could bestow upon it.

This was Katharine's view, and as she had no intention of keeping her marriage to Ralston a secret during even so much as twenty-four hours, it was neither unnatural nor unjustifiable. But in spite of all the real importance which she gave to the ceremony as a fact, it seemed so much a matter of course, and she had thought of it so long and under so many aspects, that in the chain of future events it was merely a link to be reached and passed as soon as possible. It was not the ring, nor the promise, nor the blessing, by which her life was to be changed. She knew that she loved John Ralston, and she could not love him better still from the instant in which he became her lawful husband. The difficulties began beyond that, with her intended attack upon uncle Robert. She told herself that she was sure of success, but she was not, since she could not see into the future one hour beyond the moment of her meeting with the old gentleman. That seeing into the future is the test of confidence, and the only one.

It struck her suddenly that everything which was to happen after the all-important interview was a blank to her. She paused in what she was doing—she was winding a yellow ribbon round her finger—and she looked out of the window. It was raining, for the weather had changed quickly during the afternoon. Rain in Clinton Place is particularly dreary. Katharine sat down upon the chair that stood before her little writing table in the corner by the window, and watched the grey lace veil which the falling raindrops wove between her and the red brick houses opposite.

A feeling of despair came over her. Uncle Robert

would refuse to do anything. What would happen then?
What could she do? She was brave enough to face her
father's anger and her mother's distress, for she loved
Ralston with all her heart. But what would happen?
If uncle Robert failed her, the future was no longer
blank but black. No one else could do anything. Of
what use would the family battle be? Her father could
not, and would not, do anything for her or her husband.
He was the sort of man who would take a stern delight
in seeing her bear the consequences of her mistake — it
could not be called a fault, even by him. To impose
herself on Mrs. Ralston was more than Katharine's pride
could endure to contemplate. Of course, it would be
possible to live — barely to live — on the charity of her
husband's mother. Mrs. Ralston would do anything for
her son, and would sacrifice herself cheerfully. But to
accept any such sacrifice was out of the question. And
then, too, Katharine knew what extreme economy meant,
for she had suffered from it long under her father's roof,
and it was not pleasant. Yet they would be poorer still
at the Ralstons, and she would be the cause of it.

If uncle Robert refused to help them, the position
would be desperate. She watched the rain and tried to
think it all over. She supposed that her father would
insist upon — what? Not upon keeping the secret, for
that would not be like him. He was a horribly virtuous
man, Charlotte used to say. Oh, no! he would not act a
lie on any account, not he! Katharine wondered why
she hated this scrupulous truthfulness in her father and
admired it above all things in Ralston. Jack would not
act a lie either. But then, if there were to be no secret,
and if the marriage were to be announced, what would
happen? Would her father insist upon her living at
home until her husband should be able to support her?

What a situation! She cared less than most girls about
social opinion, but she really wondered what society
would say. Her father would say nothing. He would
smile that electric smile of his, and hold his head higher
than ever. 'This is what happens to daughters who dis-
obey their parents,' he would seem to tell the world.
She had always thought that he might be like the first
Brutus, and she felt sure of it now.

It seemed like weakness to think of going to uncle
Robert that very afternoon, before the inevitable moment
was past. Yet it would be such an immense satisfaction
to have had the interview and to have his promise to do
something for Ralston. The thought seemed cowardly
and yet she dwelt on it. Of course, her chief weapon
with the old gentleman was to be the fact that the thing
was done and could not be undone, so that he could have
no good advice to give. And, yet, perhaps she might
move him by saying that she had made up her mind and
was to be married to-morrow. He might not believe her,
and might laugh and send her away — with one of his
hearty avuncular kisses — she could see his dear old face
in her imagination. But if he did that, she could still
return to-morrow, and show him the certificate of her
marriage. He would not then be able to say that she
had not given him fair warning. She wished it would
not rain. She would have walked in the direction of his
house, and when she was near it she knew in her heart
that she would yield — since it seemed like a temptation
— and perhaps it would be better.

But it was raining, and uncle Robert lived far away
from Clinton Place in a house he had built for himself
at the corner of a new block facing the Central Park.
He had built the whole block and had kept possession of
it afterwards. It was almost three miles from Alexander

Lauderdale's house in unfashionable Clinton Place —
three miles of elevated road, or of horse-car or of walking
— and in any case it meant getting wet in such a rain
storm. Moreover, Katharine rarely went alone by the
elevated road. She wished it would stop raining. If it
would only stop for half an hour she would go. Perhaps
it was as well to let fate decide the matter in that way.

Just then a carriage drove up to the door. She flat-
tened her face against the window, but could not see
who got out of it. It was a cab, however, and the driver
had a waterproof hat and coat. In all probability it
came from one of the hotels. Any one might have taken
it. Katharine drew back a little and looked idly at the
little mottled mist her breath had made upon the window
pane. The door of her room opened suddenly.

"Kitty, are you there?" asked a woman's voice.

Katharine knew as the handle of the latch was turned
that her sister Charlotte had come. No one else ever
entered her room without knocking, and no one else ever
called her 'Kitty.' She hated the abbreviation of her
name and she resented the familiarity of the unbidden
entrance. She turned rather sharply.

"Oh — is that you? I thought you were in Washington." She came forward, and the two exchanged kisses
mechanically.

"Benjamin Slayback of Nevada had business in New
York, so I came up to get a breath of my native mi-
crobes," said Charlotte, going to the mirror and beginning to take off her hat very carefully so as not to disturb
her hair. "We are at a hotel, of course — but it's nice,
all the same. I suppose mamma's at work and I know
papa's down town, and the ancestor is probably studying
some new kind of fool — so I came to your room."

"Will you have some tea?" asked Katharine.

"Tea? What wild extravagance! I suppose you offer
it to me as 'Mrs. Slayback.' I wonder if papa would.
I can see him smile — just like this — isn't it just like
him?"

She smiled before the mirror and then turned suddenly
on Katharine. The mimicry was certainly good. Mrs.
Slayback, however, was fair, like her mother, with a radi-
ant complexion, golden hair and good features, — larger
and bolder than Mrs. Lauderdale's, but not nearly so
classically perfect. There was something hard in her
face, especially about the eyes.

"It's just the same as ever," she said, seating herself
in the small arm-chair — the only one in the room. "The
same dear, delightful, dreary, comfortless, furnace-heated,
gas-lighted, 'put-on-your-best-hat-to-go-to-church' sort of
existence that it always was! I wonder how you all
stand it — how I stood it so long myself!"

Katharine laughed and turned her head. She had
been looking out of the window again and wondering
whether the rain would stop after all. She and her
sister had never lived very harmoniously together. Their
pitched battles had begun in the nursery with any
weapons they could lay hands on, pillows, moribund
dolls, soapy sponges, and the nurse's shoes. Though
Katharine was the younger, she had soon been the
stronger at close quarters. But Charlotte had the
sharper tongue and was by far the better shot with any
projectile when safely entrenched behind the bed. At
the first show of hostilities she made for both sponges —
a rag-doll was not a bad thing, if she got a chance to dip
it into the basin, but there was nothing like a sponge,
when it was 'just gooey with soap,' as the youthful
Charlotte expressed it. She carried the art of throwing
to a high degree of perfection, and on very rare occa-

sions, after she was grown up, she surprised her adorers by throwing pebbles at a mark with an unerring accuracy which would have done credit to a poacher's apprentice.

Since the nursery days the warfare had been carried on by words and the encounters had been less frequent, but the contrast was always apparent between Katharine's strength and Charlotte's quickness. Katharine waited, collected her strength, chose her language and delivered a heavy blow, so to say. Charlotte, as Frank Miner put it, 'slung English all over the lot.' Both were effective in their way. But they had the good taste to quarrel in private and, moreover, in many things they were allies. With regard to their father, Katharine took an evil and silent delight in her sister's sarcasms, and Charlotte could not help admiring Katharine's solid, unyielding opposition on certain points.

"Oh, yes!" said Katharine, answering Charlotte's last remark. "There'll be less change than ever now that you're married."

"I suppose so. Poor Kitty! We used to fight now and then, but I know you enjoyed looking on when I made a row at dinner. Didn't you?"

"Of course I did. I'm a human being." Katharine laughed again. "Won't you really have tea? I always have it when I want it."

"You brave little thing! Do you? Well — if you like. You quiet people always have your own way in the end," added Mrs. Slayback, rather thoughtfully. "I suppose it's the steady push that does it."

"Don't you have your way, too?" asked Katharine, in some surprise at her sister's tone of voice.

"No. I'm ashamed to say that I don't. No —" She seemed to be recapitulating events. "No — I don't have my way at all — not the least little bit. I have the way of Benjamin Slayback of Nevada."

"Why do you talk of your husband in that way?" enquired Katharine.

"Shall I call him Mr. Slayback?" asked Charlotte, "or Benjamin — dear little Benjamin! or Ben — the 'soldier bold'? How does 'Ben' strike you, Kitty? I know — I've thought of calling him Minnie — last syllable of Benjamin, you see. There was a moment when I hesitated at 'Benjy' — 'Benjy, darling, another cup of coffee?' — it would sound so quiet and home-like at breakfast, wouldn't it? It's fortunate that papa made us get up early all our lives. My dream of married happiness — a nice little French maid smiling at me with a beautiful little tea-tray just as I was opening my eyes — I had thought about it for years! Well, it's all over. Benjamin Slayback of Nevada takes his breakfast like a man — a regular Benjamin's portion of breakfast, and wants to feast his eyes on my loveliness, and his understanding on my wit, and his inner man on the flesh of kine — and all that together at eight o'clock in the morning — Benjamin Slayback of Nevada — there's no other name for him!"

"The name irritates me — you repeat it so often!"

"Does it, dear? The man irritates me, and that's infinitely worse. I wish you knew!"

"But he's awfully good to you, Charlie. You can't deny that, at all events."

"Yes — and he calls me Lottie," answered Charlotte, with much disgust. "You know how I hate it. But if you are going to lecture me on my husband's goodness — Kitty, I tell you frankly, I won't stand it. I'll say something to you that'll make you — just frizzle up! Remember the soapy sponge of old, my child, and be nice to your sister. I came here hoping to see you. I want to talk seriously to you. At least — I'm not sure. I want to talk seriously to somebody, and you're the most serious person I know."

" More so than your husband ? "

" He's grave enough sometimes, but not generally. It's almost always about his constituents. They are to him what the liver is to some people — only that they are beyond the reach of mineral waters. Besides — it's about him that I want to talk. You look surprised, though I'm sure I don't know why. I suppose — because I've never said anything before."

" But I don't even know what you're going to say — "

Mrs. Slayback looked at her younger sister steadily for a moment, and then looked at the window. The rain was still falling fast and steadily; and the room had a dreary, dingy air about it as the afternoon advanced. It had been Charlotte's before her marriage, and Katharine had moved into it since because it was better than her own. The elder girl had filled it with little worthless trifles which had brightened it to a certain extent; but Katharine cared little for that sort of thing, and was far more indifferent to the aspect of the place in which she lived. There were a couple of dark engravings of sacred subjects on the walls, — one over the narrow bed in the corner, and the other above the chest of drawers, and there was nothing more which could be said to be intended for ornament. Yet Charlotte Slayback's hard face softened a little as her eyes wandered from the window to the familiar, faded wall paper and the old-fashioned furniture. The silence lasted some time. Then she turned to her sister again.

"Kitty — don't do what I've done," she said, earnestly. She watched the girl's face for a change of expression,

but Katharine's impassive features were not quick to ex·
press any small feeling beyond passing annoyance.

"Aren't you happy, Charlie?" Katharine asked, gravely.

"Happy!"

The elder woman only repeated the single word, but it
told her story plainly enough. She would have given
much to come back to the old room, dreary as it looked.

"I'm very sorry," said Katharine, in a lower voice and
beginning to understand. "Isn't he kind to you?"

"Oh, it's not that! He's kind — in his way — it makes
it worse — far worse," she repeated, after a moment's
pause. "I hadn't been much used to that sort of kindness before I was married, you know — except from
mamma, and that was different — and to have it from —"
She stopped.

Katharine had never seen her sister in this mood
before. Charlotte was generally the last person to make
confidences, or to complain softly of anything she did not
like. Katharine thought she must be very much changed.

"You say you're unhappy," said the young girl. "But
you don't tell me why. Has there been any trouble —
anything especial?"

"No. You don't understand. How should you? We
never did understand each other very well, you and I. I
don't know why I come to you with my troubles, either.
You can't help me. Nobody can — unless it were — a
lawyer."

"A lawyer?" Katharine was taken by surprise now,
and her eyes showed it.

"Yes," answered Charlotte, her voice growing cold
and hard again. "People can be divorced for incompati-
bility of temper."

"Charlotte!" The young girl started a little, and
leaned forward, laying her hand upon her sister's knee.

"Oh, yes! I mean it. I'm sorry to horrify you so, my dear, and I suppose papa would say that divorce was not a proper subject for conversation. Perhaps he's right — but he's not here to tell us so."

"But, Charlie —" Katharine stopped short, unable to say the first word of the many that rushed to her lips.

"I know," said Charlotte, paying no attention. "I know exactly what you're going to say. You are going to argue the question, and tell me in the first place that I'm bad, and then that I'm mad, and then that I'm a mother, — and all sorts of things. I've thought of them all, my dear; and they're very terrible, of course. But I'm quite willing to be them all at once, if I can only get my freedom again. I don't expect much sympathy, and I don't want any good advice — and I haven't seen a lawyer yet. But I must talk — I must say it out — I must hear it! Kitty — I'm desperate! I never knew what it meant before."

She rose suddenly from her seat, walked twice up and down the room, and then stood still before Katharine, and looked down into her face.

"Of course you can't understand," she said, as she had said before. "How should you?" She seemed to be waiting for an answer.

"I think I could, if you would tell me more about yourself," Katharine replied. "I'm trying to understand. I'd help you if I knew how."

"That's impossible." Mrs. Slayback seated herself again. "But it's this. You must have wondered why I married him, didn't you?"

"Well — not exactly. But it seemed to me — there were other men, if you meant to marry a man you didn't love."

"I don't believe in love," said Charlotte. "But I

wanted to be married for many reasons — most of all, because I couldn't bear the life here."

"Yes — I know. You're not like me. But why didn't you choose somebody else? I can't understand marrying without love; but it seems to me, as I said, that if one is going to do such a thing one had better make a careful choice."

"I did. I chose my husband for many reasons. He is richer than any of the men who proposed to me, and that's a great thing. And he's very good-natured, and what they call 'an able man.' There were lots of good reasons. There were things I didn't like, of course; but I thought I could make him change. I did — in little things. He never wears a green tie now, for instance — "

"As if such things could make a difference in life's happiness!" cried Katharine, contemptuously.

"My dear — they do. But never mind that. I thought I could — what shall I say? — develop his latent social talent. And I have. In that way he's changed a good deal. You've not seen him this year, have you? No, of course not. Well, he's not the same man. But it's in the big things. I thought I could manage him, by sheer force of superior will, and make him do just what I wanted — oh, I made such a mistake!"

"And because you've married a man whom you can't order about like a servant, you want to be divorced," said Katharine, coldly.

"I knew you couldn't understand," Charlotte answered, with unusual gentleness. "I suppose you won't believe me if I tell you that I suffer all the time, and — very, very much."

Katharine did not understand, but her sister's tone told her plainly enough that there was real trouble of some sort.

"Charlie," she said, " there's something on your mind
— something else. How can I know what it is, unless
you tell me, dear ? "

Mrs. Slayback turned her head away, and bit her lip,
as though the kind words had touched her.

" It's my pride," she said suddenly and very quickly.
" He hurts it so ! "

" But how ? Merely because he does things in his
own way ? He probably knows best — they all say he's
very clever in politics."

" Clever ! I should think so ! He's a great, rough, good-
natured, ill-mannered — no, he's not a brute. He's painfully kind. But with that exterior — there's no other
word. He has the quickness of a woman in some ways.
I believe he can be anything he chooses."

" But all you say is rather in his favour."

" I know it is. I wish it were not. If I loved him —
the mere idea is ridiculous ! But if I did, I would trot
by his side and carry the basket through life, like his
poodle. But I don't love him — and he expects me to do it
all the same. I'm curled, and scented, and fed delicately,
and put to sleep on a silk cushion, and have a beautiful
new ribbon tied round my neck every morning, just like
a poodle-dog — and I must trot quietly and carry the
basket. That's all I am in his life — it wasn't exactly
my dream," she added bitterly.

" I see. And you thought that it was to be the other
way, and that he was to trot beside you."

" You put it honestly, at all events. Yes. I suppose
I thought that. I did not expect this, anyhow — and I
simply can't bear it any longer ! So long as there's any
question of social matters, of course, everything is left to
me. He can't leave a card himself, he won't make visits
— he won't lift a finger, though he wants it all properly

and perfectly done. Lottie must trot — with the card-
basket. But if I venture to have an opinion about anything, I have no more influence over him than the
furniture. I mustn't say this, because it will be repeated
that his wife said it; and I mustn't say that, because
those are not his political opinions; and I mustn't say
something else, because it might get back to Nevada and
offend his constituents — and as for doing anything, it's
simply out of the question. When I'm bored to death
with it all, he tells me that his constituents expect him
to stay in Washington during the session, and he advises
me to go away for a few days, and offers to draw me a
cheque. He would probably give me a thousand dollars
for my expenses if I wanted to stay a week with you. I
don't know whether he wants to seem magnificent, or
whether he thinks I expect it, or if he really imagines
that I should spend it. But it isn't that I want, Kitty
— it isn't that! I didn't marry for money, though it was
very nice to have so much — it wasn't for that, it really,
really wasn't! I suppose it's absurd — perfectly wild —
but I wanted to be somebody, to have some influence in
the world, to have just a little of what people call real
power. And I haven't got it, and I can't have it;
and I'm nothing but his poodle-dog, and I'm perfectly
miserable!"

Katharine could find nothing to say when her sister
paused after her long speech. It was not easy for her to
sympathize with any one so totally unlike herself, nor to
understand the state of mind of a woman who wanted the
sort of power which few women covet, who had practically given her life in exchange for the hope of it, and who
had pitiably failed to obtain it. She stared out of the
window at the falling rain, and it all seemed very dreary
to her.

"It's my pride!" exclaimed Charlotte, suddenly, after a pause. "I never knew what it meant before — and you never can. It's intolerable to feel that I'm beaten at the very beginning of life. Can't you understand that, at least ? "

" Yes — but, Charlie dear, — it's a long way from a bit of wounded pride to a divorce — isn't it ? "

"Yes," answered Charlotte, disconsolately. "I suppose it is. But if you knew the horrible sensation! It grows worse and worse — and the less I can find fault with him for other things, the worse it seems to grow. And it's quite useless to fight. You know I'm good at fighting, don't you? I used to think I was, until I tried to fight my husband. My dear — I'm not in it with him!"

Katharine rose and turned her back, feeling that she could hardly control herself if she sat still. There was an incredible frivolity about her sister at certain moments which was almost revolting to the young girl.

"What is it?" asked Charlotte, observing her movement.

"Oh — nothing," answered Katharine. "The shade isn't quite up and it's growing dark, that's all."

"I thought you were angry," said Mrs. Slayback.

"I? Why should I be angry? What business is it of mine?" Katharine turned and faced her, having adjusted the shade to her liking. "Of course, if you must say that sort of thing, you had better say it to me than to any one else. It doesn't sound well in the world — and it's not pleasant to hear."

"Why not?" asked Charlotte, her voice growing hard and cold again. "But that's a foolish question. Well — I've had my talk out — and I feel better. One must sometimes, you know." Her tone softened again, unexpectedly. "Don't be too hard on me, Kitty dear — just because you're a better woman than I am." There was a tremor in her last words.

Katharine did not understand. She understood, however, and for the first time in her life, that a frivolous woman can suffer quite as much as a serious one — which is a truth not generally recognized. She put her arm round her sister's neck very gently, and pressed the fair head to her bosom, as she stood beside her.

"I'm not better than you, Charlie — I'm different, that's all. Poor dear! Of course you suffer!"

"Dear!" And Charlotte rubbed her smooth cheek affectionately against the rough grey woollen of her sister's frock.

CHAPTER XIII.

THE rain continued to fall, and even if the weather had changed it would have been too late for Katharine to go and see Robert Lauderdale after her sister had left her. On the whole, she thought, it would probably have been a mistake to speak to him beforehand. She had felt a strong temptation to do so, but it had not been the part of wisdom. She waited for Ralston's note.

At last it came. It was short and clear. He had, with great difficulty, found a clergyman who was willing to marry them, and who would perform the ceremony on the following morning at half-past nine o'clock. The clergyman had only consented on Ralston's strong representations, and on the distinct understanding that there was to be no unnecessary secrecy after the fact, and that the couple should solemnly promise to inform

their parents of what they had done at the earliest
moment consistent with their welfare.   Ralston had
written out his very words in regard to that matter, for
he liked them, and felt that Katharine should.

John had been fortunate in his search, for he had
accidentally come upon a man whose own life had been
marred by the opposition of a young girl's family to her
marriage with him.   He himself had in consequence
never married; the young girl had taken a husband and
had been a most unhappy woman.   He sympathized with
Ralston, liked his face, and agreed to marry Ralston and
Katharine immediately.   His church lay in a distant
part of the city, and he had nothing to do with society,
and therefore nothing to fear from it.   If trouble arose
he was justified beforehand by the fact that no clergyman has an absolute right to refuse marriage to those
who ask it, and by the thought that he was contributing
to happiness of the kind which he himself had most
desired, but which had been withheld from him under
just such circumstances as those in which Ralston and
Katharine were placed.   The good man admired, too,
the wisdom of the course they were taking.   When
he had said that he would consider the matter favourably, provided that there was no legal obstacle, Ralston
had told him the whole truth, and had explained exactly
what Katharine and he intended to do.   Of course, he
had to explain the relationship which existed between
them and old Robert Lauderdale, and the clergyman,
to Ralston's considerable surprise, took Katharine's view
of the possibilities.   He only insisted that the plan
should be conscientiously carried out as soon as might
be, and that Katharine should therefore go, in the course
of the same day, and tell her story to Mr. Robert Lauderdale.   Ralston made no difficulty about that, and agreed

to be at the door of the clergyman's house on the following morning at half-past nine. The latter would open
the church himself. It was very improbable that any
one should see them at that hour, and in that distant
part of the city.

There is no necessity for entering upon a defence of
the clergyman's action in the affair. It was a case, not
of right or wrong, nor of doing anything irregular, but
possibly excusable. Theoretically, it was his duty to com-
ply with Ralston's request. In practice, it was a matter
of judgment and of choice, since if he had flatly refused,
as several others had done without so much as knowing
the names of the parties, Ralston would certainly have
found it out of the question to force his consent. He
believed that he was doing right, he wished to do what
was kind, and he knew that he was acting legally and
that the law must support him. He ran the risk of
offending his own congregation if the story got abroad,
but he remembered his own youth and he cheerfully
took that risk. He would not have done as much for
any two who might have chanced to present themselves,
however. But Ralston impressed him as a man of honour, a gentleman and very truthful, and there was just
enough of socialistic tendency in the good man, as the
pastor of a very poor congregation, to enjoy the idea that
the rich man should be forced, as a matter of common
decency, to do something for his less fortunate relation.
With his own life and experience behind him, he could
not possibly have seen things as Robert Lauderdale saw
them.

So the matter was settled, and Katharine had Ralston's
note. He added that he would be in Clinton Place at
half-past eight o'clock in the morning, on foot. They
might be seen walking together at almost any hour, by

right of cousinship, but to appear together in a carriage, especially at such an hour, was out of the question.

It would have been unlike her to hesitate now. She had made up her mind long before she had spoken to Ralston on Monday evening, and there was nothing new to her in the idea. But she could not help wondering about the future, as she had been doing when Charlotte Slayback had unexpectedly appeared in the afternoon. Meanwhile the evening was before her. She was going to a dinner-party of young people and afterwards to the dance at the Thirlwalls', of which she had spoken to Ralston. He would be there, but would not be at the dinner, as she knew. At the latter there were to be two young married women who were to chaperone the young girls to the other house afterwards.

At eight o'clock Katharine sat down to table between two typical, fashion-struck youths, one of whom took more champagne than was good for him, and talked to her of college sports and football matches in which he had not taken part, but which excited his enthusiasm, while the other drank water, and asked if she preferred Schopenhauer or Hegel. Of the two, she preferred the critic of athletics. But the dinner seemed a very long one to Katharine, though it was really of the short and fashionable type.

Then came another girls' talk while the young men smoked furiously together in another room. The two married women managed to get into a corner, and told each other long stories in whispers, while the young girls, who were afraid of romping and playing games because they were in their ball-dresses, amused themselves as they could, with a good deal of highly slangy but perfectly harmless chaff, and an occasional attempt at a little music. As all the young men smoked the very

longest and strongest cigars, because they had all been
told that cigarettes were deadly, it was nearly ten o'clock
when they came into the drawing-room. They were all
extremely well behaved young fellows, and the one who
had talked about athletics to Katharine was the only one
who was a little too pink. The dance was an early affair,
and in a few moments the whole party began to get
ready to go. They transferred themselves from one
house to another in big carriages, and all arrived within
a short time of one another.

Ralston was in the room when Katharine entered, and
she saw instantly that he had been waiting for her and
expected a sign at once. She smiled and nodded to him
from a distance, for he had far too much tact to make a
rush at her as soon as she appeared. It was not until
half an hour later that they found themselves together in
the crowded entrance hall, and Ralston assured himself
more particularly that everything was as she wished it to be.

"So to-morrow is our wedding day," he said, looking
at her face. Like most dark beauties, she looked her
best in the evening.

"Yes — it's to-morrow, Jack. You are glad, aren't
you?" she asked, repeating almost exactly the last words
she had spoken that morning as he had left her at the
door of the Crowdies' house.

"Do you doubt that I'm as glad as you are?" asked
Ralston, earnestly. "I've waited for you a long time —
all my life, it seems to me."

"Have you?"

Her grey eyes turned full upon him as she put the
question, which evidently meant more to her than the
mere words implied. He paused before answering her,
with an over-scrupulous caution, the result of her own
earnestness.

"Why do you hesitate?" she asked, suddenly. "Didn't you mean exactly what you said?"

"I said it seemed to me as though I had waited all my life," he answered. "I wanted to be — well — accurate!" He laughed a little. "I am trying to remember whether I had ever cared in the least for any one else."

Katharine laughed too. He sometimes had an almost boyish simplicity about him which pleased her immensely.

"If it takes such an effort of memory, it can't have been very serious," she said. "I'm not jealous. I only wish to know that you are."

"I love you with all my heart," he answered, with emphasis.

"I know you do, Jack dear," said Katharine, and a short silence followed.

She was thinking that this was the third time they had met since Monday evening, and that she had not heard again that deep vibration, that heart-stirring quaver, in his words, which had touched her that first time as she had never been touched before. She did not analyze her own desire for it in the least, any more than she doubted the sincerity of his words because they were spoken quietly. She had heard it once and she wanted to hear it again, for the mere momentary satisfaction of the impression.

But Ralston was very calm that evening. He had been extremely careful of what he did since Monday afternoon, for he had suffered acutely when his mother had first met him on the landing, and he was determined that nothing of the sort should happen again. The excitement, too, of arranging his sudden marriage had taken the place of all artificial emotions during the last forty-eight hours. His nerves were young and could bear the strain of sudden excess and equally sudden abstention without troubling

him with any physical distress. And this fact easily
made him too sure of himself. To a certain extent he
was cynical about his taste for strong drink. He said to
himself quite frankly that he wanted excitement and
cared very little for the form in which he got it. He
should have preferred a life of adventure and danger. He
would have made a good soldier in war and a bad one in
peace — a safe sailor in stormy weather and a dangerous
one in a calm. That, at least, was what he believed, and
there was a foundation of truth in it, for he was sensible
enough to tell himself the truth about himself so far as
he was able.

On the evening of the dance at which he met Katharine
he had dined at home again. His mother was far too
wise to ask many questions about his comings and goings
when he was with her, and it was quite natural that he
should not tell her how he had spent his day. He wished
that he were free to tell her everything, however, and
to ask her advice. She was eminently a woman of the
world, though of the more serious type, and he knew that
her wisdom was great in matters social. For the rest,
she had always approved of his attachment for Katharine,
whom she liked best of all the family, and she intended
that, if possible, her son should marry the young girl
before very long. With her temper and inherited impulses it was not likely that she should blame Ralston
for any honourable piece of rashness. Having once been
convinced that there was nothing underhand or in the
least unfair to anybody in what he was doing, Ralston
had not the slightest fear of the consequences. The only
men of the family whom he considered men were Katharine's father and Hamilton Bright. The latter could
have nothing to say in the matter, and Ralston knew
that his friendship could be counted on. As for Alexan-

der Junior, John looked forward with delight to the scene which must take place, for he was a born fighter, and quarrelsome besides. He would be in a position to tell Mr. Lauderdale that neither righteous wrath nor violent words could undo what had been done properly, decently and in order, under legal authority, and by religious ceremony. Alexander Junior's face would be a study at that moment, and Ralston hoped that the hour of triumph might not be far distant.

"I wonder whether it seems sudden to you," said Katharine, presently. "It doesn't to me. You and I had thought about it ever so long."

"Long before you spoke to me on Monday?" asked John. "I thought it had just struck you then."

"No, indeed! I began to think of it last year — soon after you had seen papa. One doesn't come to such conclusions suddenly, you know."

"Some people do. Of course, I might have seen that you had thought it all out, from the way you spoke. But you took me by surprise."

"I know I did. But I had gone over it again and again. It's not a light matter, Jack. I'm putting my whole life into your hands because I love you. I shan't regret it — I know that. No — you needn't protest, dear. I know what I'm doing very well, but I don't mean to magnify it into anything heroic. I'm not the sort of girl to make a heroine, for I'm far too sensible and practical. But it's practical to run risks sometimes."

"It depends on the risk, I suppose," said Ralston. "Many people would tell you that I'm not a safe person to —"

"Nonsense! I didn't mean that," interrupted the young girl. "If you were a milksop, trotting along at your mother's apron strings, I wouldn't look at you. Indeed, I wouldn't! I know you're rather fast, and I

like it in you.   There was a little boy next to me at dinner this evening — a dear little pale-faced thing, who
talked to me about Schopenhauer and Hegel, and drank
five glasses of Apollinaris — I counted them.   There are
lots of them about nowadays — all the fittest having sur-
vived, it's the turn of the unfit, I suppose.   But I wouldn't
have you one little tiny bit better than you are.   You don't
gamble, and you don't drink, and you're merely supposed
to be fast because you're not a bore."

Ralston was silent, and his face turned a little pale.
A violent struggle arose in his thoughts, all at once, without the slightest warning nor even the previous suspicion
that it could ever arise at all.

"That's not the risk," continued Katharine.   "Oh, no!
And perhaps what I mean isn't such a very great risk
after all.   I don't believe there is any, myself — but I
suppose other people might.   It's that uncle Robert
might not, after all — oh, well!   We won't talk about
such things.   If one only takes enough for granted, one
is sure to get something in the end.   That isn't exactly
Schopenhauer, is it?   But it's good philosophy."

Katharine laughed happily and looked at him.   But
his face was unusually grave, and he would not laugh.

"It's too absurd that I should be telling you to take
courage and be cheerful, Jack!" she said, a moment
later.   "I feel as though you were reproaching me with
not being serious enough for the occasion.   That isn't
fair.   And it is serious — it is, indeed."   Her tone
changed.   "I'm putting my very life into your hands,
dear, as I told you, because I trust you.   What's the
matter, Jack?   You seem to be thinking — "

"I am," answered Ralston, rather gloomily.   "I was
thinking about something very, very important."

"May I know?" asked Katharine, gently.   "Is it anything you should like me to know — or to ask me about, before to-morrow ? "

" To-morrow ! " Ralston repeated the word in a low voice, as though he were meditating upon its meaning.

They were seated on a narrow little sofa against the lower woodwork of the carved staircase. The hall was crowded with young people coming and going between the other rooms. Katharine was leaning back, her head supported against the dark panel, her eyes apparently half closed — for she was looking down at him as he bent forward. He held one elbow on his knee and his chin rested in his hand, as he looked up sideways at her.

" Katharine " — he began, and then stopped suddenly, and she saw now that he was turning very pale, as though in fear or pain.

" Yes ? " She paused. " What is it, Jack dear ? There's something on your mind — are you afraid to tell me ? Or aren't you sure that you should ? "

" I'm afraid," said Ralston. " And so I'm going to do it," he added a moment later. " Did you ever hear that I was what they call dissipated ? "

" Is that it ? " Katharine laughed, almost carelessly. " No, I never heard that said of you. People say you're fast, and rather wild — and all that. I told you what I thought of that — I like it in you. Perhaps it isn't right, exactly, to like a dash of naughtiness — is it ? "

" I don't know," answered Ralston, evidently not comprehending the question, but intent upon his own thoughts. In the short pause which followed he did not change his position, but the veins swelled in his temples, and his eyelids drooped a little when he spoke again. " Katharine — I sometimes drink too much."

Katharine trembled a little, but he did not see it. For some seconds she did not move, and did not take her eyes from him. Then she very slowly raised her hand and passed it over her brow, as though she were confused, and presently she bent forward, as he was bending, resting one elbow on her knee and looking earnestly into his face.

"Why do you do it, Jack? Don't you love me?" She asked the two questions slowly and distinctly, but in the one there was all her pity — in the other all her love.

Again, as more than once lately, Ralston was almost irresistibly impelled to make a promise, simple and decisive, which should change his life, and which at all costs and risks he would keep. The impulse was stronger now, with Katharine's eyes upon his, and her happiness on his soul, than it had been before. But the arguments for resisting it were also stronger. He was calm enough to know the magnitude of his temptations and his habitual weakness in resisting them. He said nothing.

"Why don't you answer me, dear?" Katharine asked softly. "They were not hard questions, were they?"

"You know that I love you," he answered — then hesitated, and then went on. "If I did not love you, I should not have told you. Do you believe that?"

He guessed that she only half realized and half understood all the meaning of what he had said. He had no thought of gaining credit in her opinion for having done what very few men would have risked in his position. The wish to speak had come from the heart, not from the head. But he had not foreseen that it must appear very easy to her for him to overcome a temptation which seemed insignificant in her eyes, compared with a life's happiness.

"Yes — I know that," she answered. "But, Jack dear — yes, it was brave and honest of you — but you don't think I expected a confession, do you? I daresay you have done many things that weren't exactly wrong and that were not at all dishonourable, but which you shouldn't like to tell me. Haven't you?"

"Of course I have. Every man has, by the time he's five and twenty — lots of things."

"Well — but now, Jack — now, when we are married, you won't do such things — whatever they may be — any more — will you?"

"That's it — I don't know," answered Ralston, determined to be honest to the very end, with all his might, in spite of everything.

"You don't know?" As Katharine repeated the words her face changed in a way that shocked him, and he almost started as he saw her expression.

"No," he answered, steadily enough. "I don't — in regard to what I spoke of. For other things, for anything else in the world that you ask me, I can promise, and feel sure. But that one thing — it comes on me sometimes, and it gets the better of me. I know — it's weak — it's contemptible, it's brutal, if you like. But I can't help it, every time. Of course you can't understand. Nobody can, who hasn't felt it."

"But, Jack — if you promised me that you wouldn't?"

Her face changed again, and softened, and her voice expressed the absolute conviction that he would and could do anything which he had given his word that he would do. That perfect belief is more flattering than almost anything else to some men.

"Katharine — I can't!" Ralston shook his head. "I won't give you a promise which I might break. If I broke it, I should — you wouldn't see me any more after that. I'll promise that I'll try, and perhaps I shall succeed. I can't do more — indeed, I can't."

"Not for me, Jack dear?" Her whole heart was in her voice, pleading, pathetic, maidenly.

"Don't ask me like that. You don't know what you're asking. You'll make me — no, I won't say that. But please don't — "

Once more Katharine's expression changed. Her face was quite white, and her grey eyes were light and had a cold flash in them. The small, angry frown that came and went quickly when she was annoyed, seemed chiselled upon the smooth forehead. Ralston's head was bent down and his hand shaded his eyes.

"And you made me think you loved me," said Katharine, slowly, in a very low voice.

"I do — "

"Don't say it again. I don't want to hear it. It means nothing, now that I know — it never can mean anything again. No — you needn't come with me. I'll go alone."

She rose suddenly to her feet, overcome by one of those sudden revulsions of the deepest feelings in her nature, to which strong people are subject at very critical moments, and which generally determine their lives for them, and sometimes the lives of others. She rose to leave him with a woman's magnificent indifference when her heart speaks out, casting all considerations, all details, all questions of future relations to the winds, or to the accident of a chance meeting at some indefinite date.

There were many people in the hall just then. A dance was beginning, and the crowd was pouring in so swiftly that for a moment the young girl stood still, close to Ralston, unable to move. He did not rise, but remained seated, hidden by her and by the throng. He seized her hand suddenly, as it hung by her side. No one could have noticed the action in the press.

"Katharine —" he cried, in a low, imploring tone.

She drew her hand away instantly. He remembered afterwards that it had felt cold through her glove. He heard her voice, and, looking past her, saw Crowdie's pale face and red mouth — and met Crowdie's languorous eyes, gazing at him.

"I want to go somewhere else, Mr. Crowdie," Katharine was saying. "I've been in a draught, and I'm cold."

Crowdie gave her his arm, and they moved on with the rest. Ralston had risen to his feet as soon as he saw that Crowdie had caught sight of him, and stood looking at the pair. His face was drawn and tired, and his eyes were rather wild.

His first impulse was to get out of the house, and be alone, as soon as he could, and he began to make his way through the crowd to a small room by the door, where the men had left their coats. But, before he had suc-ceeded in reaching the place, he changed his mind. It looked too much like running away. He allowed him-self to be wedged into a corner, and stood still, watching the people absently, and thinking over what had occurred.

In the first place, he wondered whether Katharine had meant as much as her speech and action implied — in other words, whether she intended to let him know that everything was altogether at an end between them. It seemed almost out of the question. After all, he had spoken because he felt that it was a duty to her. He was, indeed, profoundly hurt by her behaviour. If she meant to break off everything so suddenly, she might have done it more kindly. She had been furiously angry because he would not promise an impossibility. It was true that she could not understand. He loved her so much, even then, that he made excuses for her conduct, and set up arguments in her favour.

Was it an impossibility, after all? He stood still in his corner, and thought the matter over. As he considered it, he deliberately called the temptation to him to examine it. And it came, in its full force. Men who have not felt it no more know what it means than Katharine Lauderdale knew, when she accused John Ralston of not loving her, and left him, apparently forever, because he would not promise never to yield to it again.

During forty-eight hours he had scarcely tasted anything stronger than a cup of coffee, for the occurrence of Monday had produced a deep impression on him — and this was Wednesday night. For several years he had been used to drinking whatever he pleased, during the day, merely exercising enough self-control to keep out of women's society when he had taken more than was good for him, and enough discretion in the matter of hours to avoid meeting his mother when he was not quite himself. There are not so many men in polite society who regulate their lives on such principles as there used to be, but there are many still. Men know, and keep the matter to themselves. Insensibly, of course, John Ralston had grown more or less dependent on a certain amount of something to drink every day, and he had very rarely been really abstemious for so long a time as during the last two days. He had lived, too, in a state of considerable anxiety, and had scarcely noticed the absence of artificial excitement. But now, with the scene of the last quarter of an hour, the reaction had come. He had received a violent shock, and his head clamoured for its accustomed remedy against all nervous disturbances. Then, too, he was very thirsty. He honestly disliked the taste of water — as his father had hated it before him — and he had not really drunk enough of it. He was more thirsty than he had been when he had swallowed a

pint of champagne at a draught on Monday afternoon.
That, to tell the truth, was the precise form in which the
temptation presented itself to him at the present moment.
It was painfully distinct. He knew that the Thirlwalls,
in whose house he was, always had Irroy Brut, which
chanced to be the best dry wine that year, and he knew
that he had only to follow the crowd to the supper room
and swallow as much of it as he desired. Everybody
was drinking it. He could hear the glasses faintly ringing in the distance, as he stood in his corner. He let the
temptation come to see how strong it would be.

It was frightfully vivid, as he let the picture rise before
his eyes. He was now actually in physical pain from
thirst. He could see clearly the tall pint-glass, foaming
and sparkling with the ice-cold, pale wine. He could
hear the delicious little hiss of the tiny bubbles as thousands of them shot to the surface. He could smell the
aromatic essence of the lemon peel as the brim seemed to
come beneath his nostrils. He could feel the exquisite
sharp tingle, the inexpressible stinging delight of the
perfect liquid, all through his mouth, to his very throat
— just as he had seen and smelt and tasted it all on
Monday afternoon, and a thousand times before that —
but not since then.

It became intolerable, or almost intolerable, but still he
bore it, with that curious pleasure in the pain of it which
some people are able to feel in self-imposed suffering.
Then he opened his eyes wide, and tried to drive it
away.

But that was not so easy. That diabolical clinking
and ringing of distant glasses, away, far away, as it
seemed, but high and distinct above the hum of voices,
tortured him, and drew him towards it. His mouth and
throat were actually parched now. It was no longer

imagination. And now, too, the crowd had thinned, and as he looked he saw that it would be very easy for him to get to the supper room.

After all, he thought, it was a perfectly legitimate craving. He was excessively thirsty, and he wanted a glass of champagne. He knew very well that in such a place he should not take more than one glass, and that could not hurt him. Did he ever drink when there were women present, in the sense of drinking too much? On Monday the accident had made a difference. Surely, as he had often heard, the manly course was to limit himself to what he needed, and not go beyond it. All those other people did that — why should not he? What was the difference between them and him? How the thirst burned him, and the ring of the glasses tortured him!

He moved a step from the corner, in the direction of the door, fully intending to have his glass of wine. Then something seemed to snap suddenly over his heart, with a sharp little pain.

" I'll be damned if I do," said Ralston, almost audibly.

And he went back to his corner, and tried to think of something else.

CHAPTER XIV.

CROWDIE'S artistic temperament was as quick as a child's to understand the moods of others, and he saw at a glance that something serious had happened to Katharine. He had not the amateur's persistent desire to feel himself an artist at every moment. On the contrary, he had far more of the genuine artist's wish to feel himself a man of the world when he was not at his work. What he saw impressed itself upon his accurate and‐retentive memory for form and colour, but he was not always studying every face he met, and thinking of painting it. He was fond of trying to read character, and prided himself upon his penetration, which was by no means great. It is a common peculiarity of highly gifted persons to delight in exhibiting a small talent which seems to them to be their greatest, though unappreciated by the world. Goethe thought himself a painter. Michelangelo believed himself a poet. Crowdie, a modern artist of reputation, was undoubtedly a good musician as well, but in his own estimation his greatest gift was his knowledge of men. Yet in this he was profoundly mistaken. Though his reasoning was often as clear as his deductions were astute, he placed the centre of human impulses too low, for he judged others by himself, which is an unsafe standard for men who differ much from the average of their fellow-men. He mistook his quickness of perception for penetration, and the heart of men and things escaped him.

He looked at Katharine and saw that she was very angry. He had caught sight of Ralston's face, and he supposed that the latter had been drinking. He concluded that Ralston had offended Katharine, and that there was to be a serious quarrel. Katharine, too, had evidently been in the greatest haste to get away, and had spoken to Crowdie and taken his arm merely because of the men she knew he had been nearest to her in the crowd. The painter congratulated himself upon his good fortune in appearing at that moment.

"Will you have some supper?" he asked, guiding his companion toward the door.

"It's too early — thanks," answered the young girl,

almost absently. "I'd rather dance, if you don't mind,"
she added, after a moment.

"Of course!" and he directed his course towards
the dancing room.

In spite of his bad figure, Crowdie danced very well.
He was very light on his feet, very skilful and careful
of his partner, and, strange to say, very enduring.
Katharine let herself go on his arm, and they glided
and swayed and backed and turned to the right and
left to the soft music. For a time she had altogether
forgotten her strong antipathy for him. Indeed, she
had almost forgotten his existence. Momentarily, he
was a nonentity, except as a means of motion.

As she moved the colour slowly came back to her
pale face, the frown disappeared and the cold fire in
her eyes died away. She also danced well and was
proud of it, though she was far from being equal to
her mother, even now. With Katharine it was an
amusement; with Mrs. Lauderdale it was still a passion. But now she did not care to stop, and went
on and on, till Crowdie began to wonder whether she
were not falling into a dreamy and half-conscious state,
like that of the Eastern dervishes.

"Aren't you tired?" he asked.

"No — go on!" she answered, without hesitation.

He obeyed, and they continued to dance till many
couples stopped to look at them, and see how long they
would keep it up. Even the musicians became interested, and went on playing mechanically, their eyes
upon the couple. At last they were dancing quite alone.
As soon as the young girl saw that she was an object
of curiosity, she stopped.

"Come away!" she said quickly. "I didn't realize
that they were all looking at us — it was so nice."

It was not without a certain degree of vanity that Crowdie at last led her out of the room. He remembered her behaviour to him that morning and on former occasions, and he thought that he had gained a signal success. It was not possible, he thought, that if he were still as repulsive to her as he undoubtedly had been, she should be willing to let him dance with her so long. Dancing meant much to him.

"Shall we sit down somewhere?" he asked, as they got away from the crowd into a room beyond.

"Oh, yes — if there's a place anywhere. Anything!" She spoke carelessly and absently still.

They found two chairs a little removed from the rest, and sat down side by side.

"Miss Lauderdale," said Crowdie, after a momentary pause, "I wish you'd let me ask you a question. Will you?"

"If it's not a rude one," answered Katharine, indifferently, and scarcely looking at him. "What is it?"

"Well — you know — we're relations, or connections, at least. Hester is your cousin, and she's your most intimate friend. Isn't she?"

"Yes. Is it about her? There she is, just over there — talking to that ugly, thin man with the nice face. Do you see her?"

Crowdie looked in the direction indicated, though he did not in the least wish to talk about his wife to Katharine.

"Oh, yes; I see her," he answered. "She's talking to Paul Griggs, the writer. You know him, don't you? I wonder how he comes here!"

"Is that Paul Griggs?" asked Katharine, with a show of interest. "I've always wished to see him."

"Yes. But it has nothing to do with Hester —"

"What has nothing to do with Hester?" asked Katharine, with despairing absence of mind, as she watched the author's face.

"The question I was going to ask you — if you would let me."

Katharine turned towards him. He could produce extraordinarily soft effects with his beautiful voice when he chose, and he had determined to attract her attention just then, seeing that she was by no means inclined to give it.

"Oh, yes — the question," she said. "Is it anything very painful? You spoke — how shall I say? — in such a pathetic tone of voice."

"In a way — yes," answered Crowdie, not at all disturbed by her manner. "Painful is too strong a word, perhaps — but it's something that makes me very uncomfortable. It's this — why do you dislike me so much? Or don't you know why?"

Katharine paused a moment, being surprised by what he asked. She had no answer ready, for she could not tell him that she disliked his white face and scarlet lips and the soft sweep of his eyelashes. She took refuge in her woman's right to parry one question with another.

"What makes you think I dislike you?" she enquired.

"Oh — a thousand things — "

"I'm very sorry there are so many!" She laughed good-humouredly, but with the intention of turning the conversation if possible.

"No," said Crowdie, gravely. "You don't like me, for some reason which seems a good one to you. I'm sure of that, because I know that you're not capricious nor unreasonable by nature. I should care, in any case — even if we were casual acquaintances in society, and only met occasionally. Nobody could be quite indifferent to your dislike, Miss Lauderdale."

"No? Why not? I'm sure a great many people are. And as for that, I'm not so reasonable as you think, I daresay. I'm sorry you think I don't like you."

"I don't think — I know it. No — please! Let me tell you what I was going to say. We're not mere ordinary acquaintances, though I don't in the least hope ever to be a friend of yours, exactly. You see — owing to Hester — and on account of the portrait, just now — I'm thrown a good deal in your way. I can't help it. I don't want to give up painting you — "

"But I don't wish you to! I'll come every day, if you like — every day I can."

"Yes; you're very good about it. It's just because you are, that I am more sensitive about your dislike, I suppose."

"But, my dear Mr. Crowdie, how — "

"My dear Miss Lauderdale, I'm positively repulsive to you. You can't deny it really, though you'll put it much more gently. To-day, when I wanted to help you to take off your hat, you started and changed colour — just as though you had touched a snake. I know that those things are instinctive, of course. I only want you to tell me if you have any reason — beyond a mere uncontrollable physical repulsion. There's no other way of putting it, I'm afraid. I mean, whether I've ever done anything to make you hate the sight of me — "

"You? Never. On the contrary, you're always very kind, and nice in every way. I wish you would put it out of your head — the whole idea — and talk about something else. No, honestly, I've nothing against you, and I never heard anything against you. And I'm really very much distressed that I should have given you any such impression. Isn't that the answer to your question?"

"Yes — in a way. It reduces itself to this — if you never looked at me, and never heard my voice, you wouldn't hate me."

"Oh — your voice — no!" The words escaped her involuntarily, and conveyed a wrong impression; for though she meant that his voice was beautiful, she knew that its mere beauty sometimes repelled her as much as his appearance did.

"Then it's only my looks," he said with a laugh. "Thanks! I'm quite satisfied now, and I quite agree with you in that. You noticed to-day that there were no mirrors in the studio." He laughed again quite naturally.

"Really!" exclaimed Katharine, as a sort of final protest, and taking the earliest opportunity of escaping from the difficult situation he had created. "I wish you would tell me something about Mr. Griggs, since you know him. I've been watching him — he has such a curious face!"

"Paul Griggs? Oh, yes — he's a curious creature altogether." And Crowdie began to talk about the man.

Katharine was in reality perfectly indifferent, and followed her own train of thought while Crowdie made himself as agreeable as he could, considering that he was conscious of her inattention. He would have been surprised had he known that she was thinking about him.

Since Hester had told her the story of his strange illness, Katharine could not be near him without remembering her cousin's vivid description of his appearance and condition during the attack. It was but a step from such a picture to the question of the morphia and Crowdie's story, and one step further brought the comparison between slavery to one form of excitement and slavery to another; in other words, between John Ralston and the painter, and then between Hester's love for Crowdie and Katharine's for her cousin. But at this point the divergence began. Crowdie, who looked weak, effeminate and anything but manly, had found courage and strength to overcome a habit which was said to be almost unconquerable. Katharine would certainly never have guessed that he had such a strong will, but Hester had told her all about it, and there seemed to be no other explanation of the facts. And Ralston, with his determined expression and all his apparently hardy manliness, had distinctly told her that he did not feel sure of keeping a promise, even for the sake of her love. It seemed incredible. She would have given anything to be able to ask Crowdie questions about his life, but that was impossible, under the circumstances. He might never forgive his wife for having told his secret.

Her sudden and violent anger had subsided, and she already regretted what she had said and done with Ralston. Indeed, she found it hard to understand how she could have been so cruelly unkind, all in a moment, when she had hardly found time to realize the meaning of what he had told her. Another consideration and another question presented themselves now, as she remembered and recapitulated the circumstances of the scene. For the first time she realized the man's loyalty in thrusting his shortcomings under her eyes before the final step was taken. It must have been a terrible struggle for him, she thought. And if he was brave enough to do such a thing as that, — to tell the truth to her, and the story of his shameful weakness, — what must that temptation be which even he was not brave enough to resist? No doubt, he did resist it often, she thought, and could do so in the future, though he said that he could not be sure of himself. He was so brave and manly. Yet it was horrible to think of him in connection with something which appeared to be unspeakably disgusting in her eyes.

The vice was one which she could not understand. Few women can; and it would be strange, indeed, if any young girl could. She had seen drunken men in the streets many times, but that was almost all she knew of it. Occasionally, but by no means often, she had seen a man in society who had too much colour, or was unnaturally pale, and talked rather wildly, and people said that he had taken too much wine — and generally laughed. Such a man was making himself ridiculous, she thought, but she established no connection between him and the poor wretch reeling blind drunk out of a liquor shop, who was pointed out to her by her father as an awful example. She had even seen a man once who was lying perfectly helpless in the gutter, while a policeman kicked him to make him get up — and it had made a strong impression upon her. She remembered distinctly his swollen face, his bloodshot blue eyes and his filthy clothes — all disgusting enough.

That was the picture which rose before her eyes when John Ralston, putting his case more strongly than was necessary in order to clear his conscience altogether, had told her that he could not promise to give up a bad habit for her sake. In the first moment she had thought merely of the man in society who behaved a little foolishly and talked too loud, but Ralston's earnest manner had immediately evoked the recollection of her father's occasional discourses upon what he called the besetting sin of the lower classes in America, and had vividly recalled therewith the face of the besotted wretch in the gutter. She knew of no intermediate stage. To be a slave to drink meant that and nothing else. The society man whom she took as an example was not a slave to drink; he was merely foolish and imprudent, and might get into trouble. To think of marrying a man who had lain in the gutter, half blind with liquor, to be kicked by a policeman, was more than she could bear. The inevitable comic side to things is rarely discernible to those brought most closely into connection with them. It was not only serious to Katharine; it was horrible, repulsive, sickening. It was no wonder that she had sprung from her seat and turned her back on Ralston, and that she had done the first thing which presented itself as a means of distracting her thoughts.

But now, matters began to look differently to her calmer judgment. It was absurd to think that.Ralston should make a mountain of a mole-hill, and speak as he had spoken of himself, if he only meant that he now and then took a glass of champagne more than was good for him. Besides, if he did it habitually, she must have seen him now and then behaving like a typical young gentleman, and making a fool of himself. But she had never noticed anything of the kind. On the other hand, she could not believe that he could ever, under any circumstances, turn into the kind of creature who had been held up to her as an example of the habitual drunkard. There must be something between the two, she felt sure, something which she could not understand. She would find out. And she must see John again, before she left the dance. Her eyes began to look for him in the crowd.

There are times when the processes of a girl's mind are primitive in their simplicity. Katharine suddenly remembered hearing that men drank out of despair. She had seen Ralston's face when she had risen and left him, and it had 'certainly expressed despair very strongly. Perhaps he had gone at once to drown his cares — that was the expression she had heard — and it would be her fault.

Such a sequence of ideas looks childish in·this age of

profound psychological analysis, but it is just such reasoning which sometimes affects people most when their
hearts are touched. We have all thought and done very
childish things at times.

Katharine forgot all about Crowdie and what he was
saying. She had given a sort of social, mechanical attention to his talk, nodding intelligently from time to
time, and answering by vague monosyllables, or with
even more vague questions. Crowdie had the sense to
understand that she did not mean to be rude, and that
her mind was wholly absorbed — most probably with what
had taken place between her and Ralston a quarter of
an hour earlier. He talked on patiently, since he could
do nothing else, but he was not at all surprised when she
at last interrupted him.

"Would you mind looking to see if my cousin — Jack
Ralston, you know, — is still in the hall?" she asked,
without ceremony.

"Certainly," said Crowdie, rising. "Shall I tell him
you want him, if he's there?"

"Do, please. It's awfully good of you, Mr. Crowdie,"
she added, with a preoccupied smile.

Crowdie dived into the crowd, looking about him in
every direction, and then making his way straight to
Ralston, who had not left his corner.

"Miss Lauderdale wants to speak to you, Ralston,"
said the painter, as he reached him. "Hallo! What's
the matter? You look ill."

"I? Not a bit!" answered Ralston. "It's the heat,
I suppose. Where is Miss Lauderdale?" He spoke in
a curiously constrained tone.

"I'll take you to her — come along!"

The two moved away together, Ralston following
Crowdie through the press. Through the open door

of the boudoir Ralston saw Katharine's eyes looking for him.

"All right," he said to Crowdie, "I see her. Don't bother."

"Over there in the low chair by the plants," answered the painter, in unnecessary explanation.

"All right," said Ralston again, and he pushed past Crowdie, who turned away to seek amusement in another direction. Katharine looked up gravely at him as he came to her side, and then pointed to the chair Crowdie had left vacant.

"Sit down. I want to talk to you," she said quickly, and he obeyed, drawing the chair a little nearer.

"I thought you never meant to speak to me again," he said bitterly.

"Did you? You thought that? Seriously?"

"I suppose most men would have thought very much the same."

"You thought that I could change completely, like that — in a single moment?"

"You seemed to change."

"And that I did not love you any more?"

"That was what you made me think — what else? You're perfectly justified, of course. I ought to have told you long ago."

"Please don't speak to me so — Jack."

"What do you expect me to say?" he asked, and with a weary look in his eyes he leaned back in his low chair and watched her.

"Jack — dear — you didn't understand when I told Mr. Crowdie to call you — you don't understand now. I was angry then — by the staircase. I'm sorry. Will you forgive me?"

Ralston's face changed instantly, and he leaned for

ward again, so as to be able to speak in a lower
tone.

"Darling — don't say such things! I've nothing to
forgive —"

"You have, Jack! Indeed, you have — oh! why
can't we be alone for ten minutes — I'd explain it all —
what I thought —"

"But there's nothing to explain, if you love me still —
at least, not for you."

"Yes, there is. There's ever so much. Jack, why
did you tell me? You frightened me so — you don't
know! And it seemed as though it were the end of
everything, and of me, myself, when you said you
couldn't be sure of keeping a promise for my sake.
You didn't mean what you said — at least, not as I
thought you meant it — you didn't mean that you
wouldn't try — and of course you would succeed in the
end."

"I think I should succeed very soon, with you to help
me, Katharine. But that's not what a man — who is a
man — accepts from a woman."

"Her help — not her help, Jack? How can you say
so!"

"Yes, I mean it. Suppose that I should fail, what
sort of life should you lead — tied to a man who drinks?
Don't start, dear — it's the truth. We shall never talk
about it again, after this, perhaps, and I may just as well
say what I think. I must say it, if I'm ever to respect
myself again."

Katharine looked at him, realized again what his courage had been in making the confession, and she loved
him more than ever.

"Jack —" she began, and hesitated. "Since we are
talking of it, and must talk of it — can't you tell me

what makes you do it — I mean — you know ! What is it that attracts you ? It must be something very strong — isn't it ? What is it ? "

" I wish I knew ! " answered Ralston, half savagely. " It began — oh, at college, you know. I was vain of being able to stand more than the other fellows and of going home as steady as though I'd had nothing."

" But a man who can walk straight isn't drunk, Jack — "

" Oh, isn't he ! " exclaimed Ralston, with a sour smile. " They're the worst kind, sometimes — "

" But I thought that a man who was really drunk — was — was quite senseless, and tumbled down, you know — in a disgusting state."

" It's not a pretty subject — especially when you talk about it, dear — but it's not always of that description."

It shocked Ralston's refined nature to hear her speak of such things. For he had all the refinement of nervous natures, like many a man who has been wrecked by drink — even to men of genius without number.

" Isn't it quite — no, of course it's not. I know well enough." Katharine paused an instant. " I don't care if it's not what they call refined, Jack. I'm not going to let that sort of squeamishness come between you and me. It's not as though I'd come upon it as a subject of conversation — and — and I'm not afraid you'll think any the worse of me because I talk about horrid things, when I must talk about them — when everything depends on them — you and I, and our lives. I must know what it is that you feel — that you can't resist."

Ralston felt how strong she was, and was glad.

" Go on," she said. " Tell me all about it — how it began."

" That was it — at college, I suppose," he answered.

"Then it grew to be a habit — insensibly, of course. I thought it didn't hurt me and I liked the excitement. Perhaps I'm naturally melancholic and depressed."

"I don't wonder!"

"No — it's not the result of anything especial. I've not had at all an unhappy life. I was born gloomy, I suppose — and unlucky, too. You see the trouble is that those things get hold of one's nerves, and then it becomes a physical affair and not a mere question of will. Men get so far that it would kill them to stop, because they're used to it. But with me — no, I admit the fact — it is a question of will and nothing else. Just now — oh, well, I've talked enough about myself."

"What — 'just now'? What were you going to say? You wanted to go and drink, just after I left you?"

"How did you guess that?"

"I don't know. I was sure of it. And — and you didn't, Jack?"

"No, I didn't."

"Why not? What stopped you? It was so easy!"

"I felt that I should be a brute if I did — so I didn't. That's all. It's not worth mentioning — only it shows that it is a question of will. I'm all right now — I don't want it any more. Perhaps I shan't, for days. I don't know. It's a hopeless sort of thing, anyway. Sometimes I'm just on the point of taking an oath. But if I broke it, I should blow my brains out, and I shouldn't be any better off. So I have the sense not to promise myself anything."

"Promise me one thing," said Katharine, thoughtfully. "It's a thing you can promise — trust me, won't you?"

"Yes — I promise," answered Ralston, without hesitation.

"That you will never bind yourself by any oath at all, will you?"

Ralston paused a moment.

"Yes — I promise you that," he said. "I think it's very sensible. Thank you, dear."

There was a short silence after he had spoken. Then Katharine laughed a little and looked at him affectionately.

"How funny we are!" she exclaimed. "Half an hour ago I quarrelled with you because you wouldn't promise, and now I've got you to swear that you never will promise, under any circumstances."

"Yes," he answered. "It's very odd. But other things are changed, too, since then, though it's not long."

"You're mistaken, Jack," she said, misunderstanding him. "Haven't I said enough? Don't you know that I love you just as much as I ever did — and more? But nothing is changed — nothing — not the least little bit of anything."

"Dear—how good you are!" Ralston's voice was very tender just then. "But I mean — about to-morrow."

"Nothing's changed, Jack," said Katharine, leaning forward and speaking very earnestly.

But Ralston shook his head, sadly, as he met her eyes.

"Yes, dear, it's all changed. That can't be as you wanted it — not now."

"But if I say that I will? Oh, don't you understand me yet? It's made no difference. I lost my head for a moment — but it has made no difference at all, except that I respect you ever so much more than I did, for being so honest!"

"Respect me!" repeated Ralston, with grave incredulity. "Me! You can't!"

"I can and I do. And I mean to be married to you — to-morrow, just as we said. I wonder what you think I'm made of, to change and take back my word and

promise! Don't you see that I want to give you everything — my whole life — much more than I did this
morning? Yes, ever so much more, for you need me
more than I knew or guessed. You see, I didn't quite
understand at first, but it's all clear now. You're much
more unhappy — and much more foolish about it — than
I am. I don't want to go back over it all again, but won't
it be much easier for you when you have me to help you?
It seems to me that it must be, because I love you so!
Won't it be much easier? Tell me!"

"Yes — of course it would. I don't like to think of it,
because I mustn't do it. I should never have asked you
to marry me at all, until I was sure of myself. But —
well, I couldn't help it. We loved each other."

"Jack — what do you mean?"

"That I love you far too much to tie myself round your
life like a chain. I won't do it. I'll do the best I can
to get over this thing and if I do — I shan't be half good
enough for you — but if you will still have me then, we'll
be married. If I can't get over it — why then, that
means that I shall go to the devil, I suppose. At all
events, you'll be free."

He spoke very quietly, but the words hurt him as they
came. He did not realize until he had finished speaking
that the resolution had been formed within the last five
minutes, though he felt that he was right.

"If you knew how you hurt me, when you talk like
that!" said Katharine, in a low voice.

"It's a question of absolute right and wrong — it's a
question of honour," he continued, speaking quickly to
persuade himself. "Just put yourself in the position of
a third person, and think about it. What should you say
of a man who did such a thing — who accepted such a
sacrifice as you wish to make?"

"It isn't a sacrifice—it's my life."

"Yes—that's it! What would your life be, with a man on whom you couldn't count—a man you might be ashamed of, at any moment—who can't even count on himself—a fellow who's good for nothing on earth, and certainly for nothing in heaven—a failure, like me, who—"

"Stop! You shan't say any more. I won't listen! Jack, I shall go away, as I did before—"

"Well—but isn't it all true?"

"No—not a word of it is true! And if it were true twenty times over, I'd marry you—now, in spite of everybody. I—I believe I'd commit a sin to marry you. Oh, it's of no use! I can't live without you—I can't, indeed! I called you back to tell you so—"

She stopped, and she was pale. He had never seen her as she was now, and she had never looked so beautiful to him.

"For that matter, I couldn't live without you," he said, in a rather uncertain voice.

"And you shall not!" she answered, with determination. "Don't talk to me of sacrifice—what could anything be compared with that—with giving you up? You don't know what you're saying. I couldn't—I couldn't do it—not if it meant death."

"But, dear—Katharine dear—if I fail, as I shall, I'm sure—just think—"

"If you do—but you won't—well, if you should think you had—oh, Jack! If you were the worst man alive, I'd rather die with you than live for any one else! God knows I would—"

"It's very, very hard!" Ralston twisted his fingers together and bowed his head, still trying to resist her.

She bent forward again.

"Dear—tell me! A little while ago—out there—when you wanted it—wasn't that hard?"

Ralston nodded silently.

"And didn't you resist because it was a little — just a little for my sake? Just at that moment when you said to yourself that you wouldn't, you know, or just before, or just afterwards — didn't you think a little of me, dear?"

"Of course I did. Oh, Katharine, Katharine —" His voice was shaking now.

"Yes. I know now," she answered. "I don't want anything but that — all my life."

Still Ralston bent his head again, looking down at his hands and believing that he was still resisting. He could not have spoken, had he tried, and Katharine saw it. She leaned still nearer to him.

"Dear — I'm going home now. I shall be walking in Clinton Place at half-past eight to-morrow morning, as we arranged. Good-night — dear."

Before he realized what she meant to do, she had risen and reached the door. He sprang to his feet and followed her, but the crowd had closed again and she was gone.

CHAPTER XV.

KATHARINE LAUDERDALE slept sweetly that night. She had, as she thought, at last reached the crisis of her life, and the moment of action was at hand. She felt, too, that almost at the last moment she had avoided a great risk and made a good resolution — she felt as though she had saved John Ralston from destruction. Loving him as truly as she did, her satisfaction over what she had done was far greater than her pain at what he had told her of himself.

But this was not insignificant, though she wilfully made it seem as small as she could. It was quite clear that it was not a matter to be laughed at, and that Ralston did not deserve to be called quixotic because he had thought it his duty to tell her of his weakness. It was not a mountain, she was sure, but she admitted that it was not a mole-hill either. Men who exaggerated the golden letter of virtue at the expense of the gentle spirit of charity, as her father did, exaggerated also, as a rule, those forms of wickedness to which they were themselves least liable. She knew that. But she was also aware that drinking too much was not by any means an imaginary vice. It was a matter of fact, with which whole communities had to deal, and about which men very unlike her father in other ways spoke gravely. Nevertheless, though a fact, all details connected with it were vague. It seemed to her a matter of certainty that John Ralston would at once change his life and become in that respect, as in all others, exactly what her ideal of a man always had been since she had loved him.

Her mistake, if it were one, was pardonable enough. Had she become aware of his fault by accident, and when, having succumbed to his weakness, she could have seen him not himself, the whole effect upon her mind would have been very different. But she had never seen him, as she believed, in any such condition. It was as though he had told it as of another man, and she found it impossible really to connect any such ideas of inebriety as she had with the man she loved. It was as vague as though he had told her that he had once had the scarlet fever. She would have known very well what the scarlet fever was like, but she could not have associated it with him in any really distinct way. It was because

it had seemed such a small matter at first sight that she
had been suddenly overwhelmed by a sense of bitter
disappointment when he had refused to give his promise
for her sake. As soon as she had begun to understand
even a little of what he really felt, she had been as
ready and as determined to stand by him through everything as though it had been a question of a bodily illness,
for which he was not responsible, but in which she could
really help him. When she had been angry, and afterwards, when, in spite of him, she had so strongly insisted upon the marriage, she had been alike under a
false impression, though in different degrees. She had
not now any idea of what she had really undertaken to
do.

With her nature she would probably have acted just
as she did in the last case, even had she understood all,
by actual experience. She was capable of great sacrifices
— even greater than she dreamed of. But, not understanding, it did not seem to her that she had done or
promised anything very extraordinary, and she was absolutely confident of success. It was natural to her to
accept wholly what she accepted at all, and it had
always seemed to her that there was something mean in
complaining of what one had taken voluntarily, and in
finding fault with details when one had agreed, as it
were, to take over the whole at a moral valuation.

It has seemed necessary to dwell at great length on
the events which filled the days preceding Katharine's
marriage. Her surroundings had made her what she
was, and justified, if anything could justify, the extraordinary step she was about to take, and which she actually
took on the morning after the dance at the Thirlwalls'.
It is under such circumstances that such things are done,
when they are done at all. The whole balance of opinion

in her family was against her marrying John Ralston. The whole weight of events, so far as she was concerned, was in favour of the marriage.

That she loved him with all her heart, there was no doubt; and he loved her with all that his nature could give of love, which was, indeed, less than what she gave, but was of a good and faithful sort in its way. Love, like most passions, good and bad, flourishes under restraint when it is real and perishes almost immediately before opposition when it has grown out of artificial circumstances — to revive, sometimes, in the latter case, if the artificiality is resuscitated. Katharine had found herself opposed at every turn in her love for Ralston. The result was natural and simple — it had grown to be altogether the dominant reality of her life.

Even those persons who did not actively do their best to hinder her marriage, contributed, by their actions and even by their existence, to the fortifying of her resolution, as it seemed to her, but in reality to the growth of the passion which needed no resolutions to direct it. For instance, Crowdie's repulsive personality threw Ralston's undeniable advantages into higher relief. His wife's devotion to him made Katharine's devotion to John seem ten times more reasonable than it was. Charlotte Slayback's wretchedly petty and miserable life with a man whom she had not married for love, made a love match seem the truest foundation for happiness. Old Robert Lauderdale's solitary existence was itself an argument in favour of marriage. The small, daily discomfort which Alexander Junior's miserly economy imposed upon his household, and which Katharine had been forced to endure all her life, made Ralston's careless generosity a virtue by contrast. Even Mrs. Lauderdale had turned against her daughter at last, for reasons

which the young girl could not understand, either at the
time or for a long time afterwards.

She felt herself very much alone in the world, in spite
of her position. And yet, since her mother had begun to
lose her supreme beauty, Katharine was looked upon as
the central figure of the Lauderdale tribe, next to Robert
the Rich himself. 'The beautiful Miss Lauderdale' was
a personage of much greater importance than she herself
knew, in the eyes of society. She had grown used to
hearing reports to the effect that she was engaged to be
married to this man, or that, and that her uncle Robert
had announced his intention of wrapping his wedding
present in a cheque for a million of dollars. Stories of
that sort got into the papers from time to time, and
Alexander Junior never failed to write a stern denial of
the report to the editor of the journal in which the tale
appeared. Katharine was used to seeing the family
name in print on all possible occasions and paid little
attention to it. She did not know how far people must
have become subjects of general conversation before they
become the paragraphist's means of support in 'the dull
season of the year. The paragraphists on a great daily
paper have an intimate knowledge of the public taste, for
which they get little credit amongst the social lights,
who flatter themselves that the importance of the paper
in question depends very largely on their opinion of it.
Society is very much like a little community of lunatics,
who live in an asylum all by themselves, and who know
nothing whatever about the great public that lives beyond
the walls, whereas the public knows a good deal about
the lunatics, and takes a lively interest in their harmless,
or dangerous, vagaries. And in the same way society
itself forms a small public for its own most prominent
individuals, — for its own favourite lunatics, so to say, —

and watches their doings and talks about them with constant interest, and flatters them when it thinks they are agreeable, and abuses them bitterly behind their backs when it thinks they are not. The daily dinner-party conversation is society's unprinted but widely circulated daily paper. It is often quite ignorant of state secrets, but it is never unacquainted with social events, and generally has plenty of sound reasons with which to explain them. Society's comparative idleness, even in America, gives it opportunities of conversation which no equally large body of men and women can be said to possess outside of its rather elastic limits. It talks the same sort of matter which the generally busy great public reads and wishes to read in the daily press — and as talking is a quicker process than controversy in print, society manages to say as much for and against the persons it discusses, in a day, as the newspapers can say in a week, or perhaps more. As a mere matter of statistics, there is no doubt that a couple of talkative people spending an evening together can easily ' talk off' ten thousand words in an hour — which is equal to about eight columns of an ordinary big daily paper, and they are not conscious of making any great effort. It is manifestly possible to say a great many things in eight columns of a newspaper, especially if one is not very particular about what one says.

Katharine realized, no doubt, that there would some day be plentiful discussion of her rashness in marrying Ralston against the wishes of her family, and she knew that the circumstances would to some extent be regarded as public property. But she was far from realizing her own social importance, or that of the whole Lauderdale tribe, as compared with that of many people who spent enormous sums in amusing their friends, consciously and unconsciously, but who could never be Lauderdales, though it was not their fault.

At the juncture she had now reached, such considerations would have had little weight with her, but the probability is that, had she known exactly what she was doing, and how it would be regarded should others know of it, she would have vastly preferred to rebel openly and to leave New York with John Ralston on the day she married him, in uncompromising defiance of her family. Most people have known in the course of life of one or two secret marriages and must have noticed that the motives to secrecy generally seem inadequate. As a rule, they are, if taken by themselves. But in actual fact they have mostly acted upon the persons concerned through a medium of some sort of ignorance and in conjunction with an impatient passion. It is common enough, even in connection with more or less insignificant matters, to hear some one say, 'I wonder why I did that — I might have known better!' Humanity is never wholly logical, and is never more than very partially wise, even when it is old enough to 'know better.' In nine cases out of ten, when it is said of a man that 'a prophet is without honour in his own country,' the reason is that his own country is the best judge of what he prophesies. And similarly, society judges the doings of all its members by its own individual knowledge of its own customs, so that very few who do anything not sanctioned by those customs get any credit, but, on the contrary, are in danger of being called fools for believing that anything not customary can be done at all.

At half-past eight on Thursday morning Katharine left the house in Clinton Place, and turned eastward to meet John Ralston. Her only source of anxiety was

the fear lest her father should by some accident go out
earlier than usual. There was no particular reason to
expect that he should be irregular on that particular day
of all others, and she had left him over his beefsteak,
discussing the relative amounts of the nutriment — as
compared with the price per pound — contained in beef
and mutton. He had never been able to understand why
any one who could get meat should eat anything else,
and the statistics of food consumption interested his
small but accurate mind. His wife listened quietly but
without response, so that the discussion was very one-
sided. The philanthropist generally shuffled down to
breakfast when everything was cold, a point about which
he was utterly indifferent. He had long ago discovered
that by coming down late he could always be the last to
finish his meal, and could therefore begin to smoke as
soon as he had swallowed his last mouthful, which was a
habit very important to his enjoyment and very destructive to that of any one else, especially since his son had
reduced him to 'Old Virginia Cheroots' at ten cents for
five.

But Alexander Junior was no more inclined than usual
to reach his office a moment before his accustomed time.
Katharine generally left the dining-room as soon as she
had finished breakfast, and often went out immediately
afterwards for a turn in Washington Square, so that her
departure excited no remark. The rain had ceased, and
though the air was still murky and the pavements wet, it
was a decently fine morning. Ralston was waiting for
her, walking up and down on a short beat, and the two
went away together.

At first they were silent, and the silence had a certain
constraint about it which both of them felt, but did not
know how to escape from. Ralston was the first to speak.

"You ought not to have come," he said rather awkwardly, with a little laugh.

"But I told you I was coming," she answered demurely. "Didn't I ? "

"I know. That's just it. You told me so suddenly that I couldn't protest. I ran after you, but you were gone to get your things, and when you came downstairs there were a lot of people, and I couldn't speak to you."

"I saw you," said Katharine. "It was just as well. You had nothing to say to me that I didn't know, and we couldn't have begun the discussion of the matter all over again at the last instant. And now, please, Jack dear, don't begin and argue. I've told you a hundred times that I know exactly what I'm doing — and that it's I who am making you do it. And remember that unless we are married first uncle Robert will never make up his mind to do anything for us. It's never of any use to try and overcome people's objections. The only way is to ignore them, which is just what we're doing."

"There's no doubt about that," answered Ralston. "There's one thing I look forward to with pleasure, in the way of a row, though — I mean when your father finds it out. I hope you'll let me tell him and not spoil my fun. Won't you ? "

"Oh, yes, if you like. Why not ? Not that I'm at all afraid. You don't know papa. When he finds that the thing is done, that it's the inevitable course of events, in fact, he'll be quite different. He'll very likely talk of submission to the Divine will and offer to speak to Beman Brothers about letting you try the clerkship again. I know papa ! Providence has an awfully good time with him — but nobody else does."

At which piece of irreverence Ralston laughed, for it exactly expressed his idea of Alexander Junior's character.

" And there's one other thing I don't want you to speak
of, Jack," pursued Katharine, more gravely. " I mean
what you told me last night. I don't intend ever to mention it again — do you understand, dear ? I've thought
it all over since then. I'm glad you told me, and I
admire you for telling me, because it must have been hard,
especially until I began to understand. A woman doesn't
know everything, you see ! Indeed, we don't know much
about anything. We can only feel. And it did seem
very hard at first — only for a moment, Jack — that you
should not be willing to promise what I asked, when it
was to make such a difference to me, and I was willing
to promise you anything. You see how I felt, don't
you ? "

" Of course," answered Ralston, looking down at the
pavement as he walked on and listened. " It was
natural."

" Yes. I'm so glad you see it. But afterwards, when
I thought of things I'd heard — why, then I thought a
great deal too much, you know — dreadful things ! But
I understood better what it all meant. You see, at first,
it seemed so absurd ! Just as though I had asked you not
to — not to wear a green tie, for instance, as Charlotte
asked her husband. Absurd, wasn't it ? So I was frightfully angry with you and got up and went away. I'm so
ashamed of myself for it, now. But then, when it grew
clearer — when I really knew that there was suffering in
it, and remembered hearing that it was something like
morphia and such things, that have to be cured by degrees
— you know what I mean — why, then I wanted you
more than ever. You know I'd give anything to help
you — just to make it a little easier for you, dear."

" You do ! You're doing everything — you're giving
me everything," said Ralston, earnestly.

"Well — not everything — but myself, because that's all I have to give — if it's any use to you."

"Dear — as if you weren't everything the world has, and the only thing and the best thing altogether ! "

"And if I didn't love you better than anything — better than kings and queens — I wouldn't do it. Because, after all, though I'm not much, I'm all I have. And then — I'm proud — inside, you know, Jack. Papa says I'm not, because mamma and I sometimes go to the theatre in the gallery, for economy. But that's hardly a test in real life, I think — and besides, I know I am. Don't you think so ? "

"Yes — a little, in the right way. It's nice. I like it in you."

"I'm so glad. It's because I'm proud that I don't want to talk about that matter any more. It just doesn't exist for me. That's what I want you to feel. But I want you to feel, too, that I'm always there, that I shall always understand, and that if I can help you the least little bit, I mean to. I've turned into a woman all at once, Jack, in the last twenty-four hours, and now in an hour I shall be your wife, though nobody will know about it for a day or two. But I don't mean to turn into your grandmother, too, and be always lecturing you and asking questions, and that sort of thing. You wouldn't like it either, would you ? "

"Hardly ! "

Ralston laughed again, for everything she said made him feel happier and helped to destroy the painful impression of the previous night.

"Why do you laugh, Jack? Oh, I suppose it's my way of putting it. But it's what I mean, and that's the principal thing. I'd rather die than watch you all the time, to see what you do. Imagine if I were always ask-

ing questions — 'Jack, where did you go last night?'
And — 'Jack, is that your third or fourth glass of wine to-
day?' The mere idea is disgusting. No. You must just
do your best, and feel that I'm always there — even when
I'm not — and that I'm never watching you, even when I
look as though I were, and that neither you nor I are
ever going to say a word about it — from this very minute, forever! Do you understand? Isn't that the best
way, Jack? And that I'm perfectly sure that it will be
all right in the end — you must remember that, too.'

"I think you're right," said Ralston. "You've suddenly turned into a woman, and into a very clever one.
Those are just the things which most women never will
understand. They'd be much happier if they did."

The two walked on rapidly, talking as they went, and
assuredly not looking at all like a runaway couple. But
though it was very early, they avoided the streets in
which they might easily meet acquaintances, for it was
the hour when men who had any business were going to
it in various ways, according to their tastes, but chiefly
by the elevated road. They had no difficulty in reaching unobserved the house of the clergyman who had
promised to marry them.

He was in readiness, and at his window, and as they
came in sight he left the house and met them. All three
walked silently to his church, and he let them in with
his own key, followed them and locked the door behind
them.

In ten minutes the ceremony was over. The clergyman beckoned them into the vestry, and immediately
signed a form of certificate which he had already filled in,
and handed it to John without a word. John took a new
treasury note from his pocket-book and laid it upon the
oak table.

"I'm sure you must have many poor people in your parish," he said, in explanation.

"I have," said the clergyman. "Thank you," he added, placing the money in his own pocket-book, which was an old black one, much the worse for wear.

"It is we who have to thank you," answered John, "for helping us out of a very difficult situation."

"Hm!" ejaculated the elder man, rubbing his chin with his hand and fixing a penetrating glance on Ralston's face. "Perhaps you won't thank me hereafter," he said suddenly. "Perhaps you think it strange that a man in my position should be a party to a secret marriage. But I do not anticipate that you will ask me for a justification of my action. I had reasons — reasons — old reasons." He continued to rub his chin thoughtfully. "I should like to say a word to you, Mrs. Ralston," he added, turning to Katharine.

She started and blushed a little. She had not expected to be addressed by what was now her name. But she held up her head, proudly, as though she were by no means ashamed of it.

"I shall not detain you a moment," continued the clergyman, looking at her as earnestly as he had looked at John. "I have perfect confidence in Mr. Ralston, as I have shown by acceding to his very unusual request. He has told you what I said to him yesterday, and I do not wish him to doubt that I am sure that he has done so. It is merely as a matter of conscience, to satisfy my own scruples in fact, that I wish to repeat, as nearly as possible, the same words, 'mutatis mutandis,' which I said to him. I have married you and have given you my certificate that the ceremony has been duly and properly performed, and you are man and wife. But I have married you thus secretly and without witnesses — none

being indispensable—on the distinct understanding that
your union is not to be kept a secret by you any longer
than you shall deem secrecy absolutely necessary to your
future happiness. Mr. Ralston informed me that it was
your intention to acknowledge what you had done to a
near relation, the head of your family, in fact, without any delay. I am sure that it is really your intention to do so. But let me entreat you, if it is possible,
to lose no time, but to go, even at this hour, to the
person in question and tell your story, one or the
other of you, or both together. I am an old man, and
human life is very uncertain, and human honour is
rightly held very dear, for if honour means anything,
it means the social application of that truth which is
by nature divine. To-morrow I may no longer be here
to testify that I signed that document with my own
hand. To-day the person in whom you intend to confide
can come and see me and I will answer for what I have
done, or he can acknowledge your marriage without
question, whichever he chooses to do; it will be better
if it be done quickly. It always seems to me that
to-morrow is the enemy of to-day, and lies in ambush
to attack it unawares. Therefore, I entreat you to go
at once to him you have chosen and tell him what you
have done. And so good-bye, and may God bless you
and make you happy and good."

"I shall go now," said Katharine. "And we thank
you very much," she added, holding out her hand.

The clergyman lét them out and stood looking after
them for a few seconds. Then he slowly nodded twice
and re-entered the church. Ralston and Katharine
walked away very slowly, both looking down, and each
inwardly wondering whether the other would break the
silence. It was natural that they should not speak at
first. The words of the service had brought very clearly

before them the meaning of what they had done, and the clergyman's short speech, made as he said for the sake of satisfying his own scruples of conscience, had influenced them by its earnestness. They reached a crossing without having exchanged a syllable. As usual in such cases, a chance exclamation broke the ice.

"Take care!" exclaimed Ralston, laying his hand on Katharine's arm, and looking at an express wagon which was bearing down on them.

"It's ever so far off still," said Katharine, smiling suddenly and looking into his face. "But I like you to take care of me," she added.

He smiled, too, and they waited for the wagon to go by. The clouds had broken away at last and the low morning sun shone brightly upon them.

"I'm so glad it's fine on our wedding day, Jack!" exclaimed Katharine. "It was horrid yesterday afternoon. How long ago that seems! Did you hear him call me Mrs. Ralston? Katharine Ralston — how funny it sounds! It's true, that's your mother's name."

"You'll be Mrs. John Ralston — to distinguish." John laughed. "Yes — it does seem long ago. What did you do with yourself yesterday?"

"Yesterday? Let me see — I sat for my portrait, and then I went home, and then late in the afternoon Charlotte suddenly appeared, and then I dined with the Joe Allens — the young couple, you know, don't you? And then I went to the dance. I hardly knew what I was doing, half the time."

"And I hardly know why I asked the question. Isn't it funny? I believe we're actually trying to make conversation!"

"You are — I'm not," laughed Katharine. "It was you who began asking. I was talking quite sentimentally and appropriately about yesterday seeming so long ago, you know. But it's true. It does — it seems ages. I wonder when time will begin again — I feel as though it had stopped suddenly."

"It will begin again, and it will seem awfully long, before this afternoon — when uncle Robert has refused to have anything to do with us."

"He won't refuse — he shan't refuse!" Katharine spoke with an energy which increased at every syllable. "Now that the thing is done, Jack, just put yourself in his position for a moment. Just imagine that you have anywhere between fifty and a hundred millions, all of your own. Yes — I know. You can't imagine it. But suppose that you had. And suppose that you had a grand-niece, whom you liked, and who wasn't altogether a disagreeable young person, and whom you had always rather tried to pet and spoil — not exactly knowing how to do it, but out of sheer good nature. And suppose that you had known ever so long that there was only one thing which could make your nice niece perfectly happy — "

"It's all very well, Katharine," interrupted Ralston, "but has he known that?"

"I've never failed to tell him so, on the most absurdly inadequate provocation. So it must be his fault if he doesn't know it — and I shall certainly tell him all over again before I bring out the news. It wouldn't do to be too sudden, you know. Well, then — suppose all that, and that the young gentleman in question was a proper young gentleman enough, as young gentlemen go, and didn't want money, and wouldn't take it if it were offered to him, but merely asked for a good chance to work and show what he could do. That's all very simple, isn't it? And then realize — don't suppose any more — just what's going to happen inside of half an hour. The devoted niece goes to the good old uncle, and says all that over again, and calmly adds that she's done the deed and married the young gentleman and got a certificate, which she produces — by the bye, you must give it to me. Don't be afraid of my losing it — I'm not such a goose. And she goes on to say that unless the good uncle does something for her husband, she will simply make the uncle's life a perfectly unbearable burden to him, and that she knows how to do it, because if he's a Lauderdale, she's a Lauderdale, and her husband is half a Lauderdale, so that it's all in the family, and no entirely unnecessary consideration is to be shown to the victim — well ? Don't you think that ought to produce an effect of some sort? I do."

"Yes," laughed Ralston, "I think so, too. Something is certainly sure to happen."

CHAPTER XVI.

KATHARINE let Ralston accompany her within a block of Robert Lauderdale's house and then sent him away.

"It's getting late," she said. "It must be nearly ten o'clock, isn't it ? Yes. People are all going out at this hour in the morning, and it's of no especial use to be seen about together. There's the Assembly ball to-night, and of course you'll come and talk to me, but I shall see you — or no — I'll write you a note, with a special delivery stamp, and post it at the District Post-Office. You'll get it in less than an hour, and then you'll know what uncle Robert says."

"I know already what he'll say," answered Ralston. "But why mayn't I wait for you here ?"

"Now, Jack! Don't be so ridiculously hopeless about things. And I don't want you to wait, for I haven't the least idea how long it may last, and as I said, there's no object in our being seen to meet, away up here by the Park, at this hour. Good-bye."

"I hate to leave you," said Ralston, holding out one hand, with a resigned air, and raising his hat with the other.

"I like that in you!" exclaimed Katharine, noticing the action. "I like you to take off your hat to me just the same — though you are my husband." She looked at him a moment. "I'm so glad we've done it!" she added with much emphasis, and a faint colour rose in her face.

Then she turned away and walked quickly in the direction of Robert Lauderdale's house, which was at the next corner. As she went she glanced at the big polished windows which face the Park, to see whether any one had noticed her. She knew the people who lived in one of the houses, and she had an idea that others might know her by sight, as the niece of the great man who had built the whole block. But there were only two children at one of the windows, flattening their rosy faces against the pane and drumming on it with fat hands; very smartly dressed children, with bright eyes and gayly-coloured ribbons.

As Katharine had expected, Robert Lauderdale was at home, had finished his breakfast and was in his library attending to his morning letters. She was ushered in almost immediately, and as she entered the room the rich man's secretary stood aside to let her pass through the door and then went out — a quiet, faultlessly dressed young man who had the air of a gentleman. He wore gold-rimmed spectacles, which looked oddly on his young face.

Robert Lauderdale did not rise to meet Katharine, as he sat sideways by a broad table, in an easy position, with one leg crossed over the other and leaning back in his deep chair. But a bright smile came into his cheerful old face, and stretching out one long arm he took her hand and drew her down and gave her a hearty kiss. Still holding her by the hand, he made her sit in the chair beside him, left vacant by the secretary.

"I'm glad to see you, my dear child!" he said warmly. "What brings you so early?"

He was a big old man and was dressed in a rough tweed of a light colour, which was very becoming to his fresh complexion. His thick hair had once been red, but had turned to a bright sandy grey, something like the sands at Newport. His face was laid out in broad surfaces, rich in healthy colour and deeply freckled where the skin was white. His keen blue eyes were small, but very clear and honest, and the eyebrows were red still, and bushy, with a few white hairs. Two deep, clean furrows extended from beside the nostrils into the carefully brushed beard, and there were four wrinkles, and no more, across the broad forehead. No one would have supposed that Robert Lauderdale was much over sixty, but in reality he was ten years older. His elder brother, the philanthropist, looked almost as though he might have been his father. It was clear that, like many of the Lauderdales, the old man had possessed great physical strength, and that he had preserved his splendid constitutional vitality even in his old age.

Katharine did not answer his question immediately. She was by no means timid, as has been seen, but she felt a little less brave and sure of herself in the presence of

the head of her family than when she had been with
Ralston a few minutes earlier. She was not aware of the
fact that in many ways she dominated the man who was
now her husband, and she would very probably not have
wished to believe she did; but she was very distinctly
conscious that she could never, under any imaginable
circumstances, exert any direct influence over her uncle
Robert, though she might persuade him to do much for
her. He was by nature himself of the dominant tribe,
and during forty years he had been accustomed to command with that absolute certainty of being obeyed which
few positions insure as completely as very great wealth
does. As she looked at him for a moment before speaking, the little opening speech she had framed began to
seem absolutely inadequate, and she could not find words
wherewith to compose another at such short notice.
Being courageous, however, she did not hesitate long, but
characteristically plunged into the very heart of the matter by telling him just what she felt.

"I've done something very unusual, uncle Robert,"
she began. "And I've come to tell you all about it, and
I prepared a speech for you. But it won't do. Somehow, though I'm not a bit afraid of you — " she smiled
as she met his eyes — " you seem ever so much bigger
and stronger than I thought you were, now that I've got
here."

Uncle Robert laughed and patted her hand as it lay on
the desk.

"Out with it, child !" he exclaimed. "I suppose you're
in trouble, in some way or other, and you want me to help
you. Is that it?"

"You must help me," answered Katharine. "Nobody
else can. Uncle Robert — " She paused, though a
pause was certainly not necessary in order to give the

plain statement more force.   "I've just been married to
Jack Ralston."

"Good — gracious — heavens!"

The old man half rose from his seat as he uttered the
words, one by one, in his deep voice.   Then he dropped
into his chair again and stared at the young girl in down-
right amazement.

"What in the name of common sense induced you to
do such a mad thing?" he asked very quietly, as soon as
he had drawn breath.

Katharine had expected that he would be surprised, as
was rather natural, and regained her coolness and decision at once.

"We've loved each other ever since we were children,"
she said, speaking calmly and distinctly.   "You know all
about it, for I've told you before now just how I felt.
Everybody opposed it — even my mother, at last — ex
cept you, and you certainly never gave us any encouragement."

"I should think not, indeed!" exclaimed old Lauderdale, shaking his great head and beating a tattoo on the
table with his heavy fingers.

"I don't know why not, I'm sure," Katharine answered,
with rising energy.   "There's no reason in the world why
we shouldn't love each other, and it wouldn't make the
slightest difference to me if there were.   I should love
him just the same, and he would love me.   He went to
my father last year, as you know, and papa treated him
outrageously — wanted to forbid him to come to the house,
but of course that was absurd.   Jack behaved splendidly
through it all — even papa had to acknowledge that,
though he didn't wish to in the least.   And I hoped and
hoped, and waited and waited, but things went no better.
You know when papa makes up his mind to a thing, no

matter how unreasonable it is, one might just as well talk to a stone wall. But I hadn't the smallest intention of being made miserable for the rest of my life, so I persuaded Jack to marry me — "

"I suppose he didn't need much persuasion," observed the old gentleman, angrily.

"You're quite wrong, uncle Robert! He didn't want to do it at all. He had an idea that it wasn't all right —"

"Then why in the world did he do it? Oh, I hate that sort of a young fellow, who pretends that he doesn't want to do a thing because he means to do it all the time — and knows perfectly well that it's a low thing to do!"

"I won't let you say that of Jack!" Katharine's grey eyes began to flash. "If you knew how hard it was to persuade him! He only consented at last — and so did the clergyman — because I promised to come and tell you at once — "

"That's just like the young good-for-nothing, too!" muttered the old man. "Besides — how do I know that you're really married?' How do I know that you're not — "

"Stop, please! There's the certificate. Please persuade yourself, before you accuse me of telling falsehoods."

Katharine was suddenly very angry, and Robert Lauderdale realized that he had gone too far in his excitement. But he looked at the certificate carefully, then took out his note-book and wrote down the main facts with great care.

"I didn't mean to doubt what you told me, child," he said, while he was writing. "You've rather startled me with this piece of news. Human life is very uncertain," he added, using the clergyman's own words. "and it may be just as well that there should be a note made of this.

Hadn't you better let me keep the certificate itself? It will be quite safe with my papers."

"I wish you would," answered Katharine, after a moment's thought.

The production of the certificate had produced a momentary cessation of hostilities, so to speak, but the old gentleman had by no means said his last word yet, nor Katharine either.

"Go on, my dear," he resumed gravely. "If I'm to know anything, I should know everything, I suppose."

"There's not very much more to tell," Katharine replied. "I repeat that it was all I could do to persuade Jack to take the step. He resisted to the very last — "

"Hm! He seems to have taken an active part in the proceedings in spite of his resistance — "

"Of course he did, after I had persuaded him to. It was up to that point that he resisted — and even after everything was ready — even this morning, when I met him, he told me that I ought not to have come."

"His spirit seems to have been willing to have some sense — but the flesh was weak," observed the old gentleman, without a smile.

"I insist upon taking the whole responsibility," said Katharine. "It was I who proposed it, and it was I who made him do it."

"You're evidently the strong-minded member, my dear."

"In this — yes. I love him, and I made up my mind that it was right to love him and that I would marry him. Now I have."

"It is impossible to make a more direct statement of an unpleasant truth. And now that you've done it, you mean that your family shall take the consequences — which shows a strong sense of that responsibility you men-

tioned — and so you've come to me. Why didn't you come
to me yesterday ? It would have been far more sensible."

"I did think of coming yesterday afternoon — and then
it rained, and Charlotte came — "

"Yes — it rained — I remember." Robert Lauderdale's mouth quivered, as though he should have liked
to smile at the utter insignificance of the shower as compared with the importance of Katharine's action. "You
might have taken a cab. There's a stand close by your
house, at the Brevoort."

"Oh, yes — of course — though I should have had to
ask mamma for some money, and that would have been
very awkward, you know. And if I had really and truly
meant to come, I suppose I shouldn't have minded the rain."

"Well — never mind the rain now!" Uncle Robert
spoke a little impatiently. "You didn't come — and
you've come to-day, when it's too late to do anything —
except regret what you've done."

"I don't regret it at all — and I don't intend to,"
Katharine answered firmly.

"And what do you mean to do in the future ? Live
with Ralston's mother ? Is that your idea ? "

"Certainly not. I want you to give Jack something
to do, and we'll live together, wherever you make him go
— if it's to Alaska."

"Oh — that's it, is it ? I begin to understand. I suppose Jack would think it would simplify matters very
much if I gave him a hundred thousand dollars, wouldn't
he ? That would be an even shorter way of giving him
the means to support his family."

"Jack wouldn't take money from you," answered Katharine, quickly.

"Wouldn't he ? If it were not such a risk, I'd try it,
just to convince you. You seem to have a very exalted

idea of Jack Ralston, altogether. I've not. Do you know anything about his life ? "

"Of course I do. I know how you all talk about the chances you've given him — between you. And I know just what they were — to try his hand at being a lawyer's clerk first, and a banker's clerk afterwards, with no salary and — "

"If he had stuck to either for a year he would have had a very different sort of chance," interrupted the old gentleman. "I told him so. There was little enough expected of him, I'm sure — just to go to an office every day, as most people do, and write what he was told to write. It wasn't much to ask. Take the whole thing to pieces and look at it. What can he do ? What do most men do who must make their way in the world? He has no exceptional talent, so he can't go in for art or literature or that sort of thing. His father wouldn't educate him for the navy, where he would have found his level, or where the Admiral's name would have helped him. He didn't get a technical education, which would have given him a chance to try engineering. There were only two things left — the law or business. I explained all that to him at the time. He shook his head and said he wanted something active. That's just the way all young men talk who merely don't want to stay in-doors and work decently hard, like other people. An active life ! What is an active life ? Ranching, I suppose he means, and he thinks he should do well on a ranch merely because he can ride fairly well. Riding fairly well doesn't mean much on a ranch. The men out there can all ride better than he ever could, and he knows nothing about horses, nor cattle, nor about anything useful. Besides, with his temper, he'd be shot before he'd been out there a year — "

"But there are all sorts of other things, and you forget Hamilton Bright, who began on a ranch — "

"Ham-Bright is made of different stuff. He had been brought up in the country, too, and his father was a Western man — from Cincinnati, at all events, though that isn't West nowadays. No. Jack Ralston could never succeed at that — and I haven't a ranch to give him, and I certainly won't go and buy land out there now. I repeat that his only chance lay in law or business. Law would have done better. He had the advantage of having a degree to begin with, and I would have found him a partner, and there's a lot of law connected with real estate which doesn't need a genius to work it, and which is fairly profitable. But no! He wanted something active! That's exactly what a kitten wants when it runs round after its own tail — and there's about as much sense in it. Upon my word, there is!"

"You're very hard on him, uncle Robert. And I don't think you're quite reasonable. It was a good deal the old Admiral's fault — "

"I'm not examining the cause, I'm going over the facts," said old Lauderdale, impatiently. "I tried him, and I very soon got to the end of him. He meant to do nothing. It was quite clear from the first. If he'd been a starving relation it would have been different. I should have made him work whether he liked it or not. As it was, I gave it up as a bad job. He wants to be idle, and he has the means to be idle if he's willing to live on his mother. She has ten thousand dollars a year, and a house of her own, and they can live very well on that — just as well as they want to. When his mother dies that's what Jack will have, and if he chooses to marry on it — "

"You seem to forget that he's married already — "

"By Jove! I did! But it doesn't change things in the least. My position is just the same as it was before. With ten thousand a year Katharine Ralston couldn't support a family —"

"Indeed, I could! I'm Katharine Ralston, and I should be —"

"Nonsense! You're Katharine Lauderdale. I'm speaking of Jack's mother. I suppose you'll admit that she's not able to support her son's wife out of what she has. It would mean a great change in her way of living. At present she doesn't need more. She's often told me so. If she wanted money for herself, just to spend on herself, mind you — I'd give her — well, I won't say how much. But she doesn't. It's for Jack that she wants it. She's perfectly honest. She's just like a man in her way of talking, anyhow. And I don't want Jack to be throwing my money into the streets. I can do more good with it in other ways, and she gives him more than is good for him, as it is. People seem to think that if a man has more than a certain amount of money, he's under a sort of moral obligation to society to throw it out of the window. That's a point of view I never could understand, though it comes quite naturally to Jack, I daresay. But I go back. I want to insist on that circumstance, and I want you to see the facts just as they are. If I were to settle another hundred thousand dollars on Jack's mother, it would be precisely the same thing, at present, as though I'd settled it on him, or on you. Now you say he wouldn't take any money if I offered it to him."

"No. He wouldn't, and I wouldn't let him if he wanted to."

"You needn't be afraid, my dear. I've no intention of doing anything so good-natured and foolish. If anything could complete Jack's ruin for all practical purposes, that would. No, no! I won't do it. I've given Kate Ralston a good many valuable jewels at one time and another since she married the Admiral — she's fond of good stones, you know. If Jack chooses to go to her and tell her the truth, and if she chooses to sell them and give him the money, it will keep you very comfortably for a long time — "

" How can you suggest such a thing ? " cried Katharine, indignantly. " As though he would ever stoop to think of it ! "

" Well — I hope he wouldn't. It wouldn't be pretty, if he did. But I'm a practical man, my dear, and I'm an old fellow and I've seen the world on both sides of the Atlantic Ocean for over seventy years. So I look at the case from all possible points of view, fair and unfair, as most people would. But I don't mean to be unfair to Jack."

" I think you are, uncle Robert. If you've proved anything, you've proved that he isn't fit for a ranch — and so you say there's nothing left but the law or business. It seems to me that there are ever so many things — "

" If you'll name them, you'll help me," said old Lauderdale, seriously.

" I mean active things — to do with railroads, and all that — " Katharine stopped, feeling that her knowledge was rather vague.

" Oh ! You mean to talk about railroading. I don't own any railroads myself, as I daresay you know, but I've picked up some information about them. Apart from the financing of them — and that's banking, which Jack objects to — there's the law part, which he doesn't like either, and the building of them, which he's too old to learn, and the mechanical part of them, such

as locomotives and rolling stock, which he can't learn
either — and then there are two places which men covet
and for which there's an enormous competition amongst
the best men for such matters in the country — I mean
the freight agent's place and the passenger agent's.
They are two big men, and they understand their business practically, because they've learned it practically.
To understand freight, a man must begin by putting
on rough clothes and going down to the shed and
handling freight himself, with the common freight men.
There are gentlemen who have done that sort of thing —
just as fine gentlemen as Jack Ralston, but made of quite
different stuff.   And it takes a very long time to reach a
high position in that way, though it's worth having when
you get it.   Do you understand?"

"Yes — I suppose I do. But one always hears of
men going off and succeeding in some out-of-the-way
place — "

"But you hear very little about the ones who fail, and
they're the majority.   And you hear, still more often,
people saying, as they do of Jack Ralston, that he ought
to go away, and show some enterprise, and get something
to do in the West.   It's always the West, because most
of the people who talk know nothing whatever about it.
I tell you, Katharine, my dear, it's just as hard to
start in this country as it is anywhere else, though men
get on faster after they're once started — and all this
talk about something active and an out-of-door existence
is pure nonsense.   It's nothing else.   A man may have
luck soon or late or never, but the safest plan for city-
bred men is to begin at a bank.   I did, and I've not regretted it.   Just as soon as a fellow shows that he has
something in him, he's wanted, and if he has friends, as
Jack has, they'll help him.   But as long as a man hangs

about the clubs all day with a cigarette in his mouth, sensible people, who want workers, will fight shy of him. Just tell Jack that, the next time you see him. It's all I've got to say, and if it doesn't satisfy him nothing can."

The old gentleman's anger had quite disappeared while he was speaking, though it was ready to burst out again on very small provocation. He spoke so earnestly, and put matters so plainly, that Katharine began to feel a blank disappointment closing in between her and her visions of the future in regard to an occupation for John. For the rest, she would have been just as determined to marry him after hearing all that her uncle had to say as she had been before. But she could not help showing what she felt, in her face and in the tone of her voice.

" Still — men do succeed, uncle Robert," she said, clinging rather desperately to the hope that he had only been lecturing her and had some pleasant surprise in store.

"Of course they do, my dear," he answered. "And it's possible for Jack to succeed, too, if he'll go about it in the right way."

"How ? " asked Katharine, eagerly, and immediately her face brightened again.

"Just as I said. If he'll show that he can stick to any sort of occupation for a year, I'll see what can be done."

"But that sticking, as you call it — all day at a desk — is just what he can't do. He wasn't made for it, he — "

"Well then, what is he made for ? I wish you would get him to make a statement explaining his peculiar gifts — "

"Now don't be angry again, uncle Robert! This is rather a serious matter for Jack and me. Do you tell me, in real earnest, quite, quite honestly, that as far as you know the only way for Jack to earn his living is to go into an office for a year, to begin with? Is that what you mean?"

"Yes, child. Upon my word — there, you'll believe me now, won't you? That's the only way I can see, if he really means to work. My dear — I'm not a boy, and I'm very fond of you — I've no reason for deceiving you, have I?"

"No, uncle dear — but you were angry at first, you know."

"No doubt. But I'm not angry now, nor are you. We've discussed the matter calmly. And we're putting out of the question the fact that if I chose to give Jack anything in the way of money, my cheque-book is in this drawer, and I have the power to do it — without any inconvenience," added the very rich man, thoughtfully. "But you tell me that he would not accept it. It's hard to believe, but you know him better than I do, and I accept your statement. I may as well tell you that for the honour of the family and to get rid of all this nonsense about a secret marriage I'm perfectly willing to do this. Listen. I'll invite you all — the whole family — to my place on the river, and I'll tell them all what has happened and we'll have a sort of 'post facto' wedding there, very quietly, and then announce it to the world. And I'll settle enough on you, personally — not on your husband — to give you an income you can manage to live on comfortably —"

"Oh!" cried Katharine. "You're too kind, uncle Robert — and I thank you with all my heart — just as though we could take it from you — I do, indeed —"

"Never mind that, child. But you say you can't take it. You mean, I suppose, that if it were your money —

if I made it so — Jack would refuse to live on it. Let's be quite clear."

"That's exactly it. He would never consent to live on it. He would feel — he'd be quite right, too — that we had got married first in order to force money out of you, for the honour of the family, as you said yourself."

"Yes. And it's particularly hard to force money out of me, too, though I'm not stingy, my dear. But I must say, if you had meant to do it, you couldn't have invented anything more ingenious, or more successful. I couldn't allow a couple of young Lauderdales to go begging. They'd have pictures of me in the evening papers, you know. And apart from that, I'm devilish fond of you — I mean I'm very fond of you — you must excuse an old bachelor's English, sometimes. But you won't take the money, so that settles it. Then there's no other way but for Jack to go to work like a man and stick to it. To give him a salary for doing no work would be just the same as to give him money without making any pretence about it. He can have a desk at my lawyer's, or he can go back to Beman Brothers', — just as he prefers. If he'll do that, and honestly try to understand what he's doing, he shan't regret it. If he'll do what there is to be done, I'll make him succeed. I could make him succeed if he had 'failure' written all over him in letters a foot high — because it's within the bounds of possibility. But it's of no use to ask me to do what's not possible. I can't make this country over again. I can't create a convenient, active, out-of-door career at a good salary, when the thing doesn't exist. In other words, I can't work miracles, and he won't take money, so he must content himself to run on lines of possibility. My lawyer would do most things for me, and so would Beman Brothers. Beman, to please me, would make Jack a partner, as he has done

for Ham Bright. But Jack must either work or put in
capital, and he has no capital to put in, and won't take
any from me. And to be a partner in a law firm, a man
must have some little experience — something beyond
his bare degree. Do you see it all now, Katharine?"

"Indeed, I do," she answered, with a little sigh.
"And meanwhile — uncle Robert — meanwhile — "

"Yes — I know — you're married. That's the very
devil, that marriage business."

He seemed to be thinking it over. There was something so innocently sincere in his strong way of putting
it that Katharine could not help smiling, even in her
distress. But she waited for him to speak, foreseeing
what he would say, and did.

"There's nothing for it," he said, at last. "You won't
take money, and you can't live with your mother, and as
for telling your father at this stage — well, you know him!
It really wouldn't be safe. So there's nothing for it but
— I hate to say it, my dear," he added kindly.

"But to keep it a secret, you mean," she said sadly.

"You see," he answered, in a tone that was almost
apologetic, "it would be a mistake, socially, to say you
were married, and to go on living each with your own
family — besides, your father would know it like everybody else. He'd make your life very — unbearable, I
should think."

"Yes — he would. I know that."

"Well — come and see me again soon, and we'll talk it
over. You'll have to consider it just as a — I don't know
exactly how to put it — a sort of formal betrothal between
yourselves, such as they used to have in old times. And
I suppose I'm the head of the family, though your grandfather is older than I am. Anyhow, you must consider
it as though you were solemnly engaged, with the ap-

proval of the head of the family, and as though you were
to be married, say, next year. Can you do that? Can
you make him look at it in that light, child?"

"I'll try, since there's really nothing else to be done.
But oh, uncle Robert, I wish I'd come before. You've
been so kind! Why did it rain yesterday — oh, why did
it rain?"

CHAPTER XVII.

WHEN Katharine left Robert Lauderdale's house that
morning, she felt that trouble had begun and was not to
cease for a long time. She had entered her uncle's library
full of hope, sure of success and believing that John
Ralston's future depended only upon the rich man's good
will and good word. She went out fully convinced at
last that he must take one or the other of the much-
despised chances he had neglected and forthwith do the
best he could with it. She thought it was very hard, but
she understood old Lauderdale's clear statement and she
saw that there was no other way.

She sympathized deeply with John in his dislike of
the daily drudgery, for which it was quite true that he
was little fitted by nature or training. But she did her
best to analyze that unfitness, so as to try and discover
some gift or quality to balance it and neutralize it. And
her first impulse was not to find him at once and tell him
what had happened, but rather to put off the evil moment
in which she must tell him the truth. This was the first
sign of weakness which she had exhibited since that
Monday afternoon on which she had first persuaded him
to take the decisive step.

She turned into Madison Avenue as soon as she could, for the sake of the quiet. The morning sun shone full in her eyes as she began to make her way southwards, and she was glad of the warmth, for she felt cold and inwardly chilled in mind and body. She had walked far, but she still walked on, disliking the thought of being penned in with a dozen or more of unsympathizing individuals for twenty minutes in a horse-car. Moreover, she instinctively wished to tire herself, as though to bring down her bodily energy to the low ebb at which her mental activity seemed to be stagnating. Strong people will understand that desire to balance mind and body.

She was quite convinced that her uncle was right. The more she turned the whole situation over, the clearer what he had said became to her. The only escape was to accept the money which he was willing to give her — for the honour of the family. But if neither she nor John would take that, there was no alternative but for John to go to work in the ordinary way, and show that he could be steady for at least a year. That seemed a very long time — as long as a year can seem to a girl of nineteen, which is saying much.

Katharine had seen such glorious visions for that year, too, that the darkness of the future was a tangible horror now that they were fading away. The memory of a dream can be as vivid as the recollection of a reality. The something which John was to find to do had presented itself to her mind as a sort of idyllic existence somewhere out of the world, in which there should be woods and brooks and breezes, and a convenient town not far away, where things could be got, and a cottage quite unlike other cottages, and a good deal of shooting and fishing and riding, with an amount of responsibility for all these things equal in money to six or seven thousand dollars a year, out of which Katharine was sure that she could save a small fortune in a few years. It had not been quite clear to her why the responsibility was to be worth so much in actual coin of the Republic, but people certainly succeeded very quickly in the West. Besides, she was quite ready to give up all the luxuries and amusements of social existence — much more ready to do so than John Ralston, if she had known the truth.

It must not be believed that she was utterly visionary and unpractical, because she had taken this rose-coloured view of the life uncle Robert was to provide for her and her husband. There are probably a great many young women in the Eastern cities who imagine just such things to be quite possible, and quite within the power and gift of a millionaire, in the American sense of that word, which implies the possession of more than one million, and more often refers in actual use to income than merely to capital. In Paris, a man who has twenty thousand dollars a year is called a millionaire. In New York a man with that income is but just beyond the level of the estimable society poor, and within the ranks of the 'fairly well-off.' The great fortunes being really as fabulous as those in fairy tales, it is not surprising that the possession of them should be supposed to bring with it an almost fabulous power in all directions. Men like Robert Lauderdale, the administration of whose estates requires a machinery not unlike that of a small nation's treasury, are thought to have in their gift all sorts of remunerative positions, for which the principal qualifications are an unlimited capacity for enjoying the fresh air and some talent for fishing. As a matter of fact, though so much richer than ordinary men, they are so much poorer than all except the very small nations that they cannot support so many idlers.

Katharine knew a good deal about life in New York and its possibilities, but very little of what could be done elsewhere. She was perfectly well aware of the truth of all that her uncle had told her concerning the requirements for business or the law, for she had heard such matters discussed often enough. In her own city she was practical, for she understood her surroundings as well as any young girl could. It was because she understood them that she dreamed of getting out of them as soon as practicable,. and of beginning that vaguely active and remunerative existence which, for her, lay west of Illinois and anywhere beyond that, even to the shores of the Pacific Ocean. John Ralston himself knew very little about it, but he had rightly judged its mythical nature when he had told her that Robert Lauderdale would do nothing for him.

The sun warmed Katharine as she walked down Madison Avenue, but everything was black — felt black, she would have said, had she thought aloud. Ralston would not turn upon her and say, 'I told you so,' because he loved her, but she could see the expression of his face as she looked forward to the interview. He would nod his head slowly and say nothing. The corners of his mouth would be drawn down for a moment and his eyelids would contract a little while he looked away from her. He would think the matter over during about half a minute, and then, with a look of determination, he would say that he would try what uncle Robert proposed. He would not say anything against the plan of keeping the marriage a secret, now that old Lauderdale knew of it, for he would see at once that there was absolutely nothing else to be done. They had gone over the possibilities so often — there was not one which they had not carefully considered. It was all so hopelessly against

them still, in spite of the one great effort Katharine had
made that morning.

She walked more slowly after she had passed the high
level above the railway, where it runs out of the city
under ground from the central station. As she came
nearer to the neighbourhood in which John lived, she
felt for the first time in her life that she did not
wish to meet him. Though she did not admit to herself
that she feared to tell him the result of her conversation
with her uncle, and though she had no intention of
going to his mother's house and asking for him, her
pace slackened at the mere idea of being nearer to him.

Then she realized what she was doing, and with a
bitter little smile of contempt at her own weakness she
walked on more briskly. She had often read in books of
that sudden change in the aspect of the outer world
which disappointment brings, but she had never quite
believed in it before. She realized it now. There was
no light in anything. The faces of the people who
passed her looked dead and uninteresting. Every house
looked as though a funeral procession might at any
moment file out of its door. The very pavement, dry-
ing in patches in the sunshine, felt cold and unsympa-
thetic under her feet.

She began to wonder what she had better do, —
whether she should write John Ralston a long letter,
explaining everything, or whether she should write him
a short one, merely saying that the news was unfavourable — 'unfavourable' sounded better than 'bad' or 'disappointing,' she thought — and asking him to come and
see her in the afternoon. The latter course seemed
preferable, and had, moreover, the advantage of involving
fewer practical difficulties, for her command over her
mother tongue was by no means very great when sub-

jected to the test of black and white, though in conversation it was quite equal to her requirements on most
occasions. She could even entirely avoid the use of
slang, by making a determined effort, for her father
detested it, and her mother's conversational weaknesses
were Southern and of a different type. But on paper
she was never sure of being quite right. Punctuation
was a department which she affected to despise, but
which she inwardly feared, and when alone she admitted
that there were words which she seemed to spell not as
they were spelled in books — 'parallel,' for instance,
'psychology' and 'responsibility.' She avoided these
words, which were not very necessary to her, but with a
disagreeable suspicion that there might be others. Had
'develop' an 'e' at the end of it, or had it not? She
could never remember, and the dictionary lived in her
grandfather's den, at some distance from her own room.
The difficulties of writing a long letter to John Ralston,
whose mother had taught him his English before it
could be taught him all wrong at a fashionable school,
rose before her eyes with absurd force, and she decided
forthwith to send for Ralston in the afternoon.

Having come to a preliminary conclusion, life seemed
momentarily a little easier. She turned out of her way
into Fourth Avenue, took a horse-car, got transferred to
a Christopher Street one, and in the course of time got
out at the corner of Clinton Place. She wrote the shortest possible note to John Ralston, went out again, bought
a special delivery stamp and took the letter up to the
Thirteenth Street Post-Office — instead of dropping it
into an ordinary letter-box. She did everything, in short,
to make the message reach its destination as quickly as
possible without employing a messenger.

Charlotte Slayback appeared at luncheon. She pre-

ferred that meal when she invited herself, because her
father was never present, and a certain amount of peaceful conversation was possible in his absence. It was
some time since she had been in New York, and the
glimpse of her old room on the previous afternoon irresistibly attracted her again. Katharine hoped, however,
that she would not stay long, as Ralston was to come at
three o'clock, this being usually the safest hour for his
visits. Mrs. Lauderdale would then be either at work
or out of the house, the philanthropist would be dozing
upstairs in a cloud of smoke before a table covered with
reports, and Alexander Junior would be still down town.
In consideration of the importance of getting Charlotte
out of the way, Katharine was more than usually cordial
to her — a mistake often made by young people, who do
not seem to understand the very simple fact that the best
way to make people go away is generally to be as disagreeable as possible.

The consequence was that Charlotte enjoyed herself
immensely, and it required the sight of her father's
photograph, which stood upon Mrs. Lauderdale's writing-
table in the library, to keep her from proposing to spend
two or three days in the house after her husband should
have gone back to Washington. But the photograph was
there, and it was one taken by the platinum process,
which made the handsome, steely face look more metallic
than ever. Charlotte gazed at it thoughtfully, and could
almost hear the maxims of virtue and economy with
which those even lips had preached her down since she
had been a child, and she decided that she would not stay.
Her husband was not to her taste, but he never preached.

Mrs. Lauderdale had for her eldest daughter that
sentiment which is generally described as a mother's love,
and which, as Frank Miner had once rather coarsely put

it, will stand more knocking about than old boots. Charlotte was spoiled, capricious, frivolous in the extreme, ungrateful beyond description, weak where she should have been strong and strong where she should have been tender. And Mrs. Lauderdale knew it all, and loved her in spite of it all, though she disapproved of her almost at every point. Charlotte had one of those characters of which people are apt to say that they might have turned out splendidly, if properly trained, than which no more foolish expression falls from the lips of commonplace, virtuous humanity. Charlotte, like many women who resemble her, had received an excellent training. The proof was that, when she chose to behave herself, no one could seem to be more docile, more thoughtful and considerate of others or more charming in conversation. She had only to wish to appear well, as the phrase goes, and the minutest details necessary to success were absolutely under her control. What people meant when they said that she might have turned out splendidly — though they did not at all understand the fact — was that a woman possessing Charlotte Slayback's natural gifts and acquired accomplishments might have been a different person if she had been born with a very different character — a statement quite startling in its great simplicity. As it was, there was nothing to be done. Charlotte had been admirably 'trained' in every way — so well that she could exhibit the finest qualities, on occasion, without any perceptible effort, even when she felt the utmost reluctance to do so. But the occasions were few, and were determined by questions of personal advantage, and even more often by mere caprice.

On that particular day, when she lunched quietly in her old home, her conduct was little short of angelic, and Katharine found it hard to realize that she was the same woman who on the previous afternoon had made such an exhibition of contemptible pettiness and unreasoning discontent. Katharine, had she known her sister less well, would almost have been inclined to believe that Benjamin Slayback of Nevada was a person with whom no wife of ordinary sensibility would possibly live. But she knew Charlotte very well indeed.

And as the hands of the clock went round towards three, Charlotte showed no intention of going away, to Katharine's infinite annoyance, for she knew that Ralston would be punctual, and would probably come even a little before the time she had named. It would not do to let him walk into the library, after the late scene between him and her mother. The latter had said nothing more about the matter, but only one day had intervened since Mrs. Lauderdale had so unexpectedly expressed her total disapproval of Katharine's relations with John. It was not probable that Mrs. Lauderdale, who was not a changeable woman, would go back to her original position in the course of a few hours, and there would certainly be trouble if John appeared with no particular excuse.

Katharine, as may be imagined, was by no means in a normal mood, and if she made herself agreeable to her sister, it was not at first without a certain effort, which did not decrease, in spite of Charlotte's own exceptionally good temper, because as the latter grew more and more amiable, she also seemed more and more inclined to spend the whole afternoon where she was.

Hints about going out, about going upstairs to the room in which Mrs. Lauderdale painted, about possible visitors, had no effect whatever. Charlotte was enjoying herself and her mother was delighted to keep her and listen to her conversation. Katharine thought at

last that she should be reduced to the necessity of waiting in the entry until Ralston came, in order to send him
away again before he could get into the library by mistake. She hated the plan, which certainly lacked dignity,
and she watched the hands of the clock, growing nervous
and absent in what she said, as she saw that the fatal
hour was approaching.

At twenty minutes to three Charlotte was describing
to her mother the gown worn by the English ambassa-
dress at the last official dinner at the White House. At
a quarter to three she was giving an amusing account of
the last filibustering affray in the House, which she had
witnessed — it having been arranged beforehand to take
place at a given point in the proceedings — from the
gallery reserved for members' families. Five minutes
later she was telling anecdotes about a deputation from
the South Sea Islands. Katharine could hardly sit still
as she watched the inexorable hands. At five minutes to
three Charlotte struck the subject of painting, and Katharine felt that it was all over. Suddenly Charlotte herself
glanced at the clock and sprang up.

"I had forgotten all about poor little Crowdie!" she
exclaimed. "He was coming at three to take me to the
Loan Exhibition," she added, looking about her for her
hat and gloves.

"Here?" asked Katharine, aghast.

"Oh, no — at the hotel, of course. I must run as fast
as I can. There are still cabs at the Brevoort House
corner, aren't there? Thank you, my dear —" Katharine had found all her things and was already tying on
the little veil. "I do hope he'll wait."

"Of course he will!" answered Katharine, with amazing certainty. "You're all right, dear — now run!" she
added, pushing her sister towards the door.

"Do come to dinner, Charlie!" cried Mrs. Lauderdale, following her. "It's so nice to see something of you!"

"Oh, yes — she'll come — but you mustn't keep her, mamma — she's awfully late as it is!"

From a condition of apparently hopeless apathy, Katharine was suddenly roused to exert all her energies. It was two minutes to three as she closed the glass door behind her sister. Fortunately Ralston had not come before his time.

"I suppose you're going to work now, mamma?" Katharine suggested, doing her best to speak calmly, as she turned to her mother, who was standing in the door of the library.

She had never before wished that Ralston were an unpunctual man, nor that her mother, to whom she was devotedly attached, were at the bottom of the sea.

"Oh, yes! I suppose so," answered Mrs. Lauderdale. "How delightful Charlotte was to-day, wasn't she?"

Her face was fresh and rested. She leaned against the doorpost as though deciding whether to go upstairs at once or to go back into the library. With a movement natural to her she raised her graceful arms, folding her hands together behind her head, and leaning back against the woodwork, looking lazily at Katharine as she did so. She felt that small difficulty, at the moment, of going back to the daily occupation after spending an exceptionally pleasant hour in some one's company, which is familiar to all hard workers. Katharine stood still, trying to hide her anxiety. The clock must be just going to strike, she thought.

"What's the matter, child? You seem nervous and worried about something." She asked the question with a certain curiosity.

"Do I?" asked Katharine, trying to affect indifference.

Mrs. Lauderdale did not move. In the half light of
the doorway she was still very beautiful, as she stood
there trying to make up her mind to go to her work.
Katharine was in despair, and turned over the cards
that lay in a deep dish on the table, reading the names
mechanically.

"Yes," continued her mother. "You look as though
you were expecting something — or somebody."

The clock struck, and almost at the same instant
Katharine heard Ralston's quick, light tread on the stone
steps outside the house. She had a sudden inspiration.

"There's a visitor coming, mother!" she whispered
quickly. "Run away, and I'll tell Annie not to let
him in."

Mrs. Lauderdale, fortunately, did not care to receive
any one, but instead of going upstairs she merely nodded,
just as the bell rang, and retired into the library again,
shutting the door behind her. Katharine was left alone
in the entry, and she could see the dark, indistinct shape
of John Ralston through the ground-glass pane of the
front door. She hesitated an instant, doubting whether
it would not be wisest to open the door herself, send him
away, and then, slipping on her things, to follow him a
moment later into the street. But in the same instant
she reflected that her mother had very possibly gone to
the window to see who the visitor had been when he
should descend the steps again. Most women do that in
houses where it is possible. Then, too, her mother would
expect to hear Annie's footsteps passing the library, as
the girl went to the front door.

There was the dining-room, and it could be reached
from the entry by passing through the pantry. Annie
was devoted to Katharine, and at a whispered word
would lead Ralston silently thither. The closed room

between the dining-room and the library would effectually cut off the sound of voices. But that, too, struck Katharine as being beneath her — to confide in a servant! She could not do it, and was further justified by the reflection that even if she followed that course, her mother, who was doubtless at the window, would not see Ralston go away, and would naturally conclude that the visitor had remained in the house, whoever he might be.

Katharine stood irresolute, watching Ralston's shadow on the pane, and listening to Annie's rapidly approaching tread from the regions of the pantry at the end of the entry. A moment later and the girl was by her side.

" If it's Mr. Ralston, don't shut the door again till I've spoken to him," she said, in a low voice. " My mother isn't receiving, if it's a visitor."

She stood behind Annie as the latter opened the door. John was there, as she had expected, and Annie stepped back. Katharine raised her finger to her lips, warning him not to speak. He looked surprised, but stood bareheaded on the threshold.

" You must go away at once, Jack," she whispered. " My mother is in the library, looking out of the window, and I can't possibly see you alone. Wait for me near the door at the Assembly to-night. Go, dear — it's impossible now. I'll tell you afterwards."

In her anxiety not to rouse her mother's suspicions, she shut the door almost before he had nodded his assent. She scarcely saw the blank look that came into his face, and the utter disappointment in his eyes.

Seeing that the door was shut, Annie turned and went away. Katharine hesitated a moment, passed her hand over her brow, glanced mechanically once more at the cards in the china dish on the table and then went into the library. To her surprise her mother was not there, but the folding door which led to the dark drawing-room was half rolled back, and it was clear that Mrs. Lauderdale had gone through the dining-room, and had probably reached her own apartment by the back staircase of the house. Katharine was on the point of running into the street and calling Ralston back. She hesitated a moment, and then going hastily to the window threw up the sash and looked out, hoping that he might be still within hearing. But looking eastward, towards Fifth Avenue, he was not to be seen amongst the moving pedestrians, of whom there were many just then. She turned to see whether he had taken the other direction, and saw him at once, but already far down the street, walking fast, with his head bent low and his hands in the pockets of his overcoat. He was evidently going to take the elevated road up town.

"Oh, Jack — I'm so sorry!" she exclaimed softly to herself, still looking after him as he disappeared in the distance.

Then she drew down the window again, and went and sat in her accustomed place in the small armchair opposite to her mother's sofa. She thought very uncharitably of Charlotte during the next quarter of an hour, but she promised herself to get into a corner with Ralston that evening, at the great ball, and to explain all the circumstances to him as minutely as they have been explained here. She was angry with her mother, too, for not having gone up the front staircase, as she might just as well have done, but she was very glad she had not condescended to the manœuvre of introducing John into the dining-room by the back way, as she would have probably just met Mrs. Lauderdale as the latter passed through. On the whole, it seemed to Katharine that she had done as wisely as the peculiarly difficult circumstances had allowed, and that although there was much to regret, she had done nothing of which she needed to repent.

It seemed to her, too, as she began to recover from the immediate annoyance of failure, that she had gained several hours more than she had expected, in which to think over what she should say to Ralston when they met. And she at once set herself the task of recalling everything that Robert Lauderdale had said to her, with the intention of repeating it as accurately as possible, since she could not expect to say it any better than he had said it himself. It was necessary that Ralston should understand it, as she had understood it, and should see that although uncle Robert was quite ready to be generous he could not undertake to perform miracles. Those had been the old gentleman's own words.

Then she began to wonder whether, after all, it would not be better to accept what he offered — the small, settled income which was so good to think of — and to get rid of all this secrecy, which oppressed her much more since she had been told that it must last, than when she had expected that it would involve at most the delay of a week. The deep depression which she began to feel at her heart, now that she was alone again, made the simple means of escape from all her anxieties look very tempting to her, and she dwelt on it. If she begged Ralston to forget his pride for her sake, as she was willing to forget her own for his, and to let her take the money, he would surely yield. Once together, openly married before the world, things would be so much easier. He and she could talk all day, unhindered and unobserved, and plan the future at their leisure, and it was not possible that with all the joint intelligence they could bring to bear upon the problem, it should still remain unsolved.

Meanwhile, Ralston had gone up town, very much **more** disappointed than Katharine knew. Strange to say, their marriage seemed far more important in his eyes than in hers, and he had lived all day, since they had parted at ten o'clock in the morning, in nervous anticipation of seeing her again before night. He had gone home at once, and had spent the hours alone, for his mother had gone out to luncheon. Until the messenger with Katharine's specially stamped letter rang at the door, he would not have gone out of the house for any consideration, and after he had read it he sat counting the minutes until he could reasonably expect to use up the remaining time in walking to Clinton Place. As it was, he had reached the corner a quarter of an hour before the time, and his extreme punctuality was to be accounted for by the fact that he had set his watch with the Lauderdales' library clock, — as he always did nowadays, — and that he looked at it every thirty seconds, as he walked up and down the street, timing himself so exactly that the hands were precisely at the hour of three when he took hold of the bell.

There are few small disappointments in the world comparable with that of a man who has been told by the woman he loves to come at a certain hour, who appears at her door with military punctuality and who is told to go away again instantly, no adequate excuse being given for the summary dismissal. Men all know that, but few women realize it.

"Considering the rather unusual situation," thought Ralston, angrily, " she might have managed to get her mother out of the way for half an hour. Besides, her mother wouldn't have stoned me to death, if she had let me come in — and, after last night, I shouldn't think she would care very much for the sort of privacy one has in a ball-room."

He had waited all day to see her, and he had nothing to do until the evening, when he had to go to a dinner-party before the Assembly ball. He naturally thought of his club, as a quiet place where he could be alone with his annoyances and disappointments between three and four o'clock, and he took the elevated road as the shortest way of getting there.

CHAPTER XVIII.

RALSTON was in a thoroughly bad humour when he reached his club. The absurdity of a marriage, which was practically no marriage at all, had been thrust upon him on the very first day, and he felt that he had been led into a romantic piece of folly, which could not possibly produce any good results, either at the present time or afterwards. He was as properly and legally the husband of Katharine as the law and the church could make him, and yet he could not even get an interview of a quarter of an hour with his wife. He could not count, with certainty, upon seeing her anywhere, except at such a public place as the ball they were both going to that night, under the eyes of all New York society, so far as it existed for them. The position was ludicrous, or would have been, had he not been the principal actor in the comedy.

He was sure, too, that if Katharine had got any favourable answer from their uncle Robert, she would have said at least a word to this effect, even while she was in the act of thrusting him from the door. Two words, 'all right,' would have been enough. But she only seemed anxious to get rid of him as quickly as possible, and he felt that he was not to be blamed for being angry. The details of the situation, as she had seen it, were quite unknown to him. He was not aware that Charlotte Slayback had been at luncheon, and had stayed until the last minute, nor that Katharine had really done everything in her power to make her mother go upstairs. The details, indeed, taken separately, were laughable in their insignificance, and it would hardly be possible for Katharine to explain them to him, so as to make him see their importance when taken all together. He was ignorant of them all, except of the fancied fact that Mrs. Lauderdale had been at the window of the library. Katharine had told him so, and had believed it herself, as was natural. She had not had time to explain why she believed it, and he would be more angry than ever if she ever told him that she had been mistaken, and that he might just as well have come and stayed as long as he pleased. He knew that a considerable time must have elapsed between the end of luncheon and his arrival at the door of the house; he supposed that Katharine had been alone with her mother and grandfather, as usual, and he blamed her for not exerting a little tact in getting her mother out of the way, when she must have had nearly an hour in which to do so. He went over and over all that he knew of the facts, and reached always the same conclusion — Katharine had not taken the trouble, and had probably only remembered when it was too late that he was to come at three o'clock.

It must not be supposed that Ralston belonged to the class of hasty and capricious men, who hate the object of their affections as soon as they are in the least annoyed with anything she has done — or who, at all events, act as though they did. Ralston was merely in an excessively bad temper with himself, with everything he had done and with the world at large. Had he received a note from Katharine at any time later in the afternoon, telling him to come back, he would have gone instantly, with just as much impatience as he had shown at three o'clock, when he had reached Clinton Place a quarter of an hour before the appointed time. He would probably not have alluded, nor even have wished to allude, to his summary dismissal at his first attempt. But he would come. He satisfied himself of that, for he sent a message from his club to his home, directing the servant to send on any note which might come for him; and, on repeating the message an hour later, he was told that there was nothing to send.

So he sat in the general room at the club, downstairs, and turned over a newspaper half a dozen times without understanding a word of its contents, and smoked discontentedly, but without ceasing. At last, by a mere accident, his eye fell upon the column of situations offered and wanted, and, with a sour smile, he began to read the advertisements. That sort of thing suited his case, at all events, he thought. He was very soon struck by the balance of numbers in favour of the unemployed, and by the severe manner in which those who offered situations spoke of thorough knowledge and of certificates of service.

It did not take him long to convince himself that he was fit for nothing but a shoeblack or a messenger boy, and he fancied that his age would be a drawback in either profession. He dropped the paper in disgust at last, and was suddenly aware that Frank Miner was seated at a small table opposite to him, but on the other side of the room. Miner looked up at the same moment, from a letter he was writing, his attention being attracted by the rustling of the paper.

"Hallo, Jack!" he cried, cheerily. "I knew those were your legs all the time."

"Why didn't you speak, then?" asked Ralston, rather coldly, and looking up and down the columns of the paper he had dropped upon his knee.

"I don't know. Why should I?" Miner went on with his letter, having evidently interrupted himself in the midst of a sentence.

Ralston wished something would happen. He felt suddenly inclined to throw something at Miner, who generally amused him when he talked, but was clearly very busy, and went on writing as though his cheerful little life depended on it. But it was not probable that anything should happen just at that hour. There were three or four other men in different parts of the big room, writing or reading letters. There were doubtless a few others somewhere in the house, playing cards or drinking a quiet afternoon cocktail. It was a big club, having many rooms. But Ralston did not feel inclined to play poker, and he wished not to drink, if he could help it, and Miner went on writing, so he stayed where he was, and brooded over his annoyances. Suddenly Miner's pen ceased with a scratch and a dash, audible all over the room, and he began to fold his letter

"Come and have a drink, Jack!" he called out to Ralston, as he took up an envelope. "I've earned it, if you haven't."

"I don't want to drink," answered Ralston, gloomily, and, out of pure contrariety, he took up his paper again.

Miner looked long and steadily at him, closed his letter, put it into his pocket and crossed the room.

"I say, Jack," he said, in an absurdly solemn tone, "are you ill, old man?"

"Ill? No. Why? Never was better in my life.

Don't be an idiot, Frank." And he kept his paper at the level of his eyes.

"There's something wrong, anyhow," said Miner, thoughtfully. "Never knew you to refuse to drink before. I'll be damned, you know!"

"I haven't a doubt of it, my dear fellow. I always told you so."

"For a gentle and unassuming manner, I think you take the cake, Jack," answered Miner, without a smile. "What on earth is the matter with you? Let me see — you've either lost money, or you're in love, or your liver's out of order, or all three, and if that's it, I pity you."

"I tell you there's nothing the matter with me!" cried Ralston, with some temper. "Why do you keep bothering me? I merely said I didn't want to drink. Can't a man not be thirsty? Confound it all, I'm not obliged to drink if I don't want to!"

"Oh, well, don't get into a fiery green rage about it, Jack. I'm thirsty myself, and I didn't want to drink alone. Only, don't go west of Maine so long as this lasts. They're prohibition there, you know. Don't try it, Jack; you'd come back on ice by the next train."

"I'm going to stay here," answered Ralston, without a smile. "Go ahead and get your drink."

"All right! If you won't, you won't, I know. But when you're scratching round and trying to get some sympathetic person, like Abraham and Lazarus, to give you a glass of water, think of what you've missed this afternoon!"

"Dives," said Ralston, savagely, "is the only man ever mentioned in the Bible as having asked for a glass of water, and he's — where he ought to be."

"That's an old, cold chestnut," retorted Miner, turning to go, but not really in the least annoyed.

At that moment a servant crossed the room and stood before Ralston. Miner waited to see what would happen, half believing that Ralston was not in earnest, but had surreptitiously touched the electric bell on the table at his elbow, with the intention of ordering something.

"Mr. Lauderdale wishes to speak to you at the telephone, sir," said the servant.

The man's expression betrayed his respect for the name, and for a person who had a telephone in his house — an unusual thing in New York. It was the sort of expression which the waiters at restaurants put on when they present to the diner a dish of terrapin or a canvas-back duck, or open a very particularly old bottle of very particularly fine wine — quite different from the stolid look they wear for beef and table-claret.

"Which Mr. Lauderdale?" asked Ralston, with a sudden frown. "Mr. Alexander Lauderdale Junior?"

"I don't know, sir. The gentleman's at the telephone, sir."

This seemed to be added as a gentle hint not to keep any one of the name of Lauderdale waiting too long.

Ralston rose quickly, and Miner watched him as he passed out with long strides and a rather anxious face, wondering what could be the matter with his friend, and somehow connecting his refusal to drink with the summons to the instrument. Then Miner followed slowly in the same direction, with his hands in his pockets and his lips pursed as though he were about to whistle. He knew the man well enough to be aware that his refusal to drink might proceed from his having taken all he could stand for the present, and Ralston's ill temper inclined Miner to believe that this might be the case. Ralston rarely betrayed himself at all, until he suddenly became viciously unmanageable, a fact which made him always the function of a doubtful quantity, as Miner, who had once learned a little mathematics, was fond of expressing it.

The little man was essentially sociable, and though he might want the very small and mild drink he was fond of ever so much, he preferred, if possible, to swallow it in company. Instead of ringing, therefore, he strolled away in search of another friend. As luck would have it, he almost ran against Walter Crowdie, who was coming towards him, but looking after Ralston, as the latter disappeared at the · other end of the hall. Crowdie seemed excessively irritated about something.

" Confound that fellow ! " he exclaimed, giving vent to his feelings as he turned and saw Miner close upon him.

" Who ?   Me ? " enquired the little man, with a laugh. " Everybody's purple with rage in this club to-day — I'm going home."

" You ? No — is that you, Frank ? No — I mean that everlasting Ralston."

" Oh! What's he done to you ? What's the matter with Ralston ? "

" Drunk again, I suppose," answered Crowdie. " But I wish he'd keep out of my way when he is — runs into me, treads on both my feet — with his heels, I believe, though I don't understand how that's possible — pushes me out of the way and goes straight on without a word. Confound him, I say ! You used to be able to swear beautifully, Frank — can't you manage to say something ? "

" At any other time — oh, yes ! But you'd better get Ralston himself to do it for you. I'm not in it with him to-day. He's been giving me the life to come — hot — and Abraham and Isaac and Lazarus and the rich man, and the glass of water, all in a breath. Go and ask him for what you want."

"Oh — then he is drunk, is he?" asked Crowdie, with a disagreeable sneer on his red lips.

"I suppose so," answered Miner, quite carelessly. "At all events, he refused to drink — that's always a bad sign with him."

"Of course — that makes it a certainty. Gad, though! It doesn't make him light on his feet, if he happens to tread on yours. It serves me right for coming to the club at this time of day! Perdition on the fellow! I've got on new shoes, too!"

"What are you two squabbling about?" enquired Hamilton Bright, coming suddenly upon them out of the cloak-room.

"We're not squabbling — we're cursing Ralston," answered Miner.

"I wish you'd go and look after him, Ham," said Crowdie to his brother-in-law. "He's just gone off there. He's as drunk as the dickens, and swearing against everybody and treading on their toes in the most insolent way imaginable. Get him out of this, can't you? Take him home — you're his friend. If you don't he'll be smashing things before long."

"Is he as bad as that, Frank?" asked Bright, gravely. "Where is he?"

"At the telephone — I don't know — he trod on Crowdie's feet and Crowdie's perfectly wild and exaggerates. But there's something wrong, I know. I think he's not exactly screwed — but he's screwed up — well, several pegs, by the way he acts. They call drinks 'pegs' somewhere, don't they? I wanted to make a joke. I thought it might do Crowdie good —"

"Well, it's a very bad one," said Bright. "He's at the telephone, you say?"

"Yes. The man said Mr. Lauderdale wanted to speak

to him — he didn't know which Mr. Lauderdale — but
it's probably Alexander the Safe, and if it is, there's
going to be a row over the wires. When Jack's shut up
there alone in the dark in the sound-proof box with
the receiver under his nose and Alexander at the other
end — if the wires don't melt — that's all! And Alexander's a metallic sort of man — I should think he'd
draw the lightning right down to his toes."

At that moment Ralston came swinging down the hall
at a great pace, pale and evidently under some sort of
powerful excitement. He nodded carelessly to the three
men as they stood together and disappeared into the
cloak-room. Bright followed him, but Ralston, with his
hat on, his head down and struggling into his overcoat,
rushed out as Bright reached the door, and ran into the
latter, precisely as he had run into Crowdie. Bright
was by far the heavier man, however, and Ralston
stumbled at the shock. Bright caught him by one
arm and held him a moment.

"All right, Ham!" he exclaimed. "Everybody gets
into my way to-day. Let go, man! I'm in a hurry!"

"Wait a bit," said Bright. "I'll come with you — "

"No — you can't. Let me go, Ham! What the deuce
are you holding me for?"

He shook Bright's arm angrily, for between the message
he had received and the obstacles he seemed to meet at
every step, he was, by this time, very much excited.
Bright thought he read certain well-known signs in his
face, and believed that he had been drinking hard and
might get into trouble if he went out alone, for Ralston
was extremely quarrelsome at such times, and was quite
capable of hitting out on the slightest provocation, and
had been in trouble more than once for doing so, as
Bright was well aware.

"I'm going with you, Jack, whether you like it or not," said the latter, with mistaken firmness in his good intentions.

"You're not, I can tell you!" answered Ralston, in a lower tone. "Just let me go — or there'll be trouble here."

He was furious at the delay, but Bright's powerful hand did not relax its grasp on his arm.

"Jack, old man," said Bright, in a coaxing tone, "just come upstairs for a quarter of an hour, and get quiet —"

"Oh — that's it, is it? You think I'm screwed. I'm not. Let me go — once — twice —"

Ralston's face was now white with anger. The unjust accusation was the last drop. He was growing dangerous, but Bright, in the pride of his superior strength, still held him firmly.

"Take care!" said Ralston, almost in a whisper. "I've counted two." He paused a full two seconds. "Three! There you go!"

The other men saw his foot glide forward like lightning over the marble pavement. Instantly Bright was thrown heavily on his back, and before he could even raise his head, Ralston was out of the door and in the street. Crowdie and Miner ran forward to help the fallen man, as they had not moved from where they had stood, a dozen paces away. But Bright was on his feet in an instant, pale with anger and with the severe shock of his fall. He turned his back on his companions at once, pretending to brush the dust from his coat by the bright light which fell through the glass door. Frank Miner stood near him, very quiet, his hands in his pockets, as usual, and a puzzled look in his face.

"Look here, Bright," he said gravely, watching Bright's back. "This sort of thing can't go on, you know."

Bright said nothing, but continued to dust himself, though there was not the least mark on his clothes.

"Upon my word," observed Crowdie, walking slowly up and down in his ungraceful way, "I think we'd better call a meeting at once and have him requested to take his name off. If that isn't conduct unbecoming a gentleman, I don't know what is."

"No," said Miner. "That wouldn't do. It would stick to him for life. All the same, Bright, this is a club — it isn't a circus — and this sort of horse-play is just a little too much. Why don't you turn round? There's no dust on you — they keep the floor of the arena swept on purpose when Ralston's about. But it's got to stop — it's got to stop right here."

Bright's big shoulders squared themselves all at once and he faced about, apparently quite cool again.

"I say," he began, "did anybody see that but you two?" He looked up and down the deserted hall.

"No — wait a bit, though — halloa ! Where are the hall servants ? There ought to be two of them. They must have just gone off. There they are, on the other side of the staircase. Robert! And you — whatever your name is — come here!"

The two servants came forward at once. They had retired to show their discretion and at the same time to observe what happened, the moment they had seen Bright catch Ralston's arm.

"Look here," said Bright to them. "If you say anything about what you saw just now, you'll have to go. Do you understand ? As we shan't speak of it, we shall know that you have, if it's talked about. That's all right — you can go now. I just wanted you to understand."

The two servants bowed gravely. They respected Bright, and, like all servants, they worshipped Ralston.

There was little fear of their indiscretion. Bright turned to Crowdie and Miner.

"If anybody has anything to say about this, I have," he said. "I'm the injured person if any one is. And of course I shall say nothing, and I'll beg you to say nothing either. Of course, if he ever falls foul of you, you're free to do as you please, and of course you might, if you chose, bring this thing before the committee. But I know you won't speak of it — either of you. We've all been screwed once or twice in our lives, I suppose. As for me, I'm his friend, and he didn't know what he was doing. He's a deuced good fellow at heart, but he's infernally hasty when he's had too much. That's all right, isn't it? I can trust you, can't I?"

"Oh, yes, as far as I'm concerned," said Crowdie, speaking first. "If you like that sort of thing, I've nothing to say. You're quite big enough to take care of yourself. I hope Hester won't hear it. She wouldn't like the idea of her brother being knocked about without defending himself. I don't particularly like it myself."

"That's nonsense, Walter, and you know it is," answered Bright, curtly, and he turned to Miner with a look of enquiry.

"All right, Ham!" said the little man. "I'm not going to tell tales, if you aren't. All the same — I don't want to seem squeamish, and old-maidish, and a frump generally — but I don't think I do remember just such a thing happening in any club I ever belonged to. Oh, well! Don't let's stand here talking ourselves black in the face. He's gone, this time, and he'll never find his way back if he once gets round the corner. You'll hear to-morrow that he's been polishing Tiffany's best window with a policeman. That's about his pressure when he gets a regular jag on. As for me, I've been trying to get somebody to have a drink with me for just three quarters of an hour, and so far my invitations have come back unopened. I suppose you won't refuse a pilot's two fingers after the battle, Ham?"

"What's a pilot's two fingers?" asked Bright. "I'll accept your hospitality to that modest extent, anyhow. Show us."

"It's this," said Miner, holding up his hand with the forefinger and little finger extended and the others turned in. "The little finger is the bottom," he explained, "and you don't count the others till you get to the forefinger, and just a little above the top of that you can see the whiskey. Understand? What will you have, Crowdie?"

"A drop of maraschino, thanks," said the painter.

"Maraschino!" Miner made a wry face at the thought of the sugary stuff. "All right then, come in!"

They all went back together into the room in which Ralston and Miner had been sitting before the trouble began. Crowdie and his brother-in-law were not on very good terms. The former behaved well enough when they met, but Bright's dislike for him was not to be concealed — which was strange, considering that Bright was a sensible and particularly self-possessed man, who was generally said to be of a gentle disposition, inclined to live harmoniously with his surroundings. He soon went away, leaving the artist and the man of letters to themselves. Miner did not like Crowdie very much either, but he admired him as an artist and had the faculty of making him talk.

If Ralston had really been drinking, he could not have been in a more excited state than when he left the club, leaving his best friend stretched on his back in the hall. He was half conscious of having done something which

would be considered wholly outrageous among his asso-
ciates, and among gentlemen at large. The fact that
Bright was his distant cousin was hardly an excuse for
tripping him up even in jest, and if the matter were to
be taken in earnest, Bright's superior strength would not
excuse Ralston for using his own far superior skill and
quickness, in the most brutal way, and on rather slender
provocation. No one but he himself, however, even knew
that he had been making a great effort to cure himself of
a bad habit, and that although it was now Thursday, he
had taken nothing stronger than a little weak wine and
water and an occasional cup of coffee since Monday afternoon. Bright could therefore have no idea of the extent
to which his accusation had wounded and exasperated the
sensitive man — rendered ten times more sensitive than
usual by his unwonted abstention.

Ralston, however, did not enter into any such elaborate
consideration of the matter as he hurried along, too much
excited just then to stop and look for a cab. He was still
whole-heartedly angry with Bright, and was glad that he
had thrown him, be the consequences what they might.
If Bright would apologize for having laid rough hands
on him, Ralston would do as much — not otherwise. If
the thing were mentioned, he would leave the club and
frequent another to which he belonged. Nothing could
be simpler.

But he had received a much more violent impression
than he fancied, and he forgot many things — forgetting
even for a moment where he was going. Passing an up-
town hotel on his way, he entered the bar by sheer force
of habit — the habit of drinking something whenever his
nerves were not quite steady. He ordered some whiskey,
still thinking of Bright, and it was not until he had
swallowed half of it that he realized what he was doing.

With a half-suppressed oath he set down the liquor un-
finished, dropped his money on the metal table and went
out, more angry than ever.

Realizing that he was not exactly in a condition to
talk quietly to any one, he turned into a side street, lit a
strong cigar and walked more slowly for a few minutes,
trying to collect his thoughts, and at last succeeding to a
certain extent, aided perhaps by the tonic effect of the
spoonful of alcohol he had swallowed.

The whole thing had begun in a very simple way — the
gradual increase of tension from the early morning until
towards evening had been produced by small incidents
following upon the hasty marriage ceremony, which, as
has been said, had produced a far deeper impression upon
him than upon Katharine herself. The endless hours of
waiting, the solitary luncheon, the waiting again, Katharine's summary dismissal of him, almost without a word
of explanation — then more waiting, and Miner's tiresome questions, and the sudden call to the telephone,
and stumbling against Crowdie — and all the rest of it.
Small things, all of them, after the marriage itself, but
able to produce at least a fit of extremely bad temper by
their cumulative action upon such a character. Ralston
was undoubtedly a dangerous man to exasperate at five
o'clock on that Thursday afternoon.

He had been summoned by Robert Lauderdale himself,
and this had contributed not a little to the haste which
had brought him into collision with Bright. The old
gentleman had asked him to come up to his house at
once; John·had said that he would come immediately,
but on asking a further question he found the communi-
cation closed.

It immediately struck him that Katharine had not
found uncle Robert at home in the morning, that she

had very possibly gone to him again in the afternoon, and that they were perhaps together at that very moment, and had agreed to send for Ralston in order to talk matters over. It was natural enough, considering his strong desire to see Katharine before the ball, and his anxiety to hear Robert Lauderdale's definite answer, upon which depended everything in the immediate present and future, that he should not have cared to waste time in exchanging civilities in the hall of the club with Bright, whom he saw almost every day, or with Crowdie, whom he detested. The rest has been explained.

Nor was it at all unnatural that the three men should all have been simultaneously deceived into believing that he had been drinking more than was good for him. A man who is known to drink habitually can hardly get credit for being sober when he is perfectly quiet — never, when he is in the least excited. Ralston had been more than excited. He had been violent. He had disgraced himself and the club by a piece of outrageous brutality. If any one but Bright had suffered by it, there would have been a meeting of the committee within twenty-four hours, and John Ralston's name would have disappeared from the list of members forever. It was fortunate for him that Bright chanced to be his best friend.

Ralston scarcely realized how strongly the man was attached to him. Embittered as he was by being constantly regarded as the failure of the family, he could hardly believe that any one but his mother and Katharine cared what became of him. A young man who has wasted three or four years in fruitless, if not very terrible, dissipation, whose nerves are a trifle affected by habits as yet by no means incurable, and who has had the word 'failure' daily branded upon him by his discriminating relatives, easily believes that for him life is over, and that he can never redeem the time lost — for he is constantly reminded of this by persons who should know better. And if he is somewhat melancholic by nature, he is very ready to think that the future holds but two possibilities, — the love of woman so long as it may last, and an easy death of some sort when there is no more love. That was approximately John Ralston's state of mind as he ascended the steps of Robert Lauderdale's house on that Thursday afternoon.

CHAPTER XIX.

RALSTON shook himself and stamped his feet softly upon the rug as he took off his overcoat in the hall of Robert Lauderdale's house. He was conscious that he was nervous and tried to restore the balance of forces by a physical effort, but he was not very successful. The man went before him and ushered him into the same room in which Katharine had been received that morning. The windows were already shut, and several shaded lamps shed a soft light upon the bookcases, the great desk and the solid central figure of the great man. Ralston had not passed the threshold before he was conscious that Katharine was not present, as he had hoped that she might be. His excitement gave place once more to the cold sensation of something infinitely disappointing, as he took the old gentleman's hand and then sat down in a stiff, high-backed chair opposite to him — to be 'looked over,' he said to himself.

"So you're married," said Robert Lauderdale, abruptly opening the conversation.

"Then you've seen Katharine," answered the young man. "I wasn't sure you had."

"Hasn't she told you?"

"No. I was to have seen her this afternoon, but — she couldn't do more than tell me that she would talk it all over this evening."

"Oh!" ejaculated the old man. "That rather alters the case."

"How?" enquired Ralston, whose bad temper made him instinctively choose to understand as little as possible of what was said.

"Well, in this way, my dear boy. Katharine and I had a long interview this morning, and as I supposed you must have met before now, I naturally thought she had explained things to you."

"What things?" asked Ralston, doggedly.

"Oh, well! If I've got to go through the whole affair again —" The old man stopped abruptly and tapped the table with his big fingers, looking across the room at one of the lamps.

"I don't think that will be necessary," said Ralston. "If you'll tell me why you sent for me that will be quite enough."

Robert Lauderdale looked at him in some surprise, for the tone of his voice sounded unaccountably hostile.

"I didn't ask you to come for the sake of quarrelling with you, Jack," he replied.

"No. I didn't suppose so."

"But you seem to be in a confoundedly bad temper all the same," observed the old gentleman, and his bushy eyebrows moved oddly above his bright old eyes.

"Am I? I didn't know it." Ralston sat very quietly in his chair, holding his hat on his knees, but looking steadily at Mr. Lauderdale.

The latter suddenly sniffed the air discontentedly, and frowned.

"It's those abominable cocktails you're always drinking, Jack," he said.

"I've not been drinking any," answered Ralston, momentarily forgetting the forgetfulness which had so angered him ten minutes earlier.

"Nonsense!" cried the old man, angrily. "Do you think that I'm in my dotage, Jack? It's whiskey. I can smell it!"

"Oh!" Ralston paused. "It's true—on my way here, I began to drink something and then put it down."

"Hm!" Robert Lauderdale snorted and looked at him. "It's none of my business how many cocktails you drink, I suppose—and it's natural that you should wish to celebrate the wedding day. Might drink wine, though, like a gentleman," he added audibly.

Again Ralston felt that sharp thrust of pain which a man feels under a wholly unjust accusation brought against him when he has been doing his best and has more than partially succeeded. The fiery temper—barely under control when he had entered the house—broke out again.

"If you've sent for me to lecture me on my habits, I shall go," he said, moving as though about to rise.

"I didn't," answered the old gentleman, with flashing eyes. "I asked you to come here on a matter of business—and you've come smelling of whiskey and flying into a passion at everything I say—and I tell you—pah! I can smell it here!"

He took a cigar from the table and lit it hastily. Meanwhile Ralston rose to his feet. He evidently had no intention of quarrelling with his uncle unnecessarily, but the repeated insult stung him past endurance. The

old man looked up, with the cigar between his teeth, and
still holding the match at the end of it. With the other
hand he took a bit of paper from the table and held it
out towards Ralston.

"That's what I sent for you about," he said.

Ralston turned suddenly and faced him.

"What is it?" he asked sharply.

"Take it, and see."

"If it's money, I won't touch it," Ralston answered,
beginning to grow pale, for he saw that it was a cheque,
and it seemed just then like a worse insult than the first.

"It's not for you. It's a matter of business. Take it!"

Ralston shifted his hat into his left hand and took the
cheque in his right, and glanced at it. It was drawn in
favour of Katharine Lauderdale for one hundred thousand dollars. He laughed in the old man's face, being
very angry.

"It's a curiosity, at all events," he said with contempt,
laying it on the table.

"What do you mean?" cried his uncle, growing redder as Ralston turned white.

"There is no Katharine Lauderdale, in the first place,"
answered the young man. "The thing isn't worth the
paper it's written on. If it were worth money, I'd tear
it up — if it were for a million."

"Oh — would you?" The old gentleman looked at
Ralston with a sort of fierce, contemptuous unbelief.

"Yes — I would. So would Katharine. I daresay she
told you so."

Robert Lauderdale bit his cigar savagely. It was a
little too much to be browbeaten by a mere boy, when he
had been used to commanding all his life. Whether he
understood Ralston, or whether he completely lost his
head, was never clear to either of them, then, or after-

wards. He took a fresh cheque and filled it in carefully. His face was scarlet now, and his sandy eyebrows were knitted angrily together. When he had done, he scrutinized the order closely, and then laid it upon the end of the desk under Ralston's eyes.

'Pay to the order of John Ralston one million dollars, Robert Lauderdale.'

Ralston glanced at the writing without touching the paper, and involuntarily his eyes were fascinated by it for a moment. There was nothing wrong about the cheque this time.

In the instant during which he looked at it, as it lay there, the temptation to take it was hardly perceptible to him. He knew it was real, and yet it did not look real. In the progress of his increasing anger there was a momentary pause. The exceeding magnitude of the figure arrested his attention and diverted his thoughts. He had never seen a cheque for a million of dollars before, and he could not help looking at it, for its own sake.

"That's a curiosity, too," he said, almost unconsciously. "I never saw one."

A moment later he set down his hat, took the slip of paper and tore it across, doubled it and tore it again, and mechanically looked for the waste-paper basket. Robert Lauderdale watched him, not without an anxiety of which he was ashamed, for he had realized the stupendous risk into which his anger had led him as soon as he had laid the cheque on the desk, but had been too proud to take it back. He would not have been Robert the Rich if he had often been tempted to such folly, but the young man's manner had exasperated him beyond measure.

"That was a million of dollars," he said, in an odd voice, as the shreds fell into the basket.

"I suppose so," answered Ralston, with a sneer, as he

took his hat again. " You could have drawn it for fifty millions, I daresay, if you had chosen. It's lucky you do that sort of thing in the family."

" You're either tipsy — or you're a better man than I took you for," said Robert Lauderdale, slowly regaining his composure.

" You've suggested already that I am probably drunk," answered Ralston, brutally. " I'll leave you to consider the matter. Good evening."

He went towards the door. Old Lauderdale looked after him a moment and then rose, heavily, as big old men do.

" Jack! Come back! Don't be a fool, my boy!"

" I'm not," replied the young man. " The wisest thing I can do is to go — and I'm going." He laid hold of the handle of the door. "It's of no use for me to stay," he said. " We shall come to blows if this goes on."

His uncle came towards him as he stood there. Hamilton Bright was more like him in size and figure than any of the other Lauderdales.

"I don't want you to go just yet, Jack," he said, more kindly than he had spoken yet, and laying his hand on Ralston's arm very much as Bright had done in the club.

Ralston shrank from his touch, not because he was in the least afraid of being violent with an old man, but because the mere thought of such a thing offended his sense of honour, and the position in which the two were standing reminded him of what had happened but a short time previously.

" Just tell me one thing, my dear boy," began Robert Lauderdale, whose short fits of anger were always succeeded immediately by a burst of sunshiny good humour. " I want to know what induced you to go and marry Katharine in that way?"

Ralston drew back still further, trying to avoid his

touch. It was utterly impossible for him to answer that he had very reluctantly yielded to Katharine's own entreaties. Nor was his anger by any means as transient as the old man's.

"I entirely refuse to discuss the matter," he said, and paused. "Do you want a plain statement?" he asked, a moment later. "Very well. It was understood that Katharine was to tell you about the marriage, and she has done so. You're the head of the family, and you have a right to know. If I ever had any intention of asking anything of you, it certainly wasn't money. And I've asked nothing. Possibly, just now, you meant to be generous. It struck me in rather a different light. I thought it was pretty clear, in the first place, that you took me for the sort of man who would be willing to live on his wife's money, if she had any. If you meant to give her the money, there was no reason for putting the cheque into my hands — nor for writing a cheque at all. You could, and you naturally should, have written a note to Beman to place the sum to her credit. That was a mere comedy, to see what I would do — to try me, as I suppose you said to yourself. Thank you. I never offered myself to be a subject for your experiments. As for the cheque for a million — that was pure farce. You were so angry that you didn't know what you were doing, and then your fright — yes, your fright — calmed you again. But there's no harm done. You saw me throw it into the waste-paper basket. That's all, I think. As you seem to think I'm not sober, you may as well let me take myself off. But if I'm drunk — well, don't try any of those silly experiments on men who aren't. You'll get caught, and a million is rather a high price to pay for seeing a man's expression of face change. Good night — let me go, please."

During this long tirade Robert Lauderdale had walked up and down before him with short, heavy steps, uttering occasional ejaculations, but at the last words he took hold of Ralston's arm again — rather roughly this time.

"You're an insolent young vagabond!" he cried, breaking into a fresh fit of anger. "You're insulting me in my own house."

"You've been insulting me in your own house for the last quarter of an hour," retorted Ralston.

"And you're throwing away the last chance you'll ever get from me —"

"It wasn't much of a chance — for a gentleman," sneered the young man, interrupting him.

"Confound it! Can't you let me speak? I say —" He hesitated, losing the thread of his intended speech in his anger.

"You don't seem to have anything especial to say, except in the way of abuse, and there's no reason at all why I should listen to that sort of thing. I'm not your son, and I'm not your butler — I'm thankful I'm not your dog!"

"John!" roared the old man, shaking him by the arm. "Be silent, sir! I won't submit to such language!"

"What right have you to tell me what I shall submit to, or not submit to? Because you're a sort of distant relation, I suppose, and have got into the habit of lording it over the whole tribe — who would lick the heels of your boots for your money — every one of them, except my mother and Katharine and me. Don't tell me what I'm to submit to —"

"I didn't say you!" shouted old Lauderdale. "I said that I wouldn't hear such language from you — you're drunk, John Ralston — you're mad drunk."

"Then you'll have to listen to my ravings just as long

as you force me to stay under your roof," answered Ralston, almost trembling with rage. "If you keep me here, I shall tell you just what I think of you — "

"By the Eternal — this is too much — you young — puppy! You graceless, ungrateful — "

"I should really like to know what I'm to be grateful to you for," said Ralston, feeling that his hands were growing icy cold. "You've never done anything for me or mine in your life — as you know. You'd much better let me go. You'll regret it if you don't."

"And you dare to threaten me, too — I tell you — I'll make you — " His words choked him, and again he shook Ralston's arm violently.

"You won't make me forget that you're three times my age, at all events," answered the young man. "But unless you're very careful during the next ten minutes you'll have a fit of apoplexy. You'd much better let me go away. This sort of thing isn't good for a man of your age — and it's not particularly dignified either. You'd realize it if you could see yourself and hear yourself — oh! take care, please! That's my hat."

Robert Lauderdale's fury had boiled over at last and expressed itself in a very violent gesture, not intended for a blow, but very like one, and utterly destructive to Ralston's hat, which rolled shapeless upon the polished wooden floor. The young man stooped as he spoke the last words, and picked it up.

"Oh, I say, Jack! I didn't mean to do that, my boy!" said the old gentleman, with that absurdly foolish change of tone which generally comes into the voice when one in anger has accidentally broken something.

"No — I daresay not," answered Ralston, coldly.

Without so much as a glance at old Lauderdale, he quickly opened the door and left the room, as he would

have done some minutes earlier if his uncle had not held
him by the arm. The library was downstairs, and he was
out of the house before Lauderdale had sufficiently recovered from his surprise to call him back.

That, indeed, would have been quite useless, for Ralston would not have turned his head. He had never
been able to understand how a man could be in a passion
at one moment and brimming with good nature at the
next, for his own moods were enduring, passionate and
brooding.

It had all been very serious to him, much more so than
to the old gentleman, though the latter had been by far
the more noisy of the two in his anger. If he had been
able to reflect, he might have soon come to the conclusion
that the violent scene had been the result of a misunderstanding, in the first instance, and secondly, of Robert
Lauderdale's lack of wisdom in trying to make him take
money for Katharine. In the course of time he would
have condoned the latter offence and forgiven the former,
but just now both seemed very hard to bear.

After being exceptionally abstemious, — and he alone
knew at what a cost in the way of constant self-control,
— he had been accused twice within an hour of being
drunk. And as though that were not enough, with all
the other matters which had combined to affect his temper on that day, Robert Lauderdale had first tried to
make him act dishonourably, as Ralston thought, or at
least in an unmanly way, and had then tried to make a
fool of him with the cheque for a million. He almost
wished that he could have kept the latter twenty-four
hours for the sake of frightening the old man into his
senses. It would have been a fair act of retaliation, he
thought, though he would not in reality have stooped to
do it.

It was quite dark when he came out upon Fifty-ninth Street, and the weather was foggy and threatening, though it was not cold. He had forgotten his overcoat in his hurry to get away, and did not notice even now that he was without it. Half mechanically he had pushed his high hat into some sort of shape and put it on, and had already forgotten that it was not in its normal condition. His face was very pale, and his eyes were bright. Without thinking of the direction he was taking, he turned into Fifth Avenue by force of habit. As he walked along, several men who knew him passed him, walking up from their clubs to dress for dinner. They most of them nodded, smiled rather oddly and went on. He noticed nothing strange in their behaviour, being very much absorbed in his own unpleasant reflections, but most of them were under the impression, from the glimpse they had of him under the vivid electric light, that he was very much the worse for drink, and that he had lost his overcoat and had his hat smashed in some encounter with a rough or roughs unknown. One or two of his rows had remained famous. But he was well known, too, for his power of walking straight and of taking care of himself, even when he was very far gone, and nobody who met him ventured to offer him any assistance. On the other hand, no one would have believed that he was perfectly sober, and that his hat had been destroyed by no less a person than the great Robert Lauderdale himself.

He certainly deserved much more pity than he got that day. But good and bad luck run in streaks, as the winds blow across land-locked waters, and it is not easy to get across from one to the other. Ralston was drifting in a current of circumstances from which he could not escape, being what he was, a man with an irritable temper, more inclined to resent the present than to prepare the future. Presently he turned eastwards out of Fifth Avenue. He remembered afterwards that it must have been somewhere near Forty-second Street, for he had a definite impression of having lately passed the great black wall of the old reservoir. He did not know why he turned just there, and he was probably impelled to do so by some slight hindrance at the crossing he had reached. At all events, he was sure of having walked at least a mile since he had left Robert Lauderdale's house.

The cross street was very dark compared with the Avenue he had left. He stopped to light a cigar, in the vague hope that it might help him to think, for he knew very well that he must go home before long and dress for a dinner party, and then go on to the great Assembly ball at which he was to meet Katharine. It struck him as he thought of the meeting that he would have much more to tell her about their uncle Robert than she could possibly have to relate of her own experience. He lit his cigar very carefully. Anger had to some extent the effect of making him deliberate and precise in his small actions. He held the lighted taper to the end of his cigar several seconds, and then dropped it. It had dazzled him, so that for the moment the street seemed to be quite black in front of him. He walked on boldly, suspecting nothing, and a moment later he fell to his full length upon a heap of building material piled upon the pavement.

It is worth remarking, for the sake of those who take an interest in tracing the relations of cause and effect, that this was the first, the last and the only real accident which happened to John Ralston on that day, and it was not a very serious one, nor, unfortunately, a very unfrequent one in the streets of New York. But it happened to him, as small accidents so often do, at an hour which gave it an especial importance.

He lay stunned as he had fallen for more than a minute, and when he came to himself he discovered that he had struck his head. The brim of his already much injured hat had saved him from a wound; but the blow had been a violent one, and though he got upon his feet almost immediately and assured himself that he was not really injured, yet when he had got beyond the obstacle over which he had stumbled, he found it impossible to recollect which way he should go in order to get home. The slight concussion of the brain had temporarily disturbed the sense of direction, a phenomenon not at all uncommon after receiving a violent blow on the head, as many hard riders and hunting men are well aware. But it was new to Ralston, and he began to think that he was losing his mind. He stopped under a gas-lamp and looked at his watch, by way of testing his sanity. It was half past six, and the watch was going. He immediately began a mental calculation to ascertain whether he had been unconscious for any length of time. He remembered that it had been after five o'clock when he had been called to the telephone at the club. His struggle with Bright had kept him some minutes longer, he had walked to Robert Lauderdale's, and his interview had lasted nearly half an hour, and on recalling what he had done since then he had that distinct impression of having lately seen the reservoir, of which mention has already been made.

He walked on like a man in a dream, and more than half believing that he was really dreaming. He was going eastwards, as he had been going when he had entered the street, but he found it impossible to understand which way his face was turned. He came to

Madison Avenue, and knew it at once, recognizing the houses, but though he stood still several minutes at the corner, he could not distinguish which was up town and which down town. He believed that if he could have seen the stars he could have found his way, but the familiar buildings, recognizable in all their features to his practised eye even in the uncertain gaslight, conveyed to him no idea of direction, and the sky was overcast. In despair, at last, he continued in the direction in which he had been going. If he was crossing the avenue he must surely strike the water, whether he went forwards or backwards, and he was positive that he should know the East River from the North River, even on the darkest night, by the look of the piers. But to all intents and purposes, though he knew where he was, he was lost, being deprived of the sense of direction.

The confusion increased with the darkness of the next street he traversed, and to his surprise the avenue beyond that did not seem familiar. It was Park Avenue where it is tunnelled along its length for the horse-cars which go to the Central Station. It was very dark, but in a moment he again recognized the houses. By sheer instinct he turned to the right, trusting to luck and giving up all hope of finding his way by any process of reasoning. The darkness, the blow he had received when he had fallen and all that had gone before, combined with the cold he felt, deadened his senses still more.

He noticed for the first time that his overcoat was gone, and he wondered vaguely whether it had been stolen from him when he had fallen. In that case he must have been unconscious longer than he had imagined. He felt for his watch, though he had looked at it a few moments previously. It was in his pocket as well as his pocket-book and some small change. He felt comforted at finding that he had money about him, and wished he might come across a stray cab. Several passed him, but he could see by the lamplight that there were people in them, dressed for dinner. It was growing late, since they were already going to their dinner-parties. He felt very cold, and suddenly the flakes of snow began to fall thick and fast in his face. The weather had changed in half an hour, and a blizzard was coming. He shivered and trudged on, not knowing whither. He walked faster and faster, as men generally do when they have lost their way, and he turned in many directions, losing himself more completely at every new attempt, yet walking ever more rapidly, pursued by the nervous consciousness that he should be dressing for dinner and that there was no time to be lost. He did not feel dizzy nor weak, but he was utterly confused, and began to be unconscious of the distance he was traversing and of the time as it passed.

All at once he came upon a vast, dim square full of small trees. At first he thought he was in Gramercy Park, but the size of the place soon told him that he was mistaken. By this time it was snowing heavily and the pavements were already white. He pulled up the collar of his frock coat and hid his right hand in the front of it, between the buttons, blowing into his left at the same time, for both were freezing. He stared up at the first corner gas-lamp he came to, and read without difficulty the name in black letters. He was in Tompkins Square.

He had been there once or twice in his life, and had been struck by the great, quiet, open place, and he understood once more where he was, and looked at his watch. It was nearly ten o'clock. He rubbed his eyes, and then rubbed the snowflakes off the glass, for they fell so fast

that he could not hold it to the light a moment before one
of them fell into the open case. He had been wandering
for nearly three hours, dinnerless, in the snow, and he
suddenly felt numb and hungry and thirsty all at once.
But at the same time, as though by magic, the sense of
locality and direction returned. He put his watch into
his pocket again, stamped the wet snow from his shoes
and struck resolutely westward. He knew how hopeless
it was to expect to find a carriage of any sort in that poor
quarter of the city. Oddly enough, the first thing that
struck him was the absurdity of his own conduct in not
once asking his way, for he was certain that he had met
many hundreds of people during those hours of wandering. He marched on through the snow, perfectly satisfied at having recovered his senses, though he now for
the first time felt a severe pain in his head.

Before long he reached a horse-car track and waited
for the car to come up, without the least hesitation as to
its direction. He got on without difficulty, though he
noticed that the conductor looked at him keenly and
seemed inclined to help him. He paid his five cents and
sat down in the corner away from the door. It was pleasantly warm by contrast with the weather he had been facing
for hours, and the straw under his feet seemed deliciously
comfortable. He remembered being surprised at finding
himself so tired, and at the pain in his head. There was
one other man in the car, who stood near the door talking with the conductor. He was a short man, very broad
in the shoulders and thick about the neck, but not at all
fat, as Ralston noticed, being a judge of athletes. This
man wore an overcoat with a superb sable collar, and a
gorgeous gold chain was stretched across the broad ex-
panse of his waistcoat. He was perfectly clean shaven,
and looked as though he might be a successful prize

fighter.   At this point in his observation John Ralston
fell asleep.

He had two more intervals of consciousness.

He had gone to sleep in the horse-car.   He woke to find
himself fighting the man with the fur coat and the chain,
out under the falling snow, with half a dozen horse-car
drivers and conductors making a ring, each with a lan-
tern.   He thought he remembered seeing a red streak on
the face of his adversary.   A moment later he saw a vivid
flash of light, and then he was unconscious again.

When he opened his eyes once more he looked into his
mother's face, and he saw an expression there which he
never forgot as long as he lived.

CHAPTER XX.

KATHARINE looked in vain for Ralston near the door
of the ball-room that night, as she entered with her
mother, passed up to curtsy to one of the ladies whose
turn it was to receive and slowly crossed the polished
floor to the other side.   He was nowhere to be seen, and
immediately she felt a little chill of apprehension, as
though something had warned her that he was in trouble.
The sensation was merely the result of her disappointment.   Hitherto, even to that very afternoon, he had
always shown himself to be the most scrupulously exact
and punctual man of her acquaintance, and it was natural enough that the fact of his not appearing at such
an important juncture as the present should seem very
strange.   Katharine, however, attributed what she felt
to a presentiment of evil, and afterwards remembered it

as though it had been something like a supernatural warning.

When she had assured herself that he was really not at the ball, her first impulse was to ask every one she met if he had been seen, and as that was impossible, she looked about for some member of the family who might enlighten her and of whom she might ask questions without exciting curiosity. It was not an easy matter, however, to find just such a person as should fulfil the requirements of the case. Hamilton Bright or Frank Miner would have answered her purpose, and it was just possible that one or both of them might appear at a later hour, though neither of them were men who danced. Crowdie would come, of course, with his wife, but she felt that she could not ask him questions about Ralston, and Hester would hardly be likely to know anything of the latter's movements.

It was quite out of the question for Katharine to sit in a quiet corner under one of the galleries, and watch the door, as a cat watches the hole from which she expects a mouse to appear. She was too much surrounded by the tribe of high-collared, broad-tied, smooth-faced, empty-headed, and very young men who, in an American ball-room, make it more or less their business to inflict their company upon the most beautiful young girl present at any one time. Older men would often be only too glad to talk with her, and she would prefer them to her bevy of half-fledged admirers, but the older man naturally shrinks from intruding himself amongst a circle of very young people, and systematically keeps away. On the whole, too, the young girls enjoy themselves exceedingly well and do not complain of their following.

At last, however, Katharine determined to speak to

her mother. She had seen the latter in close conversation with Crowdie. That was natural enough. Crowdie thought more of beauty than of any other gift, and if Mrs. Lauderdale had been a doll, which she was not, he would always have spent half an hour with her if he could, merely for the sake of studying her face. She was very beautiful to-night, and there was no fear of a repetition of the scene which had occurred by the fireplace in Clinton Place on Monday night. It seemed as though she had recalled the dazzling freshness of other days — not long past, it is true — by an act of will, determined to be supreme to the very end. She knew it, too. She was conscious that the lights were exactly what they should be, that the temperature was perfect, that her gown could not fit her better and that she had arrived feeling fresh and rested. Charlotte's visit had done her good, also, for Charlotte had made herself very charming on that afternoon, as will be remembered by those who have had the patience to follow the minor events of the long day. Even her husband had been more than usually unbending and agreeable at dinner, and it was probably her appearance which had produced that effect on him. Like most very strong and masculine men, whatever be their characters, he was very really affected by woman's beauty. For some time he had silently regretted the change in his wife's appearance, and this evening he had noticed the return of that brilliancy which had attracted him long ago. He had even kissed her before his daughter, when he had put on her cloak for her, which was a very rare occurrence. Crowdie had seen Mrs. Lauderdale as soon as he had left Hester to her first partner and had been at liberty to wander after his own devices, and had immediately gone to her. Katharine had observed this, for she had good eyes and few things within her range

of vision escaped her. Naturally enough, too, she had
glanced at her mother more than once and had seen that
the latter was evidently much interested by some story
which Crowdie was telling. Her own mind being
entirely occupied with Ralston, it was not surprising
that she should imagine that they were talking of
him.

She watched her opportunity, and when Crowdie at
last left her mother's side, went to her immediately.
They were a wonderful pair as they stood together for
a few moments, and many people watched them. Mrs.
Lauderdale, who was especially conscious of the admiration she was receiving that night, felt so vain of herself
that she did not attempt to avoid the comparison, but
drew herself up proudly to her great height in the full
view of every one, and as though remembering and repent-
ing of the bitter envy she had felt of Katharine's youth
even as lately as the previous day, she looked down
calmly and lovingly into the girl's face. Katharine was
not in the least aware that any one was looking at them,
nor did she imagine any comparison possible between
her mother and herself. Her faults of character certainly
did not lie in the direction of personal vanity. Many
people, too, thought that she was not looking her best, as
the phrase goes, on that evening, while others said that
she had never looked as well before. She was transpar-
ently pale, with that fresh pallor which is not unbecoming
in youth and health when it is natural, or the result of an
emotion. The whiteness of her face made her deep grey
eyes seem larger and deeper than ever, and the broad, dark
eyebrows gave a look of power to the features, which was
striking in one so young. Passion, anxiety, the alterna-
tions of hope and fear, even the sense of unwonted
responsibility, may all enhance beauty when they are

of short duration, though in time they must destroy it, or modify its nature, spiritualizing or materializing it, according to the objects and reasons from which they proceed. The beauty of Napoleon's death mask is very different from that of Goethe's, yet both, perhaps, at widely different ages, approached as nearly to perfection of feature as humanity ever can.

"Well, child, have you come back to me?" asked Mrs. Lauderdale, with a smile.

There was nothing affected in her manner, for she had too long been first, yet she knew that her smile was not lost on others — she could feel that the eyes of many were on her, and she had a right to be as handsome as she could. Even Katharine was struck by the wonderful return of youth.

"You're perfectly beautiful to-night, mother!" she exclaimed, in genuine admiration.

There was something in the whole-hearted, spontaneous expression of approval from her own daughter which did more to assure the elder woman of her appearance than all Crowdie's compliments could have done. Katharine rarely said such things.

"You're not at all ugly yourself to-night, my dear!" laughed Mrs. Lauderdale. "You're a little pale — but it's very becoming. What's the matter? Are you out of breath? Have you been dancing too long?"

"I didn't know that I was pale," answered Katharine. "No, I'm not out of breath — nor anything. I just came over to you because I saw you were alone for a moment. By the bye, mother, have you seen Jack anywhere?"

It was not very well done, and it was quite clear that she had crossed the big ball-room solely for the purpose of asking the question. Mrs. Lauderdale hesitated an instant before giving any answer, and she had a puzzled expression.

"No," she said, at last. "I've not seen him. I don't believe he's here. In fact —" she was a truthful woman —"in fact, I'm quite sure he's not. Did you expect him?"

"Of course," answered Katharine, in a low voice. "He always comes."

She knew her mother's face very well, and was at once convinced that she had been right in supposing that Crowdie had been speaking of Ralston. She saw the painter at some distance, and tried to catch his glance and bring him to her, but he suddenly turned away and went off in the opposite direction. She reflected that Crowdie did not pass for a discreet or reticent person, and that if there were anything especial to be told he had doubtless confided it to his wife before coming to the ball. She looked about for Hester, but could not see her at first, neither could she discover Bright or Miner in the moving crowd. She stood quietly by her mother for a time, glad to escape momentarily from her usual retinue of beardless young dandies. Mrs. Lauderdale still seemed to hesitate as to whether she should say any more. The story Crowdie had told her was a very strange one, she thought, and she herself doubted the accuracy of the details. And he had exacted a sort of promise of secrecy from her, which, in her experience, very generally meant that a part, or the whole of what was told, might be untrue. Nevertheless, she had never thought that the painter was a spiteful person. She was puzzled, therefore, but she very soon resolved that she should tell Katharine nothing, which was, after all, the wisest plan.

Just then a tall, lean man made his way up to her and bowed rather stiffly. He was powerfully made, and moved like a person more accustomed to motion than to rest. He had a weather-beaten, kindly face, clean shaven, thin and bony. His features were decidedly ugly, though by no means repulsive. His hair was thick and iron grey, and he was about fifty years of age. Mrs. Lauderdale gave him her hand, and seemed glad to see him.

" Mr. Griggs — my daughter," she said, introducing him to Katharine, who had immediately recognized him, for she had seen him at a distance on the previous evening at the Thirlwalls' dance.

Paul Griggs bowed again in his stiff, rather foreign way, and Katharine smiled and bent her head a little. She had always wished she might meet him, for she had read some of his books and liked them, and he was reported to have led a very strange life, and to have been everywhere.

" I saw you talking to Mrs. Crowdie," said Mrs. Lauderdale. " She's charming, isn't she ? "

"Very," answered Mr. Griggs, in a deep, manly voice, but without any special emphasis. "Very," he repeated vaguely. " She was a mere girl — not out yet — when I was last at home," he added, suddenly showing some interest.

" By the bye, where is she ? " asked Katharine, in the momentary pause which followed. " I was looking for her."

" Over there," replied Mr. Griggs, nodding almost imperceptibly in the direction he meant to indicate. As he was over six feet in height, and could see over the heads of most of the people, Katharine had not gained any very accurate information.

" You can see her," he continued in explanation. " She's sitting up among the frumps ; she's looking for her husband, and there's a man with yellow hair talking to her — it's her brother — over there between the first and second windows from the end where the music is. Do you make her out?"

"Yes. How can you tell that she is looking for her husband at this distance?" Katharine laughed.

"By her eyes," answered Mr. Griggs. "She's in love with him, you know — and she's anxious about him for some reason or other. But I believe he's all right now. I used to know him very well in Paris once upon a time. Clever fellow, but he had — oh, well, it's nobody's business. What a beautiful ball it is, Mrs. Lauderdale —"

"What did Mr. Crowdie have in Paris?" asked Katharine, with sudden interest, and interrupting him.

"Oh — he was subject to bad colds in winter," answered Mr. Griggs, coolly. "Lungs affected, I believe — or something of that sort. As I was saying, Mrs. Lauderdale, this is a vast improvement on the dances they used to have in New York when I was young. That was long before your time, though I daresay your husband can remember them."

And he went on speaking, evidently making conversation of a most unprofitable kind in the most cold-blooded and cynical manner, by sheer force of habit, as people who have the manners of the world without its interests often do, until something strikes them.

A young man, whose small head seemed to have just been squeezed through the cylinder of enamelled linen on which it rested as on a pedestal, came up to Katharine and asked her for a dance. She went away on his arm. After a couple of turns, she made him stop close to Hester Crowdie.

"Thanks," she said, nodding to her partner. "I want to speak to my cousin. You don't mind — do you? I'll give you the rest of the dance some other time."

And without waiting for his answer, she stepped upon

the low platform which ran round the ball-room, and took the vacant seat by Hester's side. Hamilton Bright, who had only been exchanging a word with his sister when Griggs had caught sight of him, was gone, and she was momentarily alone.

"Hester," began Katharine, "where is Jack Ralston? I'm perfectly sure your husband knows, and has told you, and I know that he has told my mother, from the way she spoke—"

"How did you guess that?" asked Mrs. Crowdie, starting a little at the first words. "But I'm sorry if he has spoken to your mother about it—" She stopped suddenly, feeling that she had made a mistake.

She was very nervous herself that evening, and as Griggs had said, she was anxious about her husband. There was no real foundation for her anxiety, but since her recent experience, she was very easily frightened. Crowdie had spoken excitedly to her about Ralston's conduct at the club that afternoon, and she had fancied that there was something unusual in his look.

"Oh, Hester, what is it?" asked Katharine, bending nearer to her and laying a hand on hers.

"Don't look so awfully frightened, dear!" Hester smiled, but not very naturally. "It's nothing very serious. In fact, I believe it's only that Walter saw him at the club late this afternoon and got the idea that he wasn't—quite well."

"Not well? Is he ill? Where is he? At home?" Katharine asked the questions all in a breath, with no suspicion that Hester had softened the truth almost altogether into something else.

"I suppose he's at home, since he's not here," answered Mrs. Crowdie, wishing that she had said so at first and had said nothing more.

"Oh, Hester! What is it? I know it's something dreadful!" cried Katharine. "I shall go and ask Mr. Crowdie if you won't tell me."

"Don't!" exclaimed Mrs. Crowdie, so quickly and so loudly that the people near her turned to see what was the matter.

"You've told me, now — he must be very ill, or you wouldn't speak like that!" Katharine's lips began to turn white, and she half rose from her seat.

Mrs. Crowdie drew her back again very gently.

"No, dear — no, I assure — I give you my word it's not that, dear — oh, I'm so sorry I said anything!" Katharine yielded, and resumed her seat.

"Hester, what is it?" she asked very gravely for the third time. "You're my best friend — the only friend I have besides him. If it's anything bad, I'd much rather hear it from you. But I can't stand this suspense. I shall ask everybody until somebody tells me the truth."

Mrs. Crowdie seemed to reflect for a moment before answering, but even while she was thinking of what she should say, her passionate eyes sought for her husband's pale face in the crowd — the pale face and the red lips that so many women thought repulsive.

"Dear," she said at last, "it's foolish to make such a fuss and to frighten you. That sort of thing has happened to almost all men at one time or another — really, you know! You mustn't blame Jack too much —"

"For what? For what? Speak, Hester! Don't try to —"

"Katharine darling, Walter says that Jack was — well — you know — just a little far gone — and they had some trouble with him at the club. I don't know — it seems that my brother tried to hold him for some reason or other — it's not quite clear — and Jack threw Ham down, there in the hall of the club, before a lot of people — Katharine dearest, I'm so sorry I spoke!"

Katharine was leaning back against the cushion, her hands folded together, and her face set like a mask; but she said nothing, and scarcely seemed to be listening, though she heard every word.

"Of course, dear," continued Mrs. Crowdie, "I know how you love him — but you mustn't think any the worse of him for this. Ham just told me it wasn't — well — it wasn't as bad as Walter made out, and he was very angry with Walter for telling me — as though he would keep anything from me!"

She stopped again, being much more inclined to talk of Crowdie than of Ralston, and to defend his indiscretion. Katharine did not move nor change her position, and her eyes looked straight before her, though it was clear that they saw nothing.

"I'm glad it was you who told me," she said in a low, monotonous tone.

"So am I," answered her friend, sympathetically. "And I'm sure it's not half as bad as they —"

"They all know it," continued Katharine, not heeding her. "I can see it in their eyes when they look at me."

"Nonsense, Katharine — nobody but Walter and Ham —"

"Your husband told my mother, too. She spoke very oddly. He's been telling every one. Why does he want to make trouble? Does he hate Jack so?"

"Hate him? No, indeed! I think he's rather fond of him —"

"It's a very treacherous sort of fondness, then," answered Katharine, with a bitter little laugh, and changing her position at last, so that she looked into her friend's face.

"Katharine!" exclaimed Hester. "How can you talk like that — telling me that Walter is treacherous —"

"Oh — you mustn't mind what I say — I'm a little upset — I didn't mean to hurt you, dear."

Katharine rose, and without another word she left her friend and began to go up the side of the room alone, looking for some one as she went. In a moment one of her numerous young adorers was by her side. He had seen her talking to Mrs. Crowdie, and had watched his opportunity,

"No," said Katharine, absently, and without looking at him. "I don't want to dance, thanks. I want to find my cousin, Hamilton Bright. Have you seen him ?"

"Oh — ah — yes!" answered the young man, with an imitation of the advanced English manner of twenty years ago, which seems to have become the ideal of our gilded youth of to-day. "He's in the corner under the balcony — he's been — er — rather leathering into Crowdie — you know — er — for talking about Jack Ralston's last, all over the place — I daresay you've heard of it, Miss Lauderdale — being — er — a cousin of your own, too. No end game, that Ralston chap!"

Katharine lost her temper suddenly. She stopped and looked the young dandy in the eyes. He never forgot the look of hers, nor the paleness of her lips as she spoke.

"You're rather young to speak like that of older men, Mr. Van De Water," she said.

She coolly turned her back on the annihilated youth and walked away from him alone, almost as surprised at what she had done as he was. He, poor boy, got very red in the face, stood still, helped himself into countenance by sticking a single glass in his eye and then went in search of his dearest friend, the man who had just discovered that extraordinary tailor in New Burlington Street, you know.

Katharine had been half stunned by what Hester Crowdie had told her, which she felt instinctively was not more than a moiety of the truth. She had barely recovered her self-possession when she was met by what rang like an insult in her ears. It was no wonder that her blood boiled. Without looking to the right or to the left, she went forward till she was under the great balcony, and there, by one of the pillars, she came upon Bright and Crowdie talking together in low, excited tones.

Bright's big shoulders slowly heaved as in his anger he took about twice as much breath as he needed into his lungs at every sentence. His fresh, pink face was red, and his bright blue eyes flashed visibly. What the young dandy had said was evidently true. He was still 'leathering into' Crowdie with all his might, which was considerable.

Crowdie, perfectly cool and collected, leaned against the wooden pillar with a disagreeable sneer on his red mouth. One hand was in his pocket; the other hung by his side, and his fingers quietly tapped a little measure upon the fluted column. Almost every one has that trick of tapping upon something in moments of anxiety or uncertainty, but the way in which it is done is very characteristic of the individual. Crowdie's pointed white fingers did it delicately, drawing back lightly from contact with the wood, as a woman's might, or as though he were playing upon a fine instrument.

"It's just like you, Walter," Bright was saying, "to go about telling the thing to all the women. Didn't I tell you this afternoon that I was the principal person concerned, that it was my business and not yours and that if I wished it kept quiet, nobody need tell? And you said yourself that you hoped Hester might not hear it, and then the very first thing I find is that you've told her and cousin Emma and probably Katharine herself —"

"No, I've not told Katharine," said Crowdie, calmly. "I shan't, because she loves him. The Lord knows why! Drunken beast! I shall leave the club myself, since he's not to be turned out —"

Crowdie stopped suddenly, for he was more timid than most men, and his face plainly expressed fear at that moment — but not of Hamilton Bright. Katharine Lauderdale was looking at him over Bright's shoulder and had plainly heard what he had said. A man's fear of woman under certain circumstances exceeds his utmost possible fear of man. The painter knew at once that he had accidentally done Katharine something like a mortal injury. He felt as a man must feel who has accidentally shot some one while playing with a loaded pistol.

As for Katharine, this was the third blow she had received within five minutes. The fact that she was in a measure prepared for it had not diminished its force. It had the effect, however, of quenching her rising anger instead of further inflaming it, as young Van De Water's foolish remarks had done. She began to feel that she had a real calamity to face — something against which mere anger would have no effect. She heard every word Crowdie said, and each struck her with cruel precision in the same aching spot. But she drew herself up proudly as she came between the two men. There was something almost queenly in the quiet dignity with which she affected to ignore what she had heard, even trying to give her white lips the shadow of a civil smile as she spoke.

"Mr. Crowdie, I wish to speak to Hamilton a moment — you don't mind, do you?"

Crowdie looked at her with undisguised amazement and admiration. He uttered some polite but half inaudible words and moved away, glad, perhaps, to get out of the sphere of Bright's invective. Bright understood very well that Katharine had heard, and admired her calmness almost as much as Crowdie did, though he did not know as much as the latter concerning Katharines relations with Ralston. Hester Crowdie, who told her husband everything, had told him most of what Katharine had confided to her, not considering it a betrayal of confidence, because she trusted him implicitly. No day of disenchantment had yet come for her.

"Won't you come and sit down?" asked Bright, rather anxiously. "There's a corner there."

"Yes," said Katharine, moving in the direction of the vacant seats.

"I'm afraid you heard what that brute said," Bright remarked before they had reached the place. "If I'd seen you coming —"

"It wouldn't have made any difference," Katharine answered. Then they sat down side by side. "It's much too serious a matter to be angry about," she continued, settling herself and looking at his face, and feeling that it was a relief to see a pair of honest blue eyes at last. "That's why I come to you. It happened to you, it seems. Everybody [is talking about it, and I have some right to know —" She hesitated and then continued. "He's a near relation and all that, of course, and whatever he does makes a difference to us all — my mother has heard, too — I'm sure Mr. Crowdie told her. Didn't he?"

"I believe so," answered Bright. "He's just like a —oh, well! I'll swear at him when I'm alone."

"I'm glad you're angry with him," said Katharine, and her eyes flashed a little. "It's so mean! But that's not the question. I want to know from your own lips what happened — and why he's not here. I have a right to know because — because we were going to dance the cotillon together — and besides — "

She hesitated again, and stopped altogether this time.

"It's very natural, I'm sure," said Bright, who was not the type of men who seek confidences. "Crowdie has made it all out much worse than it was. He's a — I mean — I wish I'd met him when I was driving cattle in the Nacimiento Valley!"

Katharine had never seen Bright so angry before, and the sight was very soothing and comforting to her. She fully concurred in Bright's last-expressed wish.

"You're Jack's best friend, aren't you?" she asked.

"Oh, well — a friend — he always says he hasn't any. But I daresay I'd do as much for him as most of them, though, if I had to. I always liked the fellow for his dash, and we generally get on very well together. He's just a trifle lively sometimes, and he doesn't go well on the curb when he's had — when he's too lively — "

"Why don't you say when he drinks?" asked Katharine, biting on the words, as it were, though she forced herself to say them.

"Well, he doesn't drink exactly," said Bright. "He's got an awfully strong head and a cast-iron constitution, but he's a queer chap. He gets melancholy, and thinks he's a failure and tries to cheer himself with cocktails. And then, you see, having such a nerve, he doesn't know exactly how many he takes; and there's a limit, of course — and the last one does the trick. Then he won't take

anything to speak of for days together. He got a little
too much on board last Monday — but that was excusable,
and I hadn't seen him that way for a long time. I daresay you heard of it? He saved a boy's life between a
lot of carts and horse-cars, and got a bad fall ; and then,
quite naturally — just as I should have done myself —
he swallowed a big dose of something, and it went to his
head. But he went straight home in a cab, so I suppose
it was all right. It was a pretty brave thing he did —
talk of baseball! It was one of the smartest bits of field-
ing I ever saw — the way he caught up the little chap, and
the dog and the perambulator — forgot nothing, though
it was a close shave. Oh — he's brave enough! It's a
pity he can't find anything to do."

"Monday," repeated Katharine, thoughtfully. "Yes
— I heard about it. Go on, please, Ham — about to-day.
I want to hear everything there is."

"Oh — Crowdie talks like a fool about it. I suppose
Jack was a little depressed, or something, and had been
trying to screw himself up a bit. Anyway, he looked
rather wild, and I tried to persuade him to stay a little
while before going out of the club — it was in the hall,
you know. I behaved like an ass myself — you know
I'm awfully obstinate. He really did look a little wild,
though! I held his arm — just like that, you know — " he
laid his broad hand upon Katharine's glove — " and then,
somehow, we got fooling together — there in the hall —
and he tripped me up on my back, and ran out. It
was all over in a minute ; and I was rather angry at the
time, because Crowdie and little Frank Miner were there,
and a couple of servants. But I give you my word, I didn't
say anything beyond making them all four swear that
they wouldn't tell — "

"And this is the result!" said Katharine, with a sigh.

"What was that he said about being turned out of the club?"

"Crowdie? Oh — some nonsense or other! He felt his ladyship offended because there had been a bit of a wrestling match in the hall of his club, that's all, and said he meant to leave it —"

"No — but about Jack being turned out —"

"It's all nonsense of Crowdie's. Men are turned out of a club for cheating at cards, and that sort of thing. Besides, Jack's popular with most of the men. I don't believe you could get a committee to sit on his offences — not if he locked the oldest member up in the ice-chest and threw the billiard-table out of the window. He says he has no friends — but it's all bosh, you know — everybody likes him, except that doughy brother-in-law of mine!"

Katharine was momentarily comforted by Bright's account of the matter, delivered in his familiar, uncompromising fashion. But she was very far from regaining her composure. She saw that Bright was purposely making light of the matter; and in the course of the silence, which lasted several minutes after he had finished speaking, it all looked worse than it had looked before she had known the exact truth.

She felt, too, an instinct of repulsion from Ralston, which she had never known, nor dreamed possible. Could he not have controlled himself a few hours longer? It was their wedding day. Twelve hours had not passed from the time when they had left the church together until he had been drunk — positively drunk, to the point of knocking down his best friend in such a place as a club. She could not deny the facts. Even Hamilton Bright, kind — more than kind, devoted — did not attempt to conceal the fact that Ralston had been what he called 'lively.' And if Bright could not try to make him out to have been sober, who could ?

And they had been married that morning! If he had been sober — the word cut her like a whip — if he had been sober, they would at that very moment have been sitting together — planning their future — perhaps in that very corner.

She did not know all yet, either. The clock was striking twelve. It was about at that time that John Ralston was brought into his mother's house by a couple of policemen, who had found his card-case in his pocket, and had the sense — with the hope of a handsome fee — to bring him home, insensible, stunned almost to death with the blow he had received.

They had waked him roughly, the conductor and the other man, who was really a prize fighter, at the end of the run, in front of the horse-car stables, and John had struck out before he was awake, as some excitable men do. The fight had followed as a matter of course, out in the snow. The professional had not meant to hurt him, but had lost his temper when John had reached him and cut his lip, and a right-handed counter had settled the matter — a heavy right-hander just under John's left ear.

The policemen said they had picked him up out of a drunken brawl. According to them, everybody was drunk — Ralston, the prize fighter, — who had paid five dollars to be left in peace after the adventure, — the conductor, the driver and every living thing on the scene of action, including the wretched horses of the car.

There was a short account of the affair in the morning papers, but only one or two of them mentioned Ralston's name.

Katharine had yet much to learn about the doings on her wedding day, when she suddenly announced her

intention of going home before the ball was half over.
Hester Crowdie took her, in her own carriage; and Mrs.
Lauderdale and Crowdie stayed till the end.

Now against all this chain of evidence, including that
of several men who had met John in Fifth Avenue about
six o'clock, with no overcoat and his hat badly smashed,
against evidence that would have hanged a man ten times
over in a murder case, stood the plain fact, which nobody
but Ralston knew, and which no one would ever believe
— the plain fact that he had drunk nothing at all.

CHAPTER XXI.

In the grey dawn of Friday morning Katharine woke
from broken sleep to face the reality of what she had
done twenty-four hours earlier. It had snowed very
heavily during the night, and her first conscious perception was of that strange, cold glare which the snow
reflects, and which makes even a bedroom feel like a
chilly outer hall into which the daylight penetrates
through thick panes of ground glass.

She had slept very little, and against her will, losing
consciousness from time to time out of sheer exhaustion,
and roused again by the cruel reuniting of the train of
thought. Those who have received a wound by which a
principal nerve has been divided, know how intense is
the suffering when the severed cords begin to grow
together, with agonizing slowness, day by day and
week by week, convulsing the whole frame of the man
in their meeting. Katharine felt something like that
each time that the merciful curtains of sleep were sud

denly torn asunder between herself and the truth of the present.

The pain was combined of many elements, too, and each hurt her in its own way. There was the shame of the thing, first, the burning, scarlet shame — the thought of it had a colour for her. John Ralston was disgraced in the eyes of all the world. Even the smooth-faced dandy, fresh from college, young Van De Water, might sneer at him and welcome, and feel superior to him, for never having gone so far in folly. Now if such men as Van De Water knew the story, it was but a question of hours, and all society must know it, too. Society would set down John Ralston as a hopeless case. Katharine wondered, with a sickening chill, whether the virtuous — like her father — would turn their backs on Ralston and refuse to know him. She did not know. But Ralston was her husband.

The thought almost drove her mad. There was that condition of the inevitable in her position which gives fate its hold over men's minds. She could not escape. She could not go back to the point where she had been yesterday morning, and begin her life again. As she had begun it, so it must go on to the very end, 'until death them should part' — the life of a spotless girl married to a man who was the very incarnation of a disgusting vice. In those first moments it would have been a human satisfaction to have been free to blame some one besides herself for what she had done.

But even now, when every bitter thought seemed to rise up against John Ralston, she could not say that the fault had been his if she had bound herself to him. To the very last he had resisted. This was Friday morning, and on the Wednesday night at the Thirlwalls' he had told her that he could not be sure of himself. By

and by, perhaps, that brave act of his might begin to
tell in his favour with her, but not yet.   The faces, the
expressions, the words, of those from whom she had
learned the story of his doings were before her eyes and
present in her hearing now, as she lay wide awake in
the early morning, staring with hot eyes at the cold grey
ceiling of her room.

It was only yesterday that her sister Charlotte had
sat there, lamenting her imaginary woes.   How Katharine had despised her!   Had she not deliberately
chosen, of her own free will, and was she not .bound
to stand by her choice, out of mere self-respect?   And
Katharine had felt then that, come what might, for good
or ill, better or worse, honour or dishonour, she was glad
that she had married John Ralston and that she would
face all imaginable deaths to help him, even a little.
But now — now, it was different.   He had failed her at
the very outset.   It was not that others had turned
upon him, despising him wholly for a partial fault.
The public disgrace made it all worse than it might
have been, but it was only secondary, after all.   The
keenest pain was from the thrust that had entered Katharine's own heart.   It had been with him as though she
had not existed.   He had not been strong enough, for
her sake, on their wedding day — the day of days to her
— to keep himself sober from three o'clock in the afternoon until ten o'clock at night.   Only seven hours,
Katharine repeated to herself in the cold snow-glare
of the early morning — seven little hours; her lips
were hot and dry with anger, and her hands were
cold, as she thought of it.   It was not only the weakness of him, contemptible as that was — if it had at
least been weakness for something less brutal, less
beastly, less degrading.   Katharine chose the strong-

est words she could think of, and smote him with them in her heart. Was he not her husband, and had she not the right to hate and despise what he had done? It was bad enough, as she said it, and as it appeared to most people that morning. There was not a link missing in the evidence, from the moment when John had begun to lose his temper with Miner at the club, until he had been brought home insensible to his mother's house by a couple of policemen. His relations and his best friends were all convinced that he had been very drunk, and there was no reason why society in general should be more merciful than his own people. Robert Lauderdale said nothing, but when he saw the paragraph in a morning paper describing 'Mr. John R——'s drunken encounter with a professional pugilist,' he regarded the statement as an elucidatory comment on his interview with his great-nephew. No one spoke of the matter in Robert Lauderdale's presence, but the old gentleman felt that it was a distinct shame to the whole family, and he inwardly expressed himself strongly. The only one who tried to make matters look a little better than every one believed they were, was Hamilton Bright. He could not deny the facts, but he put on a cheerful countenance and made the best of them, laughing good-humouredly at John's misfortune, and asking every one who ventured an unfavourable comment whether John was the only man alive on that day in the city of New York who had once been a little lively, recommending the beardless critics of his friend's conduct to go out and drive cattle in the Nacimiento Valley if they wished to understand the real properties of alcohol, and making the older ones feel uncomfortable by reminding them vividly of the errors of their youth. But no one else said anything in Ralston's favour. He was down just then, and it was as well to hit him when everybody was doing the same thing.

Katharine tried to make up her mind as to what she should do, and she did not find it an easy matter. It would be useless to deny the fact that what she felt for Ralston on that morning bore little resemblance to love. She remembered vaguely, and with wonder, how she had promised to stand by him and help him to her utmost to overcome his weakness. How was she to help him now? How could she play a part and conceal the anger, the pain, the shame that boiled and burned in her? If he should come to her, what should she say? She had promised that she would never refer to the matter in any way, when it had seemed but the shadow of a possibility. But it had turned into the reality so soon, and into such a reality — far more repulsive than anything of which she had dreamed. Besides, she added in her heart, it was unpardonable on that day of all days. Married she was, but forgive she could not and would not. Wounded love is less merciful than any hatred, and Katharine could not help deepening the wound by recalling every circumstance of the previous evening, from the moment when she had looked in vain for John's face in the crowded room, until she had broken down and asked Hester Crowdie to bring her home.

She rose at last to face the day, undecided, worn out with fatigue, and scared, had she been willing to admit the fact, by the possibilities of the next twelve hours. Half dressed, she paused and sat down to think it all over again — all she knew, for she had yet to learn the end of the story.

She had been married just four and twenty hours. Yesterday, at that very time, life had been before her, joyous, hopeful, merry. All that was to be had glistened with gold and gleamed with silver, with the silver of dreamland and the gold of hope, having love set as a jewel in the midst. To-day the precious things were but dross and tinsel and cheap glass. For it was all over, and there was no returning. Real life was beginning, began, had begun — the reality of an existence not defined except in the extent of its suffering, but desperately limited in the possibilities of its happiness.

Katharine tried to think it over in some other way. The snow-glare was more grey than ever, and her eyes ached with it, whichever way she turned. The room was cold, and her teeth chattered as she sat there, half dressed. Then, when she let in the hot air from the furnace, it was dry and unbearable. And she tried hard to find some other way in which to save her breaking heart — if so be that she might look at it so as not to see the break, and so, perhaps — if there were mercy in heaven, beyond that aching snow-glare — that by not seeing she might feel a little less, only a little less. It was hard that she should have to feel so much and so very bitterly, and all at once. But there was no other way. Instead of facing life with John Ralston, she had now to face life and John Ralston. How could she guess what he might do next? A drunken man has little control of his faculties — John might suddenly publish in the club the fact that he was her husband.

He was not the same John Ralston whom she had married yesterday morning, and whom she had seen yesterday afternoon for one moment at her door. The hours had changed him. Instead of his face there was a horrible mask; instead of his straight, elastic figure there was the reeling, dilapidated body of the drunken wretch her father had once shown her in the streets. How could she love that thing? It was not even a man.

She loathed it and hated it, for it had broken her life. She remembered having once broken a thermometer when she had been a little girl. She remembered the jagged edge of glass, and how the bright mercury had all run out and lost itself in tiny drops in the carpet. She recalled it vividly, and she felt that she was like the broken thermometer, and the idea was not ridiculous to her, as it must be to any one else, because she was badly hurt.

Vague ideas of a long and painful sacrifice rose before her — of something which must inevitably be begun and ended, like an execution. She had never understood what the inevitable meant until to-day.

Then, all at once, the great question presented itself clearly, the great query, the enormous interrogation of which we are all aware, more or less dimly, more or less clearly — the question which is like the death-rattle in the throat of the dying nineteenth century, — 'What is it all for?'

It came in a rush of passionate disappointment and anger and pain. It had come to Katharine before then, and she had faced it with the easy answer, that it was for love — that it was all for love of John Ralston — life, its thoughts, its deeds, its hopes, its many fears — all for him, so far as Katharine Lauderdale was concerned. Love made God true, and heaven a fact, the angels her guardians now and her companions hereafter. And her love had been so great that it had seemed to demand a wider wealth of heavenly things wherewith to frame it. God was hardly good enough nor heaven broad enough.

But if this were to be the end, what had it all meant? She stood before the window and looked at the grey sky till the reflection from the dead white snow beneath her window and on the opposite roof was painful. Yet the

little physical pain was a relief. She turned, quite
suddenly, and fell upon her knees beside the corner of
the toilet table, and buried her face in her hands and
became conscious of prayer.

That seems to be the only way of describing what she
felt. The wave of pain beat upon her agonized heart,
and though the wave could not speak words, yet the
surging and the moaning, and the forward rushing, and
the backward, whispering ebb, were as the sounds of
many prayers.

Was God good? How could she tell? Was He kind?
She did not know. Merciful? What would be mercy
to her? God was there — somewhere beyond the snow-
glare that hurt so, and the girl's breaking heart cried
to Him, quite incoherently, and expecting nothing, but
consciously, though it knew more of its own bitterness
than of God's goodness, just then.

Momentarily the great question sank back into the
outer darkness with which it was concerned, and little
by little the religious idea of a sacrifice to be made was
restored with greater stability than before. She had
chosen her own burden, her own way of suffering, and
she must bear all as well as she could. The waves of
pain beat and crashed against her heart — she wondered,
childishly, whether it were broken yet. She knew it
was breaking, because it hurt her so.

There was no connected thread of thought in the torn
tissue of her mind, any more than there was any cohe-
rence in the few words which from time to time tried to
form themselves on her lips without her knowledge. So
long as she had been lying still and staring at the grey
ceiling, the storm had been brooding. It had burst now,
and she was as helpless in it as though it had been a real
storm on a real sea, and she alone on a driving wreck.

She lifted her face and wrung her hands together. It was as though some one from behind had taken a turn of rough rope round her breast — some one who was very strong — and as though the rope were tightening fast. Soon she should not be able to draw breath against it. As she felt it crushing her, she knew that the hideous picture her mind had made of John was coming before her eyes again. In a moment it must be there. This time she felt as though she must scream when she saw it. But when it came she made no sound. She only dropped her head again, and her forehead beat upon the back of her hands and her fingers scratched and drew the cover of the toilet table. Then the picture was drowned in the tide of pain — as though it had fallen flat upon the dark sands between her and the cruel surf of her immense suffering that roared up to crash against her heart again. It must break this time, she thought. It could not last forever — nor even all day long. God was there — somewhere.

A lull came, and she said something aloud. It seemed to her that she had forgotten words and had to make new ones — although those she spoke were old and good. With the sound of her own voice came a little courage, and enough determination to make her rise from her knees and face daylight again.

Mechanically, as she continued to dress, she looked at herself in the mirror. Her features did not seem to be her own. She remembered to have seen a plaster cast from a death mask, in a museum, and her face made her think of that. There were no lines in it, but there were shadows where the lines would be some day. The grey eyes had no light in them, and scarcely seemed alive. Her colour was that of wax, and there was something unnatural in the strong black brows and lashes.

. The door opened at that moment, and Mrs. Lauderdale
entered the room.   She seemed none the worse for having danced till morning, and the freshness which had
come back to her had not disappeared again.   She stood
still for a moment, looking at Katharine's face as the
latter turned towards her with an enquiring glance, in
which there was something of fear and something of
shyness.   A nervous thoroughbred has the same look, if
some one unexpectedly enters its box.   Mrs. Lauderdale
had a newspaper in her hand.

"How you look, child!" she exclaimed, as she came
forward.   "Haven't you slept?   Or what is the matter?"

She kissed Katharine affectionately, without waiting
for an answer.

"Well, I don't wonder," she added, a moment later,
as though speaking to herself.   "I've been reading
this —"

She paused and hesitated, as though not sure whether
she should give Katharine the paper or not, and she
glanced once more at the paragraph before deciding.

"What is it about?" Katharine asked, in a tired voice.
"Read it."

"Yes — but I ought to tell you first.   You know, last
night — you asked me about Jack Ralston, and I wouldn't
tell you what I had heard.   Then I saw that somebody
else had told you — you really ought to be more careful,
dear!   Everybody was noticing it."

"What?"

"Why — your face!   It's of no use to advertise the
fact that you are interested in Jack's doings.   They
don't seem to have been very creditable — it's just as
well that he didn't try to come to the ball in his condition.   Do you know what he was doing, late last night,
just about supper-time?   I'm so glad I spoke to you both

the other day. Imagine the mere idea of marrying a
man who gets into drunken brawls with prize fighters
and is taken home by the police — "

"Stop — please! Don't talk like that!" Katharine
was trembling visibly.

"My dear child! It's far better that I should tell
you — it's in the papers this morning. That sort of
thing can't be concealed, you know. The first person
you meet will talk to you about it."

Katharine had turned from her and was facing the
mirror, steadying herself with her hands upon the
dressing-table.

"And as for behaving as you did last night — he's not
worth it. One might forgive him for being idle and all
that — but men who get tipsy in the streets and fight .
horse-car conductors and pugilists are not exactly the
kind of people one wants to meet in society — to dance
with, for instance. Just listen to this — "

"Mother!"

"No — I want you to hear it. You can judge for yourself. 'Mr. John R——, a well-known young gentleman
about town and a near relation of — ' "

"Mother — please don't!" cried Katharine, bending
over the table as though she could not hold up her head.

"'— one of our financial magnates,'" continued Mrs.
Lauderdale, inexorably, "'and the hero of more than one
midnight adventure, has at last met his match in the
person of Tam Shelton, the famous light-weight pugilist.
An entirely unadvertised and scantily attended encounter
took place between these two gentlemen last night between eleven and twelve o'clock, in consequence of a
dispute which had arisen in a horse-car. It appears that
the representative of the four hundred had mistaken the
public conveyance for his own comfortable quarters, and

suddenly feeling very tired had naturally proceeded to go to bed — ' "

With a very quick motion Katharine turned, took the paper from her mother's hands and tore the doubled fourfold sheet through twice, almost without any apparent effort, before Mrs. Lauderdale could interfere. She said nothing as she tossed the torn bits under the table, but her eyes had suddenly got life in them again.

"Katharine!" exclaimed Mrs. Lauderdale, in great annoyance. "How can you be so rude?"

"And how can you be so unkind, mother?" asked Katharine, facing her. "Don't you know what I'm suffering?"

"It's better to know everything, and have it over," answered Mrs. Lauderdale, with astonishing indifference. "It only seemed to me that as every one would be discussing this abominable affair, you should know beforehand just what the facts were. I don't in the least wish to hurt your feelings — but now that it's all over with Jack, you may as well know."

"What may I as well know? That you hate him? That you have suddenly changed your mind — "

"My dear, I'll merely ask you whether a man who does such things is respectable. Yes, or no? "

"That's not the question," answered Katharine, with rising anger. "Something strange has happened to you. Until last Tuesday you never said anything against him. Then you changed, all in a moment — just as you would take off one pair of gloves and put on another. You used to understand me — and now — oh, mother! "

Her voice shook, and she turned away again. The little momentary flame of her anger was swept out of existence by the returning tide of pain.

Mrs. Lauderdale's whole character seemed to have

changed, as her daughter said that it had, between one day and the next. A strong new passion had risen up in the very midst of it and had torn it to shreds, as it were. Even now, as she gazed at Katharine, she was conscious that she envied the girl for being able to suffer without looking old. She hated herself for it, but she could not resist it, any more than she could help glancing at her own reflection in the mirror that morning to see whether her face showed any fatigue after the long ball. This at least was satisfactory, for she was as brilliantly fresh as ever. She could hardly understand how she could have seemed so utterly broken down and weary on Monday night and all day on Tuesday, but she could never forget how she had then looked, and the fear of it was continually upon her. Nevertheless she loved Katharine still. The conflict between her love and her envy made her seem oddly inconsequent and almost frivolous. Katharine fancied that her mother was growing to be like Charlotte. The appealing tone of the girl's last words rang in Mrs. Lauderdale's ears and accused her. She stretched out her hand and tried to draw Katharine towards her, affectionately, as she often did when she was seated and the girl was standing.

"Katharine, dear child," she began, "I'm not changed to you — it's only — "

"Yes — it's only Jack!" answered Katharine, bitterly.

"We won't talk of him, darling," said Mrs. Lauderdale, softly, and trying to soothe her. "You see, I didn't know how badly you felt about it — "

"You might have guessed. You know that I love him — you never knew how much!"

"Yes, sweetheart, but now — "

"There is no 'but' — it's the passion of my life — the first, the last, and the only one!"

"You're so young, my darling, that it seems to you as though there could never be anything else — "

"Seems! I know."

Though Mrs. Lauderdale had already repented of what she had done and really wished to be sympathetic, she could not help smiling faintly at the absolute conviction with which Katharine spoke. There was something so young and whole-hearted in the tone as well as in those words that only found an echo far back in the forgotten fields of the older woman's understanding. She hardly knew what to answer, and patted Katharine's head gently while she sought for something to say. But Katharine resented the affectionate manner, being in no humour to appreciate anything which had a savour of artificiality about it. She withdrew her hand and faced her mother again.

"I know all that you can tell me," she said. "I know all there is to be known, without reading that vile thing. But I don't know what I shall do — I shall decide. And, please — mother — if you care for me at all — don't talk about it. It's hard enough, as it is — just the thing, without any words."

She spoke with an effort, almost forcing the syllables from her lips, for she was suffering terribly just then. She wished that her mother would go away, and leave her to herself, if only for half an hour. She had so much more to think of than any one could know, or guess — except old Robert Lauderdale and Jack himself.

"Well, child — as you like," said Mrs. Lauderdale, feeling that she had made a series of mistakes. "I'm sure I don't care to talk about it in the least, but I can't prevent your father from saying what he pleases. Of course he began to make remarks about your not coming to breakfast this morning. I didn't go down myself until he had nearly finished, and he seemed hurt at our neglecting him. And then, he had been reading the paper, and so the question came up. But, dearest, don't think I'm unkind and heartless and all that sort of thing. I love you dearly, child. Don't you believe me?"

She put her arm round Katharine's neck and kissed her.

"Oh, yes!" Katharine answered wearily. "I'm sure you do."

Mrs. Lauderdale looked into her face long and earnestly.

"It's quite wonderful!" she exclaimed at last. "You're a little pale — but, after all, you're just as pretty as ever this morning."

"Am I?" asked Katharine, indifferently. "I don't feel pretty."

"Oh, well — that will all go away," answered Mrs. Lauderdale, withdrawing her arm and turning towards the door. "Yes," she repeated thoughtfully, as though to herself, "that will all go away. You're so young — still — so young!"

Her head sank forward a little as she went out and she did not look back at her daughter.

Katharine drew a long breath of relief when she found herself alone. The interview had not lasted many minutes, but it had seemed endless. She looked at the torn pieces of the newspaper which lay on the floor, and she shuddered a little and turned from them uneasily, half afraid that some supernatural power might force her to stoop down and pick them up, and fit them together and read the paragraph to the end. She sat down to try and collect her thoughts.

But she grew more and more confused as she reviewed the past and tried to call up the future. For instance, if John Ralston came to the house that afternoon, to explain, to defend himself, to ask forgiveness of her, what should she say to him? Could she send him away without a word of hope? And if not, what hope should she give him? And hope of what? He was her husband. He had a right to claim her if he pleased — before every one.

The words all seemed to be gradually losing their meaning for her. The bells of the horse-cars as they passed through Clinton Place sang queer little songs to her, and the snow-glare made her eyes ache. There was no longer any apparent reason why the day should go on, nor why it should end. She did not know what time it was, and she did not care to look. What difference did it make?

Her ball gown was lying on the sofa, as she had laid it when she had come home. She looked at it and wondered vaguely whether she should ever again take the trouble to put on such a thing, and to go and show herself amongst a crowd of people who were perfectly indifferent to her.

On reflection, for she seriously tried to reflect, it seemed more probable that John would write before coming, and this would give her an opportunity of answering. It would be easier to write than to speak. But if she wrote, what should she say? It was just as hard to decide, and the words would look more unkind on paper, perhaps, than she could possibly make them sound.

Was it her duty to speak harshly? She asked herself the question quite suddenly, and it startled her. If her heart were really broken, she thought, there could be nothing for her to do but to say once what she thought and then begin the weary life that lay before her — an endless stretch of glaring snow, and endless jingling of horse-car bells.

She rose suddenly and roused herself, conscious that

she was almost losing her senses.   The monstrous incon-
gruity of the thoughts that crossed her brain frightened
her.   She pressed her hand to her forehead and with
characteristic strength determined there and then to oc-
cupy herself in some way or other during the day.   To
sit there in her room much longer would either drive her
mad or make her break down completely.   She feared the
mere thought of those tears in which some women find
relief, almost as much as the idea of becoming insane,
which presented itself vividly as a possibility just then.
Whatever was to happen during the day, she must at
any cost have control over her outward actions.   She
stood for one moment with her hands clasped to her
brows, and then turned and left the room.

CHAPTER XXII.

On the present occasion John Ralston deserved very
much more sympathy than he got from the world at
large, which would have found it very hard to believe
the truth about his doings on the afternoon and night of
Thursday.   He was still unconscious when he was carried
into the house by the two policemen and deposited upon
his own bed.   When he opened his eyes, they met his
mother's, staring down upon him with an expression in
which grief, fear and disgust were all struggling for the
mastery.   She was standing by his bedside, bending over
him, and rubbing something on his temples from time to
time.   He was but just conscious that he was at home at
last, and that she was with him, and he smiled faintly at
her and closed his eyes again.

He had hardly done so, however, when he realized what a look was in her face. He was not really injured in any way, he was perfectly sober, and he was very hungry. As soon as the effect of the last blow began to wear off, his brain worked clearly enough. He understood at once that his mother must suppose him to be intoxicated. It was no wonder if she did, as he knew. He was in a far worse plight now than he had been on Monday afternoon, as far as appearances were concerned. His clothes were drenched with the wet snow, his hat had altogether disappeared in the fight, his head was bruised, and his face was ghastly pale. He kept his eyes shut for a while and tried to recall what had happened last. But it was not at all clear to him why he had been fighting with the man who wore the fur collar and the chain, nor why he had wandered to Tompkins Square. Those were the two facts which recalled themselves most vividly at first, in a quite disconnected fashion. Next came the vision of Robert Lauderdale and the recollection of the violent gesture with which the latter had accidentally knocked John's hat out of his hand; and after that he recalled the scene at the club. It seemed to him that he had been through a series of violent struggles which had no connection with each other. His head ached terribly and he should have liked to be left in the dark to try and go to sleep. Then, as he lay there, he knew that his mother was still looking at him with that expression in which disgust seemed to him to be uppermost. It flashed across his mind instantly that she must naturally think he had been drinking. But though his memory of what had happened was very imperfect, and though he was dizzy and faint, he knew very well that he was sober, and he realized that he must impress the fact upon his mother at any cost, immediately, both

for his own sake and for hers. He opened his eyes once
more and looked at her, wondering how his voice would
sound when he should speak.

"Mother dear —" he began. Then he paused, watching her face.

But her expression did not unbend. It was quite
clear now that she believed the very worst of him,
and he wondered whether the mere fact of his speaking
connectedly would persuade her that he was telling the
truth.

"Don't try to talk," she said in a low, hard voice.
"I don't want to know anything about your doings."

"Mother — I'm perfectly sober," said John Ralston,
quietly. "I want you to listen to me, please, and persuade yourself."

Mrs. Ralston drew herself up to her full height as she
stood beside him. Her even lips curled scornfully, and
the lines of temper deepened into soft, straight furrows
in her keen face.

"You may be half sober now," she answered with profound contempt. "You're so strong — it's impossible to
tell."

"So you don't believe me," said John, who was prepared for her incredulity. "But you must — somehow.
My head aches badly, and I can't talk very well, but I
must make you believe me. It's — it's very important
that you should, mother."

This time she said nothing. She left the bedside and
moved about the room, stopping before the dressing table
and mechanically putting the brushes and other small
objects quite straight. If she had felt that it were safe
to leave him alone she would have left him at once and
would have locked herself into her own room. For she
was very angry, and she believed that her anger was

justified. So long as he had been unconscious, she had felt a certain fear for his safety which made a link with the love she bore him. But, as usual, his iron constitution seemed to have triumphed. She remembered clearly how, on Monday afternoon, he had evidently been the worse for drink when he had entered her room, and yet how, in less than an hour, he had reappeared apparently quite sober. He was very strong, and there was no knowing what he could do. She had forgiven him that once, but it was not in her nature to forgive easily, and she told herself that this time it would be impossible. He had disgraced himself and her.

She continued to turn away from him. He watched her, and saw how desperate the situation was growing. He knew well enough that there would be some talk about him on the morrow and that it would come to Katharine's ears, in explanation of his absence from the Assembly ball. His mind worked rapidly and energetically now, for it was quite clear to him that he had no time to lose. If he should fall asleep without having persuaded his mother that he was quite himself, he could never, in all his life, succeed in destroying the fatal impression she must carry with her. While she was turning from him he made a great effort, and, putting his feet to the ground, sat upon the edge of his bed. His head swam for a moment, but he steadied himself with both hands and faced the light, thinking that the brilliant glare might help him.

"You must believe me, now," he said, "or you never will. I've had rather a bad day of it, and another accident, and a fight with a better man than myself, so that I'm rather battered. But I haven't been drinking."

"Look at yourself!" answered Mrs. Ralston, scornfully. "Look at yourself in the glass and see whether you have any chance of convincing me of that. Since you're not killed, and not injured, I shall leave you to yourself. I hope you won't talk about it to-morrow. This is the second time within four days. It's just a little more than I can bear. If you can't live like a gentleman, you had better go away and live in the way you prefer — somewhere else."

As she spoke, her anger began to take hold of her, and her voice fell to a lower pitch, growing concentrated and cruel.

"You're unjust, though you don't mean to be," said John. "But, as I said, it's very important that you should recognize the truth. All sorts of things have happened to me, and many people will say that I had been drinking. And now that it's over I want you to establish the fact that I have not. It's quite natural that you should think as you do, of course. But —"

"I'm glad you admit that, at least," interrupted Mrs. Ralston. "Nothing you can possibly say or do can convince me that you've been sober. You may be now — you're such a curiously organized man. But you've not been all day."

"Mother, I swear to you that I have!"

" Stop, John!" cried Mrs. Ralston, crossing the room suddenly and standing before him. "I won't let you — you shan't! We've not all been good in the family, but we've told the truth. If you were sober you wouldn't — "

John Ralston was accustomed to be believed when he made a statement, even if he did not swear to it. His virtues were not many, and were not very serviceable, on the whole; but he was a truthful man, and his anger rose, even against his own mother, when he saw that she refused to believe him. He forgot his bruises and his mortal weariness, and sprang to his feet before her. Their eyes met steadily, as he spoke.

"I give you my sacred word of honour, mother."

He saw a startled look come into his mother's eyes, and they seemed to waver for a moment and then grow steady again. Then, without warning, she turned from him once more, and went and seated herself in a small arm-chair by the fire. She sat with her elbow resting on her knee, while her hand supported her chin, and she stared at the smouldering embers as though in deep thought.

Her principal belief was in the code of honour, and in the absolute sanctity of everything connected with it, and she had brought up her son in that belief, and in the practice of what it meant. He did not give his word lightly. She did not at that moment recall any occasion upon which he had given it in her hearing, and she knew what value he set upon it.

The evidence of her senses, on the other hand, was strong, and that of her reason was stronger still. It did not seem conceivable that he could be telling the truth. It was not possible that as his sober, natural self he should have got into the condition in which he had been brought home to her. But it was quite within the bounds of possibility, she thought, that he should have succeeded in steadying himself so far as to be able to speak connectedly. In that case he had lied to her, when he had given his word of honour, a moment ago.

She tried to look at it fairly, for it was a question quite as grave in her estimation as one of life or death. She would far rather have known him dead than dishonourable, and his honour was arraigned at her tribunal in that moment. Her impulse was to believe him, to go back to him, and kiss him, and ask his forgiveness for having accused him wrongly. But the evidence stood between him and her as a wall of ice. The physical impression of horror and disgust was too strong. The outward tokens were too clear. Even the honesty of his whole life from his childhood could not face and overcome them.

And so he must have lied to her. It was a conviction, and she could not help it. And then she, too, felt that iron hands were tightening a band round her breast, and that she could not bear much more. There was but one small, pitiful excuse for him. In spite of his quiet tones, he might be so far gone as not to know what he was saying when he spoke. It was a forlorn hope, a mere straw, a poor little chance of life for her mother's love. She knew that life could never be the same again, if she could not believe her son.

The struggle went on in silence. She did not move from her seat nor change her position. Her eyelids scarcely quivered as she gazed steadily at the coals of the dying wood fire. Behind her, John Ralston slowly paced the room, following the pattern of the carpet,. and glancing at her from time to time, unconscious of pain or fatigue, for he knew as well as she herself that his soul was in the balance of her soul's justice. But the silence was becoming intolerable to him. As for her, she could not have told whether minutes or hours had passed since he had spoken. The trial was going against him, and she almost wished that she might never hear his voice again.

The questions and the arguments and the evidence chased each other through her brain faster and faster, and ever in the same vicious circle, till she was almost distracted, though she sat there quite motionless and outwardly calm. At last she dropped both hands upon her knees; her head fell forward upon her breast, and a short, quick sound, neither a sigh nor a groan, escaped her lips. It was finished. The last argument had failed; the last hope was gone. Her son had disgraced himself — that was little; he had lied on his word of honour — that was greater and worse than death.

"Mother, you've always believed me," said John, standing still behind her and looking down at her bent head.

"Until now," she answered, in a low, heart-broken voice.

John turned away sharply, and began to pace the floor again with quickening steps. He knew as well as she what it must mean if he did not convince her then and there. In a few hours it would be too late. All sorts of mad and foolish ideas crossed his mind, but he rejected them one after the other. They were all ridiculous before the magnitude of her conviction. He had never seen her as she was now, not even when his father had died. He grew more and more desperate as the minutes passed. If his voice, his manner, his calm asseveration of the truth could not convince her, he asked himself if anything could. And if not, what could convince Katharine to-morrow? His recollections were all coming back vividly to him now. He remembered everything that had happened since the early morning. Strange to say, — and it is a well-known peculiarity of such cases, — he recalled distinctly the circumstances of his fall in the dark, and the absence of all knowledge of the direction he was taking afterwards. He knew, now, how he had wandered for hours in the great city, and he remembered many things he had seen, all of which were perfectly familiar, and each of which, at any other time, would have told him well enough whither he was going. He

reconstructed every detail without effort.   He even knew
that when he had fallen over the heap of building material he had hurt one of his fingers, a fact which he had
not noticed at the time.   He looked at his hand now to
convince himself.   The finger was badly scratched, and
the nail was torn to the quick.

"Will nothing make you change your mind?" he
asked, stopping in the middle of the room.   "Will nothing I can do convince you?"

"It would be hard," answered Mrs. Ralston, shaking
her head.

"I've done all I can, then," said John.   "There's
nothing more to be said.   You believe that I can lie to
you and give you my word for a lie.   Is that it?"

"Don't say it, please — it's bad enough without any
more words."   She rested her chin upon her hand once
more and stared at the fire.

"There is one thing more," answered John, suddenly.
"I think I can make you believe me still."

A bitter smile twisted Mrs. Ralston's even lips, but
she did not move nor speak.

"Will you believe the statement of a good doctor on
his oath?" asked John, quietly.

Mrs. Ralston looked up at him suddenly.   There was
a strange expression in her eyes, something like hope,
but with a little distrust.

"Yes," she said, after a moment's thought.   "I would
believe that."

"Most people would," answered John, with sudden
coldness.   "Will you send for a doctor?   Or shall I go
myself?"

"Are you in earnest?" asked Mrs. Ralston, rising
slowly from her seat and looking at him.

"I'm in earnest — yes.   You seem to be.   It's rather

a serious matter to doubt my word of honour — even for
my mother."

Being quite sure of himself, he spoke very bitterly and
coldly. The time for appealing to her kindness, her
love, or her belief in him was over, and the sense of
approaching triumph was thrilling, after the humiliation
he had suffered in silence. Mrs. Ralston, strange to say,
hesitated.

"It's very late to send for any one now," she said.

"Very well; I'll go myself," answered John. "The
man should come, if it were within five minutes of the
Last Judgment. Will you go to your room for a moment,
mother, while I dress? I can't go as I am."

"No. I'll send some one." She stood still, watching his face. "I'll ring for a messenger," she said, and
left the room.

By this time her conviction was so deep seated that
she had many reasons for not letting him leave the house,
nor even change his clothes. He was very strong. It
was evident, too, that he had completely regained
possession of his faculties, and she believed that he
was capable, at short notice, of so restoring his appearance as to deceive the keenest doctor. She remembered
what had happened on Monday, and resolved that the
physician should see him just as he was. It did not
strike her, in her experience, that a doctor does not
judge such matters as a woman does.

During her brief absence from the room, John was
thinking of very different matters. It did not even
strike him that he might smooth his hair or wash his
soiled and blood-stained hands, and he continued to pace
the room under strong excitement.

"Doctor Routh will come, I think," said Mrs. Ralston,
as she came in.

She sat down where she had been sitting before, in the small easy chair before the fire. She leaned back and folded her hands, in the attitude of a person resigned to await events. John merely nodded as she spoke, and did not stop walking up and down. He was thinking of the future now, for he knew that he had made sure of the present. He was weighing the chances of discretion on the part of the two men who had been witnesses of his struggle with Bright in the hall of the club. As for Bright himself, though he was the injured party, John knew that he could be trusted to be silent. He might never forgive John, but he could not gossip about what had happened. Frank Miner would probably follow Bright's lead. The dangerous man was Crowdie, who would tell what he had seen, most probably to Katharine herself, and that very night. He might account for his absence from the dinner-party to which he had been engaged, and from the ball, on the ground of an accident. People might say what they pleased about that, but it would be hard to make any one believe that he had been sober when he had so suddenly lost his temper and tripped up the pacific Hamilton Bright in the afternoon.

He knew, of course, that his mother's testimony would have counted for nothing, even if she had believed him, and bitterly as he resented her unbelief, he recognized that it was bringing about a good result. No one could doubt the evidence of such a man as Doctor Routh, and the latter would of course be ready at any time to repeat his statement, if it were necessary to clear John's reputation.

But when he thought of Katharine, his instinct told him that matters could not be so easily settled. It was quite true that he was in no way to blame for having

fallen over a heap of stones in a dark street, but he knew
how anxiously she must have waited for him at the ball,
and what she must have felt if, as he suspected, Crowdie
had given her his own version of what had taken place
in the afternoon. It was not yet so late but that he
might have found her still at the Assembly rooms, and
so far as his strength was concerned, he would have gone
there even at that hour. Tough as he was, a few hours,
more or less, of fatigue and effort would make little difference to him, though he had scarcely touched food that
day. He was one of those men who are not dependent
for their strength on the last meal they happen to have
eaten, as the majority are, and who break down under a
fast of twenty-four hours. In spite of all he had been
through, moreover, his determined abstinence during the
last days was beginning to tell favourably on him, for
he was young, and his nerves had a boundless recupera-
tive elasticity. Hungry and tired and bruised as he was,
and accustomed as he had always been to swallow a stimulant when the machinery was slackened, he did not now
feel that craving at all as he had felt it on the previous
night, when he had stood in the corner at the Thirlwalls'
dance. That seemed to have been a turning-point with
him. He had thought so at the time, and he was sure
of it now. He felt that just as he was he could dress
himself, and go to the Assembly if he pleased, and that
he should not break down.

But his appearance was against him, as he was obliged
to admit when he looked at himself in the mirror. His
face was swollen and bruised, his eyes were sunken and
haggard, and his skin was almost livid in its sallow
whiteness. Others would judge him as his mother had
judged, and Katharine might be the first to do so. On
the whole, it seemed wisest to write to her early in the

morning, and to explain exactly what had happened. In the course of the day he could go and see her.

He had reached this conclusion, when the sound of wheels, grating out of the snow against the curbstone of the pavement, interrupted his meditations, and he stopped in his walk. At the same moment Mrs. Ralston rose from her seat.

"I'll let him in," she said briefly, as John advanced towards the door.

"Let me go," he said. "Why not?" he asked, as she pushed past him.

"Because — I'd rather not. Stay here!" In a moment she was descending the stairs.

John listened at the open door, and heard the latch turned, and immediately afterwards the sound of a man's voice, which he recognized as that of Doctor Routh. The doctor had been one of the Admiral's firmest friends, and was, moreover, a man of very great reputation in New York. It was improbable that, except for some matter of life and death, any one but Mrs. Ralston could have got him to leave his fireside at midnight and in such weather.

"It's an awful night, Mrs. Ralston," John heard him say, and the words were accompanied by a stamping of feet, followed by the unmistakable soft noise of india-rubber overshoes kicked off, one after the other, upon the marble floor of the entry.

John retired into his room again, leaving the door open, and waited before the fireplace. Far down below he could hear the voices of his mother and Doctor Routh. They were evidently talking the matter over before coming up. Then their soft tread upon the carpeted stairs told him that they were on their way to his room.

Mrs. Ralston entered first, and stood aside to let the

doctor pass her before she closed the door.   Doctor Routh
was enormously tall.   He wore a long white beard, and
carried his head very much bent forward.   His eyes were
of the very dark blue which is sometimes called violet,
and when he was looking directly in front of him, the
white was visible below the iris.   He had delicate
hands, but was otherwise rough in appearance, and
walked with a heavy tread and a long stride, as a strong
man marches with a load on his back.

He stopped before John, looked keenly at him, and
smiled.   He had known him since he had been a boy.

"Well, young man," he said, "you look pretty badly
used up.   What's the matter with you?"

"Have I been drinking, doctor?   That's the question."
John did not smile as he shook hands.

"I don't know," answered the physician.   "Let me
look at you."

He was holding the young man's hand, and pressing
it gently, as though to judge of its temperature.   He
made him sit down under the bright gas-light by the
dressing table, and began to examine him carefully.

Mrs. Ralston turned her back to them both, and leaned
against the mantelpiece.   There was something horrible
to her in the idea of such an examination for such a purpose.   There was something far more horrible still in
the verdict which she knew must fall from the doctor's
lips within the next five minutes — the words which must
assure her that John had lied to her on his word of honour.   She had no hope now.   She had watched the doctor
nervously when he had entered the room, and when he
had spoken to John she had seen the smile on his face.
There had been no doubt in his mind from the first, and
he was amused — probably at the bare idea that any one
could look as John looked who had not been very drunk

indeed within the last few hours. Presently he would
look grave and shake his head, and probably give John
a bit of good advice about his habits. She turned her
face to the wall above the mantelpiece and waited. It
could not take long, she thought. Then it came.

"If you're not careful, my boy —" the doctor began,
and stopped.

"What?" asked John, rather anxiously.

Mrs. Ralston felt as though she must stop her ears to
keep out the sound of the next words. Yet she knew
that she must hear them before it was all over.

"You'll injure yourself," said Doctor Routh, completing his sentence very slowly and thoughtfully.

"That's of no consequence," answered John. "What
I want to know is, whether I have been drinking or not.
Yes or no?"

"Drinking?" Doctor Routh laughed contemptuously.
"You know as well as I do that you haven't had a drop
of anything like drink all day. But you've had nothing
to eat, either, for some reason or other — and starvation's a precious deal worse than drinking any day.
Drinking be damned! You're starving — that's what's
the matter with you. Excuse me, Mrs. Ralston, forgot
you were there —"

Mrs. Ralston had heard every word. Her hands
dropped together inertly upon the mantelpiece, and she
turned her head slowly toward the two men. Her face
had a dazed expression, as though she were waking from
a dream.

"Never mind the starvation, doctor," said John, with
a hard laugh. "There's a Bible somewhere in the room.
Perhaps you won't mind swearing on it that I'm sober —
before my mother, please."

"I shouldn't think any sane person would need any

swearing to convince them!" Doctor Routh seemed to be
growing suddenly angry. "You've been badly knocked
about, and you've been starving yourself for days — or
weeks, very likely. You've had a concussion of the brain
that would have laid up most people for a week, and would
have killed some that I know. You're as thin as razor
edges all over — there's nothing to you but bone and
muscle and nerve. You ought to be fed and put to bed
and looked after, and then you ought to be sent out
West to drive cattle, or go to sea before the mast for
two or three years. Your lungs are your weak point.
That's apt to be the trouble with thoroughbreds in this
country. Oh — they're sound enough — enough for the
present, but you can't go on like this. You'll give out
when you don't expect it. Drinking? No! I should
think a little whiskey and water would do you good!"

While he was speaking, Mrs. Ralston came slowly forward, listening to every word he said, in wide-eyed wonder. At last she laid her hand upon his arm. He felt
the slight pressure and looked down into her eyes.

"Doctor Routh — on your word of honour?" she asked
in a low voice.

John laughed very bitterly, rose from his chair, and
crossed the room. The old man's eyes flashed suddenly,
and he drew himself up.

"My dear Mrs. Ralston, I don't 'know what has
happened to you, nor what you have got into your
head. But if you're not satisfied that I'm enough of
a doctor to tell whether a man is drunk or sober, send
for some one in whom you've more confidence. I'm not
used to going about swearing my professional opinion
on Bibles and things, nor to giving my word of honour
that I'm in earnest when I've said what I think about
a patient. But I'll tell you — if I had fifty words of

honour and the whole Bible House to swear on — well,
I'll say more — if it were a case of a trial, I'd give my
solemn evidence in court that Master John Ralston has
had nothing to drink.   Upon my word, Mrs. Ralston!
Talk of making mountains of mole-hills!   You're making a dozen Himalayas out of nothing at all, it seems to
me.   Your boy's starving, Mrs. Ralston, and I daresay
he takes too much champagne and too many cocktails
occasionally.   But he's not been doing it to-day, nor
yesterday, nor the day before.   That is my opinion as a
doctor.   Want my word of honour and the Bible again?
Go to bed!   Getting your old friend away from his books
and his pipe and his fire at this hour, on such a night as
this!   You ought to be ashamed of yourself, young lady!
Well — if I've done you any good, I'm not sorry — but
don't do it again.   Good night — and get that young fellow out of this as soon as you can.   He's not fit for this
sort of life, anyhow.   Don't take thoroughbreds for cart
horses — they stand it for a bit, and then they go crack!
Good night — no, I know my way all right — don't come
down."

John followed him, however, but before he left the
room he glanced at his mother's face.   Her eyes were
cast down, and her lips seemed to tremble a little.   She
did not even say good night to Doctor Routh.

CHAPTER XXIII.

It was nearly one o'clock when John Ralston let Doctor Routh out of the house and returned to his own room.
He found his mother standing there, opposite the door,

as he entered, and her eyes had met his even before he had passed the threshold. She came forward to meet him, and without a word laid her two hands upon his shoulders and hid her face against his torn coat. He put one arm around her and gently stroked her head with the other hand, but he looked straight before him at the bright globe of the gas-light, and said nothing.

There was an unsettled expression on his pale face. He did not wish to seem triumphant, and he did wish that his anger against her might subside immediately and be altogether forgotten. But although he had enough control of his outward self to say nothing and to touch her tenderly, the part of him that had been so deeply wounded was not to be healed in a moment. Her doubt — more, her openly and scornfully outspoken disbelief had been the very last straw that day. It had been hard, just when he had been doing his best to reform, to be accused by every one, from Hamilton Bright, his friend, to the people on the horse-car; but it had been hardest of all to be accused by his mother, and not to be believed even on his pledged word. That was a very different matter.

To a man of a naturally melancholic and brooding temper, as John Ralston was, illusions have a very great value. Such men have few of them, as a rule, and regard them as possessions with which no one has any right to interfere. They ask little or nothing of the world at large, except to be allowed to follow their own inclinations and worship their own idols in their own way. But of their idols they ask much, and often give them little in return except acts of idolatry. And the first thing they ask, whether they express the demand openly or not, is that their idols should believe in them in spite of every one and everything. They are not, as a rule,

capricious men. They cannot replace one object of ado-
ration by another, at short notice. Perhaps the foundation of such characters is a sort of honourable selfishness,
a desire to keep what they care for to themselves, beyond
the reach of every one else, together with an inward conviction that their love is eminently worth having from
the mere fact that they do not bestow it lightly. When
the idol expresses a human and pardonable doubt in their
sincerity, an illusion is injured, if not destroyed — even
when that doubt is well founded. But when the doubt
is groundless, it makes a bad wound which leaves an
ugly scar, if it ever heals at all.

John Ralston was very like his mother, and she knew it
and understood instinctively that words could be of no
use. There was nothing to be done but to throw herself
upon his mercy, as it were, and to trust that he would
forgive an injury which nothing could repair. And
John understood this, and did his best to meet her half
way, for he loved her very much. But he could not help
the expression on his face, not being good at masking
nor at playing any part. She, womanly, could have done
that better than he.

She wished to act no comedy, however. The thing
was real and true, and she was distressed beyond measure. She looked up at his face and saw what was in his
mind, and she knew that for the present she could do
nothing. Then she gently kissed the sleeve of his coat,
and withdrew her hands from him.

"You're wet, Jack," she said, trying to speak naturally. "Go to bed, and I'll bring you something to
eat and something hot to drink."

"No, mother — thank you. I don't want anything.
But I think I'll go to bed. Good night."

"Let me bring you something —"

"No, thank you. I'd rather not. It's all right, mother. Don't worry."

It was hard to say even that little, just then, but he did as well as he could. Then he kissed her on the forehead and opened the door for her. She bent her head low as she passed him, but she did not look up.

Half an hour later, when John was about to put out his light, he heard the little clinking of glasses and silver on a tray outside his door. Then there was a knock.

"I've brought you something to eat, Jack," said his mother's voice. "Just what I could find —"

John turned as he was crossing the room — a gaunt figure in his loose, striped flannels — and hesitated a moment before he spoke.

"Oh — thank you, very much," he answered. "Would you kindly set it down? I'll take it in presently. It's very good of you, mother — thank you — good night again."

He heard her set down the tray, and the things rattled and clinked.

"It's here, when you want it," said the voice.

He fancied there was a sigh after the words, and two or three seconds passed before the sound of softly departing footsteps followed. He listened, with a weary look in his eyes, then went to the fireplace and leaned against the mantelpiece for a moment. As though making an effort, he turned again and went to the door and opened it and brought in the tray. There were dainty things on it, daintily arranged. There was also a small decanter of whiskey, a pint of claret and a little jug of hot water. John set the tray upon one end of his writing table and looked at it, with an odd, sour smile. He was really so tired that he wanted neither food nor drink, and the sight of both in abundance was almost

nauseous to him. He reflected that the servant would
take away the things in the morning, and that his
mother would never know whether he had taken what
she had brought him or not, unless she asked him, which
was impossible. He took up the tray again, set it down
on the floor, in a corner, and instead of going to bed
seated himself at his writing table.

It seemed best to write to Katharine and send his
letter early in the morning. It was hard work, and he
could scarcely see the words he wrote, for the pain in
his head was becoming excruciating. It was necessarily
a long letter, too, and a complicated one, and his command of the English language seemed gone from him.
Nevertheless, he plodded on diligently, telling as nearly
as he could remember what had happened to him since
he had left Katharine's door at three o'clock in the
afternoon, up to the moment when Dr. Routh had pronounced his verdict. It was not well written, but on the
whole it was a thoroughly clear account of events, so
far as he himself could be said to know what had happened to him. He addressed the letter and put a special
delivery stamp upon it, thinking that this would be a
means of sending it to its destination quickly without
attracting so much attention to it as though he should
send a messenger himself. Then he put out the gas,
drew up the shades, so that the morning light should
wake him early, in spite of his exhaustion, and at last
went to bed.

It was unfortunate that the messenger who took the
specially stamped letter to Clinton Place on the following morning should have rung the bell exactly when he
did, that is to say, at the precise moment when Alexander
Junior was putting on his overcoat and overshoes in the
entry. It was natural enough that Mr. Lauderdale

should open the door himself and confront the boy, who held up the letter to him with the little book in which the receipt was to be signed. It was the worse for the boy, because Katharine would have given him five or ten cents for himself, whereas Alexander Junior signed the receipt, handed it back and shut the door in the boy's face. And it was very much the worse for John Ralston, since Mr. Lauderdale, having looked at the handwriting and recognized it, put the letter into his pocket without a word to any one and went down town for the day.

Now it was his intention to do the thing which was right according to his point of view. He was as honourable a man, in his own unprejudiced opinion, as any living, and he would no more have forfeited his right to congratulate himself upon his uprightness than he would have given ten cents to the messenger boy, or a holiday to a clerk, or a subscription for anything except his pew in church. The latter was really a subscription to his own character, and therefore not an extravagance. It would never have entered into his mind that he could possibly break the seal of Ralston's specially stamped envelope. The letter was as safe in his pocket as though it had been put away in his own box at the Safe Deposit — where there were so many curious things of which no one but Alexander Junior knew anything. But he did not intend that his daughter should ever read it either. He disapproved of John from the very bottom of his heart, partly because he did, which was an excellent reason, partly because there could be no question as to John's mode of life, and partly because he had once lost his temper when John had managed to keep his own. So far as he allowed himself to swear, he had sworn that John should never marry Katharine — unless, indeed,

John should inherit a much larger share of Robert Lauderdale's money than was just, in which case justice itself would make it right to enter into a matrimonial alliance with the millions. Meanwhile, however, Robert the Rich was an exceedingly healthy old man.

Under present circumstances, therefore, if accident threw into his hands one of Ralston's letters to Katharine, it was clearly the duty of such a perfectly upright and well-conducted father as Alexander Junior to hinder it from reaching its destination. Only one question as to his conduct presented itself to his mind, and he occupied the day in solving it. Should he quietly destroy the letter and say nothing about it to any one, or should he tell Katharine that he had it, and burn it in her presence after showing her that it was unopened? His conscience played an important part in his life, though Robert Lauderdale secretly believed that he had none at all; and his conscience bade him be quite frank about what he had done, and destroy the letter under Katharine's own eyes. He took it from his pocket as he sat in his brilliantly polished chair before his shiny table, under the vivid snow-glare which fell upon him through his magnificent plate-glass windows. He looked at it again, turned it over thoughtfully, and returned it at last to his pocket, where it remained until he came home late in the afternoon. While he sipped his glass of iced water at luncheon time, he prepared a little speech, which he repeated to himself several times in the course of the day.

In the meantime Katharine, not suspecting that John had written to her, and of course utterly ignorant of the truth about his doings on the preceding day, felt that she must find some occupation, no matter how trivial, to take her mind out of the strong current of painful thought which must at last draw her down into the very vortex of despair's own whirlpool. It seemed to her that she had never before even faintly guessed the meaning of pain nor the unknown extent of possible mental suffering. As for forming any resolution, or even distinguishing the direction of her probable course in the immediate future, she was utterly incapable of any such effort or thought. The longing for total annihilation was perhaps uppermost among her instincts just then, as it often is with men and women who have been at once bitterly disappointed and deeply wounded, and who find themselves in a position from which no escape seems possible. Katharine wished with all her young heart that the world were a lighted candle and that she could blow it out.

It must not be believed, however, that her love for John Ralston had disappeared as suddenly and totally as she should have liked to extinguish the universe. It had not been of sudden growth nor of capricious blooming. Its roots were deep, its stem was strong, its flowers were sweet — and the blight which had fallen upon it was the more cruel. A frostbitten rose-tree is a sadder sight than a withered mushroom or a blade of dried grass. It was real, honest, unsuspecting, strong, maidenly love, and it stood there still in the midst of her heart, hanging its head in the cold, while she gazed at it and wondered, and choked with anguish. But she could not lift her hand to prop it, nor to cover it and warm it again, still less to root it up and burn it.

She could only try to escape from seeing it, and she resolutely set about making the attempt. She left her room and went downstairs, treading more softly as she passed the door of the room in which her mother worked during the morning hours. She did not wish to see her again at present, and as she descended she could not help thinking with wonder of the sudden and unaccountable change in their relations.

She entered the library, but though it was warm, it had that chilly look about it which rooms principally used in the evening generally have when there is no fire in them. The snow-glare was on everything, too, and made it worse. She stood a moment in hesitation before the writing table, and laid her hand uncertainly upon a sheet of writing paper. But she realized that she could not write to John, and she turned away almost immediately.

What could she have written? It was easy to talk to herself of a 'letter; it was quite another matter to find words, or even to discover the meaning of her own thoughts. She did not wish to see him. If she wished anything, it was that she might never see him again. Nothing could have been much worse than to meet him just then, and talking on paper was next to talking in fact. It all rushed back upon her as she moved away, and she paused a moment and steadied herself against her favourite chair by the empty fireplace. Then she raised her head again, proudly, and left the room, looking straight before her.

There was nothing to be done but to go out. The loneliness of the house was absolutely intolerable, and she could not wander about in such an aimless fashion all day long. Again she went upstairs to her room to put on her hat and things. Mechanically she took the hat she had worn on the previous day, but as she stood before the mirror and caught sight of it, she suddenly took it from her head again and threw it behind her with a passionate gesture, stared at herself a moment and then buried her face in her hands. She had unconsciously put on the same frock as yesterday — the frock in which she had been married — it was the rough grey woollen one she had been wearing every day. And there were the same simple little ornaments, the small silver pin at her throat, the tiny gold bar of her thin watch chain at the third button from the top — the hat had made it complete — just as she had been married. She could not bear that.

A few moments later she rose, and without looking at herself in the glass, began to change her clothes. She dressed herself entirely in black, put on a black hat and a gold pin, and took a new pair of brown gloves from a drawer. There was a relief, now, in her altered appearance, as she fastened her veil. She felt that she could behave differently if she could get rid of the outward things which reminded her of yesterday. It is not wise to reflect contemptuously upon the smallness of things which influence passionate people at great moments in their lives. It needs less to send a fast express off the track, if the obstacle be just so placed as to cause an accident, than it does to upset a freight train going at twelve miles an hour.

Katharine descended the stairs again with a firm step, holding her head higher than before, and with quite a different look in her eyes. She had put on a sort of shell with her black clothes. It seemed to conceal her real self from the outer world, the self that had worn rough grey woollen and a silver pin and had been married to John Ralston yesterday morning. She did not even take the trouble to tread softly as she passed her mother's studio, for she felt able to face any one, all at once. If John himself had been standing in the entry below, and if she had come upon him suddenly, she should have known how to meet him, and what to say. She would have hurt him, and she would have been glad of it, with all of her. What right had John Ralston to ruin her life?

But John was not there, nor was there any possibility of her meeting him that morning. He had shut himself up in his room and was waiting for her answer to the letter which Alexander Lauderdale had taken down town in his pocket, and which he meant to burn before her eyes that evening after delivering his little speech. It was not probable that John would go out of the house until he was convinced that no answer was to be expected.

Katharine went out into the street and paused on the last step. The snow was deep everywhere, and wet and clinging. No attempt had as yet been made to clear it away, though the horse-cars had ploughed their black channel through, and it had been shovelled off the pavements before some of the houses. There was a slushy muddiness about it where it was not still white, which promised ill for a walk. Katharine knew exactly what Washington Square would be like on such a morning. The little birds would all be draggled and cold, the leafless twigs would be dripping, the paths would be impracticable, and all the American boys would be snowballing the Italian and French boys from South Fifth Avenue. The University Building would look more than usual like a sepulchre to let, and Waverley Place would be more savagely respectable than ever, as its quiet red brick houses fronted the snow. Overhead the sky was of a uniform grey. It was impossible to tell from any increase of light where the sun ought to be. The air was damp and cold, and all the noises of the street were muffled. Far away and out of sight, a hand-organ was playing 'Ah quell' amore ond'ardo'—an air which Katharine most especially and heartily detested. There was something ghostly in the sound, as though the wretched instrument were grinding itself to death out of sheer weariness. Katharine thought that if the world were

making music in its orbit that morning, the noise must
be as melancholy and as jarring as that of the miserable
hurdy-gurdy. She thought vaguely, too, of the poor old
man who has stood every day for years with his back to
the railings on the south side of West Fourteenth Street,
before you come to Sixth Avenue, feebly turning the
handle of a little box which seems to be full of broken
strings, which something stirs up into a scarcely audible
jangle at every sixth or seventh revolution. He has yellowish grey hair, long and thick, and is generally bareheaded. She felt inclined to go and see whether he were
there now, in the wet snow, with his torn shoes and his
blind eyes, that could not feel the glare. She found
herself thinking of all the many familiar figures of distress, just below the surface of the golden stream as it
were, looking up out of it with pitiful appealing faces,
and without which New York could not be itself. Her
father said they made a good living out of their starving
appearance, and firmly refused to encourage what he called
pauperism by what other people called charity. Even if
they were really poor, he said, they probably deserved to
be, and were only reaping the fruit of their own improv-
idence, a deduction which did not appeal to Katharine.

She turned eastwards and would have walked up to
Fourteenth Street in order to give the hurdy-gurdy
beggar something, had she not remembered almost immediately that she had no money with her. She never had
any except what her mother gave her for her small
expenses, and during the last few days she had not cared
to ask for any. In very economically conducted families
the reluctance to ask for small sums is generally either
the sign of a quarrel or the highest expression of sympathetic consideration. Every family has its private
barometer in which money takes the place of mercury.

Katharine suddenly remembered that she had promised Crowdie another sitting at eleven o'clock on Friday. It was the day and it was the hour, and though by no means sure that she would enter the house when she reached Lafayette Place, she turned in that direction and walked on, picking her way across the streets as well as she could. The last time she had gone to Crowdie's she had gone with John, who had left her at the door in order to go in search of a clergyman. She remembered that, as she went along, and she chose the side of the street opposite to the one on which she had gone with Ralston.

At the door of Crowdie's house, she hesitated again. Crowdie was one of the gossips. It was he who had told the story of John's quarrel with Bright. It seemed as though he must be more repulsive to her than ever. On the other hand, she realized that if she failed to appear as she had promised, he would naturally connect her absence with what had happened to Ralston. He could hardly be blamed for that, she thought, but she would not have such a story repeated if she could help it. She felt very brave, and very unlike the Katharine Lauderdale of two hours earlier, and after a moment's thought, she rang the bell and was admitted immediately.

Hester Crowdie was just coming down the stairs, and greeted Katharine before reaching her. She seemed annoyed about something, Katharine thought. There was a little bright colour in her pale cheeks, and her dark eyes gleamed angrily.

"I'm so glad you've come!" she exclaimed, helping her friend to take off her heavy coat. "Come in with me for a minute, won't you?"

"What's the matter?" asked Katharine, going with her into the little front room. "You look angry."

"Oh — it's nothing! I'm so foolish, you know. It's silly of me. Sit down."

"What is it, dear?" asked Katharine, affectionately, as she sat down beside Hester upon a little sofa. "Have you and he been quarrelling?"

"Quarrelling!" Hester laughed gaily. "No, indeed. That's impossible! No — we were all by ourselves — Walter was singing over his work, and I was just lying amongst the cushions and listening and thinking how heavenly it was — and that stupid Mr. Griggs came in and spoiled it all. So I came away in disgust. I was so angry, just for a minute — I could have killed him!"

"Poor dear!" Katharine could not help smiling at the story.

"Oh, of course, you laugh at me. Everybody does. But what do I care? I love him — and I love his voice, and I love to be all alone with him up there under the sky — and at night, too, when there's a full moon — you have no idea how beautiful it is. And then I always think that the snowy days, when I can't go out on foot, belong especially to me. You're different — I knew you were coming at eleven — but that horrid Mr. Griggs!"

"Poor Mr. Griggs! If he could only hear you!"

"Walter pretends to like him. That's one of the few points on which we shall never agree. There's nothing against him, I know, and he's rather modest, considering how he has been talked about — and all that. But one doesn't like one's husband's old friends to come — bothering — you know, and getting in the way when one wants to be alone with him. Oh, no! I've nothing against the poor man — only that I hate him! How are you, dearest, after the ball, last night? You seemed awfully tired when I brought you home. As for me, I'm worn out. I never closed my eyes till Walter came home — he

danced the cotillon with your mother. Didn't you think
he was looking ill? I did. There was one moment
when I was just a little afraid that — you know — that
something might happen to him — as it did the other
day — did you notice anything?"

"No," answered Katharine, thoughtfully. "He's
naturally pale. Don't you think that just happened
once, and isn't likely to occur again? He's been perfectly well ever since Monday, hasn't he?"

"Oh, yes — perfectly. But you know it's always on
my mind, now. I want to be with him more than ever.
I suppose that accounts for my being so angry with poor
Mr. Griggs. I think I'd ask him to stay to luncheon if
I were sure he'd go away the minute it's over. Shouldn't
you like to stay, dear? Shall I ask him? That will
just make four. Do! I shall feel that I've atoned for
being so horrid about him. I wish you would!"

Katharine did not answer at once. The vision of her
luncheon at home rose disagreeably before her — there
would be her mother and her grandfather, and probably
Charlotte. The latter was quite sure to have heard
something about John, and would, of course, seize the
occasion to make unpleasant remarks. This consideration was a decisive argument.

"Dear," she said at last, "if you really want me, I
think I will stay. Only — I don't want to be in the
way, like Mr. Griggs. You must send me away when
you've had enough of me."

"Katharine! What an idea! I only wish you would
stay forever."

"Oh, no, you don't!" answered Katharine, with a
smile.

Hester rang the bell, and the immaculate and magnificent Fletcher appeared to receive her orders about the

luncheon. Katharine meanwhile began to wonder at herself. She was so unlike what she had been a few hours earlier, in the early morning, alone in her room. She wondered whether, after all, she were not heartless, or whether the memory of all that had lately happened to her might not be softened, like that of a bad dream, which is horrible while it lasts, and at which one laughs at breakfast, knowing that it has had no reality. Had her marriage any reality? Last night, before the ball, the question would have seemed blasphemous. It presented itself quite naturally just now. What value had that contract? What power had the words of any man, priest or layman, to tie her forever to one who had not the common decency to behave like a gentleman, and to keep his appointment with her on the same evening — on the evening of their wedding day? Was there a mysterious magic in the mere words, which made them like a witch's spell in a fairy story? She had not seen him since. What was he doing? Had he not even enough respect for her to send her a line of apology? Merely what any man would have sent who had missed an appointment? Had she sold her soul into bondage for the term of her natural life by uttering two words — 'I will'? It was only her soul, after all. She had not seen his face save for a moment at her own door in the afternoon. Did he think that since they had been married he need not have even the most common consideration for her? It seemed so. What had she dreamed, what had she imagined during all those weeks and months before last Monday, while she had been making up her mind that she would sacrifice anything and everything for the sake of making him happy? She could not be mistaken, now, for she was thinking it all over quite coldly during these two minutes, while Hester was speaking to the butler. She was more

Q.—Vol. 22—Crawford

than cold. She was indifferent. She could have gone back to her room and put on her grey frock, and the little silver pin again, and could have looked at herself in the mirror for an hour without any sensation but that of wonder — amazement at her own folly.

Talk of love! There was love between Walter Crowdie and his wife. Hester could not be with any one for five minutes without speaking of him, and as for Crowdie himself, he was infatuated. Everybody said so. Katharine pardoned him his pale face, his red lips, and the incomprehensible repulsion she felt for him, because he loved his wife.

CHAPTER XXIV.

KATHARINE and Hester went up to the studio together, and Hester opened the door.

" I've brought your sitter, Walter," she said, announcing Katharine. " I've come back with a reinforcement."

" Oh, Miss Lauderdale, how do you do ? " Crowdie came forward. " Do you know Mr. Griggs ? " he asked in a low voice.

" Yes, he was introduced to me last night," explained Katharine in an undertone, and bending her head graciously as the elderly man bowed from a distance.

" Oh! that's very nice," observed Crowdie. " I didn't know whether you had met. I hate introducing people. They're apt to remember it against one. Griggs is an old friend, Miss Lauderdale."

Katharine looked at the painter and thought he was less repulsive than usual.

" I know," she answered. " Do you really want me to

sit this morning, Mr. Crowdie? You know, we said
Friday—"

"Of course I do! There's your chair, all ready for
you—just where it was last time. And the thing—it
isn't a picture yet—is in the corner here. Hester, dear,
just help Miss Lauderdale to take off her hat, won't
you?"

He crossed the room as he spoke, and began to wheel
up the easel on which Katharine's portrait stood. Griggs
said nothing, but watched the two women as they stood
together, trying to understand the very opposite impres-
sions they made upon him, and wondering with an excess
of cynicism which Crowdie thought the more beautiful.
For his own part, he fancied that he should prefer Hester's face and Katharine's character, as he judged it from
her appearance.

Presently Katharine seated herself, trying to assume
the pose she had taken at the first sitting. Crowdie disappeared behind the curtain in search of paint and
brushes, and Hester sat down on the edge of a huge divan.
As there was no chair except Katharine's, Griggs seated
himself on the divan beside Mrs. Crowdie.

"There's never more than one chair here," she explained. "It's for the sitter, or the buyer, or the lion-
hunter, according to the time of day. Other people must
sit on the divan or on the floor."

"Yes," answered Griggs. "I see."

Katharine did not think the answer a very brilliant one
for a man of such reputation. Hitherto she had not had
much experience of lions. Crowdie came back with his
palette and paints.

"That's almost it," he said, looking at Katharine. "A
little more to the left, I think—just the shade of a
shadow!"

"So?" asked Katharine, turning her head a very little.

"Yes — only for a moment — while I look at you. Afterwards you needn't keep so very still."

"Yes — I know. The same as last time."

Meanwhile, Hester remembered that she had not yet asked Griggs to stay to luncheon, though she had taken it for granted that he would.

"Won't you stay and lunch with us?" she asked. "Miss Lauderdale says she will, and I've told them to set a place for you. We shall be four. Do, if you can!"

"You're awfully kind, Mrs. Crowdie," answered Griggs. "I wish I could. I believe I have an engagement."

"Oh, of course you have. But that's no reason." Hester spoke with great conviction. "I daresay you made that particular engagement very much against your will. At all events, you mean to stay, because you only say you 'believe' you're engaged. If you didn't mean to stay, you would say at once that you 'had' an engagement which you couldn't break. Wouldn't you? Therefore you will."

"That's a remarkable piece of logic," observed Griggs, smiling.

"Besides, you're a lion just now, because you've been away so long. So you can break as many engagements as you please — it won't make any difference."

"There's a plain and unadorned contempt for social rules in that, which appeals to me. Thanks; if you'll let me, I'll stay."

"Of course!" Hester laughed. "You see I'm married to a lion, so I know just what lions do. Walter, Katharine and Mr. Griggs are going to stay to luncheon."

"I'm delighted," answered Crowdie, from behind his

easel. He was putting in background with an enormous brush. "I say, Griggs —" he began again.

"Well ?"

"Do you like Rockaways or Blue Points? I'm sure Hester has forgotten."

"'When love was the pearl of' my 'oyster,' I used to prefer Blue Points," answered Griggs, meditatively.

"So does Walter," said Mrs. Crowdie.

"Was that a quotation — or what?" asked Katharine, speaking to Crowdie in an undertone.

"Swinburne," answered the painter, indistinctly, for he had one of his brushes between his teeth.

"Not that it makes any difference what a man eats," observed Griggs in the same thoughtful tone. "I once lived for five weeks on ship biscuit and raw apples."

"Good heavens!" laughed Hester. "Where was that? In a shipwreck?"

"No; in New York. It wasn't bad. I used to eat a pound a day — there were twelve to a pound of the white pilot-bread, and four apples."

"Do you mean to say that you were deliberately starving yourself? What for?"

"Oh, no! I had no money, and I wanted to write a book, so that I couldn't get anything for my work till it was done. It wasn't like little jobs that one's paid for at once."

"How funny!" exclaimed Hester. "Did you hear that, Walter?" she asked.

"Yes; but he's done all sorts of things."

"Were you ever as hard up as that, Walter?"

"Not for so long; but I've had my days. Haven't I, Griggs? Do you remember — in Paris — when we tried to make an omelet without eggs, by the recipe out of the 'Noble Booke of Cookerie,' and I wanted to colour it with yellow ochre, and you said it was poisonous? I've often thought that if we'd had some saffron, it would have turned out better."

"You cooked it too much," answered Griggs, gravely. "It tasted like an old binding of a book — all parchment and leathery. There's nothing in that recipe anyhow. You can't make an omelet without eggs. I got hold of the book again, and copied it out and persuaded the great man at Voisin's to try it. But he couldn't do anything with it. It wasn't much better than ours."

"I'm glad to know that," said Crowdie. "I've often thought of it and wondered whether we hadn't made some mistake."

Katharine was amused by what the two men said. She had supposed that a famous painter and a well-known writer, who probably did not spend a morning together more than two or three times a year, would talk profoundly of literature and art. But it was interesting, nevertheless, to hear them speak of little incidents which threw a side-light on their former lives.

"Do people who succeed always have such a dreadfully hard time of it?" she asked, addressing the question to both men.

"Oh, I suppose most of them do," answered Crowdie, indifferently.

"'Jordan's a hard road to travel,'" observed Griggs, mechanically.

"Sing it, Walter — it is so funny!" suggested Hester.

"What?" asked the painter.

"'Jordan's a hard road'—"

"Oh, I can't sing and paint. Besides, we're driving Miss Lauderdale distracted. Aren't we, Miss Lauderdale?"

"Not at all. I like to hear you two talk — as you

wouldn't to a reporter, for instance. Tell me something more about what you did in Paris. Did you live together ? "

" Oh, dear, no! Griggs was a sort of little great man already in those days, and he used to stay at Meurice's — except when he had no money, and then he used to sleep in the Calais train — he got nearly ten hours in that way — and he had a free pass — coming back to Paris in time for breakfast. He got smashed once, and then he gave it up."

"That's pure invention, Crowdie," said Griggs.

" Oh, I know it is. But it sounds well, and we always used to say it was true because you were perpetually rushing backwards and forwards. Oh, no, Miss Lauderdale — Griggs had begun to ' arrive ' then, but I was only a student. You don't suppose we're the same age, do you ? "

"Oh, Walter!" exclaimed Hester, as though the suggestion were an insult.

" Yes, Griggs is — how old are you, Griggs ? I've forgotten. About fifty, aren't you ? "

"About fifty thousand, or thereabouts," answered the literary man, with a good-humoured smile.

Katharine looked at him, turning completely round, for he and Mrs. Crowdie were sitting on the divan behind her. She thought his face was old, especially the eyes and the upper part, but his figure had the sinewy elasticity of youth even as he sat there, bending forward, with his hands folded on his knees. She wished she might be with him alone for a while, for she longed to make him talk about himself.

" You always seemed the same age, to me, even then," said Crowdie.

"Does Mr. Crowdie mean that you were never young,

Mr. Griggs ? " asked Katharine, who had resumed her pose and was facing the artist.

" We neither of us mean anything," said Crowdie, with a soft laugh.

" That's reassuring ! " exclaimed Katharine, a little annoyed, for Crowdie laughed as though he knew more about Griggs than he could or would tell.

" I believe it's the truth," said Griggs himself. " We don't mean anything especial, except a little chaff. It's so nice to be idiotic and not to have to make speeches."

" I hate speeches," said Katharine. " But what I began by asking was this. Must people necessarily have a very hard time in order to succeed at anything ? You're both successful men — you ought to know."

" They say that the wives of great men have the hardest time," said Griggs. " What do you think, Mrs. Crowdie ? "

" Be reasonable ! " exclaimed Hester. " Answer Miss Lauderdale's question — if any one can, you can."

" It depends — " answered Griggs, thoughtfully. " Christopher Columbus — "

" Oh, I don't mean Christopher Columbus, nor any one like him ! " Katharine laughed, but a little impatiently. " I mean modern people, like you two."

" Oh — modern people. I see." Mr. Griggs spoke in a very absent tone.

" Don't be so hopelessly dull, Griggs ! " protested Crowdie. " You're here to amuse Miss Lauderdale."

" Yes — I know I am. I was thinking just then. Please don't think me rude, Miss Lauderdale. You asked rather a big question."

" Oh — I didn't mean to put you to the trouble of thinking — "

" By the bye, Miss Lauderdale," interrupted Crowdie,

"you're all in black to-day, and on Wednesday you were in grey. It makes a good deal of difference, you know, if we are to go on. Which is to be in the picture? We must decide now, if you don't mind." ·

"What a fellow you are, Crowdie!" exclaimed Griggs.

"I'll have it black, if it's the same to you," said Katharine, answering the painter's question.

"What are you abusing me for, Griggs?" asked Crowdie, looking round his easel.

"For interrupting. You always do. Miss Lauderdale asked me a question, and you sprang at me like a fiery and untamed wild-cat because I didn't answer it — and then you interrupt and begin to talk about dress."

"I didn't suppose you had finished thinking already," answered Crowdie, calmly. "It generally takes you longer. All right. Go ahead. The curtain's up! The anchor's weighed — all sorts of things! I'm listening. Miss Lauderdale, if you could look at me for one moment—"

"There you go again!" exclaimed Griggs.

"Bless your old heart, man — I'm working, and you're doing nothing. I have the right of way. Haven't I, Miss Lauderdale?"

"Of course," answered Katharine. "But I want to hear Mr. Griggs—"

"'Griggs on Struggles' — it sounds like the title of a law book," observed Crowdie.

"You seem playful this morning," said Griggs. "What makes you so terribly pleasant?"

"The sight of you, my dear fellow, writhing under Miss Lauderdale's questions."

"Doesn't Mr. Griggs like to be asked general questions?" enquired Katharine, innocently.

"It's not that, Miss Lauderdale," said Griggs, answering her question. "It's not that. I'm a fidgety old person, I suppose, and I don't like to answer at random, and your question is a very big one. Not as a matter of fact. It's perfectly easy to say yes, or no, just as one feels about it, or according to one's own experience. In that way, I should be inclined to say that it's a matter of accident and circumstances—whether men who succeed have to go through many material difficulties or not. You don't hear much of all those who struggle and never succeed, or who are heard of for a moment and then sink. They're by far the most numerous. Lots of successful men have never been poor, if that's what you mean by hard times — even in art and literature. Michael Angelo, Raphael, Leonardo da Vinci, Chaucer, Montaigne, Goethe, Byron — you can name any number who never went through anything like what nine students out of ten in Paris, for instance, suffer cheerfully. It certainly does not follow that because a man is great he must have starved at one time or another. The very greatest seem, as a rule, to have had fairly comfortable homes with everything they could need, unless they had extravagant tastes. That's the material view of the question. The answer is reasonable enough. It's a disadvantage to begin very poor, because energy is used up in fighting poverty which might be used in attacking intellectual difficulties. No doubt the average man, whose faculties are not extraordinary to begin with, may develop them wonderfully, and even be very successful — from sheer necessity, sheer hunger; when, if he were comfortably off, he would do nothing in the world but lie on his back in the sunshine, and smoke a pipe, and criticise other people. But to a man who is naturally so highly gifted that he would produce good work under any circumstances, poverty is a drawback."

"You didn't know what you were going to get, Miss Lauderdale, when you prevailed on Griggs to answer a serious question," said Crowdie, as Griggs paused a moment. "He's a didactic old bird, when he mounts his hobby."

"There's something wrong about that metaphor, Crowdie," observed Griggs. "Bird mounting hobby — you know."

"Did you never see a crow on a cow's back?" enquired Crowdie, unmoved. "Or on a sheep? It's funny when he gets his claws caught in the wool."

"Go on, please, Mr. Griggs," said Katharine. "It's very interesting. What's the other side of the question?"

"Oh — I don't know!" Griggs rose abruptly from his seat and began to pace the room. "It's lots of things, I suppose. Things we don't understand and never shall — in this world."

"But in the other world, perhaps," suggested Crowdie, with a smile which Katharine did not like.

"The other world is the inside of this one," said Griggs, coming up to the easel and looking at the painting. "That's good, Crowdie," he said, thoughtfully. "It's distinctly good. I mean that it's like, that's all. Of course, I don't know anything about painting — that's your business."

"Of course it is," answered Crowdie; "I didn't ask you to criticise. But I'm glad if you think it's like."

"Yes. Don't mind my telling you, Crowdie — Miss Lauderdale, I hope you'll forgive me — there's a slight irregularity in the pupil of Miss Lauderdale's right eye — it isn't exactly round. It affects the expression. Do you see?"

"I never noticed it," said Katharine in surprise.

"By Jove — you're right!" exclaimed Crowdie. "What eyes you have, Griggs!"

"It doesn't affect your sight in the least," said Griggs, "and nobody would notice it, but it affects the expression all the same."

"You saw it at once," remarked Katharine.

"Oh — Griggs sees everything," answered Crowdie. "He probably observed the fact last night when he was introduced to you, and has been thinking about it ever since."

"Now you've interrupted him again," said Katharine. "Do sit down again, Mr. Griggs, and go on with what you were saying — about the other side of the question."

"The question of success?"

"Yes — and difficulties — and all that."

"Delightfully vague — 'all that'! I can only give you an idea of what I mean. The question of success involves its own value, and the ultimate happiness of mankind. Do you see how big it is? It goes through everything, and it has no end. What is success? Getting ahead of other people, I suppose. But in what direction? In the direction of one's own happiness, presumably. Every one has a prime and innate right to be happy. Ideas about happiness differ. With most people it's a matter of taste and inherited proclivities. All schemes for making all mankind happy in one direction must fail. A man is happy when he feels that he has succeeded — the sportsman when he has killed his game, the parson when he believes he has saved a soul. We can't all be parsons, nor all good shots. There must be variety. Happiness is success, in each variety, and nothing else. I mean, of course, belief in one's own success, with a reasonable amount of acknowledgment. It's of much less consequence to Crowdie, for instance, what you think, or I think, or Mrs. Crowdie thinks about that picture, than it is to himself. But our opinion has a certain value for him. With an amateur, public opinion is everything, or nearly everything. With a good professional it is quite secondary, because he knows much better than the public can, whether his work is good or bad. He himself is his world — the public is only his weather, fine one day and rainy the next. He prefers his world in fine weather, but even when it rains he would not exchange it for any other. He's his own king, kingdom and court. He's his own enemy, his own conqueror, and his own captive — slave is a better word. In the course of time he may even become perfectly indifferent to the weather in his world — that is, to the public. And if he can believe that he is doing a good work, and if he can keep inside his own world, he will probably be happy."

"But if he goes beyond it?" asked Katharine.

"He will probably be killed — body or soul, or both," said Griggs, with a queer change of tone.

"It seems to me that you exclude women altogether from your paradise," observed Mrs. Crowdie, with a laugh.

"And amateurs," said her husband. "It's to be a professional paradise for men — no admittance except on business. No one who hasn't had a picture on the line need apply. Special hell for minor poets. Crowns of glory may be had on application at the desk — fit not guaranteed in cases of swelled head —"

"Don't be vulgar, Crowdie," interrupted Griggs.

"Is 'swelled head' vulgar, Miss Lauderdale?" enquired the painter.

"It sounds like something horrid — mumps, or that sort of thing. What does it mean?"

"It means a bad case of conceit. It's a good New York expression. I wonder you haven't heard it. Go on about the professional persons, Griggs. I'm not half

good enough to chaff you. I wish Frank Miner were
here. He's the literary man in the family."

"Little Frank Miner — the brother of the three Miss
Miners?" asked Griggs.

"Yes — looks a well-dressed cock sparrow — always in
a good humour — don't you know him?"

"Of course I do — the brother of the three Miss
Miners," said Griggs, meditatively. "Does he write?
I didn't know." Crowdie laughed, and Hester smiled.

"Such is fame!" exclaimed Crowdie. "But then,
literary men never seem to have heard of each other."

"No," answered Griggs. "By the bye, Crowdie, have
you heard anything of Chang-Li-Ho lately?"

"Chang-Li-Ho? Who on earth is he? A Chinese
laundryman?"

"No," replied Griggs, unmoved. "He's the greatest
painter in the Chinese Empire. But then, you painters
never seem to have heard of one another."

"By Jove! that's not fair, Griggs! Is he to be in the
professional heaven, too?"

"I suppose so. There'll probably be more Chinamen
than New Yorkers there. They know a great deal more
about art."

"You're getting deucedly sarcastic, Griggs," observed
Crowdie. "You'd better tell Miss Lauderdale more
about the life to come. Your hobby can't be tired yet,
and if you ride him industriously, it will soon be time
for luncheon."

"We'd better have it at once if you two are going to
quarrel," suggested Hester, with a laugh.

"Oh, we never quarrel," answered Crowdie. "Besides,
I've got no soul, Griggs says, and he sold his own to the
printer's devil ages ago — so that the life to come is a
perfectly safe subject."

"What do you mean by saying that Walter has no soul?" asked Hester, looking up quickly at Griggs.

"My dear lady," he answered, "please don't be so terribly angry with me. In the first place, I said it in fun; and secondly, it's quite true; and thirdly, it's very lucky for him that he has none."

"Are you joking now, or are you unintentionally funny?" asked Crowdie.

"I don't think it's very funny to be talking about people having no souls," said Katharine.

"Do you think every one has a soul, Miss Lauderdale?" asked Griggs, beginning to walk about again.

"Yes — of course. Don't you?"

Griggs looked at her a moment in silence, as though he were hesitating as to what he should say.

"Can you see the soul, as you did the defect in my eyes?" asked Katharine, smiling.

"Sometimes — sometimes one almost fancies that one might."

"And what do you see in mine, may I ask? A defect?"

He was quite near to her. She looked up at him earnestly with her pure girl's eyes, wide, grey and honest. The fresh pallor of her skin was thrown into relief by the black she wore, and her features by the rich stuff which covered the high back of the chair. There was a deeper interest in her expression than Griggs often saw in the faces of those with whom he talked, but it was not that which fascinated him. There was something suggestive of holy things, of innocent suffering, of the romance of a virgin martyr — something which, perhaps, took him back to strange sights he had seen in his youth.

He stood looking down into her eyes, a gaunt, world-worn fighter of fifty years, with a strong, ugly, deter-

mined but yet kindly face — the face of a man who has
passed beyond a certain barrier which few men ever reach
at all.

Crowdie dropped his hand, holding his brush, and gazing at the two in silent and genuine delight.   The contrast was wonderful, he thought.   He would have given
much to paint them as they were before him, with their
expressions — with the very thoughts of which the look
in each face was born.   Whatever Crowdie might be at
heart, he was an artist first.

And Hester watched them, too, accustomed to notice
whatever struck her husband's attention.   A very different nature was hers from any of the three — one reserved
for an unusual destiny, and with something of fate's shadowy painting already in all her outward self — passionate,
first, and having, also, many qualities of mercy and cruelty
at passion's command, but not having anything of the
keen insight into the world spiritual, and material, which
in varied measure belonged to each of the others.

"And what defect do you see in my soul?" asked
Katharine, her exquisite lips just parting in a smile.

"Forgive me!" exclaimed Griggs, as though roused
from a reverie.   "I didn't realize that I was staring at
you."   He was an oddly natural man at certain times.
Katharine almost laughed.

"I didn't realize it either," she answered.   "I was too
much interested in what I thought you were going to say."

"He's a very clever fellow, Miss Lauderdale," said
Crowdie, going on with his painting.   "But you'll turn
his head completely.   To be so much interested — not in
what he has said, or is saying, or even is going to say,
but just in what you think he possibly may say — it's
amazing!   Griggs, you're not half enough flattered!   But
then, you're so spoilt!"

"Yes — in my old age, people are spoiling me."
Griggs smiled rather sourly. "I can't read souls, Miss
Lauderdale," he continued. "But if I could, I should
rather read yours than most books. It has something
to say."

"It's impossible to be more vague, I'm sure," observed
Crowdie.

"It's impossible to be more flattering," said Katharine, quietly. "Thank you, Mr. Griggs."

She was beginning to be tired of Crowdie's observa-
tions upon what Griggs said — possibly because she was
beginning to like Griggs himself more than she had
expected.

"I didn't mean to be either vague or flattering. It's
servile to be the one and weak to be the other. I said
what I thought. Do you call it flattery to paint a beautiful portrait of Miss Lauderdale?"

"Not unless I make it more beautiful than she is,"
answered the painter.

"You can't."

"That's decisive, at all events," laughed Crowdie.
"Not but that I agree with you, entirely."

"Oh, I don't mean it as you do," answered Griggs.
"That would be flattery — exactly what I don't mean.
Miss Lauderdale is perfectly well aware that you're a
great portrait painter and that she is not altogether the
most beautiful young lady living at the present moment.
You mean flesh and blood and eyes and hair. I don't.
I mean all that flesh and blood and eyes and hair don't
mean, and never can mean."

"Soul," suggested Crowdie. "I was talking about that
to Miss Lauderdale the last time she sat for me — that
was on Wednesday, wasn't it — the day before yesterday? It seems like last year, for some reason or other.

Yes, I know what you mean. You needn't get into such
a state of frenzied excitement."

"I appeal to you, Mrs. Crowdie—was I talking excitedly?"

"A little," answered Hester, who was incapable of
disagreeing with her husband.

"Oh—well—I daresay," said Griggs. "It hasn't
been my weakness in life to get excited, though." He
laughed.

"Walter always makes you talk, Mr. Griggs," answered Mrs. Crowdie.

"A great deal too much. I think I shall be rude,
and not stay to luncheon, after all."

"Nonsense!" exclaimed Crowdie. "Don't go in for
being young and eccentric—the 'man of genius' style,
who runs in and out like a hen in a thunder-storm, and
is in everybody's way when he's not wanted and can't
be found when people want him. You've outgrown that
sort of absurdity long ago."

Katharine would have liked to see Griggs' face at that
moment, but he was behind her again. There was something in the relation of the two men which she found it
hard to understand. Crowdie was much younger than
Griggs—fourteen or fifteen years, she fancied, and
Griggs did not seem to be at all the kind of man
with whom people would naturally be familiar or
take liberties, to use the common phrase. Yet they
talked together like a couple of schoolboys. She
should not have thought, either, that they could be
mutually attracted. Yet they appeared to have many
ideas in common, and to understand each other wonderfully well. Crowdie was evidently not repulsive to
Griggs as he was to many men she knew—to Bright
and Miner, for instance—and the two had undoubt-

edly been very intimate in former days. Nevertheless, it was strange to hear the younger man, who was little more than a youth in appearance, comparing the celebrated Paul Griggs to a hen in a thunder-storm, and still stranger to see that Griggs did not resent it at all. An older woman might have unjustly suspected that the elderly man of letters was in love with Hester Crowdie, but such an idea could never have crossed Katharine's mind. In that respect she was singularly unsophisticated. She had been accustomed to see her beautiful mother surrounded and courted by men of all ages, and she knew that her mother was utterly indifferent to them except in so far as she liked to be admired. In some books, men fall in love with married women, and Katharine had always been told that those were bad books, and had accepted the fact without question and without interest.

But in ordinary matters she was keen of perception. It struck her that there was some bond or link between the two men, and it seemed strange to her that there should be—as strange as though she had seen an old wolf playing amicably with a little rabbit. She thought of the two animals in connection with the two men.

While she had been thinking, Hester and Griggs had been talking together in lower tones, on the divan, and Crowdie had been painting industriously.

"It's time for luncheon," said Mrs. Crowdie. "Mr. Griggs says he really must go away very early, and perhaps, if Katharine will stay, she will let you paint for another quarter of an hour afterward."

"I wish you would!" answered Crowdie, with alacrity. "The snow-light is so soft—you see the snow lies on the skylight like a blanket."

Katharine looked up at the glass roof, turning her head far back, for it was immediately overhead. When she dropped her eyes she saw that Griggs was looking at her again, but he turned away instantly. She had no sensation of unpleasantness, as she always had when she met Crowdie's womanish glance; but she wondered about the man and his past.

Hester was just leaving the studio, going downstairs to be sure that luncheon was ready, and Crowdie had disappeared behind his curtain to put his palette and brushes out of sight, as usual. Katharine was alone with Griggs for a few moments. They stood together, looking at the portrait.

"How long have you known Mr. Crowdie?" she asked, yielding to an irresistible impulse.

"Crowdie?" repeated Griggs. "Oh — a long time — fifteen or sixteen years, I should think. That's going to be a very good portrait, Miss Lauderdale — one of his best. And Crowdie, at his best, is first rate."

CHAPTER XXV.

KATHARINE was conscious that during the time she had spent in the studio she had been taken out of herself. She had listened to what the others had said, she had been interested in Griggs, she had speculated upon the probable origin of his apparent friendship with Crowdie; in a word, she had temporarily lulled the tempest which had threatened to overwhelm her altogether in the earlier part of the morning. She was not much given to analyzing herself and her feelings, but as she descended the stairs, followed by Crowdie and Griggs, she was inclined to doubt whether she were awake, or dreaming. She told herself that it was all true; that she had been married to John Ralston on the previous morning in the quiet, remote church, that she had seen John for one moment in the afternoon, at her own door, that he had failed her in the evening, and that she knew only too certainly how he had disgraced himself in the eyes of decent people during the remainder of the day. It was all true, and yet there was something misty about it all, as though it were a dream. She did not feel angry or hurt any more. It only seemed to her that John, and everything connected with him, had all at once passed out of her life, beyond the possibility of recall. And she did not wish to recall it, for she had reached something like peace, very unexpectedlv.

It was, of course, only temporary. Physically speaking, it might be explained as the reaction from violent emotions, which had left her nerves weary and deadened. And speaking not merely of the material side, it is true that the life of love has moments of suspended animation, during which it is hard to believe that love was ever alive at all — times when love has a past and a future, but no present.

If she had met John at that moment, on the stairs, she would very probably have put out her hand quite naturally, and would have greeted him with a smile, before the reality of all that had happened could come back to her. Many of us have dreamed that those dearest to us have done us some cruel and bitter wrong, struck us, insulted us, trampled on our life-long devotion to them; and in the morning, awaking, we have met them, and smiled, and loved them just the same. For it was only a dream. And there are those who have known the reality; who, after much time, have very suddenly found out that they have been betrayed and wickedly deceived,

and used ill, by their most dear — and who, in the first
moment, have met them, and smiled, and loved them
just the same. For it was only a dream, they thought
indeed. And then comes the waking, which is as though
one fell asleep upon his beloved's bosom and awoke among
thorns, and having a crown of thorns about his brows
— very hard to bear without crying aloud.

Katharine pressed the polished banister of the staircase with her hand, and with the other she found the
point of the little gold pin she wore at her throat and
made it prick her a little. It was a foolish idea and a
childish thought. She knew that she was not really
dreaming, and yet, as though she might have been, she
wanted a physical sensation to assure her that she was
awake. Griggs was close behind her. Crowdie had
stopped a moment to pull the cord of a curtain which
covered the skylight of the staircase.

"I wonder where real things end, and dreams begin!"
said Katharine, half turning her head, and then immediately looking before her again.

"At every minute of every hour," answered Griggs, as
quickly as though the thought had been in his own
mind.

From higher up came Crowdie's golden voice, singing
very softly to himself. He had heard the question and
the answer.

"'La vie est un songe,'" he sang, and then, breaking
off suddenly, laughed a little and began to descend.

At the first note, Katharine stood still and turned her
face upwards. Griggs stopped, too, and looked down at
her. Even after Crowdie had laughed Katharine did
not move.

"I wish you'd go on, Mr. Crowdie!" she cried, speaking so that he could hear her.

" Griggs is anxious for the Blue Points," he answered, coming down. "Besides, he hates music, and makes no secret of the fact."

"Is it true? Do you really hate music?" asked Katharine, turning and beginning to descend again.

"Quite true," answered Griggs, quietly. "I detest it. Crowdie's a nuisance with his perpetual yapping."

Crowdie laughed good naturedly, and Katharine said nothing. As they reached the lower landing she turned and paused an instant, so that Griggs came beside her.

"Did you always hate music?" she asked, looking up into his weather-beaten face with some curiosity.

"Hm!" Griggs uttered a doubtful sound. "It's a long time since I heard any that pleased me, at all events."

"There are certain subjects, Miss Lauderdale, upon which Griggs is unapproachable, because he won't say anything. And there are others upon which it is dangerous to approach him, because he is likely to say too much. Hester! Where are you?"

He disappeared into the little room at the front of the house in search of his wife, and Katharine stood alone with Griggs in the entry. Again she looked at him with curiosity.

"You're a very good-humoured person, Mr. Griggs," she said, with a smile.

"You mean about Crowdie? Oh, I can stand a lot of his chaff — and he has to stand mine, too."

"That was a very interesting answer you gave to my question about dreams," said Katharine, leaning against the pillar of the banister.

"Was it? Let me see — what did I say?" He seemed to be absent-minded again.

"Come to luncheon!" cried Crowdie, reappearing with

Hester at that moment. "You can talk metaphysics over the oysters."

"Metaphysics!" exclaimed Griggs, with a smile.

"Oh, I know," answered Crowdie. "I can't tell the difference between metaphysics and psychics, and geography and Totem. It is all precisely the same to me — and it is to Griggs, if he'd only acknowledge it. Come along, Miss Lauderdale — to oysters and culture!"

Hester laughed at Crowdie's good spirits, and Griggs smiled. He had large, sharp teeth, and Katharine thought of the wolf and the rabbit again. It was strange that they should be on such good terms.

They sat down to luncheon. The dining-room, like every other part of the small house, had been beautified as much as its position and dimensions would allow. It had originally been small, but an extension of glass had been built out into the yard, which Hester had turned into a fernery. There were a great number of plants of many varieties, some of which had been obtained with great difficulty from immense distances. Hester had been told that it would be impossible to make them grow in an inhabited room, but she had succeeded, and the result was something altogether out of the common.

She admitted that, besides the attention she bestowed upon the plants herself, they occupied the whole time of a specially trained gardener. They were her only hobby, and where they were concerned, time and money had no value for her. The dining-room itself was simple, but exquisite in its way. There were a few pieces of wonderfully chiselled silver on the sideboard, and the glasses on the table were Venetian and Bohemian, and very old. The linen was as fine as fine writing paper, the porcelain was plain white Sèvres. There was nothing superfluous, but there were all the little, unobtrusive, almost priceless details which are the highest expression of intimate luxury — in which the eye alone receives rest, while the other senses are flattered to the utmost. Colour and the precious metals are terribly cheap things nowadays compared with what appeals to touch and taste. There are times when certain dainties, like terrapin, for instance, are certainly worth much more than their weight in silver, if not quite their weight in gold. But as for that, to say that a man is worth his weight in gold has ceased to mean very much. Some ingenious persons have lately calculated that the average man's weight in gold would be worth about forty thousand dollars, and that a few minutes' worth of the income of some men living would pay for a life-sized golden calf. The further development of luxury will be an interesting thing to watch during the next century. A poor woman in New York recently returned a roast turkey to a charitable lady who had sent it to her, with the remark that she was accustomed to eat roast beef at Christmas, though she 'did not mind turkey on Thanksgiving Day.'

Katharine wondered how far such a man as Griggs, who said that he hated music, could appreciate the excessive refinement of a luxury which could be felt rather than seen. It was all familiar to Katharine, and there were little things at the Crowdies which she longed to have at home. Griggs ate his oysters in silence. Fletcher came to his elbow with a decanter.

"Vin de Grave, sir?" enquired the old butler in a low voice.

"No wine, thank you," said Griggs.

"There's Sauterne, isn't there, Walter?" asked Hester. "Perhaps Mr. Griggs — "

"Griggs is a cold water man, like me," answered Crowdie. "His secret vice is to drink a bucket of it, when nobody is looking."

Fletcher looked disappointed, and replaced the decanter on the sideboard.

"It's uncommon to see two men who drink nothing," observed Hester. "But I remember that Mr. Griggs never did."

"Never — since you knew me, Mrs. Crowdie. I did when I was younger."

"Did you? What made you give it up?"

Katharine felt a strange pain in her heart, as they began to talk of the subject. The reality was suddenly coming back out of dreamland.

"I lost my taste for it," answered Griggs, indifferently.

"About the same time as when you began to hate music, wasn't it?" asked Crowdie, gravely.

"Yes, I daresay."

The elder man spoke quietly enough, and there was not a shade of interest in his voice as he answered the question. But Katharine, who was watching him unconsciously, saw a momentary change pass over his face. He glanced at Crowdie with an expression that was almost savage. The dark, weary eyes gleamed fiercely for an instant, the great veins swelled at the lean temples, the lips parted and just showed the big, sharp teeth. Then it was all over again and the kindly look came back. Crowdie was not smiling, and the tone in which he had asked the question showed plainly enough that it was not meant as a jest. Indeed, the painter himself seemed unusually serious. But he had not been looking at Griggs, nor had Hester seen the sudden flash of what was very like half-suppressed anger. Katharine wondered more and more, and the little incident diverted her thoughts again from the suggestion which had given her pain.

"Lots of men drink water altogether, nowadays,"

observed Crowdie. "It's a mistake, of course, but it's much more agreeable."

. "A mistake!" exclaimed Katharine, very much astonished.

"Oh, yes — it's an awful mistake," echoed Griggs, in the most natural way possible.

"I'm not so sure," said Hester Crowdie, in a tone of voice which showed plainly that the idea was not new to her.

"I don't understand," said Katharine, unable to recover from her surprise. "I always thought that —" she checked herself and looked across at the ferns, for her heart was hurting her again.

She suddenly realized, also, that considering what had happened on the previous night, it was very tactless of Crowdie not to change the subject. But he seemed not at all inclined to drop it yet.

"Yes," he said. "In the first place, total abstinence shortens life. Statistics show that moderate consumers of alcoholic drinks live considerably longer than drunkards and total abstainers."

"Of course," assented Griggs. "A certain amount of wine makes a man lazy for a time, and that rests his nerves. We who drink water accomplish more in a given time, but we don't live so long. We wear ourselves out. If we were not the strongest generation there has been for centuries, we should all be in our graves by this time."

"Do you think we are a very strong generation?" asked Crowdie, who looked as weak as a girl.

"Yes, I do," answered Griggs. "Look at yourself and at me. You're not an athlete, and an average street boy of fifteen or sixteen might kill you in a fight. That has nothing to do with it. The amount of actual hard work in your profession, which you've done — ever since you were a mere lad — is amazing, and you're none the worse for it, either. You go on, just as though you had begun yesterday. Heaving weights and rowing races is no test of what a man's strength will bear in everyday life. You don't need big muscles and strong joints. But you need good nerves and enormous endurance. I consider you a very strong man — in most ways that are of any use."

"That's true," said Mrs. Crowdie. "It's what I've always been trying to put into words."

"All the same," continued Griggs, "one reason why you do more than other people is that you drink water. If we are strong, it's because the last generation and the one before it lived too well. The next generation will be ruined by the advance of science."

"The advance of science!" exclaimed Katharine. "But, Mr. Griggs — what extraordinary ideas you have!"

"Have I? It's very simple, and it's absolutely true. We've had the survival of the fittest, and now we're to have the survival of the weakest, because medical science is learning how to keep all the weaklings alive. If they were puppies, they'd all be drowned, for fear of spoiling the breed. That's rather a brutal way of putting it, but it's true. As for the question of drink, the races that produce the most effect on the world are those that consume the most meat and the most alcohol. I don't suppose any one will try to deny that. Of course, the consequences of drinking last for many generations after alcohol has gone out of use. It's pretty certain that before Mohammed's time the national vice of the Arabs was drunkenness. So long as the effects lasted — for a good many generations — they swept everything before them. The most terrible nation is the one that has alcohol in its veins but not in its head. But when the effects wore out, the Arabs retired from the field before nations that drank — and drank hard. They had no chance."

"What a horrible view to take!" Katharine was really shocked by the man's cool statements, and most of all by the appearance of indisputable truth which he undoubtedly gave to them.

"And as for saying that drink is the principal cause of crime," he continued, quietly finishing a piece of shad on his plate, "it's the most arrant nonsense that ever was invented. The Hindus are total abstainers and always have been, so far as we know. The vast majority of them take no stimulant whatever, no tea, no coffee. They smoke a little. There are, I believe, about two hundred millions of them alive now, and their capacity for most kinds of wickedness is quite as great as ours. Any Indian official will tell you that. It's pure nonsense to lay all the blame on whiskey. There would be just as many crimes committed without it, and it would be much harder to detect them, because the criminals would keep their heads better under difficulties. Crime is in human nature, like virtue — like most things, if you know how to find them."

"That's perfectly true," said Crowdie. "I believe every word of it. And I know that if I drank a certain amount of wine I should have a better chance of long life, but I don't like the taste of it — couldn't bear it when I was a boy. I like to see men get mellow and good-natured over a bottle of claret, too. All the same, there's nothing so positively disgusting as a man who has had too much."

Hester looked at him quickly, warning him to drop the

subject. But Griggs knew nothing of the circumstances, and went on discussing the matter from his original point of view.

"There's a beast somewhere, in every human being," he said thoughtfully. "If you grant the fact that it is a beast, it's no worse to look at than other beasts. But it's quite proper to call a drunkard a beast, because almost all animals will drink anything alcoholic which hasn't a bad taste, until they're blind drunk. It's a natural instinct. Did you ever see a goat drink rum, or a Western pony drink a pint of whiskey? All animals like it. I've tried it on lots of them. It's an old sailor's trick."

"I think it's horrid!" exclaimed Hester. "Altogether, it's a most unpleasant subject. Can't we talk of something else?"

"Griggs can talk about anything except botany, my dear," said Crowdie. "Don't ask him about ferns, unless you want an exhibition of ignorance which will startle you."

Katharine sat still in silence, though it would have been easy for her at that moment to turn the conversation into a new channel, by asking Griggs the first question which chanced to present itself. But she could not have spoken just then. She could not eat, either, though she made a pretence of using her fork. The reality had come back out of dreamland altogether this time, and would not be banished again. The long discussion about the subject which of all others was most painful to her, and the cynical indifference with which the two men had discussed it, had goaded her memory back through all the details of the last twenty-four hours. She was scarcely conscious that Hester had interfered, as she became more and more absorbed by her own suffering.

"Shall we talk of roses and green fields and angels'

loves ? " asked Griggs. " How many portraits have you painted since last summer, Crowdie ? "

" By way of reminding me of roses you stick the thorns into me — four, I think — and two I'm doing now, besides Miss Lauderdale's. There's been a depression down town. That accounts for the small number. Portrait painters suffer first. In hard times people don't want them."

" Yes," answered Griggs, thoughtfully. " Portrait painters and hatters. Did you know that, Crowdie ? When money is tight in Wall Street, people don't bet hats, and the hatters say it makes a great difference."

" That's queer. And you — how many books have you written ? "

" Since last summer ? Only one — a boshy little thing of sixty thousand."

" Sixty thousand what ? " asked Hester. " Dollars ? "

" Dollars ! " Griggs laughed. " No — only words. Sixty thousand words. That's the way we count what we do. No — it's a tiresome little thing. I had an idea, — or thought I had, — and just when I got to the end of it I found it was trash. That's generally the way with me, unless I have a stroke of luck. Haven't you got an idea for me, Mrs. Crowdie ? I'm getting old and people won't give me any, as they used to."

" I wish I had ! What do you want ? A love story ? "

" Of course. But what I want is a character. There are no new plots, nor incidents, nor things of that sort, you know. Everything that's ever happened has happened so often. But there are new characters. The end of the century, the sharp end of the century, is digging them up out of the sands of life — as you might dig up clams with a pointed stick."

" That's bathos ! " laughed Crowdie. " The sands of life — and clams ! "

"I wish you'd stick to your daubs, Crowdie, and leave my English alone!" said Griggs. "It sells just as well as your portraits. No — what I mean is that just when fate is twisting the tail of the century —"

"Really, my dear fellow — that's a little too bad, you know! To compare the century to a refractory cow!"

"Crowdie," said Griggs, gravely, "in a former state I was a wolf, and you were a rabbit, and I gobbled you up. If you go on interrupting me, I'll do it again and destroy your Totem."

Katharine started suddenly and stared at Griggs. It seemed so strange that he should have used the very words — wolf and rabbit — which had been in her mind more than once during the morning.

"What is it, Miss Lauderdale?" he asked, in some surprise. "You look startled."

"Oh — nothing!" Katharine hastened to say. "I happened to have thought of wolves and rabbits, and it seemed odd that you should mention them."

"Write to the Psychical Research people," suggested Crowdie. "It's a distinct case of thought-transference."

"I daresay it is," said Griggs, indifferently. "Everything is transferable — why shouldn't thoughts be?"

"Everything?" repeated Crowdie. "Even the affections?"

"Oh, yes — even the affections — but punched, like a railway ticket," answered Griggs, promptly. Everybody laughed a little, except Griggs himself.

"Of course the affections are transferable," he continued meditatively. "The affections are the hat — the object is only the peg on which it's hung. One peg is almost as good as another — if it's within reach; but the best place for the hat is on the man's own head. Nothing shields a man like devoting all his affections to himself."

"That's perfectly outrageous!" exclaimed Hester Crowdie. "You make one think that you don't believe in anything! Oh, it's too bad — really it is!"

"I believe in ever so many things, my dear lady," answered Griggs, looking at her with a singularly gentle expression on his weather-beaten face. "I believe in lots of goods things — more than Crowdie does, as he knows. I believe in roses, and green fields, and love, as much as you do. Only — the things one believes in are not always good for one — it depends — love's path may lie among roses or among thorns; yet the path always has two ends — the one end is life, if the love is true."

"And the other?" asked Katharine, meeting his faraway glance.

"The other is death," he answered, almost solemnly.

A momentary silence followed the words. Even Crowdie made no remark, while both Hester and Katharine watched the elder man's face, as women do when a man who has known the world well speaks seriously of love.

"But then," added Griggs himself, more lightly, and as though to destroy the impression he had made, "most people never go to either end of the path. They enter at one side, look up and down it, cross it, and go out at the other. Something frightens them, or they don't like the colour of the roses, or they're afraid of the thorns — in nine cases out of ten, something drives them out of it."

"How can one be driven out of love?" asked Katharine, gravely.

"I put the thing generally, and adorned it with nice similes and things — and now you want me to explain all the details!" protested Griggs, with a little rough laugh. "How can one be driven out of love? In many ways, I fancy. By a real or imaginary fault of the other person in the path, I suppose, as much as by anything. It won't do to stand at trifles when one loves. There's a meaning in the words of the marriage service — 'for better, for worse.' "

"I know there is," said Katharine, growing pale, and choking herself with the words in the determination to be brave.

"Of course there is. People don't know much about one another when they get married. At least, not as a rule. They've met on the stage like actors in a play — and then, suddenly, they meet in private life, and are quite different people. Very probably the woman is jealous and extravagant, and has a temper, and has been playing the ingenuous young girl's parts on the stage. And the man, who has been doing the self-sacrificing hero, who proposes to go without butter in order to support his starving mother-in-law, turns out to be a gambler — or drinks, or otherwise plays the fool. Of course that's all very distressing to the bride or the bridegroom, as the case may be. But it can't be helped. They've taken one another 'for better, for worse,' and it's turned out to be for worse. They can go to Sioux City and get a divorce, but then that's troublesome and scandalous, and one thing and another. So they just put up with it. Besides, they may love each other so much that the defects don't drive them out of it. Then the bad one drags down the good one — or, in rare cases, the good one raises the bad one. Oh, yes — I'm not a cynic — that happens, too, from time to time."

Crowdie looked at his wife with his soft, languishing glance, and if Katharine had been watching him, she might have seen on his red lips the smile she especially detested. But she was looking down and pressing her hands together under the table. Hester Crowdie's eyes were fixed on her face, for she was very pale and was evidently suffering. Griggs also looked at her, and saw that something unusual was happening.

"Mrs. Crowdie," he said, vigorously changing the subject, as a man can who has been leading the conversation, "if it isn't a very rude question, may I ask where you get the extraordinary ham you always have whenever I lunch with you? I've been all over the world, and I've never eaten anything like it. I'm not sure whether it's the ham itself, or some secret in the cooking."

Mrs. Crowdie glanced at Katharine's face once more, and then looked at him. Crowdie also turned towards him, and Katharine slowly unclasped her hands beneath the table, as though the bitterness of death were passed.

"Oh — the ham?" repeated Mrs. Crowdie. "They're Yorkshire hams, aren't they, Walter? You always order them."

"No, my dear," answered Crowdie. "They're American. We've not had any English ones for two or three years. Fletcher gets them. He's a better judge than the cook. Griggs is quite right — there's a trick about boiling them — something to do with changing the water a certain number of times before you put in the wine. Are you going to set up housekeeping, Griggs? I should think that oatmeal and water and dried herrings would be your sort of fare, from what I remember."

"Something of that kind," answered Griggs. "Anything's good enough that will support life."

The luncheon came to an end without any further incident, and the conversation ran on in the very smallest of small talk. Then Griggs, who was a very busy man, lighted a cigarette and took his departure. As he shook hands with Katharine, and bowed in his rather foreign way, he looked at her once more, as though she interested him very much.

"I hope I shall see you again," said Katharine, quietly.

"I hope so, indeed," answered Griggs. "You're very kind to say so."

When he was gone the other three remained together in the little front room, which has been so often mentioned.

"Will you sit for me a little longer, Miss Lauderdale?" asked Crowdie.

"Oh, don't work any more just yet, Walter!" cried Hester, with sudden anxiety.

"Why? What's the matter?" enquired Crowdie in some surprise.

"You know what Mr. Griggs was just saying at luncheon. You work so hard! You'll overdo it some day. It's perfectly true, you know. You never give yourself any rest!"

"Except during about one-half of the year, my dear, when you and I do absolutely nothing together in the most beautiful places in the world — in the most perfect climates, and without one solitary little shadow of a care for anything on earth but our two selves."

"Yes — I know. But you work all the harder the rest of the time. Besides, we haven't been abroad this year, and you say we can't get away for at least two months. Do give yourself time to breathe — just after luncheon, too. I'm sure it's not good for him, is it, Katharine?" she asked, appealing to her friend.

"Of course not!" answered Katharine. "And besides, I must run home. My dear, just fancy! I forgot to ask you to send word to say that I wasn't coming, and they won't know where I am. But we lunch later than you do — if I go directly, I shall find them still at table."

"Nonsense!" exclaimed Hester. "You don't want to go really? Do you? You know, I could send word still — it wouldn't be too late." She glanced at her husband, who shook his head, and smiled — he was standing behind Katharine. "Well — if you must, then," continued Hester, "I won't keep you. But come back soon. It seems to me that I never see you now — and I have lots of things to tell you."

Katharine shook hands with Crowdie, whose soft, white fingers felt cold in hers. Hester went out with her into the entry, and helped her to put on her thick coat.

"Take courage, dear!" said Mrs. Crowdie in a low voice, as she kissed her. "It will come right in the end."

Katharine looked fixedly at her for a few seconds, buttoning her coat.

"It's not courage that I need," she said slowly, at last. "I think I have enough — good-bye — Hester, darling — good-bye!"

She put her arms round her friend and kissed her three times, and then turned quickly and let herself out, leaving Hester standing in the entry, wondering at the solemn way in which she had taken leave of her.

CHAPTER XXVI.

KATHARINE's mood had changed very much since she had entered the Crowdies' house. She had felt then a certain sense of strength which had been familiar to her all her life, but which had never before seemed so real and serviceable. She had been sure that she could defy the world — in that black frock she wore — and that her face would be of marble and her heart of steel under all imaginable circumstances. She had carried her head high and had walked with a firm tread. She had felt

that if she met John Ralston she could tell him what
she thought of him, and hurt him, so that in his suffering, at least, he should repent of what he had done. .

It was different now.   She did not attempt to find reasons for the difference, and they would have been hard
to discover.   But she knew that she had been exposed
to a sort of test of her strength, and had broken down,
and that Hester Crowdie had seen her defeat.   Possibly
it was the knowledge that Hester had seen and understood which was the most immediately painful circumstance at the present moment; but it was not the most
important one, for she was really quite as brave as she
had believed herself, and what suffered most in her was
not her vanity.

The conversation at table had somehow brought the
whole truth more clearly before her, as the developer
brings out the picture on a photographer's plate.   The
facts were fixed now, and she could not hide them nor
turn from them at will.

Whether she were mistaken or not, the position was
bad enough.   As she saw it, it was intolerable.   By her
own act, by the exercise of her own will, and by nothing
else, she had been secretly married to John Ralston.
She had counted with certainty upon old Robert Lauderdale to provide her husband with some occupation
immediately, feeling sure that within a few days she
should be able to acknowledge the marriage and assume
her position before the world as a married woman.   But
Robert Lauderdale had demonstrated to her that this
was impossible under the conditions she required, namely,
that John should support himself.   He had indeed offered to make her independent, but that solution of the
difficulty was not acceptable.   To obtain what she and
Ralston had both desired, it was necessary, and she ad-

mitted the fact, that John should work regularly in some office for a certain time. Robert Lauderdale himself could not take an idle man from a fashionable club and suddenly turn him into a partner in a house of business or a firm of lawyers, if the idle man himself refused to accept money in any shape. Even if he had accepted it, such a proceeding would have been criticised and laughed at as a piece of plutocratic juggling. It would have made John contemptible. Therefore it was impossible that John and Katharine should have a house of their own and appear as a married couple for some time, for at least a year, and probably for a longer period. Under such circumstances to declare the marriage would have been to make themselves the laughing-stock of society, so long as John continued to live under his mother's roof, and Katharine with her father. The secrèt marriage would have to be kept a secret, except, perhaps, from the more discreet members of the family. Alexander Lauderdale would have to be told, and life would not be very pleasant for Katharine until she could leave the paternal dwelling. She knew that, but she would have been able to bear it, to look upon the next year or two as years of betrothal, and to give her whole heart and soul to help John in his work. It was the worst contingency which she had foreseen when she had persuaded him to take the step with her, and she had certainly not expected that it could arise; but since it had arisen, she was ready to meet it. There was nothing within the limits of reason which she would not have done for John, and she had driven those limits as far from ordinary common sense as was possible, to rashness, even to the verge of things desperate in their folly.

She knew that. But she had counted on John Ralston with that singularly whole-hearted faith which charac-

terizes very refined women. Many years ago, when ana-
lytical fiction was in its infancy, Charles de Bernard
made the very wise and true observation that no women
abandon themselves more completely in thought and
deed to the men they love, or make such real slaves of
themselves, as those whom he calls 'great ladies,' — that
is, as we should say, women of the highest refinement,
the most unassailable social position, and the most rigid
traditions. The remark is a very profound one. The
explanation of the fact is very simple. Women who
have grown up in surroundings wherein the letter of
honour is rigidly observed, and in which the spirit of
virtue prevails for honour's sake, readily believe that
the men they love are as honourable as they seem, and
more virtuous in all ways than sinful man is likely to
be. The man whom such a woman loves with all her
heart, before she has met truth face to face, cannot possibly be as worthy as she imagines that he is; and if
he be an honest man, he must be aware of the fact, and
must constantly suffer by the ever present knowledge
that he is casting a shadow greater than himself, so to
say — and to push the simile further, it is true that in
attempting to overtake that shadow of himself, he often
deliberately walks away from the light which makes him
cast it.

John Ralston could never, under any circumstances,
have done all that Katharine had expected of him,
although she had professed to expect so little. Woman
fills the hours of her lover's absence with scenes from
her own sweet dreamland. In nine cases out of ten,
when she has the chance of comparing what she has
learned with what she has imagined, she has a moment
of sickening disappointment. Later in life there is an
adjustment, and at forty years of age she merely warns

her daughter vaguely that she must not believe too much in men. That is the usual sequence of events.

But Katharine's case just now was very much worse than the common. It is not necessary to recapitulate the evidence against John's soberness on that memorable Thursday. It might have ruined the reputation of a Father of the Church. Up to one o'clock on the following day no one but Mrs. Ralston and Doctor Routh were aware that there was anything whatsoever to be said on the other side of the question. So far as Katharine or any one else could fairly judge, John had been through one of the most outrageous and complete sprees of which New York society had heard for a long time. A certain number of people knew that he had practically fought Hamilton Bright in the hall of his club, and had undoubtedly tripped him up and thrown him. Katharine, naturally enough, supposed that every one knew it, and in spite of Bright's reassuring words on the previous night, she fully expected that John would have to withdraw from the club in question. Even she, girl as she was, knew that this was a sort of public disgrace.

There was no other word for it. The man she loved, and to whom she had been secretly married, had publicly disgraced himself on the very day of the marriage, had been tipsy in the club, had been seen drunk in the streets, had been in a fight with a professional boxer, and had been incapable of getting home alone — much more of going to meet his wife at the Assembly ball.

If he had done such things on their wedding day, what might he not do hereafter? The question was a natural one. Katharine had bound herself to a hopeless drunkard. She had heard of such cases, unfortunately, though they have become rare enough in society, and she knew what it all meant. There would be years of a

wretched existence, of a perfectly hopeless attempt to
cure him. She had heard her father tell such stories,
for Alexander Junior was not a peaceable abstainer like
Griggs and Crowdie. He was not an abstainer at all —
he was a man of ferocious moderation. She remembered
painful details about the drunkard's children. Then
there was a story of a blow — and then a separation — a
wife who, for her child's sake, would not go to another
State and be divorced — and the going back to the
father's house to live, while the husband sank from bad
to worse, and his acquaintances avoided him in the street,
till he had been seen hanging about low liquor saloons
and telling drunken loafers the story of his married life
— speaking to them of the pure and suffering woman
who was still his lawful wife — and laughing about it.
Alexander had told it all, as a wholesome lesson to his
household, which, by the way, consisted of his aged
father, his wife, and his two daughters, none of whom,
one might have thought, could ever stand in need of such
lessons. Charlotte had laughed then, and Katharine
had been disgusted. Mrs. Lauderdale's perfectly classi-
cal face had expressed nothing, for she had been thinking of something else, and the old philanthropist had
made some remarks about the close connection between
intemperance and idiocy. But the so-called lesson was
telling heavily against John Ralston now, two or three
years after it had been delivered.

It was clear to Katharine that her life was ruined
before it had begun. In those first hours after the shock
it did not occur to her that she could ever forgive John.
She was therefore doubly sure that the ruin he had
wrought was irretrievable. She could not naturally
think now of the possibility of ever acknowledging her
marriage. To proclaim it meant to attempt just such a

life as she had heard her father describe. Unfortunately, too, in that very case, she knew the people, and knew that Alexander Junior, who never exaggerated anything but the terrors of the life to come, had kept within the truth rather than gone beyond it.

She did not even tell herself that matters would have been still worse if she had been made publicly John Ralston's wife on the previous day. At that moment she did not seek to make things look more bearable, if they might. She had faced the situation and it was terrible — it justified anything she might choose to do. If she chose to do something desperate to free herself, she wished to be fully justified, and that desired justification would be weakened by anything which should make her position seem more easy to bear.

Indeed, she could hardly have been blamed, whatever she had done. She was bound without being united, married and yet not married, but necessarily shut off from all future thought of marriage, so long as John Ralston lived.

She had assumed duties, too, which she was far from wishing to avoid. In her girlish view, the difference between the married and the single state lay mainly in the loss of the individual liberty which seemed to belong to the latter. She had been brought up, as most American girls are, in old-fashioned ideas on the subject, which are good, — much better than European ideas, — though in extended practice they occasionally lead to some odd results, and are not always carried out in after life. In two words, our American idea is that, on being married, woman assumes certain responsibilities, and ceases, so to say, to be a free dancer in a ball-room. The general idea in Europe is that, at marriage, a woman gets rid of as many responsibilities as she can, and acquires the liberty to do as she pleases, which has been withheld from her before.

Katharine felt, therefore, even at that crisis, that she had forfeited her freedom, and, amidst all she felt, there was room for that bitter regret. A French girl could hardly understand her point of view; a certain number of English girls might appreciate it, and some might possibly feel as she did; t an American girl it will seem natural enough. It was not merely out of a feeling of self-respect that she looked upon a change as necessary, nor out of a blind reverence for the religious ceremony which had taken place. Every inborn and cultivated instinct and tradition told her that as a married woman, though the whole world should believe her to be a young girl, she could not behave as she had behaved formerly; that a certain form of perfectly innocent amusement would no longer be at all innocent now; that she had forfeited the right to look upon every man she met as a possible admire.—she went no further than that in her idea of flirtation—and finally that, somehow, she should feel out of place in the parties of very young people to which she was naturally invited.

She was a married woman, and she must behave as one, for the rest of her natural life, though no one was ever to know that she was married. It was a very general idea, with her, but it was a very strong one, and none the less so for its ingenuous simplicity.

But the fact that she regretted her liberty did not even distantly suggest that she might ever fall in lóve with any one but John Ralston. Her only wish was to make him feel bitterly what he had done, that he might regret it as long as he lived, just as she must regret her liberty. The offence was so monstrous that the possibility of forgiving it did not cross her mind. She did not, however, ask herself whether the love that still remained was making the injury he had done it seem yet more atrocious. Love was still in a state of suspended animation — there was no telling what he might do when he came to life again. For the time being he was not to be taken into consideration at all. If she were to love him during the coming years, that would only make matters much worse.

There is not, perhaps, in the yet comparatively passionless nature of most young girls so great a capacity for real suffering as there is in older women. But there is something else instead. There is a sensitiveness which most women lose by degrees to a certain point, though never altogether, the sensitiveness of the very young animal when it is roughly exposed to the first storm of its first winter, if it has been born under the spring breezes and reared amongst the flowers of summer.

It will suffer much more acutely later, — lash and spur, or shears and knife, sharper than wind and snow, — but it will never be so sensitive again. It will never forget how the cruel cold bit its young skin, and got into its delicate throat, and made its slender limbs tremble like the tendrils of a creeper.

It was snowing again, but Katharine walked slowly, and went out of her way in her unformulated wish to lose time, and to put off the moment at which she must meet the familiar faces and hear the well-known voices at home. Until Griggs had broached the fatal subject at table, she had been taken out of herself at the Crowdies'. She must go back to herself now, and she hated the thought as she hated all her own existence. But the regions between Clinton Place and Fourth Avenue are not the part of New York in which it is best for a young girl to walk about alone. She did not like to be stared

at by the loafers at the corners, nor to be treated with
too much familiarity by the patronizing policeman who
saw her over the Broadway crossing. Then, too, she
remembered that she had given no notice of her absence
from luncheon, and that her mother might perhaps be
anxious about her. There was nothing for it but to take
courage and go home. She only hoped that Charlotte
might not be there.

But Charlotte had come, in the hope of enjoying herself as she had done on the previous day. Katharine
ascertained the fact from the girl who let her in, and
went straight to her room, sending word to her mother
that she had lunched with the Crowdies and would come
down presently. Even as she went up the stairs she felt
a sharp pain at the thought that her mother and sister
were probably at that very moment discussing John's
mishaps, and comparing notes about the stories they
had heard — and perhaps reading more paragraphs from
the papers. The shame of the horrible publicity of it
all overcame her, and she locked her door, and tried the
handle to be sure that it was fast — with a woman's distrust of all mechanical contrivances when she wishes to
be quite sure of a situation. It was instinctive, and she
had no second thought which she tried to hide from herself.

As she took off her hat and coat she grew very pale,
and the deep shadows came under her eyes — so dark
that she wondered at them vaguely as she glanced at
herself in the mirror. She felt faint and sick. She
drank a little water, and then, with a sudden impulse,
threw herself upon her bed, and lay staring at the ceiling, as she had lain at dawn. The same glare still came
in from the street and penetrated every corner, but not
so vividly as before, for the snow was falling fast, and
the mist of the whirling flakes softened the light.

It was a forlorn little room. Robert the Rich would have been very much surprised if he could have seen it. He was a generous man, and was very fond of his grand-niece, and if he had known exactly how she lived under her father's roof it would have been like him to have interfered. All that he ever saw of the house was very different. There was great simplicity downstairs, and his practised eye detected the signs of a rigid economy — far too rigid, he thought, when he calculated what Alexander Junior must be worth; a ridiculously exaggerated economy, he considered, when he thought of his own wealth, and that his only surviving brother lived in the house in Clinton Place. But there was nothing squalid or mean about it all. The meanness was relative. It was like an aspersion upon the solidity of Robert's fortune, and upon his intention of providing suitably for all his relations.

Upstairs, however, and notably in Katharine's room, things had a different aspect. Nothing had been done there since long before Charlotte had been married. The wall-paper was old-fashioned, faded, and badly damaged by generations of tacks and pins. The carpet was threadbare and patched, and there were holes where even a patch had not been attempted. The furniture was in the style of fifty years ago or more, veneered with dark mahogany, but the veneering was coming off in places, leaving bare little surfaces of dusty pine wood smeared with yellowish, hardened glue. Few objects can look more desperately shabby than veneered furniture which is coming to pieces. There was nothing in the room which Katharine could distinctly remember to have seen in good condition, except the old carpet, which had been put down when she and Charlotte had been little girls. To Charlotte herself, when she had come

in on Wednesday afternoon, there had been something
delightful in the renewal of acquaintance with all her
old dinginess of intimate surroundings.   Charlotte's
own life was almost oppressed with luxury, so that it
destroyed her independence.   But to Katharine, worn
out and heartsore with the troubles of her darkening
life, it was all inexpressibly depressing.   She stared
at the ceiling as she lay there, in order not to look at
the room itself.   She was very tired, too, and she would
have given anything to go to sleep.

It was not merely sleep for which she longed.   It
was a going out.   Again the thought crossed her mind,
as it had that morning, that if the whole world were a
single taper, she would extinguish the flame with one
short breath, and everything would be over.   And now,
too, in her exhaustion, came the idea that something less
complete, but quite as effectual, was in her power.   It
had passed through her brain half an hour previously,
when she had bidden Hester Crowdie good-bye — with a
sort of intuitive certainty that she was never to see her
friend again.   She had left Hester with a vague and
sudden presentiment of darkness.   She had assuredly
not any intention of seeking death in any definite form,
but it had seemed to be close to her as she had said
those few words of farewell.   It came nearer still as
she lay alone in her own room.   It came nearer, and
hovered over her, and spoke to her.

It would be the instant solution of all difficulties, the
end of all troubles.   The deep calm against which no
storm would have power any more.   On the one hand,
there was life in two aspects.   Either to live an existence of misery and daily torture with the victim of a
most degrading vice, a man openly disgraced, and at
whom every one she respected would forever look

askance. Or else to live out that other life of secret
bondage, neither girl nor wife, so long as John Ralston
was alive, suffering each time he was dragged lower, as
she was suffering to-day, bound, tied in every way,
beyond possibility of escaping. Why should she suffer
less to-morrow than now? It would be the same, since
all the conditions must remain unchanged. It would be
the same always. Those were the two aspects of living
on in the future which presented themselves. The torn
carpet and the broken veneering of the furniture made
them seem even more terrible. There may be a point
at which the trivial has the power to push the tragic to
the last extremity.

And on the other side stood death, the liberator, with
his white smile and far-away eyes. The snow-glare was
in his face, and he did not seem to feel it, but looked
quietly into it, as though he saw something very peaceful
beyond. It was a mere passing fancy that evoked the
picture in the weary, restless mind, but it was pleasant
to gaze at it, so long as it lasted. It was gone in a
moment again, leaving, however, a new impression —
that of light, rather than of darkness. She wished it
would come back.

Possibly she had been almost or quite dozing, seeing
that she was so much exhausted. But she was wide
awake again now. She turned upon her side with a
long-drawn sigh, and stared at the hideous furniture,
the ragged carpet, and the dilapidated wall-paper. It was
not that they meant anything of themselves — certainly
not poverty, as they might have seemed to mean to any
one else. They were the result of a curious combination of contradictory characters in one family, which
ultimately produced stranger results than Katharine
Lauderdale's secret marriage, some of which shall be

chronicled hereafter. The idea of poverty was not associated with the absence of money in Katharine's mind.
She might be in need of a pair of new gloves, and she
and her mother might go to the opera upstairs, because
the stalls were too dear. But poverty! How could it
enter under the roof of any who bore the name of Lauderdale? If, yesterday, she had begged uncle Robert to
give her half a million, instead of refusing a hundred
thousand, it was quite within the bounds of possibility
that he might have written the cheque there and then.
No. The shabby furniture in Katharine's room had
nothing to do with poverty, nor with the absence of
money, either. It was the fatal result of certain family
peculiarities concerning which the public knew nothing,
and it was there, and at that moment it had a strong
effect upon Katharine's mind. It represented the
dilapidation of her life, the literal dilapidation, the
tearing down of one stone after another from the crown-
ing point she had reached yesterday to the deep foundation which was laid bare as an open tomb to-day. She
dwelt on the idea now, and she stared at the forlorn
objects, as she had at first avoided both.

Death has a strange fascination, sometimes, both for
young and old people. Men and women in the prime
and strength of life rarely fall under its influence. It
is the refuge of those who, having seen little, believed
that there is little to see, and of the others who, having
seen all, have died of the sight, inwardly, and desire
bodily death as the completion of experience. Let one,
or both, be wrong or right; it matters little, since the
facts are there. But the fascination aforesaid is stronger
upon the young than upon the old. They have fewer
ties, and less to keep them with the living. For the
ascendant bond is weaker than the descendant in human-

ity, and the love of the child for its mother is not as her love for the child. It is right that it should be so. In spite of many proverbs, we know that what the child owes the parent is as nothing compared with the parent's debt to it. Have we all found it so easy to live that we should cast stones upon heart-broken youths and maidens who would fain give back the life thrust upon them without their consent?

Katharine clasped her hands together, as she lay on her side, and prayed fervently that she might die that day — at that very hour, if possible. It would be so very easy for God to let her die, she thought, since she was already so tired. Her heart had almost stopped beating, her hands were cold, and she felt numb, and weary, and miserable. The step was so short. She wondered whether it would hurt much if she took it herself, without waiting. There were things which made one go to sleep — without waking again. That must be very easy and quite, quite painless, she thought. She felt dizzy, and she closed her eyes again.

How good it would be! All alone, in the old room, while the snow was falling softly outside. She should not mind the snow-glare any more then. It would not tire her eyes. That white smile — it came back to her at last, and she felt it on her own face. It was very strange that she should be smiling now — for she was so near crying — nearer than she thought, indeed, for as the delicate lips parted with the slow, sighing breath, the heavy lids — darkened as though they had been hurt — were softly swelling a little, and then very suddenly and quickly two great tears gathered and dropped and ran and lost themselves upon the pillow.

Ah, how peaceful it would be — never to wake again, when the little step was passed! Perhaps, if she lay quite still, it would come. She had heard strange stories of people in the East, who let themselves die when they were weary. Surely, none of them had ever been as weary as she. Strange — she was always so strong! Every one used to say, 'as strong as Katharine Lauderdale.' If they could see her now!

She wanted to open her eyes, but the snow-glare must be still in the room, and she could not bear it — and the shabby furniture. She would breathe more slowly. It seemed as though with each quiet sigh the lingering life might float away into that dear, peaceful beyond — where there would be no snow-glare and the furniture would not be shabby — if there were any furniture at all — beyond — or any John Ralston — no 'marriage nor giving in marriage' — all alone in the old room —

Two more tears gathered, more slowly this time, though they dropped and lost themselves just where the first had fallen, and then, somehow, it all stopped, for what seemed like one blessed instant, and then there came a loud knocking, with a strange, involved dream of carpenters and boxes and a journey and being late for something, and more knocking, and her mother's voice calling to her through the door.

"Katharine, child! Wake up! Don't forget that you're to dine at the Van De Waters' at eight! It's half past six now!"

It was quite dark, save for the flickering light thrown upon the ceiling from the gas-lamp below. Katharine started up from her long sleep, hardly realizing where she was.

"All right, mother — I'm awake!" she answered sleepily.

As she listened to her mother's departing footsteps, it all came back to her, and she felt faint again. She struggled to her feet in the gloom and groped about till she had found a match, and lit the gas and drew down the old brown shades of the window. The light hurt her eyes for a moment, and as she pressed her hands to them she felt that they were wet.

"I suppose I've been crying in my sleep!" she ex‧claimed aloud. "What a baby I am!"

She looked at herself in the mirror with some curiosity, before beginning to dress.

"I'm an object for men and angels to stare at!" she said, and tried to laugh at her dejected appearance. "However," she added, "I suppose I must go. I'm Katharine Lauderdale — 'that nice girl who never has headaches and things' — so I have no excuse."

She stopped for a moment, still looking at herself.

"But I'm not Katharine Lauderdale!" she said presently, whispering the words to herself. "I'm Katharine Ralston — if not, what am I? Ah, dear me!" she sighed. "I wonder how it will all end!"

At all events, Katharine Lauderdale, or Katharine Ralston, she was herself again, as she turned from the mirror and began to think of what she must wear at the Van De Waters' dinner-party.

CHAPTER XXVII.

EVEN John Ralston's tough constitution could not have been expected to shake off in a few hours the fatigue and soreness of such an experience as he had undergone. Even if he had been perfectly well, he would have stayed at home that day in the expectation of receiving an answer from Katharine; and as it was, he needed as much rest as he could get. He had not often been at the trouble of taking care of himself, and the sensation was not altogether disagreeable, as he sat by his own fireside, in the small room which went by the name of 'Mr. Ralston's study.' He stretched out his feet to the fire, drank a little tea from time to time, stared at the logs, smoked, turned over the pages of a magazine without reading half a dozen sentences, and revolved the possibilities of his life without coming to any conclusion.

He was stiff and bruised. When he moved his head, it ached, and when he tried to lean to the right, his neck hurt him on the left side. But if he did not move at all, he felt no pain. There was a sort of perpetual drowsy hum in his ears, partly attributable, he thought, to the singing of a damp log in the fire, and partly to his own imagination. When he tried to think of anything but his own rather complicated affairs, he almost fell asleep. But when his attention was fixed on his present situation, it seemed to him that his life had all at once come to a standstill just as events had been moving most quickly. As for really sleeping in the intervals of thought, his constant anxiety for Katharine's reply to his letter kept his faculties awake. He knew, however, that it would be quite unreasonable to expect anything from her before twelve o'clock. He tried to be patient.

Between ten and eleven, when he had been sitting before his fire for about an hour, the door opened softly and Mrs. Ralston entered the room. She did not speak, but as John rose to meet her she smiled quietly and made him sit down again. Then she kneeled before the hearth and began to arrange the fire, an operation which she had always liked, and in which she displayed a singular talent. Moreover, at more than one critical moment in her

life, she had found it a very good resource in embarrass-
ment.   A woman on her knees, making up a fire, has a
distinct advantage.   She may take as long as she pleases
about it, for any amount of worrying about the position
of a particular log is admissible.   She may change colour
twenty times in a minute, and the heat of the flame as
well as the effort she makes in moving the wood will
account satisfactorily for her blushes or her pallor.   She
may interrupt herself in speaking, and make effective
pauses, which will be attributed to the concentration of
her thoughts upon the occupation of her hands.   If a
man comes too near, she may tell him sharply to keep
away, either saying that she can manage what she is doing
far better if he leaves her alone, or alleging that the prox-
imity of a second person will keep the air from the chim-
ney and make it smoke.   Or if the gods be favourable
and she willing, she may at any moment make him kneel
beside her and help her to lift a particularly heavy log.
And when two young people are kneeling side by side
before a pile of roaring logs in winter, the flames have a
strange bright magic of their own; and sometimes love
that has smouldered long blazes up suddenly and takes
the two hearts with it — out of sheer sympathy for the
burning oak and hickory and pine.

But Mrs. Ralston really enjoyed making up a fire, and
she went to the hearth quite naturally and without reflect-
ing that after what had occurred she felt a little timid in
her son's presence.   He obeyed her and resumed his seat,
and sat leaning forward, his arms resting on his knees
and his hands hanging down idly, while he watched his
mother's skilful hands at work.

"Jack dear —" she paused in her occupation, having
the tongs in one hand and a little piece of kindling-
wood in the other, but did not turn round — "Jack,

I can't make up to you for what I did last night,
can I?"

She was motionless for a moment, listening for his
reply. It came quietly enough after a second or two.

"No, mother, you can't. But I don't want to remember it, any more than you do."

Mrs. Ralston did not move for an instant after he
had spoken. Then she occupied herself with the fire
again.

"You're quite right," she said presently. "You
wouldn't be my son, if you said anything else. If I
were a man, one of us would be dead by this time."

She spoke rather intensely, so to say, but she used her
hands as gently as ever in what she was doing. John
said nothing.

"Men don't forgive that sort of thing from men," she
continued presently. "There's no reason why a woman
should be forgiven, I suppose, even if the man she has
insulted is her own son."

"No," John answered thoughtfully. "There is no more
reason for forgiving it. But there's every reason to forget it, if you can."

"If you can. I don't wish to forget it."

"You should, mother. Of course, you brought me up
to believe — you and my father — that to doubt a man's
word is an unpardonable offence, because lying is a part
of being afraid, which is the only unpardonable sin. I
believe it. I can't help it."

"I don't expect you to. We've always — in a way —
been more like two men, you and I, than like a mother
and her son. I don't want the allowances that are made
for women. I despise them. I've done you wrong, and
I'll take the consequences. What are they? It's a bad
business, Jack. I've run against a rock. I'll do any-

thing you ask. I'll give you half my income, and we can live apart. Will you do that?"

"Mother!" John Ralston fairly started in his surprise. "Don't talk like that!"

"There!" exclaimed Mrs. Ralston, hanging up the hearthbrush on her left, after sweeping the feathery ashes from the shining tiles within the fender. "It will burn now. Nobody understands making a fire as I do."

She rose to her feet swiftly, drew back from John, and sat down in the other of the two easy chairs which stood before the fireplace. She glanced at John and then looked at the fire she had made, clasping her hands over one knee.

"Smoke, won't you?" she said presently. "It seems more natural."

"All right — if you like."

John lit a cigarette and blew two or three puffs into the air, high above his head, very thoughtfully.

"I'm waiting for your answer, Jack," said Mrs. Ralston, at last.

"I don't see what I'm to say," replied John. "Why do you talk about it?"

"For this reason — or for these reasons," said Mrs. Ralston, promptly, as though she had prepared a speech beforehand, which was, in a measure, the truth. "I've done you a mortal injury, Jack. I know that sounds dramatic, but it's not. I'll tell you why. If any one else, man or woman, had deliberately doubted your statement on your word of honour, you would never have spoken to him or her again. Of course, in our country, duelling isn't fashionable — but if it had been a man — I don't know, but I think you would have done something to him with your hands. Yes, you can't deny it. Well, the case isn't any better because satisfaction is impossible, is it? I'm trying to look at it logically, because I know what you must feel. Don't you see, dear?"

"Yes. But—"

"No! Let me say all I've got, to say first, and then you can answer me. I've been thinking about it all night, and I know just what I ought to do. I know very well, too, that most women would just make you forgive as much as you could and then pretend to you and to themselves that nothing had ever happened. But we're not like that, you and I. We're like two men, and since we've begun in that way, it's not possible to turn round and be different now, in the face of a difficulty. There are people who would think me foolish, and call me quixotic, and say, 'But it's your own son — what a fuss you're making about nothing.' Wouldn't they? I know they would. It seems to me that, if anything, it's much worse to insult one's own son, as I did you, than somebody else's son, to whom one owes nothing. I'm not going to put on sackcloth and sit in the ashes and cry. That wouldn't help me a bit, nor you either. Besides, other people, as a rule, couldn't understand the thing. You never told me a lie in your life. Last Monday when you came home after that accident, and weren't quite yourself, you told me the exact truth about everything that had happened. You never even tried to deceive me. Of course you have your life, and I have mine. I have always respected your secrets, haven't I, Jack?"

"Indeed you have, mother."

"I know I have, and if I take credit for it, that only makes all this worse. I've never asked you questions which I thought you wouldn't care to answer. I've never been inquisitive about all this affair with Katharine. I don't even know at the present moment whether

you're engaged to her still, or not. I don't want to know
— but I hope you'll marry her some day, for I'm very
fond of her. No — I've never interfered with your liberty, and I've never been willing to listen to what people
wished to tell me about you. I shouldn't think it honest. And in that way we've lived very harmoniously,
haven't we?"

"Mother, you know we have," answered John, earnestly.

"All that makes this very much worse. One drop of
blood will turn a whole bowl of clean water red. It
wouldn't show at all if the water were muddy. If you
and I lived together all our lives, we should never forget last night."

"We could try to," said John. "I'm willing."

Mrs. Ralston paused and looked at him a full minute
in silence. Then she put out her hand and touched his
arm.

"Thank you, Jack," she said gravely.

John tried to press her hand, but she withdrew it.

"But I'm not willing," she resumed, after another short
pause. "I've told you — I don't want a woman's privilege to act like a brute and be treated like a spoiled child
afterwards. Besides, there are many other things. If
what I thought had been true, I should never have
allowed myself to act as I did. I ought to have been
kind to you, even if you had been perfectly helpless. I
know you're wild, and drink too much sometimes. You
have the strength to stop it if you choose, and you've
been trying to since Monday. You've said nothing, and
I've not watched you, but I've been conscious of it. But
it's not your fault if you have the tendency to it. Your
father drank very hard sometimes, but he had a different
constitution. It shortened his life, but it never seemed to

affect him outwardly. I'm conscious — to my shame — that I didn't discourage him, and that when I was young and foolish I was proud of him because he could take more than all the other officers and never show it. Men drank more in those days. It was not so long after the war. But you're a nervous man, and your father wasn't, and you have his taste for it without that sort of quiet, phlegmatic, strong, sailor's nature that he had. So it's not your fault. Perhaps I should have frightened you about it when you were a boy. I don't know. I've made mistakes in my life."

"Not many, mother dear."

"Well — I've made a great one now, at all events. I'm not going back over anything I've said already. It's the future I'm thinking of. I can't do much, but I can manage a 'modus vivendi' for us —"

"But why —"

"Don't interrupt me, dear! I've made up my mind what to do. All I want of you now, is your advice as a man, about the way of doing it. Listen to me, Jack. After what has happened between us — no matter how it turns out afterwards, for we can't foresee that — it's impossible that we should go on living as we've lived since your father died. I don't mean that we must part, unless you want to leave me, as you would have a perfect right to do."

"Mother!"

"Jack — if I were your brother, instead of your mother — still more, if I were any other relation — would you be willing to depend for the rest of your life on him, or on any one who had treated you as I treated you last night?"

She paused for an answer, but John Ralston was silent. With his character, he knew that she was quite right, and that nothing in the world could have induced him to accept such a situation.

"Answer me, please, dear," she said, and waited again.

"Mother — you know! Why should I say it?"

"You would refuse to be dependent any longer on such a person?"

"Well — yes — since you insist upon my saying it," answered John, reluctantly. "But with you, it's —"

"With me, it's just the same — more so. I have had a longer experience of you than any one else could have had, and you've never deceived me. Consequently, it was more unpardonable to doubt you. I don't wish you to be dependent on me any longer, Jack. It's an undignified position for you, after this."

"Mother — I've tried —"

"Hush, dear! I'm not talking about that. If there had been any necessity, if you had ever had reason to suppose that it wasn't my greatest happiness to have you with me — or that there wasn't quite enough for us both — you'd have just gone to sea before the mast, or done something of the same kind, as all brave boys do who feel that they're a burden on their mothers. But there's always been enough for us both, and there is now. I mean to give you your share, and keep what I need myself. That will be yours some day, too, when I'm dead and gone."

"Please don't speak of that," said John, quickly and earnestly. "And as for this idea of your —"

"Oh, I'm in no danger of dying young," interrupted Mrs. Ralston, with a little dry laugh. "I'm very strong. All the Lauderdales are, you know — we live forever. My father would have been seventy-one this year if he hadn't been killed. And as long as I live, of course, I must have something to live on. I don't mean to go begging to uncle Robert for myself, and I shouldn't care to do it for you, though I would if it were necessary. Now, we've got just twelve thousand dollars a year between us, and the house, which is mine, you know. That will give us each six thousand dollars a year. I shall see my lawyer this morning and it can be settled at once. Whenever the house is let, if we're both abroad, you shall have half of the rent. When we're both here, half of it is yours to live in — or pull down, if you like. If you marry, you can bring your wife here, and I'll go away. Now, I think that's fair. If it isn't, say so before it's too late."

"I won't listen to anything of the kind," answered John, calmly.

"You must," answered his mother.

"I don't think so, mother."

"I do. You can't prevent me from making over half the estate to you, if I choose, and when that's done, it's yours. If you don't like to draw the rents, you needn't. The money will accumulate, for I won't touch it. You shall not be in this position of dependence on me — and at your age — after what has happened."

"It seems to me, mother dear, that it's very much the same, whether you give me a part of your income, or whether you make over to me the capital it represents. It's the same transaction in another shape, that's all."

"No, it's not, Jack! I've thought of that, because I knew you'd say it. It's so like you. It's not at all the same. You might as well say that it was originally intended that you should never have the money at all, even after I died. It was and is mine, for me and my children. As I have only one child, it's yours and mine jointly. As long as you were a boy, it was my business to look after your share of it for you. As soon as you were a man,

I should have given you your share of it. It would have been much better, though there was no provision in either of the wills. If it had been a fortune, I should have done it anyhow, but as it was only enough for us two to live on, I kept it together and was as careful of it as I could be."

"Mother—I don't want you to do this," said John. "I don't like this sordid financial way of looking at it —I tell you so quite frankly."

Mrs. Ralston was silent for a few moments, and seemed to be thinking the matter over.

"I don't like it either, Jack," she said at last. "It isn't like us. So I won't say anything more about it. I'll just go and do it, and then it will be off my mind."

"Please don't!" cried Ralston, bending forward, for she made as though she would rise from her seat.

"I must," she answered. "It's the only possible basis of any future existence for us. You shall live with me from choice, if you like. It will—well, never mind— my happiness is not the question! But you shall not live with me as a matter of necessity in a position of dependence. The money is just as much yours as it's mine. You shall have your share, and—"

"I'd rather go to sea—as you said," interrupted John.

"And let your income accumulate. Very well. But I —I hope you won't, dear. It would be lonely. It wouldn't make any difference so far as this is concerned. I should do it, whatever you did. As long as you like, live here, and pay your half of the expenses. I shall get on very well on my share if I'm all alone. Now I'm going, because there's nothing more to be said."

Mrs. Ralston rose this time. John got up and stood beside her, and they both looked at the fire thoughtfully.

"Mother—please—I entreat you not to do this

thing!" said John, suddenly. "I'm a brute even to have thought twice of that silly affair last night — and to have said what I said just now, that I couldn't exactly feel as though anything could undo what had been done. Indeed — if there's anything to forgive, it's forgiven with all my heart, and we'll forget it and live just as we always have. We can, if we choose. How could you help it — the way I looked! I saw myself in the glass. Upon my word, if I'd drunk ever so little, I should have been quite ready to believe that I was tipsy, from my own appearance — it was natural, I'm sure, and — "

"Hush, Jack!" exclaimed Mrs. Ralston. "I don't want you to find excuses for me. I was blind with anger, if that's an excuse — but it's not. And most of all — I don't want you to imagine for one moment that I'm going to make this settlement of our affairs with the least idea that it is a reparation to you, or anything at all of that sort. Not that you'd ever misunderstand me to that extent. Would you?"

"No. Certainly not. You're too much like me."

"Yes. There's no reparation about it, because that's more possible. As it is, no particular result will follow unless you wish it. You'll be free to go away, if you please, that's all. And if you choose to marry Katharine, and if she is willing to marry you on six thousand a year, you'll feel that you can, though it's not much. And for the matter of that, Jack dear — you know, don't you? If it would make you happy, and if she would — I don't think I should be any worse than most mothers-in-law — and all I have is yours, Jack, besides your share. But those are your secrets — no, it's quite natural."

John had taken her hand gently and kissed it.

"I don't want any gratitude for that," she continued. "It's perfectly natural. Besides, there's no question

of gratitude between you and me. It's always been share
and share alike — of everything that was good. Now I'm
going. You'll be in for luncheon ? Do take care of yourself to-day. See what weather we're having ! And —
well — it's not for me to lecture you about your health,
dear. But what Doctor Routh said is true. You've
grown thinner again, Jack — you grow thinner every
year, though you are so strong."

"Don't worry about me, mother dear. I'm all right.
And I shan't go out to-day. But I have a dinner-party
this evening, and I shall go to it. I think I told you —
the Van De Waters' — didn't I ? Yes. I shall go to that
and show myself. I'm sure people have been talking
about me, and it was probably in the papers this morning. Wasn't it ? "

"Dear — to tell you the truth, I wouldn't look to see.
It wasn't very brave of me — but — you understand."

"I certainly shan't look for the report of my encounter
with the prize-fighter. I'm sure he was one. I shall
probably be stared at to-night, and some of them will be
rather cold. But I'll face it out — since I'm in the right
for once."

"Yes. I wouldn't have you stay at home. People
would say you were afraid and were waiting for it to
blow over. Is it a big dinner ? "

"I don't know. I got the invitation a week ago, at
least, so it isn't an informal affair. It's probably to
announce Ruth Van De Water's engagement to that foreigner — you know — I've forgotten his name. I know
Bright's going — because they said he wanted to marry
her last year — it isn't true. And there'll probably be
some of the Thirlwalls, and the young Trehearns, and
Vanbrugh and his wife — you know, all the Van De
Water young set. Katharine's going, too. She told

me when she got the invitation, some time last week.
There'll be sixteen or eighteen at table, and I suppose
they'll amuse themselves somehow or other afterwards.
Nobody wants to dance to-night, I fancy — at least none
of our set, after the Thirlwalls', and the Assembly, and I
don't know how many others last week."

"They'll probably put you next to Katharine," said
Mrs. Ralston.

"Probably — especially there, for they always do —
with Frank Miner on her other side to relieve my gloom.
Second cousins don't count as relations at a dinner party,
and can be put together. Half of the others are own
cousins, too."

"Well, if it's a big dinner it won't be so disagreeable
for you. But if you'd take my advice, Jack — however — " She stopped.

"What is it, mother ? " he asked. " Say it."

"Well — I was going to say that if any one made any
disagreeable remarks, or asked you why you weren't at
the Assembly last night, I should just tell the whole
story as it happened. And you can end by saying that
I was anxious about you and sent for Doctor Routh, and
refer them to him. That ought to silence everybody."

"Yes." John paused a moment. "Yes," he repeated,
"I think you're right. I wish old Routh were going to
be there himself."

"He'd go in a minute if he were asked," said Mrs. Ralston.

"Would he ? With all those young people ? "

"Of course he would — only too delighted ! Dear old
man, it's just the sort of thing he'd like. But I'm going,
Jack, or I shall stay here chattering with you all the
morning."

"That other thing, mother — about the money — don't
do it ! " Jack held her a moment by the hand.

"Don't try to hinder me, dear," she answered. "It's the only thing I can do—to please my own conscience a little. Good-bye. I'll see you at luncheon."

She left the room quickly, and John found himself alone with his own thoughts again.

"It's just like her," he said to himself, as he lighted a cigar and sat down to think over the situation. "She's just like a man about those things."

He had perhaps never admired and loved his mother as he did then; not for what she was going to do, but for the spirit in which she was doing it. He was honest in trying to hinder her, because he vaguely feared that the step might cause her some inconvenience here-after—he did not exactly know how, and he was firmly resolved that he would not under any circumstances take advantage of the arrangement to change his mode of life. Everything was to go on just as before. As a matter of theory, he was to have a fixed, settled income of his own; but as a matter of fact, he would not regard it as his. What he liked about it, and what really appealed to him in it all, was his mother's man-like respect for his honour, and her frank admission that nothing she could do could possibly wipe out the slight she had put upon him. Then, too, the fact and the theory were at variance and in direct opposition to one another. As a matter of theory, nothing could ever give him back the sensation he had always felt since he had been a boy—that his mother would believe him on his word in the face of any evidence whatsoever which there might be against him. But as a matter of fact, the evil was not only completely undone, but there was a stronger bond between them than there had ever been before.

That certainly was the first good thing which had come to him during the last four and twenty hours, and it had an effect upon his spirits.

He thought over what his mother had said about the evening, too, and was convinced that she was right in advising him to tell the story frankly as it had happened. But he was conscious all the time that his anxiety about Katharine's silence was increasing. He had roused himself at dawn, in spite of his fatigue, and had sent a servant out to post a letter with the special delivery stamp on it. Katharine must have received it long ago, and her answer might have been in his hands before now. Nevertheless, he told himself that he should not be impatient, that she had doubtless slept late after the ball, and that she would send him an answer as soon as she could. By no process of reasoning or exaggeration of doubting could he have reached the conclusion that she had never received his letter. She had always got everything he sent her, and there had never been any difficulty about their correspondence in all the years during which they had exchanged little notes. He took up the magazine again, and turned over the pages idly. Suddenly Frank Miner's name caught his eyes. The little man had really got a story into one of the great magazines, a genuine novel, it seemed, for this was only a part, and there were the little words at the end of it, in italics and in parenthesis, 'to be continued,' which promised at least two more numbers, for as John reflected, when the succeeding number was to be the last, the words were 'to be concluded.' He was glad, for Miner's sake, of this first sign of something like success, and began to read the story with interest.

It began well, in a dashing, amusing style, as fresh as Miner's conversation, but with more in it, and John was beginning to congratulate himself upon having found something to distract his attention from his bodily ills and his mental embarrassments, when the door opened, and Miner himself appeared.

"May I come in, Ralston?" he enquired, speaking softly, as though he believed that his friend had a headache.

"Oh — hello, Frank! Is that you? Come in! I'm reading your novel. I'd just found it"

Little Frank Miner beamed with pleasure as he saw that the magazine was really open at his own story, for he recognized that this, at least, could not be a case of premeditated appreciation.

"Why — Jack —" he stammered a moment later, in evident surprise. "You don't look badly at all!"

"Did they say I was dead?" enquired Ralston, with a grim smile. "Take a cigar. Sit down. Tell me all about my funeral."

Miner laughed as he carefully cut off the end of the cigar and lit it — a sort of continuous little gurgling laugh, like the purling of a brook.

"My dear boy" he said, blowing out a quantity of smoke, and curling himself up in the easy chair, "you're the special edition of the day. The papers are full of you — they're selling like hot cakes everywhere — your fight with Tom Shelton, the champion light weight — and your turning up in the arms of two policemen — talk of a 'jag!' Lord!"

CHAPTER XXVIII.

JOHN looked at Miner quietly for a few seconds, without saying anything. The little man was evidently lost in admiration of the magnitude of his friend's 'jag,' as he called it.

"I say, Frank," said Ralston, at last, "it's all a mistake, you know. It was a series of accidents from beginning to end."

"Oh — yes — I suppose so. You managed to accumulate quite a number of accidents, as you say."

Ralston was silent again. He was well aware of the weight of the evidence against him, and he wished to enter upon his explanation by degrees, in order that it might be quite clear to Miner.

"Look here," he began, after a while. "I'm not the sort of man who tries to wriggle out of things, when he's done them, am I? Heaven knows — I've been in scrapes enough! But you never knew me to deny it, nor to try and make out that I was steady when I wasn't. Did you, Frank?"

"No," answered Miner, thoughtfully. "I never did. That's a fact. It's quite true."

The threefold assent seemed to satisfy Ralston.

"All right," he said. "Now I want you to listen to me, because this is rather an extraordinary tale. I'll tell it all, as nearly as I can, but there are one or two gaps, and there's a matter connected with it about which I don't want to talk to you."

"Go ahead," answered Miner. "I've got some perfectly new faith out — and I'm just waiting for you. Produce the mountain, and I'll take its measure and remove it at a valuation."

Ralston laughed a little and then began to tell his story. It was, of course, easy for him to omit all mention of Katharine, and he spoke of his interview with Robert Lauderdale as having taken place in connection with an idea he had of trying to get something to do in the West, which was quite true. He omitted also to mention the old gentleman's amazing manifestation of

eccentricity — or folly — in writing the cheque which
John had destroyed. For the rest, he gave Miner every
detail as well as he could remember it. Miner listened
thoughtfully and never interrupted him once.

"This isn't a joke, is it, Jack?" he asked, when John
had finished with a description of Doctor Routh's midnight visit.

"No," answered Ralston, emphatically. "It's the
truth. I should be glad if you would tell any one who
cares to know."

"They wouldn't believe me," answered Miner, quietly.

"I say, Frank — " John's quick temper was stirred
already, but he checked himself.

"It's all right, Jack," answered Miner. "I believe
every word you've told me, because I know you don't
invent — except about leaving cards on stray acquaintances at the Imperial, when you happen to be
thirsty."

He laughed good-naturedly.

"That's another of your mistakes," said Ralston. "I
know — you mean last Monday. I did leave cards at the
hotel. I also had a cocktail. I didn't say I wasn't
going to, and I wasn't obliged to say so, was I? It
wasn't your business, my dear boy, nor Ham Bright's,
either."

"Well — I'm glad you did, then. I'm glad the cards
were real, though it struck me as thin at the time. I
apologize, and eat humble pie. You know you're one of
my illusions, Jack. There are two or three to which I
cling. You're a truthful beggar, somehow. You ought
to have a little hatchet, like George Washington — but
I daresay you'd rather have a little cocktail. It illustrates your nature just as well. Bury the hatchet and
pour the cocktail over it as a libation — where was I?

Oh — this is what I meant, Jack. Other people won't
believe the story, if I tell it, you know."

"Well — but there's old Routh, after all. People will
believe him."

"Yes — if he takes the trouble to write a letter to the
papers, over his name, degrees and qualifications. Of
course they'll believe him. And the editors will do
something handsome. They won't apologize, but they'll
say that a zebra got loose in the office and upset the type
while they were in Albany attending to the affairs of the
Empire State — and that's just the same as an apology,
you know, which is all you care for. You can't storm
Park Row with the gallant Four Hundred at your back.
In the first place, Park Row's insured, and secondly, the
Four Hundred would see you — further — before they'd
lift one of their four thousand fingers to help you out of
a scrape which doesn't concern them. You'd have to be
a parson or a pianist, before they'd do anything for you.
It's 'meat, drink and pantaloons' to be one of them, anyhow — and you needn't expect anything more."

"Where do you get your similes from, Frank!" laughed
Ralston.

"I don't know. But they're good ones, anyway. Why
don't you get Routh to write a letter, before the thing
cools down? It could be in the evening edition, you
know. There have been horrid things this morning —
allusions — that sort of thing."

"Allusions to what?" asked Ralston, quickly and
sharply.

"To you, of course — what did you suppose?"

"Oh — to me! As though I cared! All the same,
if old Routh would write, it would be a good thing. I
wish he were going to be at the Van De Waters' dinner
to-night."

"Why? Are you going there? So am I."

"It seems to be a sort of family tea-party," said Ralston. "Bright's going, and cousin Katharine, and you and I. It only needs the Crowdies and a few others to make it complete."

"Well — you see, they're cousins of mine, and so are you, and that sort of makes us all cousins," observed Miner, absently. "I say, Jack — tell the story at table, just as you've told it to me. Will you? I'll set you on by asking you questions. Stunning effect — especially if we can get Routh to write the letter. I'll cut it out of a paper and bring it with me."

"You know him, don't you?" asked Ralston.

"Know him? I should think so. Ever since I was a baby. Why?"

"I wish you'd go to him this morning, Frank, and get him to write the letter. Then you could take it to one of the evening papers and get them to put it in. You know all those men in Park Row, don't you?"

"Much better than some of them want to know me," sighed the little man. "However," he added, his bright smile coming back at once, "I ought not to complain. I'm getting on, now. Let me see. You want me to go to Routh and get him to write a formal letter over his name, denying all the statements made about you this morning. Isn't that taking too much notice of the thing, after all, Jack?"

"It's going to make a good deal of difference to me in the end," answered Ralston. "It's worth taking some trouble for."

"I'm quite willing," said Miner. "But — I say! What an extraordinary story it is!"

"Oh, no. It's only real life. I told you — I only had one accident, which was quite an accident — when

I tumbled down in that dark street. Everything else happened just as naturally as unnatural things always do. As for upsetting Ham Bright at the club, I was awfully sorry about that. It seemed such a low thing to do. But then — just remember that I'd been making a point of drinking nothing for several days, just by way of an experiment, and it was irritating, to say the least of it, to be grabbed by the arm and told that I was screwed. Wasn't it, Frank? And just at that moment, uncle Robert had telephoned for me to come up, and I was in a tremendous hurry. Just look at it in that way, and you'll understand why I did it. It doesn't excuse it — I shall tell Ham that I'm sorry — but it explains it. Doesn't it?"

"Rather!" exclaimed Miner, heartily.

"By the bye," said Ralston, "I wanted to ask you something. Did that fellow Crowdie hold his tongue? I suppose he was at the Assembly last night."

"Well — since you ask me —" Miner hesitated. "No — he didn't. Bright gave it to him, though, for telling cousin Emma."

"Brute! How I hate that man! So he told cousin Emma, did he? And the rest of the family, too, I suppose."

"I suppose so," answered Miner, knowing that Ralston meant Katharine. "Everybody knew about the row at the club, before the evening was half over. Teddy Van De Water said he supposed you'd back out of the dinner to-night and keep quiet till this blew over. I told Teddy that perhaps he'd better come round and suggest that to you himself this morning, if he wanted to understand things quickly. He grinned — you know how he grins — like an organ pipe in a white tie. But he said he'd heard Bright leathering into Crowdie — that's one of Teddy's expressions — so he supposed that things weren't as bad as people said — and that Crowdie was only a 'painter chap,' anyhow. I didn't know what that meant, but feebly pointed out that Crowdie was a great man, and that his wife was a sort of cousin of mine, and that she, at least, had a good chance of having some of cousin Robert's money one of these days. Not that I wanted to defend Crowdie, or that I don't like Teddy much better — but then, you know what I mean! He'll be calling me 'one of those literary chaps,' next, with just the same air. One's bound to stand up for art and literature when one's a professional, you know, Jack. Wasn't I right?"

"Oh, perfectly!" answered Ralston, with a smile. "But will you do that for me, Frank?"

"Of course I will. You're one of my illusions, as I told you. I'm willing to do lots of things for my illusions. I'll go now, and then I'll come back and tell you what the old chap says. If by any chance he gets into a rage, I'll tell him that I didn't come so much to talk about you as to consult him about certain symptoms of nervous prostration I'm beginning to feel. He's death on nervous prostration — he's a perfect terror at it — he'll hypnotize me, and put me into a jar of spirits, and paint my nose with nervine and pickled electricity and things, and sort of wake me up generally."

"All right — if you can stand it, I can," said Ralston. "I'd go myself — only — "

"You're pretty badly used up," interrupted Miner, completing the sentence in his own way. "I know. I remember trying to play football once. Those little games aren't much in my line. Nature meant me for higher things. I tried football, though, and then I said, like Napoleon — you remember? — 'Ces balles ne sont pas

pour moi.' I couldn't tell where I began and the football ended — I felt that I was a safe under-study for a
shuttlecock afterwards. That's just the way you feel,
isn't it? As though it were Sunday, and you were the
frog — and the boys had gone back to afternoon church?
I know! Well — I'll come back as soon as I've seen
Routh. Good-bye, old man — don't smoke too much. I
do — but that's no reason."

The little man nodded cheerfully, knocked the ashes
carefully from the end of his cigar — he was neat in everything he did — and returned it to his lips as he left the
room. Ralston leaned back in his arm-chair again and
rested his feet on the fender. The fire his mother had
made so carefully was burning in broad, smoking flames.
He felt cold and underfed and weary, so that the warmth
was very pleasant; and with all that came to his heart
now, as he thought of his mother, there mingled also a
little simple, childlike gratitude to her for having made
up such a good fire.

The time passed, and still no word came from Katharine. He was willing to find reasons or, at least, excuses,
for her silence, but he was conscious that they were of
little value. He knew, now, that there had really been
paragraphs in the papers about him, as he had expected,
and that they had been of a very disagreeable nature.
Katharine had probably seen them, or one of them,
besides having heard the stories that had been circulated by Crowdie and others during the previous evening.
He fancied that he could feel her unbelief, hurting
him from a distance, as it were. Her face, cold and contemptuous, rose before him out of the fire, and he took
up the magazine again, and tried to hide it. But it
could not be hidden.

Surely by this time she must have got his letter. There

could be no reasonable doubt of that. He looked at his watch again, as he had done once in every quarter of an hour for some time. It was twelve o'clock. Miner had not stayed long.

John went over the scene on Wednesday evening, at the Thirlwalls'. Katharine had been very sure of herself, at the last — sure that, whatever he did, she should always stand by him. Events had put her to the test soon enough, and this was the result. They had been married twenty-four hours, and she would not even answer his note, because appearances were against him.

And the great, strong sense of real innocence rose in him and defied and despised the woman who could not trust him even a little. If the very least of the accusations had been true, he would have humbled himself honestly and said that she was right, and that she had promised too much, in saying all she had said. At all times he was a man ready to take the full blame of all he had done, to make himself out worse than he really was, to assume at once that he was a failure and could do nothing right. On the slightest ground, he was ready to admit everything that people brought against him. Katharine, if he had been living as usual, would have been at liberty to reproach him as bitterly as she pleased with his weakness, to turn her back on him and condemn him unheard, if she chose. He would have been patient and would have admitted that he deserved it all, and more also. He was melancholy, he was discouraged with himself, and he was neither vain nor untruthful.

But he had made an effort, and a great one. There was in him something of the ascetic, with all his faults, and something of the enthusiasm which is capable of sudden and great self-denial if once roused. He knew what he had done, for he knew what it had cost him, mentally and physically. Lean as he had been before, he had grown perceptibly thinner since Monday. He knew that, so far, he had succeeded. For the first time, perhaps, he had every point of justice on his side. If he had been inclined to be merciful and humble and submissive towards those who doubted him now, he would not have been human. The two beings whom he loved in the world, his mother and Katharine, were the very two who had doubted him most. As for his mother, he had not persuaded her, for she had persuaded herself — by means of such demonstration as no sane being could have rejected, namely, the authoritative statement of a great doctor, personally known to her. What had followed had produced a strange result, for he felt that he was more closely bound to her than ever before, a fact which showed, at least, that he did not bear malice, however deeply he had been hurt. But he could not go about everywhere for a week with Doctor Routh at his heels to swear to his sobriety. He told himself so with some contempt, and then he thought of Katharine, and his face grew harder as the minutes went by and no answer came to his letter.

It was far more cruel of her than it had been in his mother's case. Katharine had only heard stories and reports of his doings, and she should be willing to accept his denial of them on her faith in him. He had never lied to her. On Wednesday night, he had gratuitously told her the truth about himself — a truth which she had never suspected — and had insisted upon making it out to be even worse than it was. His wisdom told him that he had made a mistake then, in wilfully lowering himself in her estimation, and that this was the consequence of that; if he had not forced upon her an unnecessary confession of his weakness, she would now have believed in his strength. But his sense of honour rose and shamed his wisdom, and told him that he had done right. It would have been a cowardly thing to accept what Katharine had then been forcing upon him, and had actually made him accept, without telling her all the truth about himself.

He had done wrong to yield at all. That he admitted, and repeated, readily enough. He made no pretence of having a strong character, and he had been wretchedly weak in allowing her to persuade him to the secret marriage. He should have folded his arms and refused, from the first. He had foreseen trouble, though not of the kind which had actually overtaken him, and he should have been firm. Unfortunately, he was not firm, by nature, as he told himself, with a sneer. Not that Katharine had been to blame, either. She had made her reasons seem good, and he should not have blamed her had she been ever so much in the wrong. There his honour spoke again, and loudly.

But for what she was doing now, in keeping silence, leaving him without a word when she must know that he was most in need of her faith and belief — for abandoning him when it seemed as though every man's hand were turned against him — he could not help despising her. It was so cowardly. Had it all been ten times true, she should have stood by him when every one was abusing him.

It was far more cruel of her than of his mother, for all she knew of the story had reached her by hearsay, whereas his mother had seen him, as he had seen himself, and his appearance might well have deceived any one but Doctor Routh. He did not ask himself whether he could ever forgive her, for he did not wish to hear in his heart the answer which seemed inevitable. As for loving her, or

not loving her, he thought nothing about it at that
moment. With him, too, as with her, love was in a
state of suspended animation. It would have been sufficiently clear to any outsider acquainted with the circumstances that when the two met that evening, something
unusual would probably occur. Katharine, indeed, believed that John would not appear at the dinner-party;
but John, who firmly intended to be present, knew that
Katharine was going, and he expected to be placed beside
her. It was perfectly well known that they were in love
with one another, and the least their greatest friends
could do was to let them enjoy one another's society.
This may have been done partly as a matter of policy,
for both were young enough and tactless enough to show
their annoyance if they were separated when they chanced
to be asked to sit at the same table. John looked forward to the coming evening with some curiosity, and
without any timidity, but also without any anticipation
of enjoyment.

He was trying to imagine what the conversation would
be like, when Frank Miner returned, beaming with enthusiasm, and glowing from his walk in the cold, wet
air. He had been gone a long time.

"Well?" asked John, as his friend came up to the fire,
and held out his hands to it.

"Very well — very well, indeed, thank you," answered
the latter, with a cheerful laugh. "I'll bet you twenty-
five cents to a gold watch that you can't guess what's
happened — at Routh's."

"Twenty-five cents — to a gold watch? Oh — I see.
Thank you — the odds don't tempt me. What did happen?"

"I say — those were awfully good cigars of yours,
Jack!" exclaimed Miner, by way of answer. "Haven't
you got another?"

"There's the box. Take them all. What happened?"

"No — I'll only take one — it would look like borrowing if I took two, and I can't return them. Jack, there's a lot of good blood knocking about in this family, do you know? I don't mean about the cigars — I'm naturally a generous man when it comes to taking things I like. But the other thing. Do you know that somebody had been to Routh about making him write the letter, before I got there?"

"What? To make him write it? Not Ham Bright? It would be like him — but how should he have known about Routh?"

"No. It wasn't Bright. Want to guess? Well — I'll tell you. It was your mother, Jack. Nice of her, wasn't it?"

"My mother!"

Ralston leaned forward and began to poke the logs about. He felt a curious sensation of gladness in the eyes, and weakness in the throat.

"Tell me about it, Frank," he added, in a rather thick voice.

"There's not much to tell. I marched in and stated my case. He's between seven and eight feet high, I believe, and he stood up all the time — felt as though I were talking to scaffold poles. He listened in the calmest way till I'd finished, and then took up a letter from his desk and handed it to me to read and to see whether I thought it would do. I asked what it meant, and he said he'd just written it at the request of Mrs. Ralston, who had left him a quarter of an hour ago, and that if I would take it to the proper quarter — as he expressed it — he should be much obliged. He's a brick — a tower of strength — a tower of bricks — a perfect Babel of a man. You'll see, when the evening papers come out —"

"Did you take it down town?"

"Of course. And I got hold of one of the big editors. I sent in word that I had a letter from Doctor Routh which must be published in the front page this evening unless the paper wanted Mr. Robert Lauderdale to bring an action against them for libel to-morrow morning. You should have seen things move. What a power cousin Robert is! I suppose I took his name in vain — but I don't care. Old Routh is not to be sneezed at, either. You'll see the letter. There's some good old English in it. Oh, it's just prickly with epithets — 'unwarrantable liberty,' 'impertinent scurrility' — I don't know what the old doctor had for breakfast. It's not like him to come out like that, not a bit. He's a cautious old bird, as a rule, and not given to slinging English all over the ten-acre lot, like that. You see, he takes the ground that you're his patient, that you had some sort of confustication of the back of your head, and that to say you were screwed when you were ill was a libel, that the terms in which the editor had allowed the thing to appear proved that it was malicious, and that as the editor was supposed to exercise some control, and to use his own will in the matter of what he published and circulated, it was wilfully published, since the city paid for places in which people who had no control over their wills were kept for the public safety, and that therefore the paragraph in question was a wilfully malicious libel evidently published with the intention of doing harm — and much more of the same kind of thing — all of which the editor would have put into the waste paper basket if it had not been signed, Martin Routh, M.D., with the old gentleman's address. Moreover, the editor asked me why, in sending in a message, I had made use of threatening language purporting to come from Mr. Robert Lauderdale. But as you had told me the whole story, I knew what to say. I just told him that you had left the house of your uncle, Mr. Robert Lauderdale, after spending some time with him, when you met with the accident in the street which led to all your subsequent adventures. That seemed to settle him. He said the whole thing had been a mistake, and that he should be very sorry to have given Mr. Lauderdale any annoyance, especially at this time. I don't know what he meant by that, I'm sure — unless uncle Robert is going to buy the paper for a day or two to see what it's like — you know the proprietor's dead, and they say the heirs are going to sell. Well — that's all. Confound it, my cigar's out. I'm a great deal too good to you, Jack!"

Ralston had listened without comment while the little man told his story, satisfied, as he proceeded from point to point, that everything was going well for him, at last, and mentally reducing Miner's strong expressions to the lowest key of probability.

"So it was my mother who went first to Doctor Routh," he·said, as though talking with himself, while Miner relighted his cigar.

"Yes," answered Miner, between two puffs. "I confess to having been impressed."

"It's like her," said John. "It's just like her. You didn't happen to see any note for me lying on the hall table, did you?" he asked, rather irrelevantly.

"No — but I'll go and look, if you like."

"Oh — it's no matter. Besides, they know I haven't been out this morning, and they'd bring anything up. I'm very much obliged to you, Frank, for all this. And I know that you'll tell anybody who talks about it just what I've told you. I should like to feel that there's a chance of some one's knowing the truth when I come into the room this evening."

"Oh, they'll all know it by that time. Routh's letter will run along the ground like fire mingled with hail. As for Teddy Van De Water, he lives on the papers. Of course they won't fly at you and congratulate you all over, and that sort of thing. They'll just behave as though nothing at all had happened, and afterwards, when we men are by ourselves, smoking, they'll all begin to ask you how it happened. That is, unless you want to tell the story yourself at table, and in that case I'll set you on, as I said."

"I don't care to talk about it," answered John. "But — look here, Frank — listen! You're as quick as anybody to see things. If you notice that a number of the set don't know about Routh's letter — that there's a sort of hostile feeling against me at table — why, then just set me on, as you call it, and I'll defend myself. You see, I've such a bad temper, and my bones ache, and I'm altogether so generally knocked out, that it will be much better to give me my head for a clear run, than to let people look as though they should like to turn their backs on me, but didn't dare to. Do you understand?"

"All right, Jack. I won't make any mistake about it."

"Very well, then. It's a bargain. We won't say anything more about it."

Miner presently took his departure, and John was left alone again. In the course of time he gave up looking at his watch, and relinquished all hope of hearing from Katharine. Little by little, the certainty formed itself in his mind that the meeting that evening was to be a hostile one.

Not very long after Miner had gone, another hand opened the door, and John sprang to his feet, for even in the slight sound he recognized the touch. Mrs. Ralston entered the room. With more impulsiveness than was usual in him he went quickly to meet her, and threw his arms round her, kissing her through her veil, damp and cold from the snowy air.

"Mother, darling — how good you are!" he exclaimed softly. "There isn't anybody like you — really."

"Why — Jack? What is it?" asked Mrs. Ralston, happy, but not understanding.

"Miner was here — he told me about your having been to old Routh to make him write — "

"That? Oh — that's nothing. Of course I went — the first thing. Didn't he say last night that he'd give his evidence in a court of law? I thought he might just as well do it. The business is all settled, dear boy. I've seen the lawyer, and he's making out the deed. He'll bring it here for me to sign when he comes up from his office, and the transfers of the titles will be registered to-morrow morning — just in time before Sunday."

"Don't talk about that, mother!" answered John. "I didn't want you to do it, and it's never going to make the slightest difference between us."

"Well — perhaps not. But it makes all the difference to me. Promise me one thing, Jack."

"Yes, mother — anything you like."

"Promise me to remember that if you and Katharine choose to get married, in spite of her father and all the Lauderdales, this is your house, and that you have a right to it. You won't have much to live on, but you won't starve. Promise me to remember that, Jack. Will you?"

"I'll promise to remember it, mother. But I'll not promise to act on it."

"Well — that's a matter for your judgment. Go and get ready for luncheon. It must be time."

Once more John put his arms round her neck, and drew her close to him.

"You're very good to me, mother — thank you!"

———

CHAPTER XXIX.

KATHARINE spent more time than necessary over dressing for dinner on that evening, not because she bestowed more attention than usual upon her appearance, but because there were long pauses of which she was scarcely conscious, although the maid reminded her from time to time that it was growing late.   The result, however, was satisfactory in the opinion of her assistant, a sober-minded Scotch person of severe tastes, who preferred black and white to any colours whatsoever, and thought that the trees showed decided frivolity in being green, and that the woods in autumn were positively improper.

It was undoubtedly true that the simple black gown, without ornament and with very little to break its sweeping line, was as becoming to Katharine's strong beauty as it was appropriate to her frame of mind.   It made her look older than she was, perhaps, but being so young, the loss was almost gain.   It gave her dignity a background and a reason, as it were.   Her face was pale still, but not noticeably so, and her eyes were quiet if not soft.   Only a person who knew her very well would have observed the slight but steady contraction of the broad eyebrows, which was unusual.   As a rule, if it came at all, it disappeared almost instantly again.   She remembered afterwards — as one remembers the absurd details of one's own thoughts — that when she had looked into the mirror for

the last time, she had been glad that her front hair did
not curl, and that she had never yielded to the temptation to make it curl, as most girls did.   She had been
pleased by the simplicity of the two thick, black waves
which lay across the clear paleness of her forehead, like
dark velvet on cream-white silk.   She forgot the thought
instantly, but, later, she remembered how severe and
straight it had looked, and the consciousness was of some
value to her — as the least vain man, taken unexpectedly
to meet and address a great assembly, may be momentarily glad if he chances to be wearing a particularly
good coat.   The gravest of us have some consciousness
of our own appearance, and be our strength what it may,
when it is appropriate to appear in the wedding garment,
it is good for us to be wearing one.

Katharine stopped at her mother's door as she descended the stairs.   Mrs. Lauderdale was dining at home,
and the Lauderdales dined at eight o'clock, so that she
was still in her room at ten minutes before the hour.
Katharine knocked and entered.   Her mother was standing before the mirror.   The door which led to her
father's dressing-room, by a short passage between two
wardrobes built into the house, was wide open.   Katharine heard him moving some small objects on his dressing-table.

"You're late, child," said Mrs. Lauderdale, not turning, for as Katharine entered, she could see her reflection in the mirror.   "Are you going to take Jane with
you?   If not, I wish you'd tell her to come here, as you
go down — I let you have her because I knew you'd be
late."

"No," answered Katharine, "I don't want her — she's
only in the way.   It's the Van De Waters', you know.
Good night, mother."

"Good night, darling—enjoy yourself—you'll be late, of course—they'll dance, or something."

"Yes—but I shan't stay. I'm tired. Good night again."

Katharine was going to the door, when her father appeared from his dressing-room, serenely correct, as usual, but wearing his black tie because no one was coming to dinner.

"I want to speak to you, Katharine," he said.

She turned and stood still in the middle of the room, facing him. He had a letter in his hand.

"Yes, papa," she answered quietly, not anticipating trouble.

"I'm sorry I could not see you earlier," said Alexander Junior, coming forward and fixing his steely eyes on his daughter's face. "But I hadn't an opportunity, because I was told that you were asleep when I came home. This morning, as I was leaving the house as usual, a messenger put this letter into my hands. It has a special delivery stamp on it, and you will see that the mark on the dial edge stands at eight forty-five A.M. Consequently, the boy who brought it was dilatory in doing his duty. It is addressed to you in John Ralston's handwriting."

"Why didn't you send it up to me, instead of keeping it all day?" enquired Katharine, with cold surprise.

"Because I do not intend that you shall read it," answered her father, his lips opening and shutting on the words like the shears of a cutting-machine.

Mrs. Lauderdale turned round from the mirror and looked at her husband and daughter. It would have been impossible to tell from her face whether she had been warned of what was to be done or not, but there was an odd little gleam in her eyes, of something which might have been annoyance or satisfaction.

"Why don't you intend me to read my letters?" asked Katharine in a lower tone.

"I don't wish you to correspond with John Ralston," answered Alexander Junior. "You shall never marry him with my consent, especially since he has disgraced himself publicly as he did yesterday. There was an account of his doings in the morning papers. I daresay you've not seen it. He was taken home last night in a state of beastly intoxication by two policemen, having been picked up by them out of a drunken brawl with a prize-fighter. To judge from the handwriting of the address on this letter, it appears to have been written while he was still under the influence of liquor. I don't mean that my daughter shall receive letters written by drunken men, if I can help it."

"Show me the letter," said Katharine, quietly.

"I'll show it to you because, though you've never had any reason to doubt my statements, I wish you to have actually seen that it has not been opened by me, nor by any one. My judgment is formed from the handwriting solely, but I may add that it is impossible that a man who was admittedly in a state of unconsciousness from liquor at one o'clock in the morning, should be fit to write a letter to Katharine Lauderdale, or to any lady, within six hours. The postmark on the envelope is seven-thirty. Am I right?" He turned deliberately to Mrs. Lauderdale.

"Perfectly," she answered, with sincere conviction.

And it must be allowed that, from his point of view, he was not wrong. He beckoned Katharine to the gas-light beside the mirror and held up the letter, holding it at the two sides of the square envelope in the firm grip of his big, thin fingers, as though he feared lest she should try to take it. But Katharine did not raise her hands, as she bent forward and inspected the address. It was assuredly not written in John's ordinary hand, though the writing was recognizable as his, beyond doubt. There was an evident attempt at regularity, but a too evident failure. It looked a little as though he had attempted to write with his left hand. At one corner there was a very small stain of blood, which, as every one knows, retains its colour on writing paper, even under gas-light, for a considerable time. It will be remembered that John had hurt his right hand.

Katharine's brows contracted more heavily. She was disgusted, but she was also pained. She looked long and steadily at the writing, and her lips curled slightly. Alexander Lauderdale turned the letter over to show her that it was sealed. Again, where the finger had hurriedly pressed the gummed edge of the envelope, there was a little mark of blood. Katharine drew back very proudly, as from something at once repulsive and beneath her woman's dignity. Her father looked at her keenly and coldly.

"Have you satisfied yourself?" he enquired. "You see that it has not been opened, do you?"

"Yes."

"I will burn it," said Alexander Lauderdale, still watching her.

"Yes."

He seemed surprised, for he had expected resistance, and perhaps some attempt on her part to get possession of the letter and read it. But she stood upright, silent, and evidently disgusted. He lifted his hand and held the letter over the flame of the gas-light until it had caught fire thoroughly. Then he laid it in the fireless grate — the room, like all the rest of the house, was heated by the furnace, — and with his usual precise interpretation of his own conscience's promptings, he turned his back on it, lest by any chance he should see and accidentally read any word of the contents as the paper curled and flared and blackened and fell to ashes. Katharine, however, was well aware that a folded letter within its envelope will rarely burn through and through if left to itself. She went to the hearth and watched it. It had fallen flat upon the tiles, and one thickness after another flamed, rose from one end and curled away as the one beneath it took fire. She would not attempt to read one of the indistinct words, but she could not help seeing that it had been a long letter, scrawled in a handwriting even more irregular than that on the envelope. The leaves turned black, one by one, rising and remaining upright like black funeral feathers, till at last there was only a little blue light far down in the heart of them. That, too, went out, and a small, final puff of smoke rose and vanished. Katharine turned the heap over with the tongs. Only one little yellow bit of paper remained unconsumed at the bottom. It was almost round, and as she turned it over, she read on it the number of the house. That was all that had not been burned.

"I'm glad to see that you look at the matter in its true light," said her father, as she stood up again.

"How should I look at it?" asked Katharine, coldly. "Good night, mother — good night," she repeated, nodding to her father.

She turned and left the room. A moment later she was on her way to the Van De Waters' house, leaning back in the dark, comfortable brougham, her feet toasting on the foot-warmer, and the furs drawn up closely round her. · It was a bitterly cold night, for a sharp frost had succeeded the snow-storm after sunset. Even inside the carriage Katharine could feel that there was

something hard and ringing in the quality of the air
which was in harmony with her own temper. She had
plenty of time to go over the scene which had taken place
in her mother's room, but she felt no inclination to analyze her feelings. She only knew that this letter of
John's, written when he was still half senseless with
drink, was another insult, and one deeper than any she
had .felt before. It was a direct insult — a sin of com-
mission, and not merely of omission, like his absence
from the ball on the previous night.

She supposed, naturally enough, that he would not
appear at the dinner-party, but at that moment she was
almost indifferent as to whether he should come or not.
She was certainly not afraid to meet him. It would be
far more probable, she thought, that he should be afraid
to meet her.

It was a quarter past eight when she reached the Van
De Waters', and she was the last to arrive. It was a
party of sixteen, almost all very young, and most of them
unmarried — a party very carefully selected with a view to
enjoyment — an intimate party, because many out of the
number were more or less closely connected and related,
and it was indicative of the popularity of the Lauderdales,
that amongst sixteen young persons there should be four
who belonged more or less to the Lauderdale tribe. There
was Katharine, there was Hamilton Bright, — the Crowdies had been omitted because so many disliked Crowdie
himself, — there was little Frank Miner, who was a near
relation of the Van De Waters, and there stood John
Ralston, talking to Ruth Van De Water, before Crowdie's
new portrait of her, as though nothing had happened.

Katharine saw him the moment she entered the room,
and he knew, as he heard the door opened, that she must
be the last comer, since every one else had arrived. With-

out interrupting his conversation with Miss Van De Water, he turned his head a little and met Katharine's eyes. He bowed just perceptibly, but she gave him no sign of recognition, which was pardonable, however, as he knew, since there were people between them, and she had not yet spoken to Ruth herself, who, with her brother, had invited the party. The elder Van De Waters had left the house to the young people, and had betaken themselves elsewhere for the evening. ·

John continued to talk quietly, as Katharine came forward. As he had expected, he had found her name on the card in the little envelope which had been handed to him when he arrived, and he was to take her in to dinner. Until late in the afternoon the brother and sister had hoped that John would not come, and had already decided to ask in his place that excellent man, Mr. Brown, who was always so kind about coming when asked at the last minute. Then Frank Miner had appeared, with an evening paper containing Doctor Routh's letter, and had explained the whole matter, so that they felt sympathy for John rather than otherwise, though no one had as yet broached to him the subject of his adventures. Naturally enough, the Van De Waters both supposed that Katharine should have been among the first to hear the true version of the story, and they would not disarrange their table in order to separate two young people who were generally thought to be engaged to be married. There were, of course, a few present who had not heard of Doctor Routh's justification of John.

Katharine came across directly, towards Ruth Van De Water, and greeted her affectionately. John came forward a little, waiting to be noticed and to shake hands in his turn. Katharine prolonged the first exchange of words with her young hostess rather unnecessarily, and then, since she could not avoid the meeting, held out her hand to John, looking straight and coldly into his eyes.

"You're to take Miss Lauderdale in, you know, Mr. Ralston," said Miss Van De Water, who knew that dinner would be announced almost immediately, and that Katharine would wish to speak to the other guests before sitting down.

"Yes — I found my card," answered John, as Katharine withdrew her hand without having given his the slightest pressure.

It was a strange meeting, considering that they had been man and wife since the previous morning, and could hardly be said to have met since they had parted after the wedding. Katharine, who was cold and angry, wondered what all those young people would say if she suddenly announced to them, at table, that John Ralston was her husband. But just then she had no definite intention of ever announcing the fact at all.

John only partly understood, for he was sure that she must have received his letter. But what he saw was enough to convince him that she had not in the least believed what he had written, and had not meant to answer him. He was pale and haggard already, but during the few minutes that followed, while Katharine moved about the room, greeting her friends, the strong lines deepened about his mouth and the shadows under his eyes grew perceptibly darker.

A few minutes later the wide doors were thrown back and dinner was announced. Without hesitation he went to Katharine's side, and waited while she finished speaking with young Mrs. Vanbrugh, his right arm slightly raised as he silently offered it.

Katharine deliberately finished her sentence, nodded and smiled to Dolly Vanbrugh, who was a friend of hers, and had been in some way concerned in the famous Darche affair three or four years ago, as Mrs. Darche's intimate and confidante.   Then she allowed her expression to harden again, and she laid her hand on John's arm and they all moved in to dinner.

"I'm sorry," said John, in a low, cold voice.   "I suppose they couldn't upset their table."

Katharine said nothing, but looked straight before her as they traversed one beautiful room after another, going through the great house to the dining-room at the back.

"You got my letter, I suppose," said John, speaking again as they crossed the threshold of the last door but one, and came in sight of the table, gleaming in the distance under soft lights.

Katharine made a slight inclination of the head by way of answer, but still said nothing.   John thought that she moved her hand, as though she would have liked to withdraw it from his arm, and he, for his part, would gladly have let it go at that moment.

It was a very brilliant party, of the sort which could hardly be gathered anywhere except in America, where young people are not unfrequently allowed to amuse themselves together in their own way without the interference or even the presence of elders — young people born to the possession, in abundance, of most things which the world thinks good, and as often as anywhere, too, to the inheritance of things good in themselves, besides great wealth —such as beauty, health, a fair share of wit, and the cheerful heart, without which all else is as ashes.

Near one end of the table sat Frank Miner, who had taken in Mrs. Vanbrugh, and who was amusing every one with absurd stories and jokes — the small change of wit, but small change that was bright and new, ringing from his busy little mint.

At the other end sat Teddy Van De Water, a good fellow at heart in spite of his eyeglass and his affectations,
discussing yachts and centreboards and fin-keels with
Fanny Trehearne, a girl who sailed her own boats at
Newport and Bar Harbor, and who cared for little else
except music, strange to say.   Nearly opposite to Katharine and John was Hamilton Bright, between two young
girls, talking steadily and quietly about society, but evidently much preoccupied, and far more inclined to look
at Katharine than at his pretty neighbours.   He had seen
Routh's letter, and had, moreover, exchanged a few words
with Ralston in the hall, having arrived almost at the
same instant, and he saw that Katharine did not understand the truth.   Ralston had begun by apologizing to
his friend for what had happened at the club, but Bright,
who bore no malice, had stopped him with a hearty shake
of the hand, and a challenge to wrestle with him any
day, for the honour of the thing, in the hall of the club
or anywhere else.

Frank Miner, too, from a distance, watched John and
Katharine, and saw that the trouble was great, though
he laughed and chatted and told stories, as though he
were thoroughly enjoying himself.   In reality he was
debating whether he should not bring up the subject
which must be near to every one's thoughts, and give
John a chance of telling his own story.   Seeing how the
rest of the people were taking the affair, he would not
have done so, since all was pleasant and easy, but he saw
also that John could not possibly have an explanation
with Katharine at table, and that both were suffering.
His kindly heart decided the question.   It would be a very
easy matter to accomplish, and he waited for a convenient
opportunity of attracting attention to himself, so as to
obtain the ear of the whole large table, before he began.

He was perfectly conscious of his own extreme popularity, and knew that, for once, he could presume upon it, though he was quite unspoiled by a long career of little social successes.

John and Katharine exchanged a few words from time to time, for the sake of appearances, in a coldly civil tone, and without the slightest expression of interest in one another. John spoke of the weather, and Katharine admitted that it had been very bad of late. She observed that Miss Van De Water was looking very well, and that a greenish blue was becoming to fair people. John answered that he had expected to hear of Miss Van De Water's engagement to that foreigner whose name he had forgotten, and Katharine replied that he was not a foreigner but an Englishman, and that his name was Northallerton, or something like that. John said he had heard that they had first met in Paris, and Katharine took some salt upon her plate and admitted that it was quite possible. She grew more coldly wrathful with every minute, and the iron entered into John's soul, and he gave up trying to talk to her — of which she was very glad.

It was some time before the occasion which Miner sought presented itself, and the dinner proceeded brilliantly enough amid the laughter of young voices and the gladness of young eyes. For young eyes see flowers where old ones see but botany, so to speak.

Katharine had not believed that it would hurt her as, it did, nor Ralston that love could seem so far away. They turned from each other and talked with their neighbours. John almost thought that Katharine once or twice gathered her black skirts nearer to her, as though to keep them from a sort of contamination. He was on her left, and he was conscious that in pretending to eat he used his right arm very cautiously because he did not wish even to run the risk of touching hers by accident.

Now, in the course of events, it happened that the subject of yachts travelled from neighbour to neighbour, as subjects sometimes do at big dinners, until, having been started by Teddy Van De Water and Fanny Trehearne, it came up the table to Frank Miner. He immediately saw his chance, and plunged into his subject.

"Oh, I don't take any interest in yacht races, compared with prize fights, since Jack Ralston has gone into the ring!" he said, and his high, clear voice made the words ring down the table with the cheery, laughing cadence after them.

"What's that about me, Frank?" asked John, speaking over Katharine's head as she bent away from him towards Russell Vanbrugh, who was next to her on the other side.

"Oh, nothing — talking about your round with Tom Shelton. Tell us all about it, Jack. Don't be modest. You're the only man here who's ever stood up to a champion prize-fighter without the gloves on, and it seems you hit him, too. You needn't be ashamed of it."

"I'm not in the least ashamed of it," answered Ralston, unbending a little.

He spoke in a dead silence, and all eyes were turned upon him. But he said nothing more. Even the butler and the footmen, every one of whom had read both the morning and the evening papers, paused and held their breath, and looked at John with admiration.

"Go ahead, Ralston!" cried Teddy Van De Water, from his end. "Some of us haven't heard the story, though everybody saw those horrid things in the papers this morning. It was too bad!"

Katharine had attempted to continue her conversation with Russell Vanbrugh, but it had proved impossible. Moreover, she was herself almost breathless with surprise at the sudden appeal to Ralston himself, when she had been taking it for granted that every one present, including his hosts, despised him, and secretly wished that he had not come.

Van De Water had spoken from the end of the table. Frank Miner responded again from the other, looking hard at Katharine's blank face, as he addressed John.

"Tell it, Jack ! " he cried. "Don't be foolish. Everybody wants to know how it happened."

Ralston looked round the table once more, and saw that every one was expecting him to speak, all with curiosity, and some of the men with admiration. His eyes rested on Katharine for a moment, but she turned from him instantly — not coldly, as before, but as though she did not wish to meet his glance.

"I can't tell a story by halves," said he. "If you really want to have it, you must hear it from the beginning. But I told Frank Miner, this morning — he can tell it better than I."

"Go on, Jack — you're only keeping everybody waiting ! " said Hamilton Bright, from across the table. "Tell it all — about me, too — it will make them laugh."

John saw the honest friendship in the strong Saxon face, and knew that to tell the whole story was his best plan.

"All right," he said. "I'll do my best. It won't take long. In the first place — you won't mind my going into details, Miss Van De Water ? "

"Oh, no — we should rather prefer it," laughed the young girl, from her distant place.

"Then I'll go on. I've been going in for reform

lately — I began last Monday morning. Yes — of course
you all laugh, because I've not much of a reputation for
reform, or anything else. But the statement is necessary because it's true, and bears on the subject. Reform
means claret and soda, and very little of that. It had
rather affected my temper, as I wasn't used to it, and I
was sitting in the club yesterday afternoon, trying to
read a paper and worrying about things generally, when
Frank, there, wanted me to drink with him, and I
wouldn't, and I didn't choose to tell him I was trying to
be good, because I wasn't sure that I was going to be.
Anyhow, he wouldn't take 'no,' and I wouldn't say
'yes' — and so I suppose I behaved rather rudely to
him."

"Like a fiend!" observed Miner, from a distance.

"Exactly. Then I was called to the telephone, and
found that my uncle Robert wanted me at once, that
very moment, and wouldn't say why. So I came back
in a hurry, and as I was coming out of the cloak-room
with my hat and coat on I ran into Bright, who generally
saves my life when the thing is to be done promptly. I
suppose I looked rather wild, didn't I, Ham?"

"Rather. You were white — and queer altogether. I
thought you 'had it bad.'"

There was a titter and a laugh, as the two men looked
at one another and smiled.

"Well, you've not often been wrong, Ham," said
Ralston, laughing too. "I don't propose to let my
guardian angel lead a life of happy idleness —"

"Keep an angel, and save yourself," suggested Miner.

"Don't make them laugh till I've finished," said Ralston, "or they won't understand. Well — Ham tried to
hold me, and I wouldn't be held. He's about twenty
times stronger than I am, anyhow, and he'd got hold of

my arm — wanted to calm me before I went out, as he thought. I lost my temper — ”

“Your family's been advertising a reward if it's found, ever since you were born,” observed Miner.

“Suppress that man, can't you — somebody?” cried Ralston, good-naturedly. “So I tripped Bright up under Miner's nose — and there was Crowdie there, and a couple of servants, so it was rather a public affair. I got out of the door, and made for the park — uncle Robert's, you know. Being in a rage, I walked, and passing Murray Hill Hotel, I went in, from sheer force of habit, and ordered a cocktail. I hadn't more than tasted it when I remembered what I was about, and promptly did the Spartan dodge — to the surprise of the bar-tender — and put it down, and went out. Then uncle Robert and I had rather a warm discussion. Unfortunately, too, just that drop of whiskey — forgive the details, Miss Van De Water — you know I warned you — just that drop of whiskey I had touched was distinctly perceptible to the old gentleman's nostrils, and he began to call me names, and I got angry, and being excited already, I daresay he really thought I wasn't sober. Anyhow, he managed to knock my hat out of my hand and smash it — ask him the first time you see him, if any of you doubt it.”

“Oh, nobody doubts you, Jack,” said Teddy Van De Water, vehemently. “Don't be an idiot!”

“Thank you, Teddy,” laughed Ralston. “Well, the next thing was that I bolted out of the house with a smashed hat, and forgot my overcoat in my rage. It's there still, hanging in uncle Robert's hall. And, of course, being so angry, I never thought of my hat. It must have looked oddly enough. I went down Fifth Avenue, past the reservoir — nearly a mile in that state.”

"I met you," observed Russell Vanbrugh. "I was just coming home — been late down town. I thought you looked rather seedy, but you walked straight enough."

"Of course I did — being perfectly sober, and only angry. I must have turned into East Fortieth or Thirty-ninth, when I stopped to light a cigar. The waxlight dazzled me, I suppose, for when I went on I fell over something — that street is awfully dark after the avenue — and I hurt my head and my hand. This finger — "

He held up his right hand of which one finger was encased in black silk. Katharine remembered the spot of blood on the letter.

"Then I don't know what happened to me. Doctor Routh said I had a concussion of the brain and lost the sense of direction, but I lost my senses, anyhow. Have any of you fellows ever had that happen to you? It's awfully queer."

"I have," said Bright. "I know — you're all right, but you can't tell where you're going."

"Exactly — you can't tell which is right and which is left. You recognize houses, but don't know which way to turn to get to your own. I lost myself in New York. I'm glad I've had the experience, but I don't want it again. Do you know where I found myself and got my direction again? Away down in Tompkins Square. It was ten o'clock, and I'd missed a dinner-party, and thought I should just have time to get home and dress, and go to the Assembly. But I wasn't meant to. I was dazed and queer still, and it had been snowing for hours, and I had no overcoat. I found a horse-car going up town and got on. There was nobody else on it but that prize-fighter chap, who turns out to have been Tom Shelton. It was nice and warm in the car, and I must have been pretty well fagged out, for I sat down at the upper end and dropped asleep without telling the conductor to wake me at my street. I never fell asleep in a horse-car before in my life, and didn't expect to then. I don't know what happened after that — at least not distinctly. They must have tried to wake me with kicks and screams, or something, for I remember hitting out, and then a struggle, and I was pitched out into the snow by the conductor and the prize-fighter. Of course I jumped up and made for the fighting man, and I remember hearing something about a fair fight, and then a lot of men came running up with lanterns, and I was squaring up to Tom Shelton. I caught him one on the mouth, and I suppose that roused him. I can see that right-hand counter of his coming at me now, but I couldn't stop it for the life of me — and that was the last I saw, until I opened my eyes in my own room and saw my mother looking at me. She sent for Doctor Routh, and he saw that I wasn't going to die, and went home, leaving everybody considerably relieved. But he wasn't at all sure that I hadn't been larking, when he first came, so he took the trouble to make a thorough examination. I wasn't really hurt much, and though I'd had such a crack from Shelton, and the other one when I tumbled in the dark, I had pretty nearly an hour's sleep in the horse-car as a set-off. Then my mother brought me things to eat — of course all the servants were in bed, and she'd rung for a messenger in order to send for Routh. And I sat up and wrote a long letter before I went to bed, though it wasn't easy work, with my hand hurt and my head rather queer. I wish I hadn't, though — it was more to show that I could, than anything else. There — I think I've told you the whole story. I'm sorry I couldn't make it shorter."

"It wasn't at all too long, Jack," said Katharine, in clear and gentle tones.

She was very white as she turned her face to him. Every one agreed with her, and every one began talking at once. But John did not look at her. He answered some question put to him by the young girl on his left, and at once entered into conversation at that side, without taking any more notice of Katharine than she had taken of him before.

CHAPTER XXX.

THE dinner was almost at an end, when John spoke to Katharine again. Every one was laughing and talking at once. The point had been reached at which young people laugh at anything out of sheer good spirits, and Frank Miner had only to open his lips, at his end of the table, to set the clear voices ringing; while at the other, Teddy Van De Water, whose conversational powers were not brilliant, but who possessed considerable power over his fresh, thin, plain young face, excited undeserved applause by putting up his eyeglass every other minute, staring solemnly at John as the hero of the evening, and then dropping it with a ridiculous little smirk, supposed to be expressive of admiration and respect.

John saw him do it two or three times, while turning towards him in the act of talking to his neighbour on his left, and smiled good-naturedly at each repetition of the trick. To tell the truth, the evident turn of feeling in his favour had so far influenced his depressed spirits that he smiled almost naturally, out of sympathy, because every one was so happy and so gay. But he was soon tired of young Van De Water's joke, before the others were, and looking away in order not to see the eyeglass fall again, he caught sight of Katharine's face.

Her eyes were not upon him, and she might have been supposed to be looking past him at some one seated farther down the table, but she saw him and watched him, nevertheless. She was quite silent now, and her face was pale. He only glanced at her, and was already turning his head away once more when her lips moved.

"Jack!" she said, in a low voice, that trembled but reached his ear, even amidst the peals of laughter which filled the room.

He looked at her again, and his features hardened a little in spite of him. But he knew that Bright, who sat opposite, was watching both Katharine and himself, and he did his best to seem natural and unconcerned.

"What is it?" he asked.

She did not find words immediately with which to answer the simple question, but her face told all that her voice should have said, and more. The contraction of the broad brows was gone at last, and the great grey eyes were soft and pleading.

"You know," she said, at last.

John felt that his lips would have curled rather scornfully, if he had allowed them. He set his mouth, by an effort, in a hard, civil smile. It was the best he could do, for he had been badly hurt. Repentance sometimes satisfies the offender, but he who has been offended demands blood money. John deserved some credit for saying nothing, and even for his cold, conventional smile.

"Jack — dear — aren't you going to forgive me?" she asked, in a still lower tone than before.

Ralston glanced up and down the table, manlike, to see whether they were watched. But no one was paying any attention to them. Hamilton Bright was looking away, just then.

"Why didn't you answer my letter?" asked John, at last, but he could not disguise the bitterness of his voice.

"I only — it only came — that is — it was this evening, when I was all dressed to come here."

John could not control his expression any longer, and his lip bent contemptuously, in spite of himself.

"It was mailed very early this morning, with a special delivery stamp," he said, coldly.

"Yes, it reached the house — but — oh, Jack! How can I explain, with all these people?"

"It wouldn't be easy without the people," he answered. "Nobody hears what we're saying."

Katharine was silent for a moment, and looked at her plate. In a lover's quarrel, the man has the advantage, if it takes place in the midst of acquaintances who may see what is happening. He is stronger and, as a rule, cooler, though rarely, at heart, so cold. A woman, to be persuasive, must be more or less demonstrative, and demonstrativeness is visible to others, even from a great distance. Katharine did not belittle the hardness of what she had to do in so far as she reckoned the odds at all. She loved John too well, and knew again that she loved him; and she understood fully how she had injured him, if not how much she had hurt him. She was suffering herself, too, and greatly — much more than she had suffered so long as her anger had lasted, for she knew, too late, that she should have believed in him when others did not, rather than when all were for him and with him, so that she was the very last to take his part. But it was hard, and she tried to think that she had some justification.

After Ralston had finished telling his story, Russell Vanbrugh, who was an eminent criminal lawyer, had commented to her upon the adventure, telling her how men had been hanged upon just such circumstantial evidence, when it had not chanced that such a man as Doctor Routh, at the head of his profession and above all possible suspicion, had intervened in time. She tried to argue that she might be pardoned for being misled, as she had been. But her conscience told her flatly that she was deceiving herself, that she had really known far less than most of the others about the events of the previous day, some of which were now altogether new to her, that she had judged John in the worst light from the first words she had heard about him at the Assembly ball, and had not even been at pains to examine the circumstances so far as she might have known them. And she remembered how, but a short time previous to the present moment, she had looked at the sealed envelope with disgust — almost with loathing, and had turned over its ashes with the tongs. Yet that letter had cost him a supreme effort of strength and will, made for her sake, when he was bruised and wounded and exhausted with fatigue.

"Jack," she said at last, turning to him again, "I must talk to you. Please come to me right after dinner — when you come back with the men — will you ? "

" Certainly," answered John.

He knew that an explanation was inevitable. Oddly enough, though he now had by far the best of the situation, he did not wish that the explanatory interview might come so soon. Perhaps he did not wish for it at all. With Katharine love was alive again, working and suffering. With him there was no response, where love had been. In its place there was an unformulated longing to be left alone for a time, not to be forced to realize how utterly he had been distrusted and abandoned when he

had most needed faith and support. There was an un-
willing and unjust comparison of Katharine with his
mother, too, which presented itself constantly. Losing
the sense of values and forgetting how his mother had
denied his word of honour, he remembered only that her
disbelief had lasted but an hour, and that hour seemed
now but an insignificant moment. She had done so much,
too, and at once. He recalled, amid the noise and laughter,
the clinking of the things on the little tray she had brought
up for him and set down outside his door — a foolish
detail, but one of those which strike fast little roots as
soon as the seed has fallen. The reaction, too, after all
he had gone through, was coming at last and was telling
even on his wiry organization. Most men would have
broken down already. He wished that he might be spared
the necessity of Katharine's explanation — that she would
write to him, and that he might read in peace and pon-
der at his leisure — and answer at his discretion. Yet
he knew very well that the situation must be cleared up
at once. He regretted having given Katharine but that
one word in answer to her appeal — for he did not wish
to seem even more unforgiving than he felt.

"I'll come as soon as possible," he said, turning to
her. "I'll come now, if you like."

It would have been a satisfaction to have it over at
once. But Katharine shook her head.

"You must stay with the men — but — thank you,
Jack."

Her voice was very sweet and low. At that moment
Ruth Van De Water nodded to her brother, and in an
instant all the sixteen chairs were pushed back simultaneously, and the laughter died away in the rustle of
soft skirts and the moving of two and thirty slippered
feet on the thick carpet.

"No!" cried Miss Van De Water, looking over her shoulder with a little laugh at the man next to her, who offered his arm in the European fashion. "We don't want you — we're not in Washington — we're going to talk about you, and we want to be by ourselves. Stay and smoke your cigars — but not forever, you know," she added, and laughed again, a silvery, girlish laugh.

Ralston stood back and watched the fair young girls and women as they filed out. After all, there was not one that could compare with Katharine — whether he loved her, or not, he added mentally.

When the men were alone, they gathered round him under a great cloud of smoke over their little cups of coffee and their tiny liqueur glasses of many colours. He had always been more popular than he had been willing to think, which was the reason why so much had been forgiven him. He had assuredly done nothing heroic on the present occasion, unless his manly effort to fight against his taste for drinking was heroic. If it was, the majority of the seven other men did not think of it nor care. But he did not deserve such very great credit even for that, perhaps, for there was that strain of asceticism in him which makes such things easier for some people than for others. Most of them, being young, envied and admired him for having stood up for a champion prize-fighter in fair combat, heavily handicapped as he had been, and for having reached his antagonist once, at least, before he went down. A good deal of the enthusiasm young men occasionally express for one of themselves rests on a similar basis, and yet is not to be altogether despised on that account.

John warmed to something almost approaching to geniality, in the midst of so much good-will, in spite of his many troubles and of the painful interview which was imminent. When Van De Water dropped the end of his cigar and suggested that they should go into the drawing-room and not waste the evening in doing badly what they could do well at their clubs from morning till night, John would have been willing to stay a little longer. He was very tired. Three or four glasses of wine would have warmed him and revived him earlier, but he had not broken down in his resolution yet — and coffee and cigars were not bad substitutes, after all. The chair was comfortable, it was warm and the lights were soft. He rose rather regretfully and followed the other men through the house to join the ladies.

Without hesitation, since it had to be done, he went up to Katharine at once. She had managed to keep a little apart from the rest, and in the changing of places and positions which followed the entrance of the men, she backed by degrees towards a corner in which there were two vacant easy chairs, one on each side of a little table covered with bits of rare old silver-work, and half shielded from the rest of the room by the end of a grand piano. It would have been too remote a seat for two persons who wished to flirt unnoticed, but Katharine knew perfectly well that most of her friends believed her to be engaged to marry John Ralston, and was quite sure of being left to talk with him in peace if she chose to sit down with him in a corner.

Gravely, now, and with no inclination to let his lips twist contemptuously, John sat down beside her, drawing his chair in front of the small table, and waiting patiently while she settled herself.

"It was impossible to talk at table," she said nervously, and with a slight tremor in her voice.

"Yes — with all those people," assented John.

A short silence followed. Katharine seemed to be

choosing her words. She looked calm enough, he thought, and he expected that she would begin to make a deliberate explanation. All at once she put out her hand spasmodically, drew it back again, and began to turn over and handle a tiny fish of Norwegian silver which lay among the other things on the table.

"It's all been a terrible misunderstanding — I don't know where to begin," she said, rather helplessly.

"Tell me what became of my letter," answered John, quietly. "That's the important thing for me to know."

"Yes — of course — well, in the first place, it was put into papa's hands this morning just as he was going down town."

- "Did he keep it?" asked Ralston, his anger rising suddenly in his eyes.

"No — that is — he didn't mean to. He thought I was asleep — you see he had read those things in the papers, and was angry and recognized your handwriting — and he thought — you know the handwriting really was rather shaky, Jack."

"I've no doubt. It wasn't easy to write at all, just then."

"Oh, Jack dear! If I'd only known, or guessed — "

"Then you wouldn't have needed to believe a little," answered John. "What did your father do with the letter?"

"He had it in his pocket all day, and brought it home with him in the evening. You see — I'd been out — at the Crowdies' — and then I came home and shut myself up. I was so miserable — and then I fell asleep."

"You were so miserable that you fell asleep," repeated Ralston, cruelly. "I see."

"Jack! Please — please listen to me — "

"Yes. I beg your pardon, Katharine. I'm out of temper. I didn't mean to be rude."

"No, dear. Please don't. I can't bear it." Her lip quivered. "Jack," she began again, after a moment, "please don't say anything till I've told you all I have to say. If you do — no — I can't help it — I'm crying now."

Her eyes were full of tears, and she turned her face away quickly to recover her self-control. John was pained, but just then he could find nothing to say. He bent his head and looked at his hand, affecting not to see how much moved she was.

A moment later she turned to him, and the tears seemed to be gone again, though they were, perhaps, not far away. Strong women can make such efforts in great need.

"I went into my mother's room on my way down to the carriage to come here," she continued. "Papa came in, bringing your letter. He had not opened it, of course — he only wanted to show me that he had received it, and he said he would destroy it after showing it to me. I looked at it — and oh, the handwriting was so shaky, and there were spots on the envelope — Jack — I didn't want to read it. That's the truth. I let him burn it. I turned over the ashes to see that there was nothing left. There — I've told you the truth. How could I know — oh, how could I know?"

John glanced at her and then looked down again, not trusting himself to speak yet. The thought that she had not even wished to read that letter, and that she had stood calmly by while her father destroyed it, deliberately turning over the ashes afterwards, was almost too much to be borne with equanimity. Again he remembered what it had cost him to write it, and how he had felt that, having written it, Katharine, at least, would be loyal to him, whatever the world might say. He would have been a little more than human if he could have then and there smiled, held out his hand, and freely forgiven and promised to forget.

And yet she, too, had some justice on her side, though she was ready and willing to forget it all, and to bear far more of blame than she deserved. Russell Vanbrugh had told her that a man might easily be convicted on such evidence. Yet in her heart she knew that her disbelief had waited for no proofs last night, but had established itself supreme as her disappointment at John's absence from the ball.

"Jack," she began again, seeing that he did not speak, "say something — say that you'll try to forgive me. It's breaking my heart."

"I'll try," answered John, in a voice without meaning.

"Ah — not that way, dear!" answered Katharine, with a breaking sigh. "Be kind — for the sake of all that has been!"

There was a deep and touching quaver in the words. He could say nothing yet.

"Of all that might have been, Jack — it was only yesterday morning that we were married — dear — and now — "

He lifted his face and looked long into her eyes — she saw nothing but regret, coldness, interrogation in his. And still he was silent, and still she pleaded for forgiveness.

"But it can't be undone, now. It can never be undone — and I'm your wife, though I have distrusted you, and been cruel and heartless and unkind. Don't you see how it all was, dear? Can't you be weak for a moment, just to understand me a little bit? Won't **you** believe me when I tell you how I hate myself and despise myself and wish that I could — oh, I don't know! — I wish I could wash it all away, if it were with my heart's blood! I'd give it, every drop, for you, now — dear one — sweetheart — forgive me! forgive me!"

"Don't, Katharine — please don't," said John, in an uncertain tone, and looking away from her again.

"But you must," she cried in her low and pleading voice, leaning far forward, so that she spoke very close to his averted face. "It's my life — it's all I have! Jack — haven't women done as bad things and been forgiven and been loved, too, after all was over? No — I know — oh, God! If I had but known before!"

"Don't talk like that, Katharine!" said Ralston, distressed, if not moved. "What's done is done, and we can't undo it. I made a bad mistake myself —"

"You, Jack? What? Yesterday?" She thought he spoke of their marriage.

"No — the night before — at the Thirlwalls', when I told you that I sometimes drank — and all that —"

"Oh, no!" exclaimed Katharine. "You were so right. It was the bravest thing you ever did!"

"And this is the result," said John, bitterly. "I put it all into your head then. You'd never thought about it before. And of course things looked badly — about yesterday — and you took it for granted. Isn't that the truth?"

"No, dear. It's not — you're mistaken. Because I thought you brave, night before last, was no reason why I should have thought you a coward yesterday. No — don't make excuses for me, even in that way. There are none — I want none — I ask for none. Only say that you'll try to forgive me — but not as you said it just now. Mean it, Jack! Oh, try to mean it, if you ever loved me!"

Ralston had not doubted her sincerity for a moment, after he had caught sight of her face when he had finished telling his story at the dinner-table. She loved him with all her heart, and her grief for what she had done was real and deep. But he had been badly hurt. Love was half numb, and would not wake, though his tears were in her voice.

Nevertheless, she had moved John so far that he made an effort to meet her, as it were, and to stretch out his hand to hers across the gulf that divided them.

"Katharine," he said, at last, "don't think me hard and unfeeling. You managed to hurt me pretty badly, that's all. Just when I was down, you turned your back on me, and I cared. I suppose that if I didn't love you, I shouldn't have cared at all, or not so much. Shouldn't you think it strange if I'd been perfectly indifferent, and if I were to say to you now — 'Oh, never mind — it's all right — it wasn't anything'? It seems to me that would just show that I'd never loved you, and that I had acted like a blackguard in marrying you yesterday morning. Wouldn't it?"

Katharine looked at him, and a gleam of hope came into her eyes. She nodded twice in silence, with close-set lips, waiting to hear what more he would say.

"I don't like to talk of forgiveness and that sort of thing between you and me, either," he continued. "I don't think it's a question of forgiveness. You're not a child, and I'm not your father. I can't exactly forgive — in that sense. I never knew precisely what the word meant, anyhow. They say 'forgive and forget' — but if forgiving an injury isn't forgetting it, what is it? Love bears, but doesn't need to forgive, it seems to me. The forgiveness consists in the bearing. Well, you don't mean to make me bear anything more, do you?"

A smile came into his face, not a very gentle one, but nevertheless a smile. Katharine's hand went out quickly and touched his own.

"No, dear, never," she said simply.

"Well — don't. Perhaps I couldn't bear much more just now. You see, I've loved you very much."

"Don't say it as though it were past, Jack," said Katharine, softly.

"No — I was thinking of the past, that's all."

He paused a moment. His heart was beating a little faster now, and tender words were not so far from his lips as they had been five minutes earlier. He could be silent and still be cold. But she had made him feel that she loved him dearly, and her voice waked the music in his own as he spoke.

"It was because I loved you so, that I felt it all," he said. "A little more than you thought I could — dear."

It was he, now, who put out his hand and touched a fold of her gown which was near him, as she had touched his arm. The tears came back to Katharine's eyes suddenly and unexpectedly, but they did not burn as they had burned before.

"I've never loved any one else," he continued presently. "Yes — and I know you've not. But I'm older, and I know men who have been in love — what they call being in love — twice and three times at my age. I've not. I've never cared for any one but you, and I don't want to. I've been a failure in a good many ways, but I shan't be in that one way. I shall always love you — just the same."

Katharine caught happily at the three little words.

"Just the same — as though all this had never happened, Jack?" she asked, bending towards him, and looking into his brown eyes. "If you'll say that again, dear, I shall be quite happy."

"Yes — in a way — just the same," answered Ralston, as though weighing his words.

Katharine's face fell.

"There's a reservation, dear — I knew there would be," she said, with a sigh.

"No," answered Ralston. "Only I didn't want to say more than just what I meant. I've been angry myself — I was angry at dinner — perhaps I was angry still when I sat down here. I don't know. I didn't mean to be. It's hard to say exactly what I do mean. I love you — just the same as ever. Only we've both been very angry and shall never forget that we have been, though we may wonder some day why we were. Do you understand? It's not very clear, but I'm not good at talking."

"Yes." Katharine's face grew brighter again. "Yes," she repeated, a moment later; "it's what I feel — only I wish that you might not feel it, because it's all my fault — all of it. And yet — oh, Jack! It seems to me that I never loved you as I do now — somehow, you seem dearer to me since I've hurt you, and you've forgiven me — but I wasn't to say that!"

"No, dear — don't talk of forgiveness. Tell me you love me — I'd rather hear it."

"So would I — from you, Jack!"

Some one had sat down at the piano. The keyboard was away from them, so that they could not see who it was, but as Katharine spoke a chord was struck, then two or three more followed, and the first bars of a waltz rang through the room. It was the same which the orchestra had been playing on the previous evening, just when Katharine had left the Assembly rooms with Hester Crowdie.

"They were playing that last night," she said, leaning toward him once more in the shadow of the piano. "I was so unhappy — last night — "

No one was looking at them in their corner. John Ralston caught her hand in his, pressed it almost sharply, and then held it a moment.

"I love you with all my heart," he said.

The deep grey eyes melted as they met his, and the beautiful mouth quivered.

"I want to kiss you, dear," said Katharine. "Then I shall know. Do you think anybody will see?"

That is the story of those five days, from Monday afternoon to Friday evening, in reality little more than four times twenty-four hours. It has been a long story, and if it has not been well told, the fault lies with him who has told it, and may or may not be pardoned, according to the kindness of those whose patience has brought them thus far. And if there be any whose patience will carry them further, they shall be satisfied before long, unless the writer be meanwhile gathered among those who tell no tales.

For there is much more to be said about John Ralston and Katharine, and about all the other people who have entered into their lives. For instance, it may occur to some one to wonder whether, after this last evening, John and Katharine declared their marriage at once, or whether they were obliged to keep the secret much longer, and some may ask whether John Ralston's resolution held good against more of such temptations as he had resisted on Wednesday night at the Thirlwalls' dance. Some may like to know whether old Robert Lauderdale lived many years longer, and, if he died, what became of

the vast Lauderdale fortune; whether it turned out to
be true that Alexander Junior was rich, or, at least, not
nearly so poor as he represented himself to be; whether
Walter Crowdie had another of those strange attacks
which had so terrified his wife on Monday night;
whether he and Paul Griggs, the veteran man of letters,
were really bound by some common tie of a former history or not, and, finally, perhaps, whether Charlotte
Slayback got divorced from Benjamin Slayback of
Nevada, or not.   There is also a pretty little tale to be
told about the three Misses Miner, Frank's old-maid
sisters.   And some few there may be who will care to
know what Katharine's convictions ultimately became
and remained, when, after passing through this five
days' storm, she found time once more for thought and
meditation.   All these things may interest a few patient
readers, but the main question here raised and not yet
answered is whether that hasty, secret marriage between
Katharine and John turned out to have been really such a
piece of folly as it seemed, or whether the lovers were
ultimately glad that they had done as they did.   It is
assuredly very rash to be married secretly, and some of
the reasons given by Katharine when she persuaded John
to take the step were not very valid ones, as he, at least,
was well aware at the time.   But, on the other hand,
such true love as they really bore one another is good,
and a rare thing in the world, and when men and women
feel such love, having felt it long, and knowing it, they
may be right to do such things to make sure of not being
parted; and they may live to look each into the other's
eyes and say, long afterwards, 'Thank God that we were
not afraid.'   But this must not be asserted of them positively by others without proof.

For better, or for worse, Katharine Lauderdale is

Katharine Ralston, and must be left sitting behind the piano with her husband after the Van De Waters' dinner-party. And if she is the centre of any interest, or even of any idle speculation for such as have read these pages of her history, they have not been written in vain. At all events, she has made a strange beginning in life, and almost unawares she has been near some of the evil things which lie so close to the good, at the root of all that is human. But youth does not see the bad sights in its path. Its young eyes look onward, and sometimes upward, and it passes by on the other side.

THE END.